Praise for *A Long Dark Night* by Lilli Sutton

"*A Long Dark Night* paints a portrait of a family teetering on the brink of destruction. Lilli Sutton delivers a tense and atmospheric thriller that is just as much a tale of survival as it is one of love and devotion."

—**Kimi Cunningham Grant**, *USA TODAY* **bestselling** author of *The Nature of Disappearing*

"Lilli Sutton's *A Long Dark Night* is a thrilling adventure through the often-unseen rough and tumble world of interior Alaska. A riveting and deeply humane novel about how we manage the complexities of family loyalty and the moral quandaries we discover in the world—I couldn't put it down."

—**Kristin Koval**, author of *Penitence*

"This is a vivid portrait of Alaska, and of a young woman brought to her breaking point fighting for what's right. I absolutely inhaled it."

—**Hayley Scrivenor**, internationally bestselling author of *Girl Falling*

Also by Lilli Sutton

Running Out of Air

A
LONG
DARK
NIGHT

a novel

LILLI SUTTON

PARK
ROW
BOOKS

PARK
ROW
BOOKS™

Recycling programs
for this product may
not exist in your area.

ISBN-13: 978-0-7783-0576-7

A Long Dark Night

Park Row Books
22 Adelaide St. West, 41st Floor
Toronto, Ontario M5H 4E3, Canada
ParkRowBooks.com

HarperCollins Publishers
Macken House, 39/40 Mayor Street Upper,
Dublin 1, D01 C9W8, Ireland
www.HarperCollins.com

Printed in U.S.A.

To Atlas, Sara, and all the other good dogs I have known.

A
LONG
DARK
NIGHT

Lilli Sutton

1

NINA DIDN'T RECOGNIZE THE MAN IN THE YARD.
She stopped a few feet back from where the floodlights reached midway down the driveway, where the line of white light melted into harsh shadow. Maybe her family had sold the house and never bothered to tell her. Years had passed since she last received one of her mother's letters. And Grant—he would have told her, she hoped, but she had no idea how he felt about her now or how he would have contacted her. By leaving, she had planted a seed of resentment—maybe it had slowly grown all these years, morphed into something worse than she dared to imagine. The old sign still stood at the end of the driveway, Ted Sanford's Sled Dogs carved into the wood, but years of relentless wind and snow had left it barely legible. Maybe the new owners hadn't even bothered to tear it down.

She needed to make a decision. Head into town, try to find someone she recognized, or try her luck with the unfamiliar man. At least he lived in Whitespur. He could point her in the right direction, tell her where her family lived now. Even if they'd left home, there was no way they'd left Whitespur. But she had to be careful. The man was chopping wood with an axe, each decisive swing splitting a log in half with a sharp crack. She didn't want to startle him. He tossed the split pieces into a pile and replaced them with another log in a smooth rhythm. Preparing for winter, because even though it was October, autumn was the final inhale before cold and darkness settled over interior Alaska.

She took a step forward at the same moment the man dropped the axe and crossed the yard to the kennel, bending forward to talk to the penned dog, who had alerted to her presence several minutes ago. With a jolt she recognized the man in profile. Like her father in old pictures from his competitive days, grinning from the runners of a dogsled after winning yet another long-distance race, he was bearded and broad-shouldered. But this man wasn't her father. He was her baby brother, Grant, fifteen when she left, twenty-four now, remade into an entirely new person.

Nina couldn't believe she hadn't registered the obvious truth. That nine years was a long time, that of course Grant wouldn't have remained frozen in time. Still—she didn't know him, didn't know how he would react to her presence again. But her entire body ached from the long truck ride up the Dalton, after days of connecting flights and layovers. She wanted desperately to sit at the worn kitchen table and spill her life to Grant, and hear his story in return, to confide in each other the way they had as teenagers, sharing gossip and dreams in equal measure. He had gone back to chopping wood, axe in hand again, as if he hadn't noticed her. But she couldn't wait any longer.

Her voice came out high, tentative, a million unspoken questions bound into his name.

Grant stopped mid-swing, processing her voice, pairing the single word to the sister he used to know. Finally, Grant turned and said her name like it was a foreign language, unfamiliar on his tongue. She met him halfway across the yard and he threw his arms around her as his body collided solidly with hers. He was taller than her, but he was when she left, the result of a growth spurt as he entered tenth grade. He smelled like woodsmoke, the strong scent long buried in his worn canvas jacket.

Nina pulled away, taking in his expression of pleasant disbelief, no hint of anger on his face.

"What the hell are you doing here?"

His voice was deeper, rougher; he sounded like all the other men in Whitespur. The town, like a rock tumbler, tossed them and polished them until they were the same man, almost, all submissive to the landscape but not to each other. No one could defy Alaska, which left only other men to best. Nina hoped he hadn't become one of them in behavior, too, getting in drunken fights at The Spur and coming home with black eyes.

Nina weighed how to answer. She could tell him the truth, complicated and simple all at once. "My restaurant closed. Months ago. There aren't many jobs available. So, I thought maybe—maybe it was time to come home."

Some of the surprise left Grant's expression. "Guess you had no other reason to visit."

She exhaled, her breath turning white in the frozen air. "Do you know how hard it is to get here? It's not easy to just visit. It's like traveling to another world. Especially now."

"No," Grant replied, "I wouldn't know." He looked past her, toward the darkened driveway. "How did you get here? I didn't hear a car."

"I hitchhiked."

Grant blinked. The brief wave of concern that washed over his face was replaced with something like hurt. "You could have called."

"You have a cell phone?"

"Yeah. I thought Mom might have given you my number, in one of those letters. There's reception in town now. I would have seen a missed call eventually." He turned away and picked up the axe and a log, readying himself to strike. "But you're right. There's nothing we can do for you anymore."

"Grant . . ." Nina tried, but she knew she was asking for too much, too soon. None of them had wanted her to leave, and she had done it anyway. So, she'd leave him alone, wouldn't make him ask her to go away. "Is anyone else home?"

"Dad's inside," he replied without looking at her. "Mom's out somewhere. Seeing a friend."

"Where's Audrey?"

"Not home."

She processed his curt response. She'd have to try her luck with a different family member; her father, maybe. He wouldn't ask many questions. "Thanks," she said, and then, because she couldn't help herself, couldn't resist pushing for a hint of forgiveness, "and we'll talk later?"

"Yeah," Grant said. "We'll talk later."

NINA OPENED THE door to silence. She paused in the mudroom, studying the pairs of dirt-encrusted rubber boots that lined the wall. One of them belonged to her, right where she'd left them years ago. Plaster had come off the walls in large chunks, revealing the logs underneath, like a wound that cut to the bone.

She set her suitcase down and moved through the next doorway to the kitchen.

The lights were off, though the sun had set half an hour ago. The low buzz of a television drew her to the living room. There hadn't been a television before. She paused in the doorway, heartbeat speeding up as she realized the moment had arrived. After nine years, she was home.

"Dad?"

A grunt came in reply. Nina swallowed the lump in her throat and stepped forward, into the periphery of his vision. Her father turned his head slowly, as if it hurt to drag his eyes away from World Series coverage, Rays versus Dodgers. "Huh. Wasn't expecting you."

Nina exhaled, flooded with equal amounts of exasperation and relief. "How are you?"

Her father studied her. Nina wondered if he had an image in his mind of her before she had left—a lot younger, and probably a lot more hopeful. She knew she must look exhausted now, bags beneath her eyes and dry, sallow skin. In turn, he had an overgrown mustache and days-old stubble lining his cheeks. He had gained weight, a lot of it. He'd always been a large man but in his racing days he'd been lean, and he'd stayed in shape her whole childhood to give tours. Maybe he'd given that up, too.

"How'd you get here?" he asked.

"I hitched a ride from Fairbanks."

Another grunt. "Long way."

"Yeah. My flight landed last night."

"Who gave you a ride?"

"A couple of people. Someone gave me a ride to the Dalton and then I got in a truck."

Her father snorted. "And you didn't have to do anything?"

Nina shifted, uncomfortable. "No. No, Dad, they were nice."

His gaze drifted back to the television. "Lucky you made it," he said under his breath. "You staying awhile?"

"Probably. I'm not sure how long." She paused, then gestured to the TV. "Who are you rooting for?"

He responded with a noncommittal noise. "Rays, I guess."

She waited for him to ask her another question, but he seemed to have nothing left to say, so she retreated from the living room. In the kitchen, she paused to breathe. Her hands shook. Her father hadn't changed much—he had always been aloof, not much of a talker unless he was talking about his dogs—but his disinterest in her return was palpable. She filled a glass with water from the kitchen sink and drank it, noticing the familiar earthy taste. She'd been drinking purified water for so long, she'd forgotten what Whitespur water tasted like.

She unpacked her suitcase in her childhood bedroom. It remained the same—two twin beds, one pushed against each wall, hers and Audrey's. Audrey had hated sharing with her younger sister, even though only two years separated them. Posters of 2000s boy bands and magazine pages depicting far-flung destinations—India, Italy, Spain—clung to the wall beside Nina's bed; Audrey's wall was bare. She thought Nina's decorations were childish, and it surprised Nina that her sister hadn't taken them down. Maybe she had missed Nina enough to keep them up after she left, or maybe she'd moved out not long after Nina had. Grant had said she wasn't home, but Nina didn't know if that meant *out* or *gone*. A handful of worn paperbacks stood atop a shelf: *The Call of the Wild, White Fang, Into the Wild*. Books chronicling both the allure and devastating power of the state where she grew up. Beside them, a haphazard pile of dust-covered cookbooks rested.

Nina studied the pages on the wall for a moment, remembering how, as a teenager, she had longed to taste authentic food from other countries, to learn to cook dishes that weren't possible at home. Her palate was well traveled now, but it always led her back to Alaska, to smoked meat and tangy berries and fresh-caught fish.

Headlights cut through the window, throwing a splash of light against the wall and signaling her mother's arrival. The engine cut out and the truck door opened and shut, but minutes later she still hadn't entered the house. Peering out the window, Nina saw a light on in the kennel.

In the mudroom she found her old down jacket. It had a couple of rips, but those were ones that she herself had made—it didn't appear to have been worn since she left. She zipped it on, thankful that it still fit, and stepped out into the night.

The cold seized her, again, going straight through her jeans and pricking her skin. Grant was still chopping wood, though the pile of remaining logs was greatly reduced. As she approached, he looked up.

"I didn't tell her," he said, anticipating her question. "Go surprise her."

"Thanks," she replied, breath fogging in the air. She hesitated, as if there was more to say, but Grant tossed two pieces of wood on the pile, drew the tarp over it, and brushed past her, heading toward the house. Still not in the mood for conversation.

Her lungs hurt as she hurried across the yard, to the haphazard white building that leaned at a strange angle. Each step on the frozen ground jolted her bones. She thought only of warmth as she opened the door. A cacophony of noise exploded: dogs barking, howling, whining, a pure wall of sound. Nina paused, staring in awe at the well-lit kennel interior. Another thing that hadn't changed.

Across the kennel her mother straightened up, a squirming black puppy in her hands. "Well. I'll be damned."

"Hi," Nina said, shutting the door behind her. "I know this is a surprise."

"That's an understatement. Here," she said, quickly covering the distance between them and handing Nina the puppy. "Hold him. He's got an infected cut."

The puppy in her hands twisted and squeaked. His right front paw was inflamed. "How old?"

"Six weeks. A pain in my ass."

"What's the theme?"

"International cities. That one's London." Her mother returned with a syringe of ointment and carefully applied it to the paw, then wrapped it in vet tape. "Maybe that'll hold," she said, taking London back and returning him to the kennel with his mother. "Probably his siblings will chew it right off." She spent a minute cleaning up the supplies before refocusing her attention on Nina. "So. Want to tell me what you're doing here?"

"It's a long story," Nina replied, the shake returning to her voice. "I was hoping I could stay for a while."

"Hmm." Her mother laughed as she turned away to grab a broom and began sweeping the aisle, bitterness dripping from her voice. "That's funny. How long?"

"I don't know."

"New York didn't work out so well?"

Nina hesitated. Her mother had said New York because that's where Nina had been the last time they'd spoken, nearly five years ago. She didn't have the heart to explain that she'd moved to a little city in Maine, fallen in love with the gray-yellow beaches and sturdy brick buildings. That for almost four years, 4950 had been her life, her dream fully realized, until the world had ripped it away.

"Mom, the pandemic, it's . . . I know it's nothing here, but a lot of places shut down. So many people are sick. I've barely been outside in months."

"So?"

"So, I lost my job." Her shoulders sagged as she admitted it, close to the whole truth.

Her mother's head snapped up. "You got fired because some people are sneezing?"

"It's worse than that. A lot of people are dying. Don't you watch the news?"

"Only when I can pry your father away from the TV." She paused, leaning on the broom. "I understand that it's worse out there. But that's it? You gave up and came back?"

"Not exactly." Nina sighed, fiddling with the zipper on her coat. Even inside the kennel, it was cold enough to warrant the extra layer. "I lost my job in May. I've been looking for a new one this whole time, but there aren't any, not in the city. I couldn't afford rent anymore. I had to break my lease." The search had extended beyond Portland. She had sent out applications to New York, Chicago, New Orleans, anywhere that was hiring. Most places never responded, or sent her an apologetic form email stating that the position had already been filled, or worse, the restaurant had closed its doors. Micah landing a sous-chef role at a James Beard Award–winning restaurant in Austin had been the last straw. She couldn't wither away in Portland alone, not without Micah's odd brand of pessimistic optimism to keep her going. She missed the scent of his menthol cigarettes when she sat in the backyard late into the night, swirling a lonely glass of wine on the patio table. And as much as she valued their friendship, she couldn't follow him across the country without the promise of an income of her own. An unfamiliar city was daunting enough without the additional risk of an empty bank account.

"It's interesting that you chose to come home now, after all these years." Her mother began sweeping again, her shoulders rigid. Nina knew anger simmered beneath her mother's carefully restrained demeanor. "No visits. No letters. No money. Nothing to give until we have something to offer you."

"I tried, Mom. It costs so much just to exist out there. I didn't have any extra money, especially after I lost my job."

"But you said you would, Nina. You said you'd send money home. And you didn't." She paused again, looking at Nina directly. "And you stopped writing back."

Nina's heart sank. The letters had arrived in her mailbox a few times a year, postmarked from Whitespur, a few short sentences scrawled in her mother's neat handwriting. Never anything that seemed worth writing about—updates on a few of the dogs, maybe a mildly interesting bit of news about the town. Nina wrote back while in culinary school, and the letters followed her to her first apartment after graduating. But eventually she'd moved again, and stopped receiving them. She'd written once or twice from her new address, but maybe those letters never made it home. The thought of her mother's letters piling up in the mailroom, only to be thrown away, made her stomach turn.

"I moved," she said, her voice quiet. "I got caught up in—in life, in trying to stay afloat. I could never cut ties with you on purpose. But I had to leave. You know that."

Her mother shook her head. "Audrey didn't have to leave. Grant didn't have to leave."

"But I had the chance—"

She lifted a hand. "I know. I know. I admit not thinking the scholarship was worth anything at the time." She coughed once, into her elbow.

Nina's mind jumped to the virus, as it always did these days, filled with the sound of sirens wailing outside her apartment windows and the scent of Clorox wipes as she sanitized groceries from her twice-monthly trips to the store. She'd had to stop watching the news after Micah moved out, the images of packed emergency rooms and crying nurses sending her into a depressive spiral, overwhelmed with anxiety and a feeling of powerlessness. But its impact on Alaska had been limited so far, she reminded herself, and her mother always coughed in the colder months, her throat irritated from the woodstove. She sensed that some of the tension had left the room and glanced down at one of the kennels, recognizing the light brown dog curled up inside. "Honey. She was a youngster when I left."

"She won't let us retire her," her mother replied, peering around Nina's shoulder into the kennel. "Too much energy for a dog her age."

Nina crouched down and said Honey's name. The dog lifted her head, one ear floppy, the other straight like a cone. In an instant she bounced to her feet, wriggling with excitement, emitting a high-pitched whine as she pressed up against the chain-link door to get closer to Nina. She laughed, trying to tamp down the sadness rising in her throat. Honey remembered her. It had been so hard to leave the dogs, and she knew many of them must have passed away while she was gone—but Honey remembered her.

"She missed you," her mother observed.

Nina pushed her fingers through the wire diamonds, scratching Honey's chest. Honey twisted and licked Nina's fingers. "How are the tours going?"

The broom clattered against the wall as her mother tossed it back to its resting place. "Not well. There have hardly been any tourists this year. From the virus, I guess. And with the oil drilling in Brooks Valley, we can't use some of the old routes. I've been trying to sell some dogs, but it's a long way out here from Anchorage or even Fairbanks. People won't come."

"I read about the drilling. It's awful."

A scoff in response. "You read about it. We have to live with it."

"I could drive some dogs to the city," Nina offered. "To Anchorage, even. See if anyone's interested."

"You'd need your father to sell them. You're nobody." Before Nina could respond, her mother strode past her, waving a hand. "Come on. I'm going to heat up some chili for dinner."

Her comment about Nina being unable to sell dogs stung, but her mother was right. Her father had won the Iditarod in the '80s, and the Yukon Quest twice. Even though he was long retired from sled racing, his name adorned that worn sign in front of their house and the brochures that her mother mailed out to travel agencies across the state, and to the companies across the country that offered Alaskan tours. Nina, on the other hand, hadn't mushed since she was seventeen. Her mother was right—she was nobody.

After dinner, full of chili—her first home-cooked meal in three days—Nina wandered back to her room. She stopped at the familiar creak and groan of the floorboards beneath heavy footsteps in the hallway. Grant had been quiet through dinner, but they all had. Her mother had asked a few questions about New York, about the restaurants she had worked in. Nina didn't mention 4950—not yet—because she couldn't square that vibrant, life-giving place with cold, desolate Whitespur. She would tell them one day, if she stayed home long enough. Her father had been silent, but Nina couldn't tell if he was glowering or simply deep in his thoughts. When she asked him to pass the butter—twice—he didn't respond, and Grant had reached across the table to slide the dish over, without looking at her. Now she turned to face him.

"What's up?"

He indicated her room. "Can we talk?"

Nina stifled a yawn. The time difference had caught up to her and she'd hardly slept in three days. She wanted, more than anything, to curl up beneath the heavy quilts on her bed and sleep until she felt capable of making her family appreciate her presence. She'd figure out something—training the dogs, fixing the house up, convincing mushers to purchase their stock. She pushed the bedroom door open and let Grant follow her in.

Grant wandered over to Audrey's bed and sat down. "I want to apologize."

"For what?"

"For being rude to you earlier. It's just—I didn't know how to react. I mean, I haven't seen you in so long. And I had a lot on my mind."

"Like what?"

He shrugged. "It's not important. I'm just saying sorry for being an ass."

"Thanks," Nina replied, deciding not to push it. "So, where are you working?" she asked, resuming her unpacking. A long moment passed; Grant remained silent. Nina glanced over her shoulder and saw the expression on his face. "What?"

"You're not going to like it."

"That never stopped you from telling me something."

"Alright." He exhaled. "I'm working on the oil field."

Nina tossed a shirt onto her bed. "Grant. Seriously?"

He raised his hands in defense. "It's good money. Insanely good. Otherwise, I'd be working on the trucks that come through or I'd be off to Fairbanks. There's not much I can do without a degree, besides manual labor. At least this pays well."

"Yeah, but from what I've read, it's destroying the refuge."

"And it's building back the town. That TV Dad's always watching? The oil company paid for satellites in town. I even get cell service by The Spur. People have money for food, can afford to fix up their houses. It's a necessary evil, in my opinion."

"Couldn't you work on, like, wind turbines?"

"There's a lot of people who want those jobs. Way more than are willing to work on a rig. And again, I'd have to leave Whitespur."

"Right." Nina stared at her hands for a moment. *As if leaving Whitespur was the worst thing in the world.*

"Enough about me. What happened to you?"

"What do you mean?"

"Your big New York job. Living the life."

Nina hesitated. Maybe she could tell Grant the truth, or at least part of it. "New York was great, for a while. But that's not where I've been for the last few years. I was working at a restaurant in Portland, Maine."

"What was that like?"

"Incredible in the summer. Cold in the winter. We got a few nor'easters, they're called. Like a snowstorm, but worse because of the sea."

Grant nodded. "And?"

"What?"

"I feel like there's something you're not telling me."

Nina laughed, a little in awe that he could see through her so clearly even after so many years apart. "You're right, there's more to it. But I don't want to explain it all right now. All you need to know is that the restaurant closed and I ran out of money. The pandemic changed everything."

"It's weird," Grant said, "hearing about all that. It's like it doesn't exist here. I think most of the cases are in the bigger cities."

"Mom said the tourists stopped showing up."

"Yeah. No money from them. And Dad's disability checks are hardly anything." He shook his head. "Mom just had that litter born a few weeks ago. I don't know where she thinks the money is going to come from."

"Disability checks?"

Grant's brow furrowed. "Yeah. He broke his leg a few years ago. Got run into a tree while mushing some young, excited dogs. Smashed the sled and shattered his leg. He hasn't been the same since." He paused. "He's different. I'm sure you noticed."

"I can't believe no one told me."

"Well. You weren't exactly easy to reach."

Nina closed her eyes for a moment, putting a pin in an argument that could last an entire night—her family had been difficult to reach, not her. She had lived in a world of technology, of instant access to anyone in the world. Except the people she loved the most, the ones she'd hurt by leaving. She felt a twinge of guilt as she remembered the many nights spent drinking and dancing with Micah, surrounded by swirling lights, loud music, and enough disposable income to spend on *fun*. That was never something her family had been able to afford. But when his words sank in, her eyes snapped open again.

"I did notice, about Dad. Something is off with him, like he's in a trance. And he looks different." She paused. "I wouldn't worry about Mom. She's tough. She's survived being poor before."

Grant snorted. "We've never *not* been poor. She's never known what it's like to have money."

"You're right," Nina said, unpacking her last shirt and

collapsing on the bed beside the pile of clothes. "I feel so bad, for not being able to help more. It's like the last nine years disappeared. It all amounted to nothing."

"I'm glad you're back," Grant said, and his sincerity briefly warmed Nina's heart.

She sat up on her elbow. "What's Audrey been up to?"

The smile left Grant's face, and Nina's stomach flipped.

2

NINA HUGGED HER ARMS AROUND HER CHEST, ducking her head to shield her face from the wind that blew relentlessly around her. A weak sun hung low in the sky, providing some light but little warmth through the thin layer of clouds. She reached up a hand to wrangle her hair back down over her shoulders. The small deck outside the second-story apartment was unshielded from the elements. Beside her, Grant knocked on the worn brown door a second time but was met again with only silence and the whistle of the wind.

"She must not be home," Grant said.

They were halfway down the shoddy wooden staircase when the door creaked open. Nina turned quickly and jogged back up the stairs, Grant on her heels. In the doorway stood a woman with box-dye black hair, dressed in a gray sweatshirt and sweatpants. She gazed at the siblings and raised an eyebrow.

"Looking for Audrey?"

"Yeah," Grant replied. "Hi, Katrina," he added, no sense of pleasantry in his tone. The name jogged Nina's memory—one of Audrey's childhood friends. She couldn't remember them hanging out much as teenagers, but maybe they'd befriended each other again in adulthood. Katrina's hair had been light brown back then.

"Grant." Katrina gave a curt nod, her expression unchanging. "She's not here," she said, leaning against the doorframe. "Think she went down to the bar."

In the middle of the day? Nina wondered. Maybe she had gone for lunch. Nina imagined the crisp exterior of a salty French fry between her teeth and realized she was hungry. Last night, her first night back home, she'd slept soundly, but her internal clock was off, and she hadn't eaten breakfast. She thanked Katrina and turned to follow Grant down to the dirt road. Nina shot a quick glance at the faded green truck they'd left parked by the converted house, then jogged to catch up with Grant. The walk to The Spur was a short one, but the biting cold made her long for whatever heat the truck cab could provide.

"Do they live together?" she asked.

Grant nodded. "They've been roommates for a few months now. I don't know Katrina well, though." He paused, and Nina sensed that he wanted to say more. "It's nice to have someone looking out for Audrey who isn't using her in some other way. At least as far as I know."

Nina kept her mouth shut. The reality of Audrey's situation was making her more uneasy by the minute, and she hadn't even seen her sister yet. They'd never been close—Audrey took pride in being the oldest and therefore the most mature, which meant she'd frowned upon Nina's hobbies of reading and playing with whatever litter of puppies happened to be around. Nina had always thought of Audrey as clever and ambitious, too good for Whitespur. But maybe the time away from home had clouded her opinion, made her idealize Audrey when in fact she was always destined for the kind of life Whitespur offered.

No vehicles passed by as they walked, snow squeaking under their boots, the silence almost as loud as the city streets Nina had grown used to. They passed the general store and the Protestant church, both housed in low-slung wooden buildings, the church only distinguishable by the small gold cross above its door. Nina suspected that most people were home, hurrying to get through as many chores as possible in the few hours of soft daylight that late October provided. There was firewood to chop, windows to seal, meat to smoke. Later, when darkness fell, the street would come alive as the residents converged on the bar and Mexican restaurant that comprised the town's only social scene.

A few snow machines were parked outside the bar. When her classmates at culinary school asked how she passed the time in Alaska, she'd mentioned snow machines and gotten confused looks—eventually she gathered that what Alaskans called snow machines, the rest of the country called snowmobiles, yet another in a long line of differences. She hadn't ridden one since leaving, but hadn't forgotten the sensation of skimming over the snow at high speed, shifting her weight to balance into the turns. She preferred the dogsled, but snow machines made quicker work of traveling on roads.

Grant stopped walking and turned to face Nina. "You sure you want to go in?"

"Yeah. Of course."

Grant looked like he wanted to say something more but seemed to think better of it. He shouldered the door open and Nina followed him into the dimly lit interior. Most of the tables in the middle of the floor space were empty, though a few men sat along the bar. Fuzzy classic rock played through an old speaker system. There were booths along the back that were difficult to see from the doorway, curving along a wide hallway that led to the pool tables in a separate room. The air smelled of oil and onions, bringing her instantly back to her teenage years, evenings after school spent crowded around a table with her friends, drinking sweet soda and eating too many cheese fries. The bulletin board on the nearest wall caught her eye. Seeing it was like opening a time capsule—it had been there for as long as Nina could remember, available for anyone to tack up anything they wanted. Mostly it was people selling stuff, like preserves or firewood, or posters for lost pets. But a different kind of poster caught her attention.

She mouthed the word as she read it. A massive headline, white letters on a gray background: MISSING. Beneath it, a black-and-white photograph of a smiling man who might have been in his thirties, with short curly hair and a beard. *Last seen February 27th, 2019, leaving the Brooks Valley oil field at 5 PM wearing dark blue pants and a white sweatshirt.* There were more details, his height and age, and a number to call with any information.

"I'm surprised that's still up." Grant must have followed her gaze.

"He went missing from the oil field?"

"Yeah. He was never found. They searched for a while but . . . you know how it goes here. He could be anywhere."

Anywhere, including somewhere safe. Maybe he got tired of the endless darkness and cold and left, went back home or somewhere warmer. Or maybe he froze to death, or drove a snow machine off a cliff, or suffered a heart attack while out hunting and no one knew where to search. It wasn't difficult to imagine ways to die in Alaska.

She noticed something beneath the flyer and lifted its corner—another missing person poster was underneath. This one was in full color, and the person in the photograph was more a boy than a man, a blond-haired teenager grinning with palm trees and an ocean behind him, on vacation somewhere, so incongruous with Whitespur. Benjamin Weber was his name, last seen the morning of July 9, 2018, in the cafeteria of the Brooks Valley oil field, where he had worked for less than six months. Nina studied his face.

"I recognize him. Wasn't he on the news?"

Grant hesitated, then shrugged. "Maybe. His parents flew out and stayed here for months, hassling the police and the higher-ups at the field. They brought in reporters from Seattle, made a big fuss. They never found him, either."

"He looks so young." Nina was certain now that she had seen his picture on the news, interspersed with video interviews of his teary-eyed parents and a solemn reporter asking them questions. Why hadn't she reached out to her family then, asked if they knew Benjamin, if they'd joined the search parties? What had seemed like an insurmountable distance between Nina and her family now felt tiny, a threshold capable of being crossed with a single step.

"He was. Just out of high school. I think he was saving up money for college. I didn't work with him, but, you know, his story got around. I felt so bad for his family."

"This happened after you started working there?"

"Yeah. I started a few months before he did, I guess."

Nina sensed that he didn't want to talk about it anymore and turned away from the bulletin board. She spotted Audrey alone at a table near the back.

She tried to recall the last time she had seen her sister, to connect that image to the woman sitting across the room. Audrey had been twenty-one when Nina left, still living at home in their shared bedroom, helping with the sled tours. Of the three of them, Audrey had been the least interested in mushing, but she was outgoing and good with the tourists, chatting to them about where they were from with genuine interest. She had wanted to become a flight attendant or work on a cruise ship, a people-oriented job that took her to new destinations, and it seemed a cruel twist of fate that she'd ended up here, at the greasy bar in the tiny town where she'd been born and raised. Her mother's letters had stopped mentioning Audrey after the first year, and now Nina knew why.

She nudged Grant. "There."

He nodded and weaved through the tables scattered across the middle of the floor. Audrey was slumped over, a few beer bottles clustered to the side of the table and one between her hands. She was awake enough to look up as they approached, a smile flitting over her face when she saw Grant but dropping as her gaze shifted to Nina.

"No fucking way."

Nina's older sister straightened up, pushing the half-full bottle of beer away before clambering out of her chair to pull Nina into a loose, beer-scented hug. Nina held her breath and waited until Audrey released her, taking a step back to evaluate her sister. She looked worn, Nina thought. Her hair was bleached a few shades short of white—Katrina's work?—and deep, dark semicircles punctuated the undersides of her eyes. Her skin was spotty and dry, worked over by the harsh Alaskan cold.

Nina became aware that Audrey was saying something to her. "What?" she managed, trying to match the person who stood before her to the vibrant, self-sufficient sister she had left behind nine years ago. Grant's subtle hints hadn't done much to prepare her.

"What are you doing here?" Audrey sank back into her chair, knocking over the half-full bottle and sending beer across the table. Grant grabbed a wad of napkins and began mopping it up. "I told everyone you'd never come back. You're rich."

"I'm not as successful as Mom may have led you to believe,"

Nina said gently, trying futilely to make eye contact with Grant. "My restaurant closed. I'm going to be back home for a little while, maybe until spring."

Audrey stared at her for a moment, and then laughed. Her gaze flicked to her brother. "Grant. I'm behind on rent again."

His face darkened. He set the soaked wad of napkins on the table and grabbed another fistful of clean ones from the dispenser. "Let's talk about this another time, Audrey."

Nina cleared her throat. "I don't have much money right now. But I can try to help you."

Audrey mumbled something and looked away. She waved her left hand in their direction, still muttering under her breath.

"What?" Nina asked. "I can't hear you."

"I said get out of here," Audrey replied, her words half choked by a sob. "I don't want you to see me like this."

Nina reached to touch Audrey's shoulder, tentatively, but drew back sharply when Audrey hissed under her breath. She knocked an empty bottle to the floor; it shattered by Nina's feet.

She sensed the eyes of everyone at the bar on them. "Sorry," Nina mumbled, more to the quiet room than to Audrey. Anger flared in her chest. Audrey had no right to act this way toward her, not when Nina had done nothing to wrong her. Before she had time to unleash a flicker of her irritation, a waitress hurried over, dropping down to sweep up the pieces with a broom and dustpan. Nina backed away; Grant hesitated for a moment and then stepped beside her. She wanted to leave before Audrey caused a bigger scene, but something about the waitress felt familiar. When she stood up, Nina smiled in spite of the situation.

"Ila?"

The woman blinked, then returned Nina's smile. "Nina? Wow, I had no idea you were visiting."

"I'm back for a little while, actually," Nina replied, as they slowly moved toward the bar. "I'm sorry about—" she started, then gestured back to where Audrey sat.

"Don't worry about it. She's in here most days."

"Yeah, I . . ." Nina shot a quick glance at Grant, but his face was stony. "I gathered."

"I can't believe it." Nina thought the shimmer in Ila's eyes was genuine excitement. "How long has it been?"

"Nine years," Nina replied, the number spilling off her tongue with none of the heaviness she felt when she thought of those long years rolling out like a red carpet delivering her back home. "Hey, when are you free? It'd be nice to catch up."

Ila grinned. "I'd love that. Maybe on Sunday?"

"Sure, swing by. Same place."

"I'll see you then," Ila said, reaching over to squeeze Nina's arm. "Don't worry about Audrey," she said quietly. "I keep an eye on her."

Nina tried to hold on to that reassurance as she followed Grant out of The Spur, but one last look at Audrey confirmed what she knew to be true: Her sister was merely a ghost of her former self.

3

"YOU'D BETTER HOLD HIM, OR YOU'RE GETTING dragged halfway to Fairbanks."

Nina dug her heels into the snow, leaning all her weight back against River's harness, trying to muscle the black dog back half an inch so she could clip him to the tug line. The four dogs behind River, already hooked to the gang line, barked up a deafening racket, only adding to the frenzy. His front paws churned in the snow as he unleashed a blood-curdling yelp. Nina cursed under her breath, annoyed that she'd unhooked River in the first place: The lead dog was supposed to be the first one on the line. She'd disrupted their routine, and had lost all authority over the team.

"Here." Grant's large hands brushed past hers, fingers disappearing in the tufted fur around River's neck, and together they dragged the dog back. Nina clipped on the tug line and stepped away, shaking out her hands.

"You didn't have to take pity on me."

"Nina. Your options were standing there all day or letting him go, and I wasn't about to chase him down." At the edge of the floodlit yard, Grant's face was cast in harsh shadow, his teeth white against the darkness. With the limited daylight in autumn and winter, running the dogs in the dark was often unavoidable. He'd mentioned earlier that he usually took them out at night now, when he got back from work. The dogs were used to it; their eyes adjusted easily to the faint light of the moon and stars. Nina and Grant both wore headlamps, the beams of which helped them to keep an eye on how the dogs were running. But on the cloudless nights of her childhood, Nina had often turned off the headlamp and let her eyes adjust, savoring in how the features of the landscape became visible through the darkness.

"Whatever," Nina mumbled, her status as an older sibling not allowing her to thank him even begrudgingly. She checked the contents of the basket one more time, making sure that the Remington shotgun was nestled properly beside the sled bag. Close to a decade had passed since she had shot a gun, but she remembered the weight of it in her hands, the chill of the cold metal through her gloves. Necessary protection in the backcountry where there were bears, moose, and wolves to consider. Satisfied, she faced Grant again. "Are you ready?"

Grant glanced at the quintet of dogs hooked to his own sled, standing quietly. "Yeah, I'd say so."

Nina pulled her gloves, then her mittens back on and stepped behind her sled. She eyed the steel snow hook set into the ground, the only thing keeping her dogs from tearing hell-bent out of the yard and into the wilderness. She stepped aboard the sled runners, took a deep breath, and extended her foot to kick the hook loose.

It came out instantly, as she had anticipated. Then came the explosion: the furious scramble of twenty paws digging into the snow for traction, followed by a bone-rattling jolt as the sled bounced forward into motion.

Nina had time to think *they're out of control* before the sled careened around a corner of the yard and bounced off a tree, needle-laden branches thwacking against her face. The sled teetered on the left runner and Nina's heart caught as she threw her weight to the right, counterbalancing, and then the right runner slammed to the ground. An image of her father's accident flashed through her mind. The sled wobbled again, Nina still holding her breath, and then they were off, rushing relatively smoothly into the night.

"Easy!" Nina called, again and again, although her pleas did nothing to slow the dogs down. She hit the brake a few times, but it was futile. The fastest way to tire out Alaskan huskies, she knew, was to let them run. The huskies weren't a defined breed, more of a mutt engineered over generations to be lightweight and fast, with a warm coat, tough paws, and a hearty appetite—everything necessary to excel at long-distance travel through the unforgiving Alaskan landscape. Her family's dogs came from a mix of Siberian husky, greyhound, Labrador retriever, border collie, and native Alaskan dogs.

The sound of barking prompted her to steal a glance over her shoulder. Grant's dogs were approaching at a dead run, quickly gaining ground on her team. It made sense—they were conditioned. Nina had chosen mostly older dogs, the ones used for tour-giving who were supposed to be calm and sensible. That clearly wasn't the case. Grant had warned her that they weren't getting as much exercise these days. She should have listened.

"I thought you wanted me to lead!" Grant shouted as he drew closer, and Nina gestured, hoping he understood that he could go past. A minute later, his sled drew even, making use of the wide, packed-down road of snow that went out past the lake and toward the mountains, maintained by the hunters and trappers. Plenty of dog teams had traveled the road since the last big snowfall.

Nina stepped on the brake a few more times and finally the dogs slowed, allowing Grant's team to take the lead. Nina exhaled and let herself take in her surroundings—the endless white snow, the dark lines of the forest off to her right, the massive, ice-covered Bow Lake to her left. Some people kept part of the lake plowed once the ice was thick enough, so the few kids in the town could skate and play hockey. The huge mountains straight ahead, the Brooks Range, drew Nina's attention again. It would take all night to reach them, even though they covered half the sky. For a moment she was arrested—awed by the sheer beauty, the scale, the wildness—by the place she called home. How was it that the East Coast had prevented her from coming back? But what kept her from visiting was fear—of Whitespur sinking its claws in again, slow and deep, trapping her there.

Ahead, Grant bore right, following another trail that climbed up a slight incline into the forest. "Gee!" Nina called the familiar command, feeling a rush of relief when River obeyed and turned. Or maybe he was only following his kennelmates ahead.

The other dogs were moving well. She'd put Sugar and Sage in the swing positions, behind River to each side. In the wheel spot were Shadow—another older, experienced dog—and Wilder, a youngster, still learning the ropes according to her mother's records. Despite the cold, Nina was warmed by memories of her childhood, the hundreds of nights spent like this, racing across the snow beneath a bright moon and a clear star-filled sky. She'd had her own team of dogs then, as Grant had his now. She'd asked her mother about them at dinner that night, and to her credit, she kept immaculate records of each dog. Nina had gone to the kennel office earlier and flipped through a few boxes of files, traveling down a memory lane lined with familiar canine faces. She had felt immense guilt for leaving them behind, but after listening to friends talk about their pets, she became aware of the differences in the relationship with her own dogs. They were more like coworkers than pets—tools, even, a necessity for navigating the Alaskan wilderness and also her family's source of income. But she loved them, knew their personalities and quirks, and had often wished as a child that she could sneak her favorite dog into the house, if only for a night. She recognized too, eventually, that the dogs weren't lying around missing her after she left. They had a whole family caring for them, and a job to do. Working dogs weren't the type to pine.

Grant had slowed ahead. He threw his snow hook down and Nina called to the dogs, asking them to slow down, and set her snow hook, like a boat's anchor. The dogs were calmer now, and once they halted, they alternated biting the snow and rolling in it, trying to cool down. Even though the temperature hovered in the low teens, good weather for sled travel, the dogs still overheated when they overexerted themselves, as they'd done leaving the yard.

Nina stepped off the runners and made her way over to Grant. "What's up?"

"I'm checking Briar's foot," he replied, bending down over a small gray dog. "Yeah, can you hand me some booties? She's getting ice."

Nina found a bag containing booties in his sled and returned with a set of four, handing them one by one to her brother as he attached each covering to the dog's paws, securing the Velcro straps around her ankles. As soon as he straightened up, Briar began gnawing on the booties, pulling at the straps with her front teeth.

"I guess she's just going to eat them."

"Not if we get moving again."

"Hang on," Grant said. "I want to show you something."

Nina followed him into the trees, listening to the snow crunching beneath her boots. The wind that had blown so hard that morning had died down. Nina felt as if every noise she made, even the sound of her own breathing, was an affront to the exquisite stillness that had settled over the land.

They emerged from the trees to overlook the valley. Nina took in the smattering of buildings and the oil rigs, standing like towers on the massive pads throughout the valley. They were too far away to hear, but she could imagine the creaking of the mechanical beasts as they drew up the oil. It resembled a miniature town, all the buildings lit up, casting soft glows through their windows, turning the surrounding snow and even the sky a faint orange.

"This is where you work?" Nina asked, and Grant nodded.

"Those buildings," he said, pointing at some long rectangles, "are dorms. A bunch of people live there now, anyone who came from out of town or even out of state. Whitespur's population has almost tripled if you count them."

Nina stayed quiet, trying not to shiver as the cold crept into her bones. She thought of the East Coast, how her friends had complained of thirty-degree weather. How she'd adapted to scuttling between buildings, artificial heat warming her body and lulling her to sleep. She felt more alive in Alaska, where there was no one to save her from her own poor decisions.

"Where do they come from? All those workers."

"Other states. Some from Canada. A lot have worked on oil fields before and want higher pay. Some are entirely new. I guess they're desperate." He paused for a moment too long. "They hire a lot of ex-convicts. Felons. Guys who don't have a lot of other options."

"That's not a bad thing. They deserve opportunities for a better future."

"As long as they don't bring their pasts with them."

Nina thought he was bordering on judgmental, but realized she didn't know—he had spent years on the oil field, while she had only arrived home yesterday. "You're always calling the other workers 'the guys,' 'the men,'" she said. "Do any women work there?"

He nodded. "A few. Some in the administrative side of things, some in the cafeteria. And I know there's a couple on the rigs. One of the engineers. But the majority are men. And the dorms, they're single occupancy, and they're not allowed to bring a wife or a girlfriend or anything. I get the vibe that a lot of these guys are unattached."

As far as Nina knew, Grant was also unattached. "Those posters in The Spur. The missing people. Does it scare you?"

"No," Grant replied, without hesitation. "Everyone who's gone missing has been from out of state. Guys who are totally unfamiliar with Alaska. It wouldn't take much for something to go wrong. They get the idea to go off on a hike and end up lost and dehydrated."

"Everyone? There's been more than two?"

He shot her a look, as if annoyed that she'd focused on only a part of what he'd said. "There were a couple others. People who just didn't show up to work one day, and no one came looking for them. Like I said, they're unattached."

"But not that Benjamin kid. Or Eric Riley. Someone cared about them enough to make posters."

"Yeah. Don't get me wrong—it's sad. I just think people expect Whitespur to be like the rest of the country, but they don't know. This isn't just some state park with well-marked hiking trails—this is big, rugged wilderness," he said, gesturing to the isolated valley, the looming mountains. "Sometimes people make a huge deal of an injury at work. The rigs are dangerous, you know? It's a lot of heavy machinery. I think it's the same thing with the disappearances. People who aren't from here don't understand that you can't just walk into the woods. Especially in winter."

Injuries. Plural. Nina turned the word over in her mind. "And you're sure you feel safe working there?"

"I do," Grant said, firmly.

"But how many people have gotten hurt? Have gone missing?"

"Missing, four or five. Injured . . . I don't know. A handful."

"Doesn't that seem like a lot? It's been operating, what, six years?"

This time, Grant paused before replying. "Maybe."

Not quite agreement, but acknowledgment. Nina tucked away the dangerous nature of his job for another time. Maybe she could get him to reconsider, to look for work elsewhere. "Why do you stay at home, if Audrey moved out? Can't you afford your own place?"

Grant sighed, squatting to sit in the snow. "The oil work is good money, yeah. But I've been giving most of it to Mom and Dad. Especially these last few months . . . I mean, winter is the bulk of the sled tours, right? But there are still busloads of tourists in the summer. And we usually sell some dogs. But there's been nobody, Nina. Mom was worried she might have to sell all the dogs and find a job. And there aren't any."

"Right." She paused, lowering herself to sit beside him. "I get all that. But how does Audrey afford it?"

"She's had a few different jobs. I think she's cleaning houses right now. She's had various boyfriends pay her rent. For a year she got it together and worked at the Interpretive Center in the wildlife refuge, helping out the tourists. But then . . ." He trailed off, and Nina sensed that he didn't want to go on. Grant cleared his throat. "She had this boyfriend, this junkie, and that's when she was at her worst. I don't know if she was using. I've only ever heard her talk about drinking. But believe it or not, what you saw today is not her lowest point."

Nina drew a breath, thinking of her sister when they were younger, her bubbly, confident personality. If she'd asked back then, her family would have bet on Audrey, not Nina, being the one to leave home and thrive in a big city. An ache of sadness rose in her chest as she thought of Audrey slumped over the table that morning, slurring her speech. Anger, too, though she wasn't sure if it was directed at Audrey, for not living up to her potential, or at Whitespur, for claiming another victim. "How long ago was that?"

"Last winter, so almost a year ago. That guy got caught moving his 'product' on the Dalton," Grant said, with air quotes, "and is supposedly in prison in Fairbanks now. She hasn't mentioned him since then."

"Do you see her a lot?"

Grant shrugged. "A few times a month, usually at The Spur. I try to check up on her, but she's kind of elusive. Hardly at her apartment. Doesn't ever come over for dinner."

Nina snorted. "Yeah. I bet Mom isn't too happy with her."

"It's tearing her apart," he said, and Nina felt a twinge of regret for making light of the situation. "She tried to help Audrey for a while, but now she's just trying to keep her own head above water."

"That's the thing about Alaska. No matter how much you love it, it's always trying to drown you."

A moment passed before a small smile spread across his face. "Isn't that the truth." He reached over to pat her shoulder. "It's too bad you had to come back."

THE OIL FIELD WAS LIKE ITS OWN TOWN. GRANT HAD never gotten used to it, even though he'd worked there for almost three years and knew every corner of camp—the warehouses, the administrative offices, the cafeteria, the dorms, the workshops. He remembered, in his final years of school, sneaking out while his parents were asleep to watch the buildings go up, from the same spot he'd taken Nina yesterday. The entire valley had been illuminated by huge vehicles with spotlights parked all around, so they could work through the long nights in autumn and spring. The glow stopped at the tree line, allowing Grant to hide in the shadows between the branches. Summers, of course, provided more than enough light, and in winter it was too cold to build, the frozen earth impenetrable. But the rest of the year was a twenty-four-hour operation, no time for rest; extracting the oil was a profitable and therefore urgent business.

At first Grant didn't think much of it. He wanted to go to college, like Nina, though he had no strong urge to leave the state and would have settled for one of the University of Alaska campuses. He had no clue what he wanted to major in, but he read in the brochures that *undecided* was an option, and he liked the idea of putting off big decisions for his older, wiser self to choose. But he received a rejection letter in the mail. Embarrassed, he'd worked a handful of odd jobs and observed the oil field slowly draw his friends in with its lucrative pay. A better alternative than going up to Prudhoe Bay or one of the other faraway fields, or worse, crabbing in the Bering Sea. At least they could live at home, maybe buy or build a house in town, stay close to friends and families. Less of a life than he had wanted, but a familiar one, at least. So, after three years of resistance—long enough for Nina to get her degree and start working in a restaurant, long enough for Grant to know he couldn't spin his wheels any longer—he had applied for a job and been hired as a floor hand, the lowest of the low. The other workers didn't even call the position by its proper name—they called the floor hands roughnecks, and watched as the roughnecks scrambled around, mopping and power washing (in the warm months) and lugging parts to the mechanics. The more senior employees rarely looked Grant in the eye, but he didn't mind the invisibility. Back then, his friends were roughnecks too, and after the exhausting days, bone weary, they'd go to The Spur and put away three beers each and marvel over how much money they had made and how much more was to come.

Grant yanked open the door to Warehouse A and stepped into the massive heated interior. A small mercy—that all the buildings had heat, that in the coming winter he would only have to spend brief amounts of time outside, moving between the warehouses and the garages and the cafeteria. He'd been promoted to maintenance tech last year, though he was still learning the ropes from Doc, a man in his fifties who'd been brought in from Oklahoma to work in the shop. Doc hated Alaska and used every opportunity to disparage Grant's state. Grant put up with it—he couldn't imagine being brought to Alaska unwillingly. The people who loved it were either born here or chose to move. And not everyone born in Alaska loved it.

Grant thought of Nina as he changed into his oil-stained navy jumpsuit in the locker room. He couldn't get a read on her, how happy she was to be back. He could guess: not very. The question still lingered—if the restaurant hadn't closed, would she have stayed away forever? Like Audrey, she'd always been starry-eyed, always wanted to travel the world. New York had almost been too predictable, too commonplace of a landing spot. But he couldn't say that to her, not when she'd worked hard through years of school far from home and finally earned the career she'd always wanted. It would be cruel to belittle her accomplishments. Besides, she'd been in Maine for the last few years, working at her own restaurant. He still hadn't gotten the full story out of her, didn't know much about her life after culinary school, but he was curious. And envious—that she'd always had a clear purpose and known how to follow it.

Grant made his way back through the warehouse, brushing past the throngs who were gathering for the changeover, night shift to day. He usually worked days but sometimes they put him on nights, and three nights of 5:00 p.m. to 5:00 a.m. usually rendered him useless for the following three days he would have off. He remembered viscerally his first week on the job, every muscle in his body on fire, too exhausted to eat and shower after work; all he'd wanted to do was sleep. Running after a boss's orders turned out to be more difficult than homestead chores. Then he'd adapted, like flicking a switch. At least he wasn't a roughneck anymore, at everyone's beck and call, scurrying between odd jobs like a rat. Since he'd been promoted, they'd hired dozens more roughnecks, mostly guys from out of state or at least out of Whitespur, anonymous faces that Grant couldn't bother to memorize. Faces like Benjamin Weber, who he'd forgotten about until Nina uncovered his poster yesterday. Some would stay for years, and some would quit in weeks, determined to find a job that didn't break them down mentally and physically. Most, he hoped, wouldn't simply disappear.

"Morning," Grant called to Doc, the aptly named equipment doctor, as he entered the garage, blasted as always by the acrid smell of oil and gasoline. That was one part he hadn't gotten used to. After a full day in the shop, he always dealt with lingering headaches, like the chemicals he inhaled had slipped into his brain and were wrapping their tendrils around the soft tissue. He didn't allow himself to worry about what it might mean long-term, what might grow from the unnatural things he forced himself to do. The smell clung to his jumpsuit no matter how many times he washed it, as did the dark stains.

Doc straightened up and indicated the trio of F-350s lining the right wall. "Those came in yesterday. Can you check them over?"

Grant nodded, relieved that he wouldn't go straight to working on drilling equipment that morning. He still wasn't fully familiar with a lot of the equipment, how it should look and function, which necessitated a lot of time with Doc peering over his shoulder and Grant guessing the wrong answers. Trucks, he knew his way around for the most part. He couldn't fix all the problems, but he could diagnose them.

He glanced over his shoulder at Doc as he popped the hood of the first truck, but the older man was already back to work on a worn hunk of metal. Grant didn't know Doc's real name; no one did.

The morning passed. One truck needed a new battery and catalytic converter, another a new set of spark plugs. The third was in serviceable shape, though rusty. The trucks all had around a hundred thousand miles, castoffs from their original jobs, ready to take the full brunt of the near-arctic wasteland. No point in sending pricey new vehicles to Brooks Valley, where the snow and ice would break them down in due time, just as the difficult labor of extracting the oil would break down the men. He could forget that's what he was doing here, most of the time. Working on trucks, he was only a mechanic. And the pieces of equipment—they were nothing but disembodied metal objects, difficult to identify as drilling machinery. He did a lot of pretending but it made his days easier.

He reminded himself that in twenty years he could be done with all this, an early retirement, rich by rural Alaska standards. He could travel, he could go to college and get a degree in environmental sciences. Atone for the harm he'd done to the earth by learning how to heal it. Hope he lived long enough to fix the mistakes he made.

"Can you drive those over to Site Fourteen?"

Grant turned at the sound of Doc's voice. Doc tilted his head, indicating a truck parked against the opposite wall. Grant eyed the bed full of metal pipes and nodded. He didn't like visiting the well sites—they forced him to confront the truth. There, he had to hear the drilling rig moving, the mechanical scraping as it drew the liquefied remains of ancient organisms up to the surface. But it gave him a reason to drive through the refuge, too, to marvel at the mountains and the millions of acres of smooth snow. He settled into the driver's seat and grabbed the keys from where they rested on the dashboard.

He turned onto the packed snow road heading out of camp and followed it west. The sites were all labeled with metal signs stuck into the snow, although with how frequently conditions changed, they often tipped over and got swept away by strong winds. It was a roughneck's job to replace them, driving all over the refuge with a stack of numbered signs, but it was a low priority task and so often the sites were left unmarked for weeks. But Grant knew the closest sites, One through Twenty, by heart. The higher numbers, the newest sites, were deeper in the refuge and he had yet to visit all of them. Along the road ran the many miles of pipeline that carried the oil away from its point of origin.

Site Fourteen was near a stand of trees. Shelter for a passing moose or fox, maybe, before the oil company had moved in and taken it over. Two trailers were stationed aside the massive drill pad that spanned twelve acres, the wells spreading out to cover many more miles underground. Grant parked the truck beside one of the trailers and switched off the headlights. He'd have to wait for the rig workers to unload the pipes, but maybe he could remain inside the cab for however long it took.

Then he spotted the site foreman, standing with his arms folded in front of the stairs that led up and into the rig, staring through the windshield at Grant. Elias Woodsman. A known hard-ass, the boss no one ever wanted to get stuck with. He wasn't the only difficult supervisor, but he had been around since the Brooks Valley drilling opened and he had a reputation. He'd given Grant plenty of grief when Grant was a roughneck, and he wasn't about to give Elias a reason to write him up for being lazy. Grant pulled on his gloves, threw open the truck door, and climbed out, resigning himself to help unload the pipes.

Several men joined Grant at the truck. They worked alongside each other silently, carrying the pipes inside and stacking them on the drilling rig floor. Elias supervised them in silence. Despite how long he had worked at the oil field, Grant had crossed paths with him in town only a few times, always at the small general store. Plenty of the other foremen would go to The Spur for a drink on their days off, but not Elias, as far as Grant could tell. He seemed downright antisocial—lived in one of the dorms and stuck around camp. Some people had no interest in acclimating to their oil towns, always mentally already living in the next one, even when jobs took years.

The last pipe clattered onto the stack. Elias met Grant's eyes and gave him a curt nod. Job done, Grant turned, eager to head back to the relative civilization of camp.

A noise made him stop in his tracks. An unusual sound, a hiss, like steam escaping, and a high-pitched whistle. The hair on the back of his neck stood up—the sound, it was so distinctly *not right*. He turned around as it happened.

A rush of steam thundered toward the ceiling, filling the building with hot, cloudy air, and then the fireball followed with such an explosive force that Grant was knocked off his feet as he stumbled backward, hands covering his ears as he ducked from the great angry colors of red and black that licked across the metal pipes. Then the deafening whistle again. Then shouting, Elias calling orders, men running from all directions to shut off the rig and assess the damage.

His ears were ringing. A high-pitched, disorienting sound; he couldn't tell if it came from the rig equipment or from his own body. He pressed his hands harder against his ears and then dropped them, but the whine didn't change. He pushed up on his forearms and turned.

Grant looked again and saw what no one else did. A body lying on the floor, a hundred feet from the rig. Thrown by the explosion. Before Grant could think he was running, covering the distance to the body even as the hot, damp air choked his lungs. He threw off his gloves as he landed on his knees beside the man.

Look for a pulse. He knew that much. He'd gone through

two weeks of safety training at the start of this job, but little of it had been first aid. He couldn't remember how to give CPR. There were medics on staff, people who made it their purpose to save lives. They could call one of the medics and wait for the colorful lights of the modified ambulance to illuminate the snow outside.

Only there was no pulse. Grant held the man's wrist in his hand and waited, but there was nothing. The skin was warm. Blood was starting to pool beneath the man's head. He made himself place his fingers on the man's neck, though something in his primal body protested—*don't touch the dead, don't touch the dead.*

"Sanford?"

He flinched at the sound of his own last name as if he'd forgotten he existed. Elias loomed over him, looking not at the body but at Grant.

"He's dead," Grant managed.

Elias frowned. "Are you sure?"

What a question. Grant wanted to offer Elias his position, kneeling on the hard concrete floor, to say: *See for yourself.* But he only nodded.

"Okay." Grant thought a shadow of fear passed across Elias's face before he rearranged his expression into something neutral, something in control. Elias turned and Grant followed, taking in the small crowd of men who were watching, waiting. "Listen up. Death on-site is a big deal. If this gets out, it's not going to look good. I don't need to remind you that we've had more than a few safety investigations over the years. Another, and they might revoke the company's contract. We could *all* lose our jobs." He had their attention now, and paused, calculating. "Do any of you know him?"

There was a long silence. "That's Churchy," someone offered. A nickname.

"Churchy. He had a drinking problem, right?"

Grant's stomach sank, a shimmering ball of anxiety swirling inside him. He thought he understood what Elias was doing, but he didn't want to believe it.

"Sharpe," Elias said, tilting his head. One of the men broke off and jogged up the stairs. Grant wondered where he was going, what the head tilt meant. It was like they were speaking a different language, and Grant couldn't learn it fast enough to understand. "The last time any of us saw him was two nights ago. He was blasted drunk. Stumbling around, waving a whiskey bottle. We tried to talk him into going to bed, but he must have wandered off. Didn't show up to work *yesterday*. Didn't show up *today*, either. And *today*, there was an explosion at Site Fourteen. A small one. But enough to warrant an inspection." He paused. "Tomorrow, I'll write him up as missing. I meant to today, but with all this nonsense," he said, gesturing at the now still and silent drill, "I forgot. You can see how that might happen."

Sharpe reentered the building, the door clanging shut behind him, and held aloft a half-empty bottle of whiskey. It must have come from one of the trailers, but it felt like they had planned it. Grant opened his mouth, wanted to ask Elias if he was insane, to declare that he would tell the truth of the man's death. But he couldn't bring himself to speak.

"We'll take him to the forest down the scout road. No one needs to know about this, alright? If you want to keep your jobs and keep making money, no one says a word. This," Elias said, pointing at Churchy's body, "means nothing. He was a nobody. And the environmentalists are itching for a good reason like this to shut down drilling in the Valley. But they're not gonna pay our bills, and they're not gonna give us new jobs after they take all this away. Don't let them win."

To Grant's shock, the men all nodded, as if Elias's plan made perfect sense, as if *of course* the body belonged in the woods to be scavenged by wolves. As if Elias could read Grant's mind, he turned, his expression dark. "You'll drive," he said, no hint of a question in his voice.

Grant wanted to protest. He wanted to insist that the accident should be reported, that the man, no matter how anonymous, deserved better. Maybe he had family back home, waiting for news of another safe day on the oil field. Instead, they would hear nothing. But the men, the living men, were shouldering around him, lifting the body, carrying it up the stairs and to the truck, leaving a dark pool of blood behind on the concrete floor. And Elias was staring at Grant, his jaw set, reveling in Grant's fear, daring him to object. Saying: *If anyone finds out, I'll know it was you.*

So, Grant lifted the keys from his pocket. And he drove.

5

NO ONE SPOKE ON THE WAY OUT TO THE SCOUT road. The truck tires rolled smoothly over the snow and then bounced as the road became rougher, less frequently traveled out where there were no drilling sites yet. Grant could almost let himself forget how terrified he was, how wrong it was to participate in this cover-up. The three other men in the truck, all strangers, hadn't said a word. They'd taken off their hats and unzipped their thick jackets, revealing faces he recognized, people he'd seen around camp and town. Grant cleared his throat.

"Are we . . . are we just not going to report this?"

The man in the passenger seat coughed. "Fuck no."

"That guy, what'd we call him? Churchy? Weird religious freak. Wouldn't talk except to try to convert us."

"But . . ." Grant trailed off, hating that they spoke so casually about the dead, how they didn't use his real name. "What if he has a family?"

Silence. Then the one who had said Churchy's nickname spoke again. "Can't remember if he does. Like I said, he didn't talk much. He was from some little town in Canada, right? I got the sense he didn't have a lot to go home to."

Grant wanted them to talk about the man, about Churchy, hoping to appeal to their humanity. He wanted them to imagine themselves as the dead body losing blood in the back of the truck, about to be dumped in the woods and forgotten about. But another half mile down the road, the man in the front seat waved his hand, indicating the thick forest up ahead.

"There."

"The road ends," Grant said.

"Just get as close as you can."

Grant drove until the truck strained to move forward. A wild thought crossed his mind—he could get the truck stuck, strand them out by the woods so that someone had to come get them and the cover-up would be revealed. But it would only be Elias, probably—no one else knew where they were.

Grant put the truck in Park. Without a word, the men zipped their jackets and pulled their hats and gloves back on, shoving open the truck doors and slamming them shut again. Then Grant was alone.

Thank God they hadn't asked him to help. But here he was, skin prickling at the back of his neck, not allowing himself to look as thuds and grunts sounded from the back of the truck, from the difficult task of maneuvering a body. He thought again about the blood spreading beneath Churchy's head on the rig floor. The blood that would have been dripping out the entire bumpy ride to the end of the scout road, staining the truck bed. Blood that he would have to find a way to clean without Doc noticing.

He thought of something else, too, a black-and-white image of a smiling man. *Eric Riley*. And the younger face behind, in color, Benjamin Weber. Yesterday, Nina had stood before the bulletin board in The Spur, asking Grant about the missing men, who he had all but forgotten about. Now he wondered— had Eric and Benjamin actually disappeared, or had they too died and been carted off into the woods in neat cover-ups? He tried to remember who Eric had worked for, or what his job even was, but couldn't. Maybe his disoriented mind was jumping to conclusions, trying to make connections that weren't there. A couple of missing people had nothing to do with this man's death. Just yesterday, Grant had reassured Nina that a few disappearances were to be expected in Alaska. Still—Elias and the other men had seemed so practiced, so prepared for this to happen. He couldn't shake the feeling that they had done this before. How many other bodies were waiting in the woods?

The thud of the tailgate closing brought Grant back to the present. He pulled his phone from his pocket, slowly, waiting until they walked past with the body between them, then opened up the camera and hit Record. The camera wouldn't focus at first and he cursed under his breath, tapping the screen, but finally the image sharpened and he zoomed in, hands shaking, catching their last few yards of journey across the open snow before they entered the dark woods. The seconds ticked into minutes at the top of the screen. How deep would they go? Far enough to ensure the body wouldn't be spotted by anyone else coming up the road. But this was the end. No one ever came this far.

Close to ten minutes later they reemerged. Grant managed to stop the video and put his phone away. The men walked in a line, hunched against the cold. They didn't look like they were returning from covering up a murder; they had no air of guilt.

The cold rushed in as the truck doors opened again. They said nothing to him, simply waited for him to turn the truck around and get going. Grant's eyes stung, frustration and panic threatening to spill into tears. He ran the back of his hand across his face.

"Don't say anything, kid," the man next to him said. "Or you'll end up out here, too." He chuckled and slapped Grant's arm.

The other men laughed, and Grant played along, forcing himself to smile. But he knew they weren't joking.

6

ON A NORMAL NIGHT, ENTERING THE SPUR WAS A relief—the wash of heated air, the soft yellow lights, the familiar oldies playing at a gentle volume. But tonight, a wave of anxiety made Grant stop in the doorway. He knew most everyone in the building—unfamiliar faces in The Spur were always new hires on the oil field, never tourists these days. Usually, he liked the small-town familiarity—no introductions to make, nothing but friends or people to steer clear of. But tonight, he wished for invisibility, the opportunity to drink a beer alone with his thoughts, without his friends cracking jokes and making plans for a hunting trip. His options after work had been home or the bar, and he'd chosen the bar, because the thought of sitting at the dinner table and acting normal was unbearable.

He spotted Michael and Orson and made his way over before they had a chance to call to him, the anxiety sinking like a small stone in his stomach. Grant had decided he wouldn't say anything about the cover-up. The oil men had nothing to lose. Clearly Churchy hadn't mattered to them; why would Grant? He had a life here, sure, a family, friends who would ask questions, but he could still picture his dead body lying beside Churchy's.

Michael was the loudest one of his friends. Maybe Grant could get him talking, enough that he wouldn't be the center of conversation. He hoped news of the explosion hadn't already spread.

He settled onto a stool beside Orson, who glanced at him. "You look rough."

"Long day," he muttered.

"Doc working you too hard?"

"Something like that." The bartender, Shauna, placed a beer in front of him. He took a sip, barely tasting it, and remembered that he hadn't eaten dinner. The alcohol would bypass his empty stomach and go straight to his head. He'd have to be careful that he didn't get too drunk to drive home. Though he was unlikely to pass a single other car on the five-mile drive, he didn't want to crash into a tree. He took another drink and said, "I don't know if you heard, but Nina's back home."

Michael looked up from his phone. Orson raised his eyebrows. "When would we have heard?"

Grant shrugged. "We were here yesterday. Word travels fast."

"That's cool," Michael said. "How's she doing?"

Grant considered his question. "Okay, I guess. She didn't come back by choice. She lost her job because of the pandemic and hasn't been able to find a new one. She said it's really bad in the cities."

Michael whistled. "Damn. It's still all over the news. Like a lot of people are dying. I hope she's not sick."

"She seems fine to me."

"Yeah, but it's been, what, a couple days?" Michael continued. "Maybe she picked it up on the plane."

"She said she had to wear a mask."

"And I heard those don't do anything," he muttered.

On the wall opposite the bar was a flat-screen TV tuned to a news channel where the anchors always insinuated the pandemic was a hoax and suggested that the vaccines in development would cause a whole host of other problems. Grant usually ignored it, focused instead on the TV behind the bar, which showed sports, but maybe Michael paid more attention. Plenty of other residents got all their news from that single TV, the ones who didn't live within range of the satellite or even have cell phones.

"Will she be here for a while?" Orson asked.

"I don't know. At least through winter, I'd guess." He flinched as a hand touched his shoulder.

"You're jumpy today," Ila said, stopping beside him.

"Sorry. I didn't see you."

"I'm on break. Want to come outside?"

Grant didn't particularly want to leave the warmth of the bar, but outside was the only place they could be alone. He pushed his beer toward Orson. "Drink it while it's still cold."

In a narrow alleyway behind The Spur, they were mostly shielded from the wind, but the evening was still bitter. The ground was littered with cigarette butts—most of the staff smoked, hence the allowance for occasional short breaks. Ila had never told anyone she didn't.

"How are you?"

Grant liked that she always asked him that question and he loved the directness of her brown-eyed gaze whenever it settled on him. But tonight, he couldn't meet her eyes. His thoughts were a fragmented spiral of images. Steam. Fire. Body. Keys. Road. Forest. The blood he had scrubbed from the truck bed after returning to the shop. He had busied himself near the truck until Doc took lunch, and thankfully none of the other mechanics paid Grant much attention—at least, that he was aware of. Maybe someone had watched with curious eyes as he took the bucket of pale red soapy water and dumped it down the drain of one of the slop sinks.

He couldn't tell Ila. She hated the drilling in the Brooks Valley more than anyone, enough so that he was surprised she'd said yes to a first date. She would tell someone, tell the whole town, call in reporters, anything to shut down the drilling. And as much as Grant wanted that, too, he had no other job prospects. And even if the oil company was ousted, another would fight for the contract and take its place. So, he wouldn't tell her, but he would answer as truthfully as he could.

"I've been better. Work was rough today. There was some problem with one of the rigs, a fire or something. Stressed everyone out."

Her brow furrowed. "No one got hurt?"

"No," Grant replied. He didn't let himself hesitate. The knit of her brow still showed concern. He placed a hand on her shoulder, slid it behind her head, rested it on the back of her neck. "I missed you."

"I missed you, too." She shifted closer to him. "Have you told Nina about us yet?"

The question Grant had been dreading. "No. Sorry. It . . . hasn't come up."

Ila rolled her eyes but smiled. "Grant. She's not going to kill you. I just think she deserves to hear it from you, okay? Her brother." She paused. "I'm not even sure if she'll care at all. She's gone and lived an entire life and I've been here. Staying the same."

"You lost touch?"

She made a face. "I always called her when I was in Fairbanks or anywhere with service. Sometimes she'd answer. She'd text me, but I wouldn't get it for a month. I'm sure she's an entirely different person now. Feels like time stood still for me for nine years."

The pain and longing were clear in her voice. "You sound envious."

"I am," she replied. "I mean, Whitespur will always be home. But of course, I want to travel. Of course, I still want to go to college. I think I'd come back to Alaska. Just maybe not here. Somewhere coastal." She smiled, though it was the saddest Grant had ever seen her. "But what are the chances of that? It's easier to try to be happy in Whitespur, while I'm here."

"You and I could move somewhere," Grant offered. "Seward or Homer. It'd be a little easier to get to Anchorage, hop on a plane and travel." She eyed him skeptically. "You could work at a restaurant. I could do something that doesn't involve oil. I don't know what, but anything else."

They hadn't discussed their future much yet. As he realized this, it struck Grant as strange that he didn't know what Ila wanted, if she ever wanted to get married and have kids. They had lived remarkably in the present, spending time with each other almost daily but also both absorbed in the town they'd always lived in. That she wanted to leave wasn't shocking— she'd said as much before—but could she picture Grant going with her?

She didn't respond for a long moment, and the silence made Grant uneasy. Maybe he'd said too much, pushed too far by including himself in the scenario.

"That sounds nice," she said, her voice flat. "But I don't think I could leave my family. Lusa is still a mess. She needs so much help with the kids." Her sister's husband had died while fishing for king crab in the Bering Sea two years ago, his absence still a raw wound. Even her parents were locked in grief. Ila rolled her shoulders and glanced at the door. "I should get back to it. You sticking around?"

"I'll have a beer, yeah. But I'll probably head home early tonight."

Ila nodded, her expression clouded by some private concern. Grant reached for her, and to his relief she came willingly, tilting her head up and kissing him. Her lips were warm and soft and for a moment he forgot about the explosion, the body, his role in a crime. For a moment, it was just Ila, and he pondered why, if she brought him this much comfort and peace, he'd put no thought into their future.

He let her go. She squeezed his hand and then grabbed the door handle, pulling off her gloves and hat as she stepped back inside. Grant followed, engulfed by the warmth and the music once again. Orson was still at the bar, finishing the last of Grant's beer, but Michael was gone.

Orson was kind enough to buy Grant a replacement beer, which he drank, and convinced him to share an order of poutine. Grant picked at the French fries smothered in gravy and cheese curds, shoving them around on the plate with his fork. Orson shook his head and finished the meal off on his own.

"It's almost eight. I'm gonna head out," Grant said. He liked to be in bed by nine when he could, rising a little past four in the morning to make his way to the oil field. But he suspected he wouldn't get much sleep that night. The day sat heavy on his shoulders, impelling him down toward the earth where the man's body rested. He wondered if Churchy had been found yet, if his scent had drawn in a desperate predator.

"See you," Orson said. Grant felt a small relief that he had hidden his anxiety well; Orson seemed oblivious to it.

As Grant pushed through the front door, he nearly bumped into someone. "Sorry," he mumbled, stepping aside and holding the door propped to let the person through. But they didn't move.

"Grant?"

He blinked and let the door fall shut. It was Audrey, bundled in a tan puffy coat, face mostly obscured by a black hat and scarf. She smiled tentatively up at him.

"It's nice to see you."

"Yeah, you too." Grant shifted, gazing past her down the street to where the truck was parked.

Audrey's expression fell. "You can talk to me. I'm not drunk."

"Sorry. It's not . . . I was on my way out."

"I know." She folded her arms across her chest. "I upset Nina yesterday, didn't I?"

Grant froze, wondering how he could answer the question. Of course, Nina was upset, seeing her older sister drunk and out of it, slumped over a table on a weekday afternoon. But he thought she'd moved past it already. She hadn't mentioned it to him again, at least, hadn't said much on the way home from the bar. But maybe it was still bothering her. Grant coughed, stalling for time.

"It's okay," Audrey said, reaching out to touch his arm. "She has every right to be upset with me."

Grant studied her, surprised that she spoke so coherently. He hadn't seen her completely sober in a long time—over a year, maybe. Or maybe it was the first day she hadn't had anything to drink in over a year. He held himself back from asking.

"Are you ever going to come over for dinner again?" Grant blurted out.

The left corner of Audrey's mouth lifted, but her eyes relayed a different story. "I don't think so. Mom doesn't want me around until I'm sober. And . . ." She lifted her shoulders in a shrug. "You know how that goes."

Grant didn't, but he could guess. Without thinking, he pulled Audrey into a hug, surprised by how little of her there was beneath the bulky jacket. He stepped back quickly, but she grinned, her eyes dancing with an energy he forgot was once familiar. "Take care of yourself," he managed. "See you soon."

"You too, Grant. Stay safe on that oil field."

As if she knew. Grant's heart sped up, but Audrey brushed past him—probably in a hurry for her first drink of the day. She didn't know, of course not. He worked a dangerous job. It wasn't the first time he'd been told to stay safe. But the words carried a different meaning now. Grant couldn't help looking over his shoulder as he walked to the truck, but what he was looking for, he didn't know.

7

NINA LIFTED THE CUTTING BOARD AND DUMPED THE chopped whitefish into the last of forty-something bowls. Her head pounded from the chorus of barking, whining, and howling that had been her soundtrack for the last half hour, as she prepared dinner for the dogs. Her mother was in the house, cooking their dinner—Nina had offered to help, but her mother had made a snide comment about not having the ingredients Nina was used to, and she had taken the hint and opted to prepare the dogs' meal instead.

Now she amused herself by imagining what she would say to Micah if he were here—that maybe the dogs would prefer their fish julienned or brunoised, that the dinner crowd sure was raucous tonight, that they hadn't ordered enough kibble for the evening rush. Dumb jokes that would have gotten an eye roll and a flick of a shiny knife in her direction.

Nina wiped her brow with the back of her wrist and closed the freezer, pausing to survey the array of bowls and buckets on the floor. Each one was labeled, but she still feared giving a dog the wrong food or leaving out an important supplement, the same way she used to fear forgetting an allergy in a guest's dish. She picked up the first two bowls and proceeded down the aisle, opening each kennel door and sliding the bowl in, praying that her fingers wouldn't become a casualty of the snapping teeth that greeted each dinner.

During their twice-weekly trips to the fish market, Micah would sometimes pick up a king crab and shake it so that its claws waggled in her direction, threatening to pinch—only if he was in a good mood, if the restaurant was doing well, if the sun was shining. He hated wintertime, even cloudy days. That was how they met—on a dreary day in October, Nina's second month of culinary school. She'd gone down to stand on the bank of the Hudson one evening after class had ended, feeling overwhelmed and insecure and far from home. The sky was a flat uniform gray, the leafy trees an array of muted colors—red, orange, gold. Nina had never known autumn like this before, as anything other than the first act of winter. The air was cool and smelled like rain and smoke. The scent led her to Micah, sitting on a bench, a cigarette between his fingertips. She lifted a hand. She knew of him, as she knew of everyone in her Culinary Fundamentals course. Nina had yet to make a friend, but she thought Micah was as good a candidate as any.

He saw her looking and smiled, a grin that would grow as familiar as Bow Lake, as the Brooks Range. "Want one?"

It took her a moment to realize he meant a cigarette. "Oh. Sure."

Nina had never smoked before, and it burned her throat and made her cough. Micah seemed not to notice. "God. It's fucking cold here."

She almost laughed. He had made room on the bench for her and she sat, feeling the chilled iron through her jeans.

Fifty degrees wasn't cold, although already her perspective was shifting. She had worn a light jacket down to the river.

"Wait. You're the Alaska girl, right? Don't make fun of me."

Nina didn't mind being identified as *the Alaska girl*—when they'd done icebreakers on the first day in some of her classes, she'd mentioned it as one of her fun facts. A few people had since told her that they'd visited, though none as far north as Whitespur. "I won't," she replied.

"I'm from Hawai'i," he said, and raised his eyebrows when she asked which island. "Oahu. Honolulu."

Nina nodded. "I always wanted to visit Hawai'i. I thought it must be the exact opposite of Alaska." She had hoped, even then, that their geography might be the foundation for a connection—because they were both American, but disconnected from the majority of the country. She had overheard Micah call it the "mainland"; in Alaska they called it the lower forty-eight. Different words for the same thing, the experience of being separate from the rest, belonging but not fully.

Micah exhaled a puff of smoke, his expression thoughtful. "I bet we could cook some good shit together. Alaskan-Hawaiian fusion."

They didn't know it then, but that idea would eventually become 4950, their little restaurant tucked away on a side street in downtown Portland. It came after years of working in New York, in high-pressure kitchens with verbally abusive head chefs and enough oven burns to tell their profession from a glance. At their first job together, at Nocturne—a popular, well-respected restaurant in the West Village that had been around since the '80s—they would greet each other solemnly each day with "Chef" and then dissolve into laughter, partially in disbelief that they had made it, that they had come so far, physically and mentally, and ended up in a kitchen together sweating and shouting and churning out good food.

But Micah only lasted eight months at Nocturne. "Those guys are fucking pricks, Nina," he said one night, when they were seated at their favorite dive bar in the wee hours, the clock somewhere between midnight and close. It was May, and spring had the city in its grasp, spreading more daylight on the streets and unspooling fresh green leaves from the tree branches. The air felt too hopeful for Micah's pessimism. "I can't do it anymore. I'm interviewing at Root & Stone next week."

Nina stayed quiet for what felt like several minutes, stirring the ice in her third drink of the night. Micah had a smaller tolerance for being treated poorly; she had known that from the days when he complained about the behavior of even their milder culinary school instructors. She could usually ignore it and focus on the cooking, as she had always done—inventing new recipes and learning all the ways to cook an ingredient had been her lifeline growing up, a way to mentally block out the exceptional cold and darkness of winter. But she understood Micah was right in this case—she'd left Nocturne in tears so many times, dampening her shirtsleeves as she cried in the alley-way beside the building, counting up the ways she had failed.

"I'm going to stay," she told Micah. "I want more experience before I try to go somewhere else."

He sipped his drink and set it back on the table. "Your bullshit tolerance is so much higher than mine."

What Nina had been thinking, but it made her smile to hear him say it out loud. "What can I say. I'm hardened." She paused, then said, "Is it weird that it bothers me more when it happens to other people? Like, when Castle yells at me, it makes me feel worthless and incompetent. But when he yells at you, or Elise, it makes me angry. Like I want to take a knife to that uniform he's so proud of." Ian Castle was the sous-chef at Nocturne and never refrained from hurling any insult that crossed his mind.

Micah snorted. "Just wait until he's not wearing it, at least."

Nina had no real plans to commit an act of vandalism. She was only marginally saddened, too, when Micah left Nocturne. They still shared a city, still lived in apartments only a few blocks apart. Nina couldn't fathom that they wouldn't end up in the same kitchen again, eventually. And they did, but not in New York. Micah's secret weapon was his previous career, a short-lived but lucrative stint in the Silicon Valley tech industry. He'd left with a desire to chase his passion for cooking and a handful of rich friends with money to burn. When he'd pitched the idea for 4950—behind Nina's back—they were in. And that money had certainly burned, all of it, trying and failing to keep the restaurant afloat for just a few months in the pandemic.

But for a few years, Nina's dream had been realized. She'd never expected to become so close with Micah, but his wise-cracking, self-assured attitude had softened her hard exterior. She'd learned to have fun in her years away, she thought, pausing to pet Honey before delivering her dinner. Not that growing up in Whitespur hadn't been fun, but she couldn't deny that she loved stepping into a different social class, being a chef, drinking expensive liquor at trendy bars and always knowing that Micah was looking out for her, making sure she didn't get too drunk and didn't leave her wallet on the bar top. In those days they never rested. When the bars closed down, they walked to their shared apartment in South Portland and cooked up the wildest dishes they could imagine—saimin with smoked caribou sausage, fry bread topped with soft squares of haupia—until one of them declared the resulting meal a success or an incredible failure, and then they retreated to their respective rooms and slept like the dead. They would wake at noon the next day to do it all over again.

When the dogs had finished eating, she retrieved each bowl and rinsed it in the sink. A space heater aimed at the wall hummed, working overtime to keep the pipes from freezing. When it got cold enough in the winter, the pipes sometimes froze regardless, even if the power didn't go out. But when the power did—Nina remembered how cold it got one winter, near fifty below, and her mother had thrown up her hands and brought all the dogs inside. Many had to be separated so they wouldn't fight. It was their nature—they were high-energy dogs, and without an outlet for that energy, they sometimes turned on each other. But Nina and Audrey had brought a few of the sweet, older ones into their bedroom, piled all the blankets on the floor, and slept in the nest of dogs. Her wish come true, for one night.

Guilt wound its way through Nina when she thought of Audrey the day before, drunk in the afternoon, asking Grant for money. Her own relationship with alcohol was—had been—so different. She never drank to get through the day but as a celebration, to revel in the lifestyle she had earned, to connect with friends after a hard week or even a hard night in the kitchen. Never once had she felt dependent on it. But Audrey wasn't the first alcoholic in Whitespur. The winters were harsh, too much darkness, too much cold. Alcohol warmed the body and numbed the mind. Though it didn't matter, she wondered when Audrey had turned the corner—when Alaska became too much, when trying to leave became too difficult. Nina wanted to talk to her sister again, alone, to try to figure out if there was some way she might help. Another task on her growing to-do list.

Nina finished cleaning up and turned off the light. She paused outside in the yard, craning her neck up at the cloudy sky. It had seemed like the only option, coming back here, but now she remembered what a trap it was, to be stuck out in the bush without internet, without cell service. More than anything, she wanted to call Micah and hear his voice telling her that it would all be fine, that she would find her way back. Whitespur was more claustrophobic than New York. There was no room to be anonymous here; everyone had watched her grow up and knew all the details of her life. Until she left. Then she had become simply another story, one of the fabled ones who got away.

NINA LOOKED UP from the sink of soapy water as Grant stomped inside. "Saved you a plate," she said, gesturing with her chin toward the counter.

Grant's eyes grazed over it. "Yeah, thanks." The kitchen was empty except for Nina. Her dad had parked in front of the television as soon as he'd finished eating, and her mom had gone into town for a few essential groceries from the general store. Neither of her parents had seemed surprised that Grant hadn't shown up for dinner—when Nina commented on his absence, her mother remarked that he was likely with his friends. Nina tried not to let it sting that after only a day, her presence at home had become old news. Since dinner ended, she had adjusted to the quiet, the soft murmur of the TV through the walls, and now Grant's demeanor was too loud and off-kilter. "Can I talk to you about something?" he asked, coming closer.

Nina turned off the faucet. "Yeah, of course."

"Not here," he said. "Let's go to the kennel."

A few minutes later, once the dogs had quieted down, Nina leaned against the prep counter as Grant paced the aisle. A kind of nervous energy radiated off her younger brother. Nina was reminded of the time he'd crashed the family snow machine when he was fourteen and come home in tears, begging Nina to help him break the news to their parents. Perhaps even then, he'd sensed that Nina would be more reliable than Audrey. She'd taken pity on him and sat beside him on the couch as he described the accident, going too fast on a downhill turn and rolling the machine. After confirming that he was uninjured, Ted had revoked his driving privileges for the rest of the winter, and Mary had put him on kennel-cleaning duty for the next three months. Grant, always eager to do the right thing, hadn't complained once.

"What's wrong?" she asked.

He hesitated. "I don't know how to tell you."

"That's ominous," Nina replied, trying to keep her tone light as she wondered what he could possibly be so worried about. Her mind went to Audrey, the myriad of bad situations that her alcoholic older sister might have gotten herself into.

He said nothing and continued to pace. Nina moved from the counter to sit on a bench pushed against the wall. Finally, she could no longer take it. "Grant. Spill."

"Sorry," he said. "I'm trying to figure out where to start." He paused his pacing and stared at the ceiling for a long moment before looking at her. "You're going to hear about a fire."

"What?"

"A fire. Because there was one, today, at one of the drilling sites. An explosion. A small one, I guess. It was over in seconds."

"Okay." Nina failed to see how this could cause him so much upset.

"It's not the full story." He exhaled. "Someone died."

"What?" Nina said, again, except this time the word left her mouth like a squeak. She sat up, watching Grant with more attention.

"This guy, he's—he was—new. Newer than me. I don't know what happened, exactly, but there was all this steam and then an explosion and then flames. I wasn't that close to the drill and it

knocked me over. Anyway, it went out and there was . . . a body."
He paused, like he was choking back a sob. "No one seemed to
notice him except for me. I took his pulse but . . . you know.
I guess he was closer and the explosion threw him pretty hard."

Nina swallowed and nodded, trying to push away the sick-
ening images that Grant's story had sprouted in her mind.
"What about you? Are you okay?"

"I'm here, aren't I?" he replied, though his tone didn't inspire
much confidence.

"Why were you there? At a rig, I mean? I thought you
worked in a shop."

Grant stared at her. "I had to deliver some pipes." He took a
breath. "So, I'm looking at this, at this body, and it's the worst
thing I've ever seen. I mean, people get injured, it happens all
the time, like I told you yesterday. But this was different. I've
never—I've never seen someone die before. And the rig foreman came up with this story, to make it look like he'd gotten
too drunk and wandered off. He said it would be bad for all of
us if word got out. There'd be too many questions, too much
chance they'd shut the rig down. 'Take him down the scout
road,' he said. And no one questioned him." Grant closed his
eyes. "A few of the guys, they grabbed the body and they made
me drive the truck out to the woods. And that's it."

"Wait. Drive the truck out to the woods and do what?
Leave him there? Why?" Nina asked, unwilling to believe
what Grant had told her, that he would go along with it. She
couldn't bring herself to say *you*, to accuse him outright—not
Grant. But the sinking sensation in her stomach told her that
she might understand where his story was headed.

"Yeah. This guy, he's not—he wasn't popular. From what
the other guys said, he came from out of town, no family or
friends that he ever talked about. I don't know if that's true,

or just a way to make themselves less guilty. But now he's dead, and no one will ever know, even if he does have someone back home."

"You're going to say something, right? Report it?"

"God, I don't know," Grant said. "To who?"

"The police. The oil oversight people. They have those, right? Someone above the foreman."

"I don't know," Grant repeated, sitting beside her on the bench. He folded forward, head in his hands. One of the dogs barked, a sharp sound, but Grant didn't lift his head. "I mean, yes, they exist. But no one else cared. It was like, 'yep, normal day on the job.' And they're going to report him as missing using that story they made up." He paused. "I took a video. Of them carrying the body into the woods, and coming back to the truck. But I don't know if their faces are even visible. If I show that video to anyone, if I report it differently . . ." He trailed off, words strangled by a ragged breath. "They'll know it was me."

A video. Smart of Grant to take one. She tucked its existence away for later—he was too worked up for her to ask to watch it now. The dog barked again, pushing against its kennel door. "Does it matter? Is that the type of place you want to work?"

His head shot up. "Nina. A man died and they dumped his body in the woods. What do you think they'd do to me?"

"Covering up an accident and a murder are two different things," Nina protested, but the fear in his eyes was real. She hesitated, and then asked, "You said some of the people who work there are felons, right? Ex-convicts? Is that why you're afraid?"

Grant's eyes narrowed and he shook his head. "No. I mean, yes, the oil company does hire people with criminal records. But as far as I know, Elias doesn't have one. I think he's one of the career oil guys. Besides, it doesn't matter what they've done in their past," he said, with a sweeping gesture, as if to encompass everything he'd told her.

"Sorry. You're right." Nina drew a breath, thought of the other missing men and the multiple *injuries* that Grant had alluded to the day before. Grant had said that the other workers had seemed unbothered, practiced, even, at orchestrating a cover-up. Perhaps it wasn't the first time a dead body had landed at their feet. "Okay, so, you're not going to report it. Are you going to quit?"

"And go where?"

"Another oil field. You could go to Texas or North Dakota. Get the hell out of here."

"Because that worked out so well for you. Sorry," Grant said reflexively, before Nina could even process the comment. "Look. I don't think leaving is the answer. I think I just have to keep my mouth shut and cope with this fucked-up thing."

Nina stayed quiet, trying to imagine a way to bring attention to the man's death without implicating her brother. A different dog whined, a pitiful sound, and Nina wished she had a similar noise to express helplessness. She glanced at Grant, then blurted, "What if I reported it?"

"No," he said quickly, "no, don't do that."

"They wouldn't know who it came from."

"No," he repeated, more firmly this time. "You were young when you left. Maybe you don't remember how things work around here. But the police won't care about one death in a town this small. Not when it happened during a dangerous job. It's how it goes with any accident that gets reported. They might come out and poke around, but they won't seriously investigate, not when the oil contracts bring in so much money. But you know who will care? Everyone whose work gets interrupted because the police come sniffing around."

Nina tried to control the indignation in her voice. "You're making it sound like the Wild West. I'm not naive. It might take the police a while to get here, but they'll come." Grant seemed to think she was still the same innocent—relatively speaking—eighteen-year-old she'd been when she left for school. A small part of her questioned if she should have tried harder to find work before coming home. She could have remained in blissful oblivion to her family's problems. But guilt came with that thought—she had to help Grant, not throw him to the wolves. "Do you really think everyone at the oil field feels the same way?"

"All the oil people, they might shop at the general store and hang out at The Spur, but they don't belong here. They have no obligation to protect me, to protect us. The oil people have more money and more resources. They have ways of figuring it out." He stood up, running his hands through his hair. Though he said *people*, plural, Nina sensed that he was referring to the foreman, the leader of the cover-up. "Besides, a report wouldn't come from you. It'd come from me. Understand?"

Nina felt the weight of Grant's fear. Though she didn't understand the politics of the oil field, she could tell he felt strongly that he'd be a target if he went to the police. Maybe it was only the adrenaline coursing through his veins. If she gave him some time, he might come around to doing the right thing. "Yeah. I get it." She paused. "Are you sure you're okay?"

"Yeah," he replied, a little too quickly. "I need to get some sleep. Sorry for telling you all this."

"It's okay," Nina said, but he was already halfway down the aisle.

The sound of the door closing resonated after he left. Nina studied the kennel as her thoughts roamed—the stained concrete floors, the thick log walls, the bulletin board outside the office, covered in notes in her mother's handwriting and a few photos of her father's race victories. The dogs were agitated again, whining and pawing at their kennel doors in the wake of Grant's absence. They wanted attention; they wanted to run.

Someone died, Nina thought, again and again, as if that idea was somehow less comprehensible than the cover-up. It wasn't that she was unfamiliar with death. Growing up, there had been hunting accidents, snow machining accidents, deaths on faraway offshore drilling rigs. Someone's brother or uncle or cousin. This felt different, because no matter how much she resisted, she kept imagining Grant in that man's place—his body, lifeless on the rig floor. His body, loaded into the back of a pickup truck and carted off into the wilderness, left as food for a pack of wolves or a thin old bear, late to hibernation. Or maybe only a vagrant vulture would show interest. Another Alaskan tragedy, another life taken by human greed.

No. That would never happen. Grant was a local with a family who loved him. He couldn't just disappear. *Or could he? They could lie. Say he never showed up for work. It might take weeks to find the body.*

Sick to her stomach, Nina forced herself to stand. The evening was still young and she faced another long night. She'd been working on her résumé and plotting a trip to the nearest library with internet, to apply for jobs. Maybe she'd find work in Fairbanks, stay within driving distance of home for a while. With the state her family was in, she could no longer justify fleeing to the farthest possible opportunity.

WHEN NINA STEPPED OUT OF THE KENNEL BUILDING
the next evening, she noticed a figure standing by the front
door of the house. She hung back in the shadows to avoid
triggering the floodlights. The figure knocked on the door,
waited for a moment longer, and then turned away. A sliver
of face showed from between the hat and coat hood wrapped
around the person's head—a woman, Nina thought.

"Hello?" she called, stepping forward. The floodlight
snapped on, turning the yard into a well-lit stage.

"Nina?" the woman replied, hopefully. "It's Ila."

Nina jogged across the yard to meet her. "Hi. Sorry, I
couldn't tell."

"Are you surprised to see me?"

"Of course not," Nina said. "You've always kept your
promises." She studied Ila's face, still unnerved by how different Ila looked after nine years—herself, but a woman, lines on
her forehead and around her mouth and some worry carried in

her eyes. At some point in Nina's absence, she had stepped into adulthood, just as Grant had done. And in turn, Nina.

Ila walked to a black Subaru sitting idle in the driveway. She reached into the passenger seat and produced a pair of skates. "What do you think?"

"I think that's a great idea."

AN HOUR LATER, Nina called "whoa" to the dogs and set the snow hook by Bow Lake. She switched off her headlamp, giving her eyes a minute to adjust to the darkness. A few clouds had drifted in and now shed snow, light flurries that were barely noticeable unless Nina sought them. The clouds themselves commanded more attention—they were orange.

"Is that light from the oil field?" Nina asked, pointing at them.

"Yeah," Ila replied as she clambered out of the sled basket. "It's not so bad when the sky is clear, but they have huge lights out there, and we're close enough to see them."

The strangely colored clouds made Nina think of how bright the oil field camp had been when Grant had taken her to see it from above. With Ila's help, she checked the dogs, making sure their paws were in good shape and offering each dog a piece of frozen whitefish.

"It's beautiful, isn't it?" Ila asked when they were done, pulling off her gloves and mittens to quickly change from boots to ice skates. Nina did the same, hoping her fingers wouldn't freeze before it was time to lace the skates. The evening air hovered around eighteen degrees and Nina was happy to slip her gloves back on a minute later.

"It reminds me of when we were kids," she replied, taking a few unsteady steps onto the ice before her strides settled into a gliding motion. Nina had gone ice-skating a few times since she left, mostly in big ugly rinks when friends wanted to go. Once, in winter, she'd traveled upstate with Micah and skated on a frozen lake, although not wild like this one—there had been houses surrounding the lake, plenty of eyes watching from the windows. She had been anxious rather than relaxed and free, the way she felt now, although some of that anxiety stemmed from trying to teach Micah to skate. He had not been an easy student, with two left feet and more confidence than skill.

"I'm sure everything does, right? You've been away for so long." Ila caught up to her as they moved out toward the interior of the lake. A dense forest of mostly spruce trees flanked the left side, stretching out to meet the mountains in the distance. Nina turned slowly as she skated, keeping an eye on the dogs, but they had curled up beside the sled, content to sleep until it came time to work again.

"It's an unusual way to grow up, from what I've gathered." Nina had met only a few other people from Alaska, mostly 4950 customers who wanted to personally thank her for highlighting their state's cuisine. Many people claimed to be from Alaska but hedged when pushed and finally admitted that they'd spent a few years in Anchorage or moved away in childhood. She hadn't met anyone else who had lived their entire life in the bush.

"But special, right?"

Nina thought about her childhood spent in the long dark night, the freezing temperatures, the sweet blip of a mild near-arctic summer. The looming mountains, the uniform trees, the wild tundra that tumbled out in all directions. She thought of the caribou and the grizzly bears she'd known as neighbors.

And the people—the strange, gruff, soulful people whose entire existence was a battle against nature. They lived in a place almost inhospitable to humans and yet managed to survive, to raise families and hold meager jobs and celebrate a kid's first moose harvest. The people who were born and raised here, like her and Ila, or who for some reason chose to forgo structured society and rely on only themselves for survival. And yet she had left.

"Yeah, it's special," she replied, slowing to match Ila's pace.

"I'm glad you're back," Ila said. "Even if you don't stay for long. I missed you."

"I missed you, too." In all the years away, Nina had never met someone who understood her as easily as Ila did, no doubt because of the way they grew up. Even Micah, who she considered the friend equivalent of a soulmate—she had to explain things to him all the time, because his childhood in Hawai'i bared little resemblance to hers in Alaska. And she didn't understand his history, either. They taught each other who they were through food and through stories. But Ila already knew.

Ila glanced toward Nina, her brow furrowed as they traced a slow circle in the center of the lake. "Can I tell you something? You might not like it."

"Sure," Nina replied, bracing herself for more news about Audrey, undoubtedly, that her drinking habit was worse than it appeared or that she'd been caught using some drug in The Spur.

"Grant's never going to tell you, so I will. We're seeing each other."

Nina skated a couple of awkward steps, the blades shaving through the top layers of ice. "What? You and Grant?" Disbelief washed over her, not for the fact of the relationship but because Grant had hidden it from her.

"Yeah. It's been, oh, a year. That probably makes it worse." Ila smiled sheepishly. "He was worried you'd be upset. I said you were allowed to be. But again, I didn't think he'd ever get around to telling you, and you deserve to know."

Nina failed to suppress a laugh. "It's a little bit horrifying to think about Grant dating anyone, let alone you. But I guess he's grown up now. Why would I be upset?"

"You know Grant. He worries about everything." She paused. "But he's more mature than most of the men here. I dated a couple of the oil guys when they first started coming into town, but I felt like I couldn't trust any of them, like they all had families or at least girlfriends back home. They just wanted to get their big check, have a little fun while they were at it, and get the hell out of Alaska. They didn't want anything serious."

"I probably don't need to remind you, but Grant works at that same oil field."

Ila skated closer to bump Nina's shoulder. "You and I both know he's not like that. He doesn't want to be there. But it's the only place that pays."

"I know," Nina said, and she did, despite every ounce of her being that hated the oil field's existence, especially after what Grant had told her yesterday. "Well. I'm happy for you guys. It just might take me a minute to wrap my head around it." She wondered why Grant hadn't told her sooner, but he was prone to worrying about nothing. She'd have to ask him how serious they were, if he saw them getting married. She liked the idea of Ila becoming her sister-in-law.

"What about you?" Ila asked, putting distance between them with a few quick strides. "Did you leave anyone behind?"

"No," Nina replied, images of the empty city clouding her mind. It wasn't what Ila meant, but the pandemic sometimes gave the impression that she was the only person left on earth, wandering the picked-through aisles of an abandoned grocery store. It was startling sometimes to round a corner and see a pair of eyes staring back above a blue mask. "I've dated people, but I was single when I left. My last real relationship ended a few years ago. I was dating this girl—"

"Girl?" Ila said, immediately, glancing at Nina with raised eyebrows and a smile.

"Yeah. I've dated both, you know, men and women since I left."

"Very metropolitan of you."

"Something like that," Nina replied. She recognized Ila's comment was intended to be harmless, but it still stung, because Nina hadn't known that part of her identity existed until she left home. She cleared her throat. "Anyway, I really liked her. But she was an actress, and she decided to give LA a go, and we couldn't make long distance work."

"An actress! Is she famous?"

"Not yet. But then again, I haven't checked social media since I got home. Maybe she's become a star in the last few days."

Ila laughed, her voice carrying in the quiet air. "If you've been dating movie stars, the options in Whitespur are going to be awfully disappointing."

Nina hadn't thought much about Miriam in months. They had dated in New York, when she'd worked for Nocturne after graduating. Miriam had been fun, and beautiful, and ambitious. But after she moved to Los Angeles and they broke up, Nina found herself more focused on work than dating. And when 4950 became reality—she went on dates, sometimes, but she was an unappealing mix of focused and exhausted that pushed people away even as she tried to pull them in. She had more fun with Micah than with most of the people she dated, anyway, and the idea of a romantic relationship became an afterthought, like the can of beans she might pick up just to keep the pantry stocked.

"By the way, I told August you're home," Ila continued.

His name made Nina's heart skip a beat, even after years of trying not to think about him. August, who she'd been so certain she'd spend her whole life with, if only she hadn't wanted to leave Alaska. August loved Alaska like it was air, like he needed it to live. Even leaving interior Alaska had been difficult for him to imagine. He'd been devastated by her choice to go to New York. She hadn't seen him since the day before she left home nine years ago and hadn't spoken to him since sophomore or junior year of college—he rarely updated his social media beyond posting a picture of a scenic landscape once or twice a year. Still—even after so long, the idea of him tugged at her heartstrings and called to mind a future with a warm cabin, long walks in the snow, and a quiet symbiosis with the land.

"You're blushing," Ila remarked.

"It's freezing out," Nina replied, quick to protest the accurate observation. "What's he doing now?"

"He's a biologist at the refuge. Studies tundra plants. He's around The Spur most nights, if you ever want to ask him about it." Ila winked and reached up to tug her hat lower over her ears.

Nina nodded, but her mind kept shifting to other thoughts. Ila seemed in awfully high spirits—had Grant told her about the accident, the body? It seemed unlikely, but then again, Nina was doing her best to laugh and project normalcy even as she remembered Grant's palpable anxiety the night before. Maybe that knowledge was lurking behind Ila's smile as well. She hadn't had a chance to talk to him today; he left for work early in the morning, and Ila had shown up before Grant returned home. But maybe she could talk to Ila about it without saying much at all. She cleared her throat.

"Ila, can I ask you something?"

"Fire away," her friend replied, whirling a circle around Nina.

"What would you do if you knew about something bad that had happened, but also knew there would be consequences if you said something?"

Ila slowed now, regarding Nina seriously. "Are you okay?"

"Yeah, I'm okay. This is hypothetical."

"Is this about the rig explosion?"

Nina's heart skipped another beat. "You heard about it?"

Ila snorted. "Nina, I work at the only legal bar in town. Ten different guys came in this afternoon and were talking about it. Mimicking the explosion." She made a face and waved her arms, throwing herself off-balance. "They were all so casual about it. I thought, maybe this isn't the whole story."

"And you thought I would know?"

"Come on. Think about the question you just asked me. I can put two and two together." Ila stopped skating entirely and placed a hand on Nina's arm. "Is Grant in trouble?"

"No, no," Nina said, shaking her head. "He would tell you if he was."

"Are you sure? I know that word about it spread fast, but why would he tell you—"

A sudden frenzy of barking and howling made them both whip around. "The dogs!" Nina called, and they were off, slicing across the center of the lake. They'd skated far from shore and Nina could barely make out the sled and dogs—like little dots bouncing in the distance. Their cries echoed through the valley, amplified by the lake's topography.

"Wait!"

Nina jolted as Ila caught her arm, nearly slipping. She followed her friend's pointed finger and her breath caught in her throat.

Wolves.

Three of them, trotting in a line along the shore, away from the dogsled. The light of the quarter moon caught the silver in their fur and made them shine, even against the white snow. They were moving at a steady pace, but not hurried. As they came closer, they leaped onto the frozen lake one by one and cut a track across the center, heading toward the forest on the far shore. They never paused but kept a wide berth.

"Wow," Nina breathed. She'd seen wolves only once before, as a kid, on a camping trip way out in the mountains with her father. In the summer twilight, she'd stolen away from the campsite to gather more kindling for the fire. From a hill above the tundra, she had watched a pack of wolves move soundlessly across the valley, their mottled fur blending with the red-green grass that waved in the soft breeze. She stayed still until they disappeared—whether they ducked out of sight or she simply lost track, she was never sure.

The women stared at each other in disbelief. Then Ila's face cleared, as if she had just remembered something.

"Somebody needs to report the explosion at the rig," she said, and skated to the shore.

9

GRANT STOPPED AT THE SIGHT OF DOC SITTING IN A folding camp chair in the middle of the shop floor. The big garage was silent except for the fans running overhead, circulating the artificially warm air. Doc raised his eyebrows at Grant and gestured for him to come over.

"Did you clock in?"

"Yeah. What's going on?"

Doc grunted. "Inspectors showed up. Closed the whole operation down for an unspecified amount of time. All the rigs are shut off."

Grant's pulse quickened. "Why?"

Doc shrugged. "Guess it had to do with that explosion at Site Fourteen. Standard protocol, I imagine. I would have thought Elias would keep his mouth shut about it, but there you go."

"Yeah," Grant mumbled, trying his best not to let the churning in his stomach turn to nausea. He knew that Elias was going to report the explosion, just as he had reported Churchy—real name, Clyde Lee—missing. Some staff had been recruited to search the woods close to the dorm buildings yesterday, following the logic that a man stumbling drunk wouldn't go far. Grant hadn't been asked to join the search team, but he had overheard talk of it in the cafeteria. Throughout the day he caught glimpses of them trudging back to the buildings to warm up and plan their next route. He had been awash with guilt, knowing the search team wouldn't find the body. At least not yet. Yesterday he had heard whispers of the search expanding to include the area around town—another logical conclusion, that a drunk man might wander toward the bar. It could take days, or weeks, but maybe the search would move to the forest at the end of the scout road.

He cleared his throat. "So, what do we do?"

"Well, you might as well sit, 'cause you're not gonna get paid." Doc grunted. "You can go home, I guess. Go to the bar, go eat till you're sick in the cafeteria. Just don't lift a finger for free, as far as I'm concerned."

"How will we know when work will start up again?"

"Better stick around if you're worried about that. Sleep in the dorms. But I'll shoot you a text. You won't miss too much."

Grant considered. He didn't want to sleep in an unfamiliar bed, surrounded by his coworkers who would no doubt be just as restless. But he didn't want to miss the return to work, either, be stranded at home for more days than he had to. He'd have to make periodic trips into town to check his messages. It shouldn't take long for the inspectors to diagnose the problem with the rig, or declare it safe. In the meantime, he could ask what chores his parents needed help with around the house.

"When did they get here? The inspectors."

"Late last night."

Grant wiped a hand across his face and tried to present a

neutral expression to Doc. "I'm going to head back home to wait this out. Shouldn't take too long, right?"

Doc raised a scruffy gray eyebrow at him. Grant knew he was babbling, trying too hard to appear casual. "Don't go too far. They might want to talk to you. Since you were out at Site Fourteen when it happened."

Grant froze. Doc had been the one to tell Grant to take the truck to that site to deliver the pipes. And it had taken him a suspiciously long time to return, the truck's mileage higher than it should have been for that trip. Doc hadn't said anything, but maybe he'd pieced together that something had gone awry. Doc was meticulous with his machines; he would notice anything unusual.

"Yeah," Grant managed to say. "I'm sure the guys on the rig know more, but I'll talk to the inspectors if they ask me to." He waited for Doc to say something, but the older man remained silent, his face impassive. Maybe he wanted to be alone in the relative quiet of the shop, a rare moment of peace. Grant lifted a hand to signal his departure and walked back to the shop doors, trying to keep his pace from quickening. Every instinct told him to run far, far away from the oil field, from the inspectors. If they wanted to question him, he wasn't sure he would be able to hold the story in. The truth would come spilling out; he would lead the inspectors into the woods himself, searching for the frozen remains, anything to free his guilty conscience. But he wouldn't go to them first, not when the other men had insinuated a threat. The consequences would be the same, unless a trooper took him directly to jail. If he confessed the truth, and remained free, word would spread, the men would find him, and he might meet a fate similar to Churchy's. But if he kept the story a secret for as long as he could, maybe even forever—that seemed the only sure way to protect himself, and his family.

Grant paused outside the shop, the cold air hitting him like an electric shock. He wasn't even supposed to be at work today but had picked up a shift from another maintenance tech whose wife was pregnant and needed to be driven to an appointment in Fairbanks. If Grant hadn't come in today, he might have lived blissfully oblivious to the inspection for several more days. Or, more likely, he would have heard via gossip at The Spur. His breath fogged in the darkness for a second longer before he stepped away from the soft yellow glow of the lamps out-side the garage. He went to the cafeteria and tried to eat a small breakfast. But he was too distracted to focus on the food, couldn't help but feel as if the eyes of all the other men in the building were on him, watching him eat alone, vulnerable. He cleaned up his plate and walked quickly to the warehouse, swiping his card to clock back out. As he changed out of his jumpsuit, someone brushed past him, roughly, and Grant had to suppress a yelp, certain he was going to be slammed against the lockers. But the man kept moving down the row without so much as looking back. Grant drew deep breaths, trying to slow his racing heart.

His snow machine was parked by all the others in the lot outside the warehouse. The inspectors' trucks were parked nearby, engines off, the ALASKA OIL AND GAS AUTHORITY logo printed on the doors. The inspectors must have taken other vehicles out to Site Fourteen, or they were inside one of the buildings. Grant swung a leg over the snow machine and pulled on his helmet, turned on the engine, and headed toward home. Halfway there, he thought better of it, and pulled onto the packed road that led up the hillside where he'd taken Nina the week before.

The snow machine made quicker work of going up the hill than the dogsled, but the road through the trees hadn't been traveled in some time so rather than risk getting stuck, he parked it and walked. The snow crunched under his footsteps and spruce branches reached out to brush his arms as he passed. His boots began to sink into the snow and he gave up, already tired of laboring through the darkness. He ducked into the trees and half crawled to the ledge, lying on his stomach in the snow.

Grant kept a small pair of binoculars in the inner pocket of his coat and he pulled them out now, adjusting them until the camp below pulled into focus. The magnification wasn't great and the darkness worked against him, but the buildings below were visible, illuminated by floodlights. There were little signs of activity; probably everyone was using the morning to sleep in. He trained the binoculars on the main office's door and waited.

Time passed, enough for a damp chill to seep into Grant's bones, enough for him to consider the appeal of falling asleep in the snow. But he forced himself to stay awake, to pay attention. And then the door opened.

Warm light spilled out first, turning the snow golden. Then a quartet of people stepped outside. Two were dressed in the same uniform—thick brown coats, beanies, snow boots. Grant didn't recognize them but guessed they were the inspectors. The other uniform—a bright blue shirt, a navy felt hat—he did recognize. A trooper. Was his presence a routine part of the inspection, or because of the missing person report? He hadn't noticed a police car in the lot. The last person was Elias. Grant drew a breath, wishing the binoculars had better zoom. But he had no doubt that it was Elias, his tall, willowy body taking long strides beside the inspectors. They were headed for the parking lot, toward one of the trucks. Undoubtedly on their way out to Site Fourteen.

Grant sat up and stashed the binoculars in his pocket. Would Elias implicate him? Elias wouldn't bring up Churchy's death— disappearance—himself, but maybe the inspectors would ask questions. Maybe that was why the police were already involved. Grant made an effort to slow his breathing. He had nothing to worry about. They were only investigating the explosion, making sure that it wouldn't happen again. The distance from camp had cleared his head somewhat, and he didn't know why he had been so worried about talking to the inspectors. He could keep a secret, one that his livelihood—and even his life—depended on. If he was called for questioning, he would tell them the barest version of the truth. *I came to deliver some pipes. There was an explosion. That's all I know.*

If he believed hard enough, he could make it true.

10

NINA HAD GONE TO THE POLICE. OF COURSE, SHE
had—it was the right thing to do. The morning after her
conversation with Ila, she'd borrowed the truck and driven
three and a half hours down the Dalton to the nearest trooper
station. Nina knew there was probably a cop or two stationed
closer to Whitespur, but she had no idea how to find them.
She wasn't about to make the call from outside the general
store or The Spur, the only places she could get enough cell
service. The drive was long enough to make her question
herself more than a hundred times. She couldn't tell if she was
nauseated and lightheaded from the early morning or from
nerves. The magnitude of what she needed to do wasn't lost
on her—get the troopers to come investigate, without implicating Grant, and ideally without shutting down the oil field
permanently. As much as she hated the oil field's existence,
she had come to appreciate how much her family depended
on Grant's income, at least while the tourists weren't able to

visit. Every word had to be carefully chosen to keep the officer from realizing she had family employed at the oil field. Maybe that wasn't even possible, maybe they would collect her information and trace her right back to Grant. She could be writing her brother a ticket to jail.

The station was in a small town off the highway, nothing more than a trucking depot. A cluster of buildings greeted Nina—a gas station, a grocery store, some ramshackle houses, and the station itself, housed in an old brick building, which also contained the post office. She sat outside for what felt like an hour, rehearsing what she was going to say, but it took snow falling on the windshield to get her out of the truck and into the building. As she walked through the doors, Nina felt marginally more confident that she could get through the conversation in a way that kept Grant safe.

Inside, a few officers sat behind a glass partition, typing on outdated computers and filing paperwork. The waiting area was empty. Nina approached the window and cleared her throat. An older woman, not in uniform, gazed up at her from behind a desk. A long moment passed.

"Yes?" the woman said.

"Oh. Hello. I'm here to, uh, report an incident." Nina could have kicked herself for sounding so uncertain. She had meant to come in projecting confidence, even as her stomach turned over with anxiety. If she appeared suspicious, the entire conversation might slip out of her control. She swallowed and tried to arrange her facial features into something neutral, if not brave.

"What type of incident?" The woman had begun opening a drawer full of report forms.

This was the part that had tripped Nina up in the truck. "Uh. An accident at an oil field. I didn't witness it, but I spoke to a witness. I believe it needs to be investigated."

She had the woman's attention now. "Where are you coming from, hun?"

A deep breath helped to steady her. "Whitespur. It's a few hours north of here."

She nodded. "I know Whitespur. Hold on." She left her desk and walked around the corner, out of Nina's sight. A minute later she reappeared at a door on the left, which she opened, beckoning Nina through. "I'm going to have you talk to one of the senior officers. This is Trooper Peterson."

Nina thanked her and walked through the door into a small office straight out of the 1960s, complete with wood paneling, and a hideous green couch shoved up against one wall facing a massive walnut desk. It reminded Nina more of a therapist's office than a police officer's, which put her slightly at ease, as if it guaranteed the conversation would be to her benefit. The trooper seated behind the desk, a middle-aged man with thinning brown hair, gestured to the couch. Nina took a seat and waited.

"Talk," the man barked. Nina flinched.

"Well. I'm here to report an incident. But I'd like to remain anonymous." Peterson looked at her. "I don't want to get involved. But someone needs to know what happened."

"Kid," he drawled, "you're giving me a whole lot of nothing. Get to the point."

Nina resisted the urge to roll her eyes. He reminded her of executive chefs she had worked for in the past, men with too much power who thought they could intimidate their employees into behaving how they wanted. "The day before yesterday, Saturday, outside of Whitespur, in the Brooks Valley refuge, there was a fire at the oil field. A small explosion. It was put out. That's the story, that's what everyone heard." She took a breath. "But I know someone who works in the oil field. And he—they—told me that someone died. Because of the explosion. And instead of reporting it, the boss asked some workers to put the body in a truck and drive it into the woods. And only the rig malfunction got reported."

Peterson leaned back in his chair, drawing his hands together on his desk. His weathered face was impassive, everything about him agonizingly still. Nina waited, biting her tongue, until he spoke. "And why should I believe you?" He leaned forward again, his attention trained on Nina. "I know there's a lot of folks who aren't too happy about the drilling up there. Maybe you're just trying to get them shut down."

Nina wanted a second to refocus herself but held his gaze. "You're right. I'm not happy about the drilling. But I'm even less happy that someone died. And because he didn't have a family, a life in Whitespur, he was treated as disposable." She paused again, trying to read Peterson's face. "Go to Whitespur. Ask anyone about the fire. They all know it happened."

"What was his name?"

"Who?"

"The man who died."

"I don't know," Nina admitted.

"And this witness? Name?"

"I can't tell you," Nina said, finally letting her eyes slide down to her lap. "They fear retribution."

"Mmm-hmm." Peterson sat, hands clasped together, looking at Nina like she was the most amusing part of his day. "I've heard of environmentalists who chain themselves to equipment or glue themselves to buildings. I appreciate you taking this more straightforward approach."

Nina's stomach sank as Peterson rose, gesturing at the door. "Wait!" She remained on the couch, gripping the armrest with her left hand, like that small tether would keep her grounded as Peterson walked away. "Please." He turned to face her, folding his arms over his chest, and waited. Nina studied his bright blue uniform, the badge on his shoulder. "I grew up in Whitespur," she said, her voice quavering despite her best effort to hold steady. "I've been away for a few years, but it's hard to overstate the impact of the oil field. A lot of people work there. I have family there." That was as close as she could come to identifying herself, identifying Grant. She wondered if she had said too much, but pushed on. "I don't want those people to lose their jobs. I want the oil company to understand that they can't do something so—so vile, so cruel, and get away with it. Other people who worked there have gone missing. Maybe the same thing happened to them."

Peterson waited, like he wanted to be sure she was finished. He closed his eyes for a long moment, his round face drooping from a life of hard work. When he opened his eyes again, something on his face had softened. His expression held pity, but Nina didn't care, if it brought him closer to listening. "I know about the other disappearances. Worked those cases myself. But we never found anything. If what you say is true," he said, "if they covered up a death, all the workers involved will lose their jobs. The oil field will shut down, maybe not forever, but long enough to hurt the people that rely on it. You don't get to dump a body in the woods and go on your merry way."

"I know that. I guess what I want to believe is that it's better for us, for Whitespur, to lose the oil jobs than to live in the shadow of a company that everyone fears. Or at least, to make sure that something like this never happens again. I'm not naive. I'm sure another company will take over the contract and the drilling will continue. I just don't want these people to get away with what they did." She waited, but Peterson only looked at her. "Please send someone. Your newest trooper, I don't care."

"Can't promise anything," Peterson grunted, gesturing again for her to stand.

Reluctantly, Nina followed Peterson out of his office, wishing he had been more encouraging. Outside, snow continued to fall, coating the vehicles in the parking lot. She entered the truck and watched her breath cloud in the cab as she let the engine warm, waiting for the heat to kick on. Midafternoon dusk had fallen already, nighttime creeping back in from its short vacation. She backed the truck from the parking spot and pulled onto the highway, starting the long journey home, her mind tumbling over every word she had said, fear creeping up through her chest. She had the sensation of flicking over the first domino in a chain that stretched out of sight—as much as she tried to plan the ending, she had no idea what would come next. She could only hope that she had said enough, but not too much—that her family would be safe, and that justice would be brought to the dead man. She could only hope, despite her doubts, that she had done the right thing.

11

NINA WOKE TO THE SOUND OF THE FLOORBOARDS creaking.

She sat up, momentarily disoriented, listening for the sound of traffic swishing by on the street below. She missed her second-story apartment in the cheery yellow house that overlooked a tree-lined, shady street in South Portland, a block away from a park. In the summertime she would lie with the window open, breathing in the humid ocean-washed air, and listen to the neighbors talk and play guitar as they grilled on the patio. Micah would play music from speakers in the living room, the two songs intermingling pleasantly, the air sweet with corn and hot dogs. After dark, almost every yard on the street was lit by string lights, substitutions for the stars that the city's glow outshone.

The floorboards groaned again, drawing Nina from the edges of her memories. She sat up and instinctively reached for her phone on the bedside table, which she kept charged despite not having cell service at home. Her screen time had plummeted since coming back to Alaska, which had to be good for her eyesight, at least.

The phone clock read 4:14 a.m. Nina rose from bed and bent toward the floor to scoop an oversize sweatshirt and pull it over her head. She'd slept in a T-shirt and shorts, but already the bare skin of her legs prickled with goose bumps. The cold was always there to remind her of the long winter that awaited.

Nina tiptoed to the door and pressed her ear against it, listening, but couldn't make out any more sounds. She eased the door open and stepped into the hallway, alert in the exquisite quiet. No lights were on in the house and the TV was off, which meant her father was asleep. The house was like a cave, each room a passage to the unknown.

Something thumped in Grant's room. Nina walked down the hallway and pressed her hand against the door, surprised when it swung open. Grant whirled to face her. He was in the center of the room, lit by the dim glow of a lamp on his dresser. He wore thick insulated work pants and a white T-shirt.

"Nina. What are you doing?"

His voice was low, and she answered in the same quiet tone, not quite a whisper. "Sorry. I heard . . ." She trailed off, realizing she didn't have a good explanation for opening the door. "You woke me up. I could ask you the same question, though."

"I'm going to work. The oil field reopened yesterday. I got a text from Doc last night."

Nina nodded, trying to ignore the sinking sensation in her stomach. "So, the inspection . . . It's over?"

"Yeah. They cleared it." He turned away from her and pulled an orange wool sweater over his T-shirt. "Look, I know it's not what you wanted to hear. But I have to go back to work."

Disappointment flooded through Nina. Trooper Peterson

hadn't listened. A few days had passed and as far as she knew, the troopers had never shown up. Only the inspectors, which had nothing to do with her—Elias had reported the explosion. Business as usual.

"Is it what you wanted to happen?"

Grant froze, his back still to her. The rigid set of his shoulders told her that she'd struck a nerve. He exhaled and turned back to face her, slowly. The expression on his face made her breath catch—at once so young and so old, her baby brother and a man much older than twenty-four years. The weight of his choices hung from his fingertips, pulling him down toward the ground. She stepped closer to him, wanting to comfort him in some way, then hesitated.

"It's not too late. You can tell them the truth."

Grant shook his head. "No. They didn't even call me in for questioning. I thought it would be a bigger process, but . . ." He shrugged. "They checked it out, interviewed the guys from Site Fourteen, and that's it. They didn't find anything unusual."

Nina hoped her expression didn't convey the frustration she felt. She couldn't reveal that she had gone to the troopers hoping for more, a legitimate investigation—not now, maybe not ever. Grant wouldn't understand. "Will the man's family ever know?"

Grant reached for his backpack and slung it over his shoulders. "I don't know," he replied, not meeting her eyes. "Elias reported him missing. I'm sure they've told his family, if he has one. There're a thousand ways to disappear in Alaska."

"And that's it? The search team gave up?"

"I don't know, Nina," Grant said, his voice brittle like broken glass. He sounded exhausted and angry, as if she represented all the things in the world he was mad at. "I have to go, okay?"

He brushed past her, and Nina stepped back from the doorway to let him go.

A FEW HOURS LATER, still under the cover of darkness, Nina returned from a run and unhooked the five exhausted, panting dogs. She had tested out a new leader—Sage, a slender dog with light brown fur, white on her chest and legs. In her usual spot in the swing position next to her mother, Sage was always a step ahead of Sugar, pulling harder, listening more closely for Nina's commands. That attentiveness had translated well to leading a team through the regular training route.

She put the dog away last after checking her large paws for any injuries. She ran a hand through the thick ruff at Sage's neck. She had more fur than most of the other huskies, more Siberian husky in her lineage. But she didn't get as hot as some of the other heavy-coated dogs did, the ones who were relegated to the easier sled-tour lifestyle rather than designated as racing prospects.

"Good girl," Nina said, half-heartedly, because Sage never reacted much to praise, gave not so much as a single tail wag in response to Nina's voice. Nina led Sage to her kennel and shut the latch, pausing to rub her eyes with the back of her hand.

She'd been unable to fall back asleep after talking to Grant, though she'd tried, tossing back and forth in bed for an hour before giving up and trudging to the kennel. After feeding the dogs early—they hadn't minded—she had run her small team for an hour, relishing the big darkness at the edges of her headlamp's glow, the tears streaming down her cheeks from the wind, its icy fingers tracing the edges of her face. Now she returned to reality, facing another long day of waiting.

Back in the house, she scrounged for food, settling on toast and eggs, which were an expensive commodity in Whitespur.

Her mother was close friends with one of the few families who went through the effort of keeping chickens alive in the Far North, and thus reaped the benefits in exchange for jars of crowberry jam.

Her mother wandered into the kitchen as Nina cracked the second egg into a bowl. "Make some for me?"

Nina glanced over her shoulder. "Sure. How many?"

"Two eggs, two pieces of toast, please."

"Do you have any smoked salmon?"

She was met with a stare. "Salmon, yes. The spare freezer is full of it. Smoked, no."

"Too bad. It's good with eggs."

"Never tried it," her mother said. "We haven't used the smoker the last few years. Too much work." She took a seat and reached for the first piece of mail from a stack on the table. Nina had sorted through it all already—just bills and campaign mail for the upcoming election. "You're up early."

Nina poured the beaten eggs into the sizzling pan, making a mental note to offer to go to the post office soon. Her mother, or sometimes Grant, went a few days a week to collect the mail; it wasn't delivered house to house. "Yeah. Grant woke me up leaving for work."

"The oil field is open again?"

"Apparently. The inspectors cleared it."

Her mother made a sound of acknowledgment. "Good." She paused. "You know, with all these bills."

"Not so off-the-grid anymore, huh?"

In Nina's early childhood they hadn't had indoor plumbing or electricity. She remembered the terror of having to use the outhouse in the dead of winter in the dark hours—which was most of the time. The kids were instructed to wake up one of their parents to stand sentinel with a shotgun at the back door, lest a hungry pack of wolves be waiting in the shadows.

That never happened, but it didn't stop Nina from picturing monsters in every darkened corner. She remembered, too, the acute thrill of racing back to the house, of diving beneath a warm pile of blankets and sinking back to sleep, cradled by the night's long arms.

But the town had changed as Nina grew up, becoming a bigger depot for the truckers who took the Dalton to and from Prudhoe Bay. The road connecting Whitespur to the Dalton was now maintained by the state. The gas station expanded, and a motel was built behind it. Streetlamps lit up the main street through the winter and the general store offered more grocery options than it used to, even shipping in beef and chicken, though many of the families still hunted moose, deer, and caribou for their meat. Most of them were no longer true homesteaders, especially with the extra infusion of resources from the oil field. But life in Alaska remained harsher than most in the lower forty-eight could imagine—Nina knew, from telling stories to her friends and coworkers, their eyes widening in disbelief.

"It's not just the utility payments. You know how much it costs to feed the dogs. It feels like it's tripled in the time you've been away. I might have to . . ." She trailed off, as if she didn't want to say what came next. "I don't want to, but I might need to find homes for some of the tour dogs. Give them away for free. I don't know if we can afford to keep them through winter."

Nina absorbed her words in silence as she divided the scrambled eggs between two plates, then pulled the golden-brown slices of bread from the buttery skillet. Focusing on the food had pulled her out of her swirling thoughts, if only briefly, but now they poured back in. Her family had never given away dogs of value for free before, only retired dogs. Who would even take them? Any other sled tour operations were probably experiencing the slowdown from the pandemic, too.

She was still disappointed that the oil field was reopened, that there seemed to have been no legitimate attempt to investigate her report. But hearing her mother talk about the expenses, about how much they needed Grant's income, she wondered if she had thrown her family onto the train tracks, and only by some miracle had the train gone a different route. It was hard not to think in what-ifs, but she felt more than a little sick to her stomach at the thought of making her family's situation worse. She set the plates on the table in front of her mother and then divvied up silverware, finally sliding into the chair opposite her mother and taking a bite of the eggs. They were a little bland—the seasoning cabinet had offered underwhelming options—but they would do.

"I'm taking your father to a doctor's appointment this morning," her mother said, peering at Nina over the top of her reading glasses. "I'll have the truck for a couple of hours."

"A couple of hours? Don't you need to go to like, Fairbanks?"

Her mother shook her head. "There's a doctor's office at the oil field. It's heavily discounted for family members, but Grant added your father to his insurance, so it's practically free."

"Wow," Nina said. Another benefit of the oil field that was difficult to argue with, and one she wished she'd known about before going to the police. She might have gone anyway, but at least her consciousness would have known exactly how much guilt to carry. "What does he need?"

"What doesn't he need?" she replied with a sigh. "He's having all kinds of issues with that leg. Back pain now, too. This doctor wants to recommend him for another surgery, but the specialist is in Anchorage. I don't think your father will go for it. He had such a hard time healing from the first one."

"I'm sorry I wasn't here," Nina said as her throat tightened. "I could have helped."

"Well, we didn't tell you." Her mother paused to cough. "Besides, he was in a real state that first year. Probably good you weren't around. Grant took the brunt of it, poor thing."

"What about Audrey?"

A moment passed before she replied. "I told her she wasn't allowed back here until she was sober. That was four years ago. But even before that, around the time Ted was injured, we hardly saw her." She took a sip of water and then stood abruptly, carrying her empty plate to the sink. "I hate to say it, but your sister has never been quite right."

The surprise Nina felt must have registered on her face. She opened her mouth to defend Audrey but her mother breezed past, heading to the living room. She didn't believe that her mother felt that way about Audrey, who had always been so helpful with the dog tours growing up, sociable with the tourists and easy for them to talk to. Sure, Audrey had been defiant as a teenager, sleeping over at friends' houses without permission and arguing about doing her homework, but Nina didn't think her mother held that kind of resentment for her oldest daughter. Perhaps too much had happened while Nina was away for Mary to think of those memories from a time when Audrey was younger, before her addiction carved the great rift between them. She had an urge to unearth a box of family photos, to dig up all the ones of Audrey innocent and smiling, to remind her mom of the child who still existed within the troubled adult.

Her mother said something to Ted, her voice carrying as she urged him up from the chair. Nina took one more bite of toast and scraped her half-eaten breakfast into the trash, her appetite suddenly deserting her. Wasting food would have gotten her a chewing-out in childhood, but no one was there to witness, so she tamped down the guilt and washed the plates, setting them beside the sink to dry.

Half an hour later and her parents were gone, the truck engine fading away to nothing as it rumbled down the driveway. Through the kitchen window snow began to fall, lazy flakes spiraling down to top off the blanket of white that already covered the earth. An overwhelming surge of loneliness washed over Nina. She wished for the city, the ability to jog down the stairs and step into a world populated by people. She didn't have to speak to them, to know them, she just wanted to be around them. And when she did want comfort and familiarity, the restaurant brought it—the rhythm of bodies in the kitchen, shouted questions and returned affirmations, the sound of chopping knives and sizzling oil, the first drink of the night poured when the kitchen closed. Nina hadn't felt this alone since 4950 shut its doors.

She considered a late morning nap, but stopped outside her bedroom. The door to Grant's room was cracked, weak morning light from the windows spilling into the dark hallway. She took a few more steps and pushed the door open as she'd done that morning, half expecting to find Grant again, for a repeat of their hushed conversation to play out. But of course, the room was empty, the bed unmade, piles of clothing strewn on the floor. She took a step back, embarrassed that her boredom had led to snooping, like she was a kid again, home sick from school, trying to find Audrey's journal and read her secrets.

Then something caught her eye.

Grant's phone, face down on the dresser. Had he meant to leave it? She should bring it to him. He worked in a garage; he'd be easy enough to find. She picked up the phone and turned it over. The screen lit up—a picture of Ila, bundled in a heavy winter coat, hat, and scarf, kneeling in the snow, her arm around Briar. Ila was smiling, her brown eyes warm and inviting, her clothes and hair dusted with snowflakes, and Briar was too, her mouth open in a husky grin. The phone vibrated. It didn't recognize Nina's face.

I took a video. Of them carrying the body into the woods, and coming back to the truck.

Grant's words echoed through Nina's mind. She hadn't asked to watch the video yet, had forgotten it existed. Until now. Somewhere in Grant's camera roll, that key piece of evidence waited. Even if the faces of the men weren't visible, as Grant suspected, it might be enough to get the troopers to search the area.

The password input appeared and without thinking, her fingers typed of their own accord: 5593. Ila's birthday. The little dots at the top of the screen turned clear and shook, indicating an incorrect attempt. She tried Grant's birthday next, then the last four digits of his phone number, then 1234, just in case. Nothing worked.

Nina set the phone back on the dresser, forcing herself to slow down. That morning, she had tried to accept that her attempt had failed, that the cover-up wouldn't be investigated. She'd come to understand how much her family needed the oil field to remain open. But like she'd said to the officer a few days ago, it seemed unlikely that even proving the cover-up would result in a permanent closure, even if they discovered evidence about the other disappearances, too. The oil beneath the refuge's surface was valuable, not just to the town, but to the state, the country. The stubborn part of her, the part that had practiced chopping techniques in culinary school until her fingers blistered and bled, flared up. She had been given this second chance for a reason, and she wouldn't let it go to waste.

She didn't know how many attempts remained before the phone locked for either a period of time, or permanently. She suspected her own password was easy to guess for people who knew her well—4950. What did Grant care about, beyond Ila, his friends, and the dogs?

In the mirror, she noticed a framed photograph hanging on the wall opposite Grant's bed. A black-and-white image of their father after his first Yukon Quest win, squatting in front of his sled with an arm around his lead dog, Ranger. He still wore his racing bib, the number *27* emblazoned in bold black font. Grant had admired their father so much as a child, had wanted to follow in his footsteps and become a champion musher. *27*. What had his number been the year of his second Quest win?

The living room was quiet, the television off for once. Nina hit the light switch and stood before the almost identical image of her father post–second Quest victory. He crouched beside a different lead dog this time, pure white and serious-looking. Her father's beard was longer. And his bib number was again two digits: *16*.

Back in Grant's room, she typed the four numbers with hesitant fingers.

2716.

Once again, it didn't work.

Nina swallowed. One more try.

1627.

The phone unlocked.

Nina stared at it in her hands. She should set it down, turn it off, and put it in her pocket and take it to Grant. Ask about the video then. Leave it alone if he refused. Her index finger hovered above the screen, her heart hammering in her chest. She tapped the Photos app.

The most recent ones were of dogs, Grant's team resting on a run, tongues lolling as they sat and panted in the snow. There was a slightly blurry picture of Michael and Orson in The Spur, arms around each other's backs, each holding a beer in his free hand, no doubt drunk out of their minds. Then she saw it.

A video, ten minutes long. The cover image showed a shadowy stand of trees and snowy ground. Nina tapped the video, hit Pause, scrolled down to check the date. October 24.

The recording started off blurry, a rapid zoom in on a patch of forest, before it slowly came into focus. A trio of men disappeared into the trees. Two of them were carrying something. It was hard to tell what, but Nina knew. She scrubbed the video forward, holding her breath, but the image remained mostly the same. Grant's hand shook as he held the phone, the camera focused on the same stand of trees, until, in the last seconds, a trio of men emerged from the forest. They wore blue jumpsuits with green reflective patches—the rig workers' uniform, Nina guessed—and walked through the snow with their heads down. The phone lowered abruptly, cut to black, and the video ended. Nina let it play from the beginning again, trying to make out any distinguishing features of the men, but the video was too shaky, too far away, to see them clearly.

Nina stared at the screen for a minute longer. When she looked up, her reflection stared back from the mirror above Grant's dresser, wild-eyed and guilty. There was no way to set the phone down and forget what she had seen. The Oil and Gas inspectors had left; the search team hadn't located the body. Nina held in her hand the power to make them look again, and she wouldn't let it slip through her fingers.

Ten minutes later, she fired up the snow machine and skimmed the main trail toward town, racing through the light blue dawn, the gentle snow. She parked outside The Spur and waited, but the street was deserted. The bar was closed until noon and so most everyone was home or at work.

Nina pulled both phones from her pockets. She unlocked

Grant's and texted the video to herself, muttering "please send, please send" under her breath as the bar at the top of the screen inched along in excruciating slowness. Finally, her phone buzzed, a new text from Grant popping up on her screen. She deleted the conversation from Grant's messages and sat, heart racing, before she had the wherewithal to pull her gloves back over her beet-red hands. There was something she needed to do before she went back to the police. Years ago she'd read an article about dating safety, how you weren't supposed to send any pictures or videos to people you didn't know well because they could find the location of your house, or your favorite restaurant, through the metadata. She still had a metadata scrubber downloaded from her dating app days. She remembered carefully scrubbing the first selfie she sent to Miriam, though she later realized that Miriam could have Googled her name, which would have resulted in Nina's picture and bio on the Nocturne website popping up as the first result. It had been difficult to hide her occupation.

But she'd have to figure out some other time to use the scrubber. She didn't want to spend another second in front of The Spur.

"Nina?"

She jumped and almost dropped both phones. She shoved Grant's in her pocket as she looked up. It took her a moment to recognize the man who stood a few feet away on the sidewalk in front of her. He wore a hat, a coat, a thick wool scarf—so much of him covered, but she would have only needed to see his eyes to remember him.

"August," she breathed out.

In New York and Portland, she hardly ever ran into an ex. Once she stopped dating someone, the cities reabsorbed them, tucking them away in hidden pockets. There were enough bars and restaurants that she could avoid her usual spots for a few weeks until she decided to brave a visit, and she usually didn't run into anyone from her past, didn't have to force her way through awkward small talk. She and Miriam hadn't broken up until after Miriam had moved to LA, the thousands of miles between them guaranteeing no surprise run-ins. So, she hadn't thought about August since she'd gotten home, and didn't even consider if he was still in Whitespur until Ila had told her. In nine years, she had thought of him less and less, which surprised her now that he stood in front of her, more handsome than she had imagined he would one day be. She blushed, not for his sudden appearance but because she felt like a child caught eating cookies from the jar. Grant's phone burned a hole in her pocket, reminding her that she couldn't wait around. She needed to drop the phone with him and clear her conscience, at least partially.

But August was standing in front of her. "I didn't know you stayed in Whitespur," she said, managing to keep her voice level. A partial truth—she hadn't known until the other night.

"I'd say I didn't know you were back, but that isn't true." A grin spread across his face. "Ila told me. Offered to pass along a hello from me, but I said I didn't know if you'd want to see me."

"She told me you were here, too," Nina admitted. Then, "Why wouldn't I?"

"Oh, I don't know." His gaze shifted, his expression turning sheepish. "Maybe the fit I threw when you said you were leaving?"

"I wouldn't call it a fit." But Nina remembered it clearly: how he had cried when she told him about the scholarship, about her chance to get out of Whitespur. Maybe that was all he was ashamed of, shedding tears, cracking that hard exterior that most men seemed desperate to maintain. A failure in stoicism. But Nina carried her own shame—that August had always loved her more. They were together for three years, as teenagers, yes, but August had always been an old soul. Everyone said that—his parents, her parents, their teachers. It shouldn't have surprised her that by their last year of high school he had laid out a plan for their life together: buy one of the old hunting cabins up Back Creek and fix it up, acquire their own team of sled dogs for hunting and trapping, have a kid or two by their mid-twenties. Never mind college, never mind that August was as smart as Nina. He applied, too, got into the University of Alaska. But he had little interest in going. His sense of security, his certainty that Whitespur was home—it scared her. She couldn't blame herself for wanting to run.

"But I never apologized. And I'd like to do that. You were following your dream, and I should have supported you regardless. You've accomplished so much. I've been proud of you from afar, all these years."

"I appreciate it." She paused to swallow the lump in her throat. It was intended as a compliment, but still—after everything she had achieved, she had still ended up here, at home, facing August as if nothing had changed. "So, did you? Stay in Whitespur?"

He tilted his head side to side. "I left. Came back. I did go to UAA, but I got tired of the city. Worked in Lake Clark for a couple of years after I graduated, but that was too far away." He smiled again. "I missed Whitespur. Can you believe it?"

Nina nodded. She could believe it; though she hadn't come back willingly, she also didn't try as hard as she could to stay away. Instead, she'd come home, let Whitespur sink its teeth into her again. "And what do you do now?"

"I work in Brooks Valley. Resident biologist."

"So, you did study biology?"

"Yeah. Boreal and tundra ecosystems. I'm supposed to coordinate between the oil company and the Fish and Wildlife Service. Make sure everyone's needs are being met. It's a lot of work."

"I bet." Nina placed her hands on the snow machine's handle-bars.

"Sorry," he said. "I'm yammering. Anyway, we should . . ." He trailed off, as if he'd thought better of presenting an invitation.

"Get dinner sometime?" Nina finished. To her surprise, she wanted to see him again. Maybe nothing would come of it—maybe they'd only talk once, or maybe they'd become friends again. Part of her also wanted to tell him about her life away from home, to prove to him that it had been worth it to leave. That even though she had ended up back in the same place, she was a different person now. They made plans for Monday night, a little over a week away, dinner at Los Padres. Nina tried not to think of it as a date as August walked away, as she started the snow machine engine. She had so much else to worry about—like the video, like returning Grant's phone. Before she could go to the police again, she had to go to the oil field.

12

GRANT NEARLY JUMPED OUT OF HIS SKIN WHEN NINA sat down across from him. She shouldn't be allowed, he thought, to just show up without warning in the cafeteria, cheeks flushed red from the cold, eyes loaded with intense purpose. Before he had a chance to ask why she was there, she unzipped her coat, pulled something from an interior pocket, and slid it across the table to him without saying a word.

"Oh," Grant said, recognizing the object as his phone. "Thanks." He thought briefly of the video, as he often did now when he saw his phone—the video, which he kept meaning to delete, his finger hovering over the trash-can icon before he turned off the screen. He didn't know why he couldn't let it go. Maybe that he wanted proof, in case things slipped out of his control. "You didn't need to come all the way out here for this."

He had realized he had forgotten it after arriving at work that morning, when he'd popped in his wireless earbuds and patted through his pockets—nothing. He usually listened to music or an NPR podcast while he worked. He downloaded new playlists and episodes whenever he had cell service, but he could survive a day without drowning out the background sounds of the shop. Besides providing entertainment, he didn't use his phone much at work, and he'd planned to swing by home once his shift ended to grab it. Now he wondered how Nina had found it, where he'd left it.

"I walked past your room and saw it on your dresser," Nina said before he could ask. "I thought you'd get bored out here without it." She paused. "I didn't have anything better to do so I thought I'd drop it off."

A fair explanation—his dresser was visible from the hallway, though he wasn't sure how she had noticed his phone amid all the clutter and couldn't resist the urge to give her a hard time.

"You were snooping?"

He could have sworn Nina's cheeks turned a brighter shade of red. "No. Why would I do that?"

He thought again of the video, a quick flash of panic. But his phone had a password, one he'd added when he started working at the oil field, in case he dropped it somewhere and a stranger picked it up. He shrugged, trying to appear nonchalant. "I don't know. Bored out of your mind?"

She relaxed a little, sitting back in the chair. "Yeah. But I wasn't snooping." Her focus shifted, traveling around the cafeteria, the sheet metal walls, the bright fluorescent lights, taking it in with interest. Grant tried to view it through her eyes, how expansive and industrial it must look. "So, this is the oil field."

"The most or least exciting part of it, depending on who you ask. How did you find me?"

She pointed at the door. "I walked in. Well, I told the guy at the gate that I was your sister and I had something to bring you from home. He didn't even ask for my ID. Anyway, I remembered you said you usually take lunch early. I thought I'd check here first. And I was right." She paused. "Do you have time to show me around?"

Grant laughed. It was a ridiculous request, and Nina must realize it. He imagined her asking out loud, *Remind me, which site did that guy die at?* Even the idea of her being here made him nervous. He wanted to keep her visit as short as possible. "No, sorry. That's not exactly allowed. But get something to eat if you want. They won't ask for your ID, either."

Nina wrinkled her nose at Grant's half-eaten meal. "Is that pot roast?"

"Come on. You weren't a food snob before you left."

"And I'm not one now," Nina replied. "I was going to stop by the store on the way home. Get a few things for dinner." She paused, looked down at her hands. "Guess who I ran into?"

He didn't have the energy to rattle through a list of suspects. "Just tell me."

"August," Nina said, and Grant thought a trace of a smile crossed her face.

"Did he know you were back?"

"Yeah, Ila told him." She paused. "Are you friends?"

"Sort of." He wouldn't have called August a friend, but he supposed they were. August, by virtue of being three years older, ran with a different crowd when they were kids, hung out with people Nina's age and sometimes even Audrey's. Two years didn't make a difference, but for some reason three did, and Grant's group of friends was totally separate. But he had seen August around plenty since he had taken the biologist position in Brooks Valley, sometimes chatting to the higher-ups at the oil field, sometimes riding a snow machine on the same paths Grant ran his dogs. He'd always thought August was a little quiet, a little difficult to talk to, even when he'd dated Nina in high school. But he'd always been enamored with Nina, ready to build a life around her—as long as that life involved staying in Alaska.

"Well," Nina said, unfazed by Grant's noncommittal answer, "we're getting dinner next week."

"A date?"

"God, I don't know," she replied, and her tone made Grant wonder if he'd struck a nerve. Did she *want* it to be a date, when it clearly wasn't? Or maybe August was still in love with her and Nina wanted to be left alone. "Well, that's all I came for," Nina said, starting to stand up and rezip her jacket. She reached across the table, grabbed a piece of pot roast off Grant's plate with her fingers, and narrowed her eyes as she chewed. "I thought the food here was supposed to be good."

Grant laughed. "It's good for Whitespur. Want me to walk you out?"

She shook her head. An expression that Grant couldn't quite read passed over her face, and just as quickly, it vanished. "I'm a big girl. Thanks, though. See you at home?"

It crossed his mind that maybe she was going to poke around the oil field on her own. Maybe she had a fantasy of conducting her own investigation, of discovering the frozen body lying in the woods. But she wouldn't get far; the cafeteria was the only place she could wander into without attracting attention. The security guard at the entrance might not do the best job of checking IDs, but maybe he didn't need to—without the proper uniforms, any interlopers stuck out, and if someone showed up where they weren't supposed to be, people asked questions. It was how Grant had discovered he was in the wrong place several times during his first year—getting borderline interrogated by a rig boss that wasn't his.

"What are you making for dinner?"

"4950 moose burgers, minus the Hawaiian flare."

"So, 49 burgers?"

Nina rolled her eyes. "Very funny."

"Sounds good. I'll be there."

She grew smaller and smaller as she strode through the big building. The idea of Nina entering his room without him there unsettled him, but he didn't have a good reason why, besides the basic invasion of privacy. He had told her about the video on the day of the accident, but he didn't want to believe that she might go looking for it. Though if anyone could guess his password, that person would be Nina. He unlocked the phone quickly and scrolled through his camera roll. The video was still there. He changed the password to a string of numbers that meant nothing to him, random digits, and hoped he would remember it. He turned off the screen, exhaled, and set the phone face down on the table.

He still wasn't used to living with one of his sisters again. Nina's pots of moisturizer and dropper bottles of serum had been dwindling on the bathroom countertop, her expensive skincare slowly running out. The products were new—it was hard to find anything other than Bag Balm and Vaseline on the shelves at the general store—but the clutter wasn't. Back when both Nina and Audrey lived at home, there was never an inch of free counter space, and Grant often didn't get to even look in the mirror before heading to school. At least now he left for work so early that sharing bathroom space was never a problem.

But they'd all grown up practically sharing rooms, Audrey and Nina lounging on Grant's bed or Grant falling asleep on their floor until his sisters woke him up by lightly kicking him in the stomach, insisting that he went back to his own room. After all, his room had belonged to Nina before he was born, and then she'd been forced to share with Audrey. *Too many kids for this house*, their mom used to say.

Grant ate another bite of his now-cold meal and stood up to clock back in, trying to shake the feeling that he was forgetting something. With the inspectors gone and the oil field reopened, he had nothing to worry about, in theory. But there was still a body in the woods.

13

"PLEASE." NINA FOLDED HER ARMS ACROSS HER chest, projecting what she hoped was an imploring expression at the woman behind the counter. She wasn't the same woman Nina had pleaded her case to five days ago, and Nina hadn't yet determined if that was better or worse. This woman was younger, but her patience was thinner. Her eyes kept drifting to the computer screen to her right, and Nina swore that a Facebook page was reflected in the woman's glasses. The walls of the office behind the plexiglass had been decorated with strings of paper bats, ghosts, and pumpkins, the latter's bright orange washed out by the fluorescent lights. "I'm telling you. I have new evidence."

The woman sighed and shifted her weight to one hip. "Who did you say you spoke to?"

"Officer Peterson," Nina replied, a spark of hope shooting through her chest. "Is he in?"

The woman's mouth formed a flat line. "Hold on." She made

a big show of crossing the open office to pick up a landline phone from its cradle on the opposite desk. Through the plexiglass, Nina watched with her heart in her throat as the woman dialed. She moved the phone to her ear and spoke, though she was angled away and Nina couldn't read her lips. After an agonizing minute, she put the phone down and disappeared, then opened the door to the left. Nina had the strange sensation of time looping as she stepped into the familiar vintage office with its wood-paneled walls and green couch. Trooper Peterson once again didn't acknowledge her presence, but Nina didn't wait for his instructions this time. She sat and spoke.

"I have new evidence regarding the death of the man in Brooks Valley."

Peterson blinked up at her like a basset hound, all droopy skin and sad eyes. "Why are you here again?"

Nina tilted her head. "I told you. I have a—"

Peterson held up a hand. "You came here a week ago to tell us about the 'incident'—" air quotes "—and I listened to you. I sent a trooper. In fact, that was in addition to those sent when we received an unrelated missing person report. They investigated, they interviewed, they found no wrongdoing. Why am I supposed to listen to you all over again?"

Nina hated being dismissed. She was once again reminded of the chefs she'd worked with before, powerful men who believed that they could learn nothing of importance from anyone else, especially a young woman. But that was part of it, too—she couldn't raise her voice and demand attention or Peterson would brush her off as hysterical. She'd been called that before, and worse, for crying on overwhelming days in the kitchen, when she'd cut her fingers more times than she could count, every step sent pain shooting up her legs, and she still couldn't produce a sauce that made the head chef happy. Nina had quickly learned to remain quiet even when the tears flowed, letting them mix with steam and sweat on her cheeks. Push through, remain steady, don't raise your voice, and dear God, whatever you do, don't show any emotion. She tried to draw on some of that now, to remain as calm and collected as possible.

That a trooper had been sent to the oil field was news to her, but it didn't change her course. She scooted forward on the couch and pulled her phone from her pocket. She glanced away for only a second, waiting for the camera to scan her face and unlock her phone. Peterson stewed in annoyance, but Nina could handle that, as long as he didn't tip over into outright anger toward her. She tapped the screen, pulled up the video, stood, and stepped to the front of Peterson's desk.

"Please. Just watch this."

He sighed and took the phone, squinting at the screen as though he were trying to read some small text. He watched in silence for a long minute, then looked up at her. Angling her body over the desk so that Peterson could still view the screen, Nina dragged the bar at the bottom of the video, scrubbing it forward. Peterson's eyebrows shot up with interest at the final few seconds of the video, as the men emerged from the woods and the screen cut to black. He leaned back and drummed his fingers on the desk.

"Who took that?"

"I can't say," Nina said, sitting back down. "I mean, it's the same source who told me about this. But like I said last time, they're worried about potential consequences."

To Nina's immense relief, Peterson tugged a yellow legal pad loose from a stack of notebooks and wrote something down. She wiped her damp palms against her jeans in a way that she hoped was inconspicuous.

"Do you know approximately where that video was taken?"

"No. In Brooks Valley, for sure. But I've never been to the

oil field—at least, not past the main area with all the buildings," she corrected herself.

"Explain to me what you think is happening in this video."

He was trying to trip her up. He wanted a name, something concrete to go after. But Nina couldn't implicate Grant. She wouldn't put him in danger, because she still believed that it was possible to bring justice for the dead man without revealing her brother's involvement. It wasn't his fault, anyway. He had only gone along with a bad idea. "The anonymous source is the one filming. Those three men are dumping the body in the woods. The man who died at Site Fourteen."

Peterson stopped writing and tapped his pen against the notepad. "You didn't mention Site Fourteen last time."

"My mistake. That's where the fire happened."

"Show me that video again." There was new interest in his voice.

She waited in silence as he watched the video in full. He coughed once, covering his mouth with his arm, and handed her phone back. "Okay. I'll tell you what. You seem real shook up about this. And though that video doesn't show much, it gives us something more solid to go by. We'll send some of our officers out. Bypass the oil people altogether. They won't like it, and I'm sure we'll get on their bad side," he continued, suppressing a laugh, "but maybe they do have something to hide."

Nina ignored his condescension and pocketed the phone. "I appreciate you looking into this more," she managed to say.

Peterson tapped the desk. "I'm going to need a copy of that video."

She drew a breath. She had prepared for this moment, yesterday, as she left the oil field. She had glanced at the phone, at the three bars of service on the top right of the screen, and ducked into the nearest bathroom to hide in a stall. Given

Grant's anxiety, not just about his job but about his safety, and the extent to which her family relied on the oil field remaining open, it wasn't worth the risk to leave any information attached to the video.

The scrubber took a few minutes to process the large file, but once it was done, she had deleted the original copy of the video, leaving only the clean one. Nina left the oil field feeling more secure in her plan than before—she had both the evidence the troopers needed to investigate and protection for Grant. As she had believed all along, there was a way to make things right without implicating her brother.

Nina had checked a thousand times that the information linked to the video had been removed. Now she held her breath and sent the file to the number Peterson gave her.

Peterson frowned down at his desk; his forehead creased with layers of wrinkles. "It would be good if you could get your source to talk to us," he said. "Real, real good."

Nina stilled. She knew, without a doubt, that Grant wouldn't talk to the police. He wanted to protect his job, and himself, above anything else, and she couldn't blame him. She had gone out of her way to make sure the police couldn't track him down. Perhaps there was a way for him to share his story and still remain safe, but Grant was so adamant that he couldn't get involved. She nodded slowly, her mind tumbling over itself like a dog too eager to run. "I can't promise anything."

"Neither can I," Peterson replied, standing up and stepping around his desk to show her to the door. "But we'll take a look."

BEFORE GOING HOME, Nina stopped at the Whitespur general store to settle herself. Nothing calmed her quite like wandering the aisles, thinking of possible recipes. She had spent a lot of time in the tiny store before leaving home and knew the rows by heart, both what they contained and what they lacked—there wasn't a lot of fresh produce, for starters. She had spent her culinary school summers driving to every farmers' market in Dutchess County, reveling in the abundance of heirloom tomatoes and lettuce varieties and berries ripe enough to burst. Nothing compared to biting into a fresh apple in October beneath a maple tree alive with fiery red and orange leaves. But the general store was its own small miracle, how far most of the food had traveled to sit on its shelves, the ways the products could be coddled to survive the long trip north. And since March, each trip to the grocery store had been fraught with anxiety—face masks and hand sanitizer and nervous glances at people who stepped too close. To wander through the store without fear of the virus hanging over her was a relief.

Nina turned a corner and stopped. August stood in the aisle, a red basket on one arm, assessing the boxes of pasta. She hesitated, but then August looked up and saw her and such a genuine smile spread across his face that some part of Nina softened and forgot the day she'd had. She walked toward him.

"I guess this is going to keep happening," August said.

"Small town," Nina replied. She stepped beside him, angling herself to see the shelf from his perspective, but not before noting what was already in his basket. Canned tomatoes, garlic, a plastic container of fresh basil—expensive, she knew from experience—an onion, and a wedge of parmesan. "Sauce from scratch?" she asked.

"Oh, yeah. I've been trying to perfect my own recipe. Don't laugh."

"I'm not laughing," she said, though the corners of her mouth turned up involuntarily. "You need a secret ingredient."

"Maybe I already have one. Maybe I pick it up last, so snoops like you don't steal it for themselves."

Nina flushed, not at the suggestion that she would steal his recipe, but because the snoop label was all too accurate. "Fair enough," she muttered, then added, "I thought you were super busy?"

"I am. But I still have to eat. If you were that desperate to get dinner with me sooner, you should have said something." He nudged her arm and Nina smiled.

"I can wait a few more days." She picked up a box of angel hair and set it in his basket. "My favorite, do you remember?"

"How could I ever forget?" A moment passed. "So, what should my secret ingredient be?"

Nina tilted her head. "That's personal to every chef. Besides, you made it sound like you already had one picked out."

"I was testing your confidence in me."

Nina met his eyes for a moment, still startled by the familiarity reflected in them. So many memories were layered there, her teenage years full of hope and anxiety in equal measure. She had made it out of Whitespur, but here she was, standing shoulder to shoulder with August in the general store as if no time had passed. A light bulb flickered overhead, and Nina shivered. "Fully confident," she said. "I always thought you'd be a good cook one day. You come from a family of them."

"Yeah, well. I never had to put much effort in, between my mom and Harvey." His brother. Nina remembered him as aloof and serious, an older, more solidified version of August. "And you."

"Tell Harvey I want one of his caribou roasts while I'm back home."

August smiled again. "Are you kidding? He'd love to cook for you." His gaze moved to his wristwatch, visible at the edge of his coat sleeve, and then back up to Nina. "Sorry. I don't mean to overemphasize how busy I am, but I've got a mountain of paperwork waiting back at my cabin."

"And I've kept you from it long enough," Nina replied, shoving her hands into her pockets. She was thankful for the conversation, for the serendipity of bumping into August when she was at her most distracted and distressed. "See you in a few days?"

He exhaled. "I wish we could stay right here forever."

The admission reminded Nina that August had never shied from speaking his feelings out loud. And as nice as it sounded—to stand in eternity looking at pasta and talking about cooking—she didn't want to give him false hope that she was anything other than the girl who would always want to leave. In the past, she had hurt him, and she didn't know if she should allow herself the opportunity to do it again.

"Let's start with dinner, before you decide to let me monopolize all your free time."

She turned away before he could respond, tracing her way back out of the aisle, and lingered in the produce section until she glimpsed August push through the store's front door and into the evening. Nina allowed herself to purchase two exorbitantly priced green apples, because she needed a fraction of the joy that New England had brought her.

At the checkout counter, she stared out the window as the clerk rang up the apples, worry gnawing at her insides. She couldn't stop picturing Peterson's face as he watched the video, the interest gleaming in his eyes. If the video didn't convince him to investigate further, nothing would. Grant would continue working at the site of a crime, there would be no justice for the dead man's family, and Nina would have wasted her time and worried her brother for nothing.

She carried the bag of apples out into the cold autumn air, letting the memory of the short conversation with August keep her warm.

14

THE FIRST THING GRANT NOTICED WERE THE LIGHTS.
They came swirling through the windows of the shop as dawn broke, painting the walls and floors blue and red. Doc lifted his head. The other mechanics and techs stopped what they were doing, set down wrenches, and slid out from beneath trucks. No one said a word for a long moment.

It could be about something else, Grant told himself. *Maybe someone else got hurt.* But Whitespur didn't have a police force, didn't have ambulances to call when someone was injured, only the emergency transport vehicles at the oil field, adorned with red and white lights. Not blue.

"Shit," someone muttered under their breath.

Without thinking, Grant abandoned his tools and wove his way through the shop, pushing open the front door. No one tried to stop him; he suspected they followed him instead, footsteps dull and muffled at the edges of his mind, over-whelmed by the lights. He had to see them for himself.

In the big lot across campus a handful of police SUVs had parked. They had a logo he didn't recognize painted on the side, Cold Creek Troopers. Probably the nearest town with a station; he remembered passing a sign for Cold Creek on the way to Fairbanks. Two of the troopers stood outside the cars, lit by the rotating lights and the weak, low sun, mostly obscured by clouds. They were talking to a foreman and one of the HSE managers, though Grant couldn't tell who; their backs were to him. He wasn't sure if he would recognize the HSE manager, anyway; they spent most of their time holed up in warm, bright offices on the first floor of the dorm building, emerging only to run safety courses for new hires and handle paperwork about dangerous incidents.

Except for the one Grant had witnessed.

Slowly the lights on the cars shut off as the engines quieted. Soon the sun provided the only light, the whole world bathed in quiet gray. More officers got out of their vehicles, gathering into a small group. Grant was aware of his coworkers behind and beside him, all watching in fascinated silence. They probably had more questions than he did.

One of the officers broke off and headed in their direction. His light blue uniform was almost friendly, a clear sky on a summer day. He stopped a few feet away.

"Good morning, sir. How can we help you?"

Grant flinched at the sound of Doc's voice, too cheery and formal. Doc rarely spoke in full sentences.

"Morning. We're here to investigate a report of an incident. I can't say much more than that right now, but don't worry, we're not shutting down operations today. We'll likely ask all of you questions over the next few days. Even if you don't know anything, even if you have no idea what I'm talking about, speaking to us will be a huge help."

His smile didn't put Grant any more at ease. His stomach

churned and he wondered if he would vomit right there, onto the spotless snow at the trooper's feet. He thought of Nina's visit the other day and part of him was glad that she wasn't there to see this, though he suspected that she would be happy about another investigation. Doubt swirled within him, but he pushed it away, trying to put Nina out of his mind. Beside him, some of the men shifted. Everyone knew about the Site Fourteen explosion by now. Was that where their minds had gone? Had they heard rumors of something more?

The trooper said something else, but Grant couldn't focus on his words.

"Get back to work, boys," Doc said. "I'll send one of you out next when I'm done."

Doc followed the trooper to a small administrative building. Grant sensed his coworkers turning away, the surge of heat as one of them opened the door to reenter the shop. They were talking over each other, voices lapping like waves on a lakeshore. His vision swam, and his stomach turned again. He followed the others back inside.

Sweat dripped off his forehead. His hand shook when he picked up a wrench. He wanted to leave, to go home, to hide until all the troopers left. But he would only look suspicious. They would find him, make him talk, and Grant didn't know if he could lie to an officer. He had settled on going to his grave with the secret of what he had witnessed. But deep down, hadn't he expected this to happen? Hadn't he been preparing for this moment since the second he got behind the wheel of the truck, with Churchy's body in the bed?

He didn't have to wait long to find out. Doc returned to the shop, strode purposefully across it, and clapped a hand on Grant's shoulder. "It's about that Site Fourteen nonsense," he grumbled. "You're up."

Grant hoped the terror didn't show on his face. He sensed

a few pairs of eyes on him as he walked across the shop, back into the sparkling chill of late morning, and tried to conjure an air of neutrality, or even mild annoyance, like he had better things to do than answer questions in a stuffy office. *I could still run*, he thought. Take some dogs and head into the wilderness for a few days, until they found the men who had actually done it, who had carried Churchy's body into the woods. Then he would be safe.

But the idea was ridiculous. To flee would be to implicate himself, and he didn't want to leave his family worried.

Grant walked a straight line to the building Doc had told him to go to. Inside, he waited in the lobby for only a minute until the trooper poked his head out and motioned Grant in. In the HSE office, the walls were painted white and were bare except for framed certificates and a single bookshelf stuffed full of manuals. The trooper was a young guy, maybe only a year or two older than Grant. The skin on his face looked soft, clean-shaven. Like he woke up each morning with plenty of time and nothing to worry about. He gestured for Grant to sit at the chair facing the desk and picked up a pen, poised to write on the yellow legal pad in front of him.

"I'm Officer Fisher. And you are—Grant? Is that correct?"

Grant nodded. "Sanford," he added, his voice small. "My last name."

"Grant Sanford," Fisher said, writing it down. "So, Grant. Doc tells me you went out to Site Fourteen on October twenty-fourth? Is that correct?"

"Yeah." Grant shifted, unsure of how much information to offer. He decided on as little as possible. Wasn't saying too much the easiest way to get caught in a lie?

Fisher looked at him. "What were you doing?"

Getting caught up in a crime. "Doc—that's my boss, I don't actually know his real name—he asked me to drive some pipes out to Site Fourteen, so I did."

Fisher nodded slowly. "There was an explosion at Site Fourteen during the time you were gone. Did you witness it?"

He could lie, but maybe someone else would tell the truth, Elias or one of the other crew members at the rig. He chose a half-truth. "I did. I had finished helping unload the pipes and started driving away. I heard a loud sound and some shouting. I stopped and got out but they had it under control, so I went back to the shop."

The trooper let a long silence pass between them. Grant knew the tactic, waiting someone out so they would speak. He kept his mouth shut. Eventually, Fisher spoke again. "Doc said you were gone for a while."

"Because I stopped to make sure everything was okay."

He nodded slowly. "And nothing else of note, besides the explosion?"

Grant hesitated. He had come in with his mind made up: He wouldn't say anything. Let the other men tell the truth if they wanted to, let them point fingers at him, but he would protect his own innocence and, in turn, that of his family. But now the moment had arrived, the chance to come clean, to lay it out for the officer and let him choose what to do. To help Churchy's family, if he had one. Maybe Grant would spend some time in jail, or maybe he'd get some kind of bargain for giving up the names of the men who had carried Churchy's body to the woods. Except he didn't know their names, but all he had to say was—the Site Fourteen men. Someone would check the schedule and determine who had been working on October 24th.

It would have been easy, at least in comparison to the secrets he'd been keeping. But that's not what he did. "No, nothing of note." Guilt and anxiety crushed his chest, but he reminded himself that without the oil field, his family would have nothing.

If Fisher noticed Grant's brief hesitation, it didn't show in his expression. He wrote something down and clicked his pen a few times before placing it on the desk and looking back up at Grant. "Do you know why we're here?"

Grant took his time answering. He'd come too far to say the wrong thing now. "The explosion. Guess the Oil and Gas authorities didn't do their job."

"They did their job," Fisher replied. "But we've received reports of a death related to the explosion, and a possible cover-up of that death." He paused, letting his words hang in the air between them. "Have you heard anything that might be related to such an incident?"

Reports. Plural. Grant's heart sped up. His palms were slick—his emotional discomfort starting to manifest physically. "No," he replied. "I haven't heard anything about that."

"What about Clyde Lee?"

Grant's pulse accelerated again at the sound of Churchy's real name. Another opportunity for innocence. "Who?"

Fisher's expression remained neutral. "He was reported missing on October twenty-fifth. He was scheduled to work at Site Fourteen on October twenty-fourth. Did you see him there?"

Grant shook his head. "I don't know who he is." He paused, then offered more. "I've been working in the shop for a couple years now, and I live at home. I haven't met many of the newer rig workers."

Fisher nodded once, as if satisfied. And to Grant's surprise and relief, he stood up, extending his hand across the desk to shake Grant's. His sweaty hand. Grant could blame it on the warm room after a morning in the poorly heated shop. But Fisher said nothing. He stepped around his desk and opened the door, ushering Grant out silently and waving for the next person in the lobby to come in. Grant glanced at the occupied chair and his chest constricted yet again. Elias sat, back rigid, blue eyes fixed solemnly on the wall across from him. He turned his head slowly, gaze sweeping to meet Grant's for a second, before he stood up, rearranging his expression into something affable, and stepped around Grant to greet the trooper. Grant didn't look over his shoulder as he left, but he swore Elias's eyes burned a hole in his back.

15

"GO IN," NINA COMMANDED, STARING DOWN AT THE blue-eyed black dog. Wilder locked eyes with her, tongue lolling from his mouth, indignant at the thought that he should return to his kennel after a long run. *You should be exhausted,* Nina thought. "Please," she tried, gently nudging his hind end with her knee, and Wilder relented, stepping inside the kennel. Nina quickly shut the door behind him and leaned against it, closing her eyes in a moment of relief as she listened to him lap from his water bowl. It was midafternoon, but Nina was hungry and tired after her third run of the day, different configurations of dogs to make sure they all got enough exercise. The amount of time outside was for her own benefit, too, to distract her from the anxiety she'd felt ever since handing over the video file. As far as she knew, nothing had come of it yet, but she was still on edge.

It didn't help that when she ran the dogs close to dusk, she was reminded of the time, as a teenager, she'd fallen off the sled and watched her dogs head deep into the forest. There was nothing to stop them—the dogs would run until they grew tired or got stuck. She was ten miles from home with no way of calling and staring into a long night of near-zero temperatures. She had to get the dogs back.

An hour later, deep in the spruce forest, voice raw from calling out, ice had shot up her spine. At first Nina thought it was some effect of the cold, her body starting to shut down from too much exposure. Already her gloved hands neared numbness, her face icy. But then the hairs on the back of her neck stood up. Her heart raced. Her palms, cold as they were, began to sweat. Nina turned and saw the bear.

A knock on the door startled her from her memories. *I wonder if Mom is expecting anyone.* She straightened up, checking the wall clock—3:00 p.m. Audrey? She didn't expect her sister to show her face at home, and doubted she would knock, but maybe she needed something.

She opened the door and peered up at the man who stood outside. His face was weathered, wrinkles on his brow and around his eyes. On his wrist, where the left shirtsleeve pushed back a little, was what Nina guessed to be an expensive watch. A gray beard trimmed close to his skin. But he wasn't old, just middle-aged. He looked like someone who had spent a lot of time working outside. He looked like any other man from Whitespur.

"Hi," Nina said. "Can I help you?"

"Mary Sanford?"

"No, I'm her daughter. Nina." She extended her hand and the man shook it.

"I thought you might be a little young. Name's Frankie."

The driveway behind him was empty save for her family's truck. *He must have parked up the drive,* Nina thought. Sometimes people feared the entire driveway wouldn't be clear of snow and didn't want to get stuck. "Do you have an appointment? Need some help?"

"No, no appointment," Frankie replied. "I'm in the market for a sled dog or two and I was passing through and I thought—why not check out Sanford Sled Dogs?"

"Passing through, huh? Not many people pass through Whitespur. Where are you headed?" Nina regretted that her small talk sounded accusatory. Her mother was inside the house, but Nina didn't want to go retrieve her, not with this golden opportunity in front of her. If she could convince this man to purchase a dog, she could accomplish what she'd wanted to do since arriving home—help her family. The trained, race-capable sled dogs weren't cheap. But she didn't yet know what kind of dog he wanted. Maybe only a puppy, too unproven to charge much money for. The puppies of the city litter were eight weeks old now and ready to be weaned. She would check with her mother, of course, before letting any dogs go. But she suspected Mary would welcome any money she could get.

The man smiled, taking it in stride. His teeth were straight and white. "Coming back, actually, from Prudhoe Bay. Had some business up there, going back to Fairbanks now, then home."

He was in the oil industry, then. She decided not to ask if he had any connection to the Brooks Valley field. "Well, good idea to stop in. We've got dogs. Although I'll have to double-check with my family before I sign off on selling any." She stepped aside, gesturing for Frankie to enter the kennel building. "Are you looking for recreational dogs? Do you run a trapline?"

"I want Yukon Quest dogs. I want dogs that can cover a long distance, fast."

Nina regarded him. He wasn't cracking a joke. Still, people sometimes got ideas in their heads about running long distance races like the Yukon Quest or the Iditarod but never made it as far as the starting line and left behind a set of unconditioned, neglected dogs. She tried to ignore the dollar signs and gather more information. "What did you say your last name was?"

"I didn't. It's Campbell," he replied. "Not a name you'll recognize. I haven't raced in Alaska yet."

"So, you're from . . ."

"Montana," Frankie supplied, a neutral expression still on his face. Nina wished she had the convenience of the internet to verify that he had raced before and knew how to care for dogs, but she'd have to do without. "I've got a good team back home. But I need the edge. I don't want to just make it to Fairbanks. I want to be in the money."

Nina tilted her head, running through a mental list of the dogs. She couldn't offer him any of Grant's dogs. The dogs she'd mushed as a teenager were retired or dead now. She thought of Honey. "We have a solid, race-bred leader. She's fast and she's good down a trail. I've been using her a lot the last few weeks." She led him to Honey's kennel, indicating the brown dog, who was curled up in a ball. "She's ten, though. Still fit, with tons of experience, but she may only race for another year or two. Her sister, Sugar, is still running great, too. They're bred for stamina and longevity."

"Only a few weeks?"

Nina hesitated, momentarily confused, and then nodded. "Oh. Yeah. I've been away from home for a while. I recently got back. My mom, she knows the dogs better, but she's filled me in on their conditions."

"You were away? At college?"

"Yeah," Nina replied, trying to shift his attention back to the dogs. She didn't know why he was so interested in her whereabouts. But maybe he was only making conversation and she was being cagey and unfriendly. She had never sold dogs on her own before. "I'd offer to let you take Honey out, but we just got back from a run. That's why she's sleeping. Normally she's a bundle of energy."

Frankie turned his attention back to the dog. "Does she eat before she sleeps?"

He must know something about mushing, Nina thought. "Yes. Always. She's got a great appetite. Here," she continued, side-stepping down the aisle past a few kennels. "This is Wilder. He's three. I've been using him as a wheel dog because he's small, but I think he'd be fine in any position. Maybe even a leader one day."

Wilder stood up from his bed as soon as they stopped in front of his kennel. He pressed against the door, wagging his tail so hard his entire body wriggled, and let out a high-pitched whine. His bright blue eyes were stark against his black fur. Nina reached through the chain link to scratch his face.

"What's the theme with that one?"

After a moment of confusion, Nina gathered he must have picked up on the litter themes—Honey and Sugar, and the various others from the name plaques on each kennel door. "None," she replied. "He was the only one in his litter. My dad said he was wilder than any puppy he'd ever seen, and it stuck."

A hint of a smile crossed Frankie's face. "Better than some of the ones I've ended up with. Years ago, I bought a pair of dogs from a kennel near Great Falls. Theme was 'dogs in literature.' I ended up with Cujo and White Fang."

Nina laughed. "I hope they were nicer than their name-sakes."

Frankie's expression cleared, as if he realized he had gotten sidetracked. Refocusing on Wilder, he said, "He is small."

"Yeah, well, that's what makes him a good wheel dog." Nina suspected that Frankie wasn't really concerned about the dog's size. He might be preparing to lowball her. "He's agile," Nina continued. "He stays out of the sled's way."

"You think he could lead one day?"

"I do. He has the drive and instinct. I think if you put him up front with Honey for a season, let her show him the ropes, he'd get the hang of it eventually. He'd be ready to replace Honey by the time she retires."

Frankie was quiet for a long time, studying Wilder. "What else you got?" he said, finally, and Nina obliged him, showing off the other dogs. She didn't know them as well, the ones she'd run less frequently since she'd been home, but she ducked into the office to grab the record book and rattled off their conditioning history. Her mother had a grading system for categories such as drive, energy, appetite, teachability—letters penciled in her sloped handwriting, A or B+, a dreaded D on occasion. Frankie listened in silence. She reminded herself that there was nothing to worry about. She was home, with her parents steps away inside the house. Frankie was just there to buy a dog.

He paused in front of Sage's kennel, indicating the dog who sat near the back. "I like the look of this one."

"Oh." Nina hesitated. "She's a real problem child, unfortunately. She tends to pick fights with the other dogs. Not one you'd want on a race team."

Nina held her breath, but Frankie merely nodded. When she finished going through the list, Frankie laughed, a deep, rumbling sound. "I think," he said, "you gave me the best options first."

Nina smiled. "What can I say. I like to be up front."

"How much are you thinking?"

Nina paused, begging her brain to remember the pricing system her mother always used. She had to factor in their past and future performances, their age, any potential litters they might have. "Honey's a proven race dog," she said. "And good leaders are hard to find. Five thousand for her. Wilder's younger, less proven. I'll let him go for three."

Frankie didn't react, just stared at her, his blue eyes devoid of emotion. Nina shivered, wishing he was a little more convivial, a little easier to read.

"They're good dogs, right? You wouldn't lie to me about that?"

"We have a thirty-day money-back guarantee," Nina replied, inching away from him and ducking into the office to grab a contract. "It's all in here," she said, handing him a stapled stack of papers. "You can read through it. We'll take the dogs back for most reasons. Sickness, behavioral issues, failure to mesh with your other dogs. But not for something like losing a race. You'll need to fill this out before you take them home."

Frankie scanned the first page and then looked back at Nina. "Alright. You've got a deal."

Nina's heart skipped a beat. Her mother would be over the moon. Since Nina had arrived home, she'd heard a thousand times that the dogs hadn't sold well over the last couple of years, even before the pandemic. Her mother was digging into the family's savings, buying cheaper food and less of it, leaving the lights off as much as possible. Barely scraping by. Eight thousand dollars could take them a long way through winter.

"Great." She glanced down at his extended hand. "Let me confirm with my mom. She's inside. It won't be an issue, but I want her to know which dogs are leaving."

Frankie withdrew his hand. "Could I come inside," he said, "for a glass of water?"

Nina hesitated, then nodded. There wasn't any reason this man couldn't step inside the dingy interior of their home. If anything, it might make him feel better about forking over eight grand—maybe they could repaint the kitchen or replace the missing shingles on the roof. "Come on," she said, heading down the aisle.

Inside the house, she filled a glass from the kitchen faucet and handed it to him. "Tap water's okay to drink."

Frankie nodded once, absently. His gaze traveled to the sink stacked full of dirty dishes from breakfast and lunch that had yet to be washed. Someone had tracked mud across the floor. One of Grant's sweaters, the orange one he'd worn the day the oil field reopened, was thrown carelessly over the back of a chair, a sleeve dangling over the table. Least excusable were the peeling paint on the walls and the water-stained cabinets, some with doors off their hinges. Nina resisted the urge to apologize for the state of the house. It wasn't her fault—things hadn't been so bad nine years ago. Maybe she wouldn't have left if the house had been in disrepair. Or maybe she would have only been more desperate to start over somewhere new. Nina waited for Frankie to drink the water.

"Sorry," he said, as if realizing he'd been frozen. "I do a lot of contracting work. I was just thinking . . ." He trailed off, as if embarrassed.

"We'll work on it in the spring," Nina said, exhaling when he lifted the glass to his mouth. "I'll be right back, okay?"

She walked past the doorway to the living room, television blaring, and down the hallway. She knocked on her parents' bedroom door and heard a muffled response.

"Mom?" She pushed the door open and stepped into the dim bedroom.

"What's the matter, Nina?" Mary asked, sitting up in bed. "I don't need the truck right now."

"No, it's not about the truck. There's a man here—"

"A man?" Her voice hinted at panic, and Nina wondered where her mind had gone—something to do with Audrey, maybe, bad news about her daughter.

"He's here about dogs," Nina said, and her mother visibly

relaxed. "I've been talking to him for a while, out in the kennel. He wants two dogs for a long-distance sled team."

"Hmm," her mother said, eyebrows raised. "And?"

"I think I made him a deal. For Honey and Wilder."

Her mother coughed and looked away. "Honey is your dog, Nina."

"And you always said we could sell our dogs if we wanted to." She waited, but her mother didn't respond. "She was a puppy when I left, Mom. It's not like we have a bond." But Honey had remembered her, even after all those years, and guilt licked its way through her the same way Honey had licked her fingers on her first day home. She had been raised to understand that the dogs were a business, and to never get too attached. She hadn't thought twice about selling Honey, but something had held her back from selling Sage, from telling the truth about the talented, tireless leader she knew Sage to be. Sage was younger and would adapt easier to a new home. Honey would get used to it, eventually—but would she miss Nina's mother, who had cared for her for ten years, and her kennelmates?

"She's a good dog," her mother replied, after a long moment of silence. "I spent a lot of time training her."

"I don't have to sell her—"

"No. She's the right dog, for what he wants." She coughed again. Nina was struck by how small her mother seemed, swallowed by the comforter and a huge old sweater, probably her father's. "Your dad bred Wilder's litter. You should talk to him. He likes that dog."

Nina thought of interrupting her father, planted in front of the television. He wouldn't care. Just lift a hand and tell her that the dogs were meant to be sold. "Okay," she replied. "I'd better get back out there; I don't want to leave him waiting."

"Hold on. How much?"

"Five thousand for Honey, three thousand for Wilder."

"Did you ask for more?"

Nina hesitated, then admitted the truth. "No. I was thinking of what they would have gone for when I was a kid."

"Well. Nothing you can do about it now. The money will still help." She seemed like she might want to try talking him into a higher price, but then she relaxed back against the pillows. "Good job, Nina."

She carried that with her down the hallway, *good job, Nina*, the first praise she'd received from her mother in years. Those weren't words she'd heard when she got into culinary school, on a scholarship that covered most of her tuition, and not when she'd graduated, the first in her family to do so. In the last letter she had written to her mother, she had told her about the job at Nocturne. In response, her mother had talked only about the town, about the oil field that was getting ready to begin drilling, about a litter of recent puppies. She hadn't written a word about Nina's accomplishments. Sometimes she wondered if her mother had ever gotten the letter, or if Nina had received her letters out of order. But she remembered now that there was only one way to contribute in her mother's eyes—to sell dogs, to send Sanford Sled Dog lines into the world and let them prove themselves. Honey and Wilder would run the Yukon Quest and maybe even place. She had no idea how good Frankie's other dogs were, but she knew how good Honey was and how good Wilder could be.

Good job, Nina. Eight thousand dollars and two fewer mouths to feed through winter.

When Nina returned, the kitchen was empty. The glass, empty too, had been placed atop the pile in the sink. *He must have gone back to the kennel*, she thought. He probably wanted to spend time with his new dogs, get to know them. She let the door swing shut behind her and strode across the yard, each breath clouding before her face.

The lights were still on in the kennel. Nina paused in the doorway, scanning the aisle. "Frankie?" she called. A few dogs whined in response, a chorus longing for attention. She stepped forward, a sinking sensation in her chest, the hairs on her arms standing up beneath her coat.

Nina pushed the office door open again, called Frankie's name. Empty. Letting her eyes drift down the aisle, her stomach clenched, a wave of nausea followed by fear. Honey's kennel was empty—door shut, but empty. Her vision jumped again. Wilder was gone, too.

Before she bolted, something caught her eye. On the prep table lay an envelope. White, unmarked. She reached for it, hand shaking, and opened it, slid out a stack of cash. She counted it as quickly as she could. All of it was there, all eight thousand dollars. But Frankie and the dogs were gone.

Nina ran from the kennel and down the driveway, calling out at the top of her lungs, all three of their names on a repeat. She thought maybe the dogs would respond, their barks leading to where he'd parked his truck. Nothing but the silent night answered her. She paused halfway down the driveway, doubled over, gasping in cold air that shocked her lungs with each breath. A ball of rage unfurled in her chest, and she resisted the urge to throw back her head and howl.

She thought again of the bear all those years ago, the same tightness in her chest, the galloping fear. It had been early fall, maybe the last week of September. Still some daylight, though she'd been out as night fell. The second snow, finally enough of a layer to use a real sled and not the rusty old ATV that the dogs pulled in the summer. Late in the season for a bear. The bears who weren't hibernating yet had something wrong—old or weak or sick, unable to find enough food to sustain themselves for winter. They knew that hibernation might kill them, or they'd wake up in the dead of winter with no food sources left. So, they scavenged, drew closer to towns, hunted for easier prey. Like Nina.

Had she been easy prey to Frankie, too?

What does it matter? she asked herself. *He paid. If the money is real.* It had looked real, worn, money that had passed hands. But she'd have to drive hours to get to a bank, somewhere that could verify if it was legit. The stores in Whitespur didn't even have counterfeit pens at the register.

Back in the kennel, she recounted the money, confirming again that it was all there. The unsigned contract sat on the table. That was the part that stung—the dogs were now virtually untraceable. The contract had everything in it—breeding rights, what food the dogs should eat, their normal training regime, a clause that stated they must be returned to Sanford Sled Dogs rather than resold. Nina wondered if Frankie Campbell was even his real name. Why would he flee with the dogs if he had nothing to hide?

Maybe he was in a hurry.

But what situation could prompt this kind of urgency? Not even a note—*here's my address, mail me the contract and I'll mail it back.* The fact that he'd left the money made it stranger. He wasn't stealing the dogs, not truly. He was just a man with money and something to hide.

Nina flinched when her mother walked through the kennel door. Dressed in jeans, a fitted sweater, and a jacket, she was fully awake now and ready for business. Her eyes scanned the empty aisle quickly and settled on Nina, on the envelope in Nina's hand.

"I thought I heard shouting."

Nina shook her head. "The dogs caused a ruckus when they saw Honey and Wilder leave." She thrust the envelope toward her mother.

She counted the money and looked at her daughter again.

"This is a huge relief, Nina. I'm sad to see those two go, but now we can finally afford some of the repairs to winterize the house a bit. I'm going to Bill's tomorrow to ask when he's free." Bill was their contractor, an older man with an immaculate cabin on the refuge border. He sometimes boasted that he'd worked on every house in Whitespur. "It's strange seeing Honey's kennel empty. She's been here for so long."

Tears sprang to Nina's eyes. *I didn't even get to say goodbye. And I have no idea where she's going or what's going to happen to her.* She forced herself to smile. "I know. But she's going to be treated well. That man—Frankie—he was so excited to have her."

As her mother turned away, Nina's heart sank. Why hadn't she kept a better eye on the stranger? She'd been too eager, tripping over herself to help her family. In the process, she had failed Honey and Wilder, and now she would never see them again.

On her way back to the house she stopped and stared into the dark trees. The bear had been off the trail, observing her. Nina's mind had gone blank. *Grizzly, play dead.* Was that all? Surely if she lay down, the bear would come investigate. She had studied its long muzzle, its rounded ears. *Like a teddy bear*, she thought.

Nina had been told many times to always make noise in the woods, to never surprise a bear. She'd been calling the dogs every couple of minutes, shouting out for her leader, Danish, a smart gray dog who knew the territory well. Then, Nina had hoped Danish wasn't on her way back toward Nina. She thought of how appetizing the dogs would look to the bear, all strung up on a line like a kebab.

"Hey, bear," she said, taking a couple of slow steps backward. The bear didn't move but stared at her with casual interest. "I know it's autumn, and you're hungry, but I'm sure you can find something else to eat." She kneeled in the snow, stretched out her legs, propped herself up with her hands like a yoga pose. She thought of the canister of bear spray on the sled, useless to her now. "I saw caribou yesterday, a whole bunch, down in the valley. One of them would keep you full all winter."

The bear hadn't moved. Nina took a quiet breath and dropped down onto her elbows, tucking her face against her arms. How long would it take her family to realize she'd gone missing? August would search for her tirelessly once he knew she hadn't come home. He had a deep knowledge of the refuge land, spent so much time riding and skiing the trails. The thought of him finding her half-eaten corpse, guts spilled out on the snow, was too terrible to entertain. She muttered a quiet prayer and waited, expecting every second for warm breath to touch the back of her neck, perhaps a lick like an approximation of a kiss, and then teeth. And then—

But it never came. After an eternity, convinced she was frozen to the snow, Nina lifted her head and scanned the dark woods. The bear was gone, as far as she could tell. Melted away into the forest. She stood up shakily and continued down the trail, calling out, until half an hour later she spotted the sled, the dogs tangled up in some bushes half off the trail. Another hour passed in detangling the lines from the branches, longer still because Nina couldn't stop looking over her shoulder for the bear. She never saw it again, or any other bear at such close range.

But she remembered the feeling. And now it had come back to haunt her once again.

16

"THE POLICE," GRANT REPEATED, PUSHING HIS FOOD around on his plate like he used to when he was much younger—except now his appetite had left from fear, not boredom. "No warning. A bunch of troopers rolled up and started doing interviews. We thought the oil field would be shut down by now, but they're keeping it open and camping out there." He hadn't seen much of his family since Sunday. He'd gone to The Spur after work the past two days, to hang out with Orson and Michael and speculate on why the police were conducting an investigation. Grant mostly kept his mouth shut, letting them talk, only murmuring agreement with their theories. By the time he got home those nights, his parents and sister were asleep. But he had decided to brave their company today, mostly because he couldn't face another evening of biting his tongue around his friends, unable to tell them what he knew about the explosion.

Nina shifted in her chair, her expression neutral. "Because of the fire?"

"Yes." Grant looked at her pointedly. "Because of the fire."

"Isn't that how it's supposed to work?" their mother asked. "An accident happens, someone reports it, there's an inspection, you're cleared to keep working?"

"There was already an inspection." Grant couldn't keep the agitation out of his voice. "The rig was cleared to keep operating. This must be about something else."

Nina met his eyes and shook her head the tiniest bit, almost imperceptible. Grant didn't know if he believed her. His opinion had changed a thousand times the past few days. Nina had reported it. She hadn't. It had been one of the rig workers. No way, they had too much at stake. Elias himself had reported it, trying to keep himself clear of any repercussions as foreman. No, he would never take that risk, not when he'd already fabricated a story about Churchy's disappearance.

"Nina sold two dogs today," his mother said, standing up to put her plate in the sink. "Made eight grand."

"Who?" Grant asked. Nina didn't answer right away. She glanced at their father, who was hunched over his plate, eating in silence as he did most nights.

"Honey and Wilder," Nina said, quiet, but Ted's head shot up.

"First I'm hearing of this," he grunted, setting down his fork.

"I'm sorry," Nina began. "I talked to Mom about it—"

"And I told you to tell your father," Mary said, leaning against the counter, arms folded across her chest.

Nina looked to Grant for help, but he had nothing to say in her defense. He couldn't take his eyes off her, either, waiting for some sign that she'd spilled the truth about the body to someone else, that the investigation was, in some way, her fault. He barely caught their conversation, too focused on his own anxieties.

"Wilder was supposed to be my leader," their father continued, staring straight ahead. "I bred that litter. My two best race dogs and they gave me one puppy. One goddamn puppy. And you sold him?"

Grant knew what Nina wanted to say: *You're never going to race again.* But an unsettling quiet entered the kitchen, each member of his family rigid. The tension made him sick. He wanted to get up and walk out of the kitchen, like leaving a painting, to go back to reality where people moved and spoke instead of sitting in frozen silence. But they remained, waiting, until their father stood up and threw his plate against the wall.

Shattered bits of ceramic scattered across the floor. Ted left, back to the living room, back to the television that held him captive. Nina's mouth hung open, her eyes wide, as if she wanted to tell him to look at himself, at his broken body that hadn't stood on sled runners for years. But Grant knew he wouldn't listen. In his mind, the Iditarod was tomorrow, and he was the favorite, and she'd sold his entire team from under his nose. Grant thought of reaching across the table to touch Nina's arm, to console her in some way, but she shut her jaw, a dark expression clouding her face. She didn't look upset; she looked angry.

"I'll clean it up," Grant offered, and Mary nodded and left the room.

With a broom, he swept up the pieces, bending down to brush them into the dustpan. Nina took her plate to the trash can, scraped her fork against it as she ushered her leftover food into the garbage. "So. Does that happen a lot? I mean, what the fuck was that about?"

"I think he's pretty clearly upset at you," Grant replied, stepping beside her to shake the dustpan into the can. "Not that you deserve it. But he's been through a lot."

"Throwing a plate at the wall, though? He's never done something like that."

The fist-sized hole in the living room wall begged to differ. Grant had hung a framed family photograph over it; Nina would have no idea it was there. "He's angrier than he used to be. He won't hurt you, if that's what you're worried about."

"I'm not," Nina muttered. She wandered back to the table, resting her fingers on its surface. It dawned on Grant that she was already hurt, even if the violence hadn't affected her physically. He set the broom back in the closet and drew a breath. His sister didn't turn to face him.

"Nina," he said, his voice low but urgent. "Did you report it? What I told you?"

She shook her head.

"Please. I have to know."

She straightened up and turned, meeting his gaze. "No. I didn't report it."

"Okay." He ran his hands through his hair, still struggling to believe her. Could she be that good of a liar? "Okay. I'm sorry to accuse you. I just—I guess one of the guys I work with must have. Or they told someone else, like I told you."

"Word got out about the fire, Grant. More than a few people aren't happy about the drilling in the refuge. Anyone could have made a report."

"You're right." He watched her closely, but her face still revealed nothing. Maybe she was telling the truth. "You're right. They're interviewing everyone, though. I'm worried I'll say the wrong thing. And I'm worried about not getting paid if they shut the drilling down again."

"I made us eight thousand dollars today," Nina said, glancing at him. "I wouldn't worry about the money right now."

The comment stung—he didn't understand why she couldn't grasp how much he had sacrificed to keep their family afloat the last few years. She had been dismissive and critical of his work at every turn, even though he'd made it clear the oil field was his only option. His happiness, his health, his safety, even his life now—he'd set it all at stake to pay the bills for his parents, and for Audrey. And Nina, in a stroke of luck, had made more cash in a single day than he had in months.

"You know that money won't last forever, right? Maybe not even until spring. Do you understand how necessary my job is?"

"I do. I know what shape the house is in. I can only imagine it'd be worse without your job."

She hadn't apologized, but he hadn't asked her to. Grant swallowed his indignation. "I'm glad you sold a couple of dogs, even though I'll miss them. I'm sorry Dad reacted like that. I should have said something. But I thought you—"

"I get it." She lifted a hand to silence him. "Dad will forget about it in a day or two. But, Grant?" She paused, waiting until he looked at her. "I know you need your job. But if you're that worried about saying something, about spilling the accident, maybe it means you should. The police will protect you. So, don't protect your bosses. You're not going to gain anything from it."

He tapped his fingers against the Formica counter. When he imagined telling the truth, it didn't end like the picture Nina painted. It ended with him in jail, or dead. Nina's view of the law was far rosier than his, and didn't include the fact that his coworkers had covered up a death like it was a routine part of their job. "I already told you. This is the only job that's viable for me. I can't stand against them and continue working there." Nina's jaw was rigid, her forehead creased. She looked both like his older sister and a stranger, like the span of time she'd been away had turned her into someone unrecognizable. "I'm sorry. I know you want me to do the right thing. Maybe this is the right thing for me." She didn't respond. As he turned away, the sight of the empty table jogged his memory. "Hey, didn't I leave a sweater here?"

"Yeah," Nina replied, her voice flat. "Maybe Mom brought it to your room?"

It was one of his favorites, but he didn't push it. In his bedroom, the overhead light pulsed and died when he flipped the switch. He left it dark, not bothering with the bedside lamp or to rummage for his sweater, and let his guilt fester. He could never say the right thing. He hadn't reported the body, hadn't even refused to cart it off to the woods. He hadn't defended Nina from their father's senseless bullying. It wasn't too late—he could get up now, pull the remote from his father's hands, and force him to talk. Unspool the dark presence of his misery that had hung, cloudlike, over this house since the day he shattered his leg.

But Grant knew it was useless. Mushing had been his entire life, and with that gone, with a leg that never healed right and a body that no longer stood up to the rigors of hours on a dogsled, Ted Sanford believed he had nothing left to live for. The dogs in the kennel existed only as dreams, as projections for the future. Grant knew his father had still held hope when he bred Wilder's litter, when his mother was still driving him to weekly physical therapy sessions in Fairbanks after his surgery. But it was too late. He hadn't been able to go for an entire winter, trapped by the ferocious snow, the impassable Dalton. By spring his leg had healed wrong and the physical therapist could only try to help him in his limited range of mobility. Grant remembered how his father's anger had boiled over that summer, his rage burning white-hot through every room in the tiny house. Grant was working at Brooks Valley by then and spent as little time at home as possible. In those days, he'd been glad that both Nina and Audrey were gone. Now he tried to imagine what Audrey would have done had she been there— probably thrown her own plate at the wall, shown their father the childish nature of his actions. Demanded that he apologize and start acting like an adult. But he couldn't know for sure; she hadn't eaten a meal at their house in years.

Sometimes the generational divide between himself and his father felt as clean as a knife slicing through whitefish. Ted had made his living off the land, hunting and fishing and raising champion sled dogs. His family had lived without running water, without electricity, without plumbing. Everything had shifted rapidly after Grant was born. His sisters might even remember the days of the outhouse, but Grant didn't. Unlike his father, who lived with the land, Grant's job was to exploit it, or at least assist the exploitation, make it easier to extract the valuable resources and damage the environment in the process. And damage the people, too. Though Ted kept his mouth shut and accepted the money from each of Grant's paychecks, he imagined that his role at the oil field only added to his father's discontent. Grant had tried many times to think of ways to improve Ted's mental health, at least, but talking to him had become near impossible. They watched TV together, sometimes, had stilted conversations. Each year, the summers had become a little easier. The extra daylight and warmth helped Ted, sometimes pulling him from the dim recesses of the living room to the sun-washed back stoop. Once in a while they'd drink a beer together and Ted would comment on the colors of the backyard tundra.

His sister didn't understand what lurked beneath the surface of her father's anger. Grant knew he should knock on Nina's door, apologize, and explain, try to help her comprehend the depth of their father's pain. But once more, he couldn't move, couldn't speak, couldn't bring himself to do the right thing. It was becoming a pattern, one he felt too weak to break.

17

FOR THREE DAYS, NINA KEPT HER HEAD DOWN, running the dogs and completing chores, and listening to Grant's reports of the developments on the oil field. He was anxious, a fuse waiting to be lit, since more troopers had arrived. Maybe the extra pressure would convince him to come clean, and the whole ordeal could end. Handing it over to the proper authorities still seemed like the right thing to do, but the increased police presence had clearly set her brother on edge, and Nina didn't like seeing him so stressed. Then again, she didn't like anything about the situation.

In the meantime, Nina desperately needed to get out of the house. Her father still hadn't spoken to her, and her mother operated with a kind of indifferent coolness. Any pride in Nina's salesmanship had dissipated with her father's anger. Nina didn't have the energy to remind her mother that this was exactly what she had wanted—more money and fewer dogs to feed. Nor could she tell her parents the truth, that the man had vanished with the dogs and left an unsigned contract. She couldn't bear the thought of any more anger or disappointment directed at her. And she still held out hope that maybe it had been a mistake, that the man would return to fill out the contract and the problem would solve itself.

Now, at 7:00 a.m., she rolled past Cold Creek and continued down the Dalton highway, heading toward Fairbanks. The threat of a snowstorm made it risky to drive the Dalton in early November, but the sky above was cloudless, and she had wasted enough time. There was little money left in her bank account, and the longer she remained at home, the more claustrophobic she felt. She needed to find a job.

That the nearest library was in Fairbanks complicated the process. Nina had crawled out of bed at 3:30 to leave by 4:00 a.m., and though she'd brought enough coffee to fuel an army, her eyelids still drooped. The road was mostly empty, save for the occasional long-haul trucker who roared past on the opposite side, blazing into the frozen North. The first hints of light had yet to creep in and illuminate the landscape of scrubby trees and low mountains that stretched to the horizon, so for now she drove through endless darkness, the truck's headlights spotlighting only the road in front of her. Close to Fairbanks, when the sky did begin to lighten, she welcomed the sight of gradually taller trees, birch intermingling with spruce.

Nina had performed this process twice in high school, borrowing the truck to submit college applications in Fairbanks. At least colleges sent acceptance letters the old-fashioned way, snail mail, so eventually she'd gotten the thick envelope from the Culinary Institute of America. Now she'd have to find job applications that included that convenient little box: *Is there anything else you'd like to tell us?*

Yes, she thought, *by virtue or bad luck I live farther north than any sensible person should. Please help.* She'd ask for their response by mail. Employers within Alaska, she suspected, would be more understanding of her circumstances.

Midmorning, after stopping for more coffee and a plate of gummy, overcooked pancakes, Nina pulled into the library parking lot, in front of the large brick building. A steady stream of cars rolled past on the road, and Nina marveled to once again be immersed in humanity, the infrastructure built where people gathered. At a moment's notice, she could have anything she wanted.

She steeled herself for the blast of cold air and opened the truck door. Inside the library, after filling out a guest pass, she removed her gloves, coat, hat, and thick wool sweater, creating a mountain of clothes on the empty chair beside her assigned computer desk. Left in a long-sleeve T-shirt, she felt almost naked.

Nina pulled up every job board website she could think of and scrolled through the postings. To her surprise, half the openings that popped up were for positions at various oil fields, including Brooks Valley. Apparently, an army of chefs was needed to feed the workers, but she couldn't entertain the thought of supporting the oil industry, even in a small way. She found a few chef positions worth applying for: at a lodge near Denali National Park, at a hotel in Anchorage, at a restaurant in Homer. Before applying to each one she closed her eyes and tried to imagine herself there, cooking in an unfamiliar kitchen, with strangers all around her. Serving food to customers she didn't know, lying down to sleep at night in a new bed. Where would she live? The lodge and the hotel both offered housing, presumably a standard room, maybe a suite if she was lucky. In Homer, she'd have to make her own way. The thought of doing any of it without Micah was painful. Still, she typed answers to the questions, filled out the required boxes, and uploaded copies of her résumé, reminding herself to text him when she was finished.

An hour and a half later, she leaned back in her chair, spent from the effort of selling herself. Behind her closed lids she saw, cruelly, Honey and Wilder, curled up together in the snow. Black dog and brown dog, four eyes peering up at her, begging her for help. *I don't even know where you are*, she almost whispered, and then her eyes snapped open.

She Googled Frankie Campbell, then Frank Campbell, then Franklin Campbell, then Francis Campbell. She added "Montana" to each query, then "musher," then just "dogs." One of the searches pulled up a Frank Campbell in Missoula, an investment banker, but he looked nothing like the man Nina had met and when she skimmed the page, she realized it was an obituary.

Nina stared at the monitor, breathing quickly, a chill sliding up her spine. He wasn't real. He had used a fake name. Whoever he was, he had taken her dogs and stolen off into the long dark night with them, no paperwork to trace him back. But why? He wouldn't spend eight thousand dollars to do something horrible to the dogs. But he must be up to something. Trapping without a license, maybe, but if he had eight thousand dollars to spare, he certainly had twenty-five dollars for a license. Or—if what he said was true, and he was from Montana—he wouldn't shy from the higher nonresident fee. Maybe he was trapping or hunting illegal game, then, taking wolves or bears from areas where their populations were protected. That would explain why he wanted race dogs—a quick getaway.

With a sinking feeling, she realized there was nothing more she could do. He had given her no other information, no identifying clues. And he had paid for the dogs—she couldn't technically report them as stolen. If she somehow found him, she wouldn't even ask for the dogs back; her family needed the money more. As long as the dogs were safe and treated well, all she needed was the signed contract, a way to trace them. The fact that he had no internet presence clouded her previous hope that he simply hadn't understood the contract—leaving it blank now seemed entirely intentional.

Nina swallowed her fear, grabbed her belongings, and headed home.

THE NEXT MORNING, minutes before noon, Nina waited on the exposed landing outside her sister's apartment, thin snowflakes falling on all sides. Thankfully, it hadn't started snowing until last night, after she was home in bed, exhausted from her journey to Fairbanks. This morning, nearly a foot of fresh snow had made her morning chores more difficult as she trudged back and forth across the yard.

Nina knocked once more. She had shown up unannounced, but she had been meaning to visit Audrey for a while, to spend some time with her sister outside of the bar.

Just before she lifted her fist again the door opened. Audrey blinked at the sight of Nina and then grinned. Her hair was up in a bun and she wore a faded black sweatshirt and sweatpants. Dark circles rimmed the undersides of her eyes. "Sorry. Katrina usually gets the door, but she's at work. It's hard to hear from my room. What's up?"

"Just thought I'd stop by," Nina said. "Were you sleeping? Sorry if I woke you up." She realized she didn't know her sister's schedule, if Audrey typically slept until midday. If she spent her nights drinking, it wasn't difficult to imagine that she might have a hard time getting out of bed in the morning.

"Not sleeping," she replied, but offered no clarification. "Anyway, come in." She stepped back, making space for Nina to pass through the doorway.

"Thanks," Nina said, stamping the snow off her boots before she crossed the threshold. "Do you have any coffee? It's freezing out there."

"Instant," Audrey said. The apartment was small, and densely decorated, a couch covered in blankets, string lights illuminating a blue-green mandala tapestry on the wall, and an old TV propped up on an empty crate.

"Instant is fine." She removed her boots and set them atop the pile of shoes beside the door. "Isn't it weird having a TV? I watched way too much when I first moved away."

"The oil company paid for those satellites. Why not use it? I probably do watch too much, but you know how boring it is here."

Boring wasn't how Nina would describe her time home, not with the trouble Grant was in and the borderline stolen dogs. She'd thought of them the entire drive home yesterday, analyzed every sentence she could remember Frankie saying to her, and still had no idea where to look next, or if there was anything more she could do to find out where they'd gone. She had even given more thought to telling her mother, but didn't want to worry her. As far as she was concerned, the money was a life raft in the white-water rapids of the coming winter.

As she sat on the couch, shoving blankets aside, Nina's phone buzzed in her pocket. To her surprise, several notifications lit up the screen, including a text from Micah. **So sick of Austin!! Tired of these pretentious cowboys. Get me out of here!!!**

He had sent it the night before, in response to her text sent from the library asking how he was doing. She typed a quick sympathetic response. "You have service here?" she asked Audrey, who had filled a kettle and set it on the stove.

"Yeah. Isn't that wild? I guess I'm close enough to the center of town." She turned back to the kitchen and a thought crossed Nina's mind. It was a long shot, but she had to try.

She opened the internet app on her phone and typed into the search bar the one distinct detail she remembered from her conversation with Frankie: Cujo and White Fang sled dogs Great Falls Montana.

The page took a long time to load. The sound of Audrey moving through the kitchen, setting mugs and spoons on the counter, reminded Nina why she had come here in the first place. But finding any information she could about Frankie Campbell now took precedence. When the search finally loaded, she scrolled through the results. The third one down linked to a pedigree page for a dog named White Fang, a purebred Siberian husky from a kennel in—Nina held her breath—Augusta, Montana. The dog's siblings were listed, among them a dog registered under the name Man Killer. That must be Cujo. The other littermates were all named after fictional dogs, too. Another agonizingly slow search showed her it wasn't all that far from Great Falls. The kennel that had registered the dogs was called Willow Creek, a name she saw reflected on the map for more than one body of water. Audrey hummed to herself in the kitchen and Nina wondered how much time she had before the coffee was ready and she would have to devote her attention to her sister.

One more search revealed a website for Willow Creek Kennel, somewhat outdated, plain black text on a white background with poorly sized, low-resolution images of husky dogs and links to the web pages of various sponsors. The site wasn't formatted for a mobile phone, but after zooming in, she found the phone number at the bottom of the screen. Nina walked to the kitchen and saw that the water on the stove was simmering. She noticed, too, that there were no bottles of alcohol on the counter or on top of the refrigerator. Maybe Audrey kept them tucked away in a cabinet.

"Sorry, do you mind if I make a call? It'll be quick."

Audrey nodded. "Go ahead. I'll wait in here until you're done."

Glad that her sister hadn't asked questions, Nina retreated back to the living room and sat on the far end of the couch, pulling a knit blanket over her lap. She drew a few deep breaths before typing the number into her phone, then hesitated. Maybe she was being paranoid. Only four days had passed. Frankie—if that was his real name—could still realize he forgot to fill out a contract and come back. But his actions had been so deliberate, and quick. He hadn't wasted any time leaving the envelope of cash and disappearing with both dogs. Nina tapped the call button and pressed the phone to her ear.

Someone answered on the third ring. "Hello, this is Maureen," said a gruff voice. When no further greeting came, no mention of a business name, Nina began to doubt that she had the right number.

She cleared her throat. "Hi. I'm trying to reach—Willow Creek Kennel?"

"You have," replied Maureen. She sounded downright uninterested, but Nina relaxed a tiny bit. At least she contacted the right place.

"I'm calling—I'm calling about . . ." Nina trailed off, trying to organize her thoughts. She hadn't learned her lesson from the trooper station about needing to rehearse. "I have a buyer interested in some dogs and I'm doing a background check. You were listed as a kennel he previously bought dogs from. I'm Nina Sanford, from Sanford Sled Dogs," she added, hoping she sounded legitimate enough to hold the woman's attention.

"Sure. Where are you from? I don't recognize the name."

"Whitespur, Alaska. My client, he's from Montana." *Client* sounded too formal, but she pushed through. "His name is Frankie Campbell. He said he bought two dogs named Cujo and White Fang several years ago. Cujo's registered name was Man Killer? It says they were born in 2008?"

Maureen laughed, a thick sound from deep in her throat. "I remember them. Total sweethearts. But hey, I didn't sell them to a man named Frankie. Normally I'd have to go look at my records when so much time has passed, especially the ones I sell young. They were a year old, I think. Anyway, the guy I sold them to was named Waylon Turcotte, and I remember because five or so years ago he was busted in some big drug raid down in Billings. It was all over the news."

Nina wanted to ask if she was sure, because she couldn't believe that the answer hadn't been a straightforward yes—she had hoped that Frankie was simply old-fashioned and had escaped having any internet presence. She listened carefully as Maureen continued.

"He must have sold them to whoever you're talking to, maybe before he was arrested. Frank, you said his name was? Yeah, definitely not him. I remember Waylon. Thought he was handsome. The crazy ones always are."

Nina listened to the woman prattle on, turning the new information over in her mind. A chill raced up her spine, her body reacting before her brain. "He did say he bought the dogs from you, though."

"Sure, but he probably got them secondhand and didn't want to admit that. Or maybe he's buddies with Waylon." She laughed. "Sorry, hun, but I can't tell you anything about your Frank. Hope you have some other places to check. Or hey, just ask him. I bet he'll have a good story about how he got those dogs."

"Do you know where Waylon is now?"

"No idea. Never got the dogs back from him, either. I guess he's still in prison. I only saw the news coverage back when it happened."

Nina thanked the woman and hung up. She stared at the screen for a moment, her brain working overtime. Maybe Maureen was right, and Frankie had gotten those dogs, White Fang and Cujo, through dodgy means. Maybe he was used to acquiring dogs secondhand, without paperwork, and that's why he'd disappeared without signing a contract. But another, darker thought pulsed at the center of her mind. Frankie Campbell had no internet presence that she could find. He hadn't signed a contract. What if—what if it was the same man, using a fake name? The thought bordered on too absurd to indulge. How could he have made it to a different state undetected? Why wasn't he in prison? Nina's finger hovered over her phone as she willed herself to search Waylon Turcotte's name.

She flinched at the sound of Audrey's footsteps across the living room, then set her phone down and accepted a mug of coffee.

"You're done, right?"

"Yeah. Sorry about that." Her mind still raced, her heart rate elevated, but Nina willed herself to slow her breathing. She had to search for Waylon Turcotte later, but for now, she needed to focus on her sister.

"It's fine," Audrey said, settling in the chair opposite the couch. "But since when do we ever do background checks on customers?"

Nina hadn't realized that Audrey had been listening. "Oh, it's . . . this guy bought a couple dogs the other day, and when I searched his name yesterday, I couldn't find anything about him. But he mentioned these dogs he had bought in Montana, so I called that woman to verify."

Audrey raised her eyebrows. "But you told her he hadn't bought the dogs yet."

Nina shrugged. "I didn't want her to think I was snooping instead of doing my due diligence."

"Is Mom worried about it?"

Nina hesitated, then shook her head. "No." Some instinct told her not to confide that Frankie hadn't signed a contract and was entirely untraceable.

Her sister accepted that answer. "So, how's life since you've been home?"

It dawned on Nina that, though she had anticipated another unpleasant interaction with Audrey, she felt herself starting to relax. Despite the tension from the phone call and her worry about Frankie's identity, she enjoyed being in her sister's apartment, surrounded by the things that kept her company. Audrey seemed at ease, too, twirling a lock of hair around her finger as she gave Nina her undivided attention. She wasn't drunk, that was for sure, unless she'd poured some alcohol into her coffee. Though she'd been a little disheveled when she'd answered the door, she was more awake now, more present.

But her question was a difficult one to answer. Between the mystery of Frankie and the ongoing drama at the oil field, the last two weeks hadn't exactly been peaceful. "Fine, I guess. I hear a lot about Grant's job."

Audrey nodded, her nose wrinkling. "I don't like that he's working there. *He* doesn't like that he's working there. But I'm sure Mom and Dad do."

"Mom likes the money. I have no idea what Dad thinks." She paused. "Mom is really worried about being able to feed the dogs through this winter. Did she ever ask you about taking one?"

Her sister shook her head, her expression falling as she stared down at her mug. "No. She doesn't talk to me. She probably doesn't trust me to keep a dog alive."

Audrey's change in demeanor made Nina switch the subject. "Do you ever overhear stuff, at The Spur, about what goes on at the oil field?"

"I've been trying to spend less time there," Audrey replied with a laugh. "But sure, sometimes. I mean, I heard about the explosion pretty quickly. If someone gets injured, someone else is always there to reenact it in bloody detail."

"Does that happen often? People getting injured?"

"Sometimes," Audrey replied, after a moment. "Every few months, I'd say. Maybe more often. It seems like dangerous work, though. There was one guy who had a pretty bad injury, had to have his arm amputated. After he had the surgery, he came back to town and talked big about suing the company. At first, people listened, but his case got dismissed, and everyone got tired of hearing from him. Eventually, he left. Went back home, I guess. I don't know all the details of the case, but the judge siding with the oil company sent a pretty clear message."

Nina absorbed the new information. "I have a feeling, sometimes, that there's more going on at the field than they let on."

"Maybe you do watch too much TV. Anyway, The Spur isn't where people bring their secrets. It's where Morgan goes to brag about catching the biggest trout." Audrey smiled, but it quickly left her lips. "I mean, this guy Clyde isn't the first person to go missing from there. A few other people have, years ago, and they were never found. They put up flyers in The Spur and act like that's the best they can do."

"I saw the posters for Eric and Benjamin. I remember seeing Benjamin on the news. Grant told me they brought in a bunch of reporters."

"Yeah, I remember that," Audrey said, nodding. "Cameras everywhere. They interviewed anyone who would talk, but most of the oil field workers wouldn't. I think the best clip they got was of Shauna. She was so excited to be on TV." She paused. "I felt so bad for his family. Sometimes his mom and dad would come to The Spur at night and they always looked so . . . devastated. No one would really talk to them. I think most people felt like they were jeopardizing our one big opportunity by bringing so much negative attention to the oil field."

"I can't imagine what they were going through. It's sad that they never found him."

"It is, but that's Alaska, right? People go missing."

Nina nodded. She knew the statistics, that more people went missing in Alaska than any other state each year. There was so much wilderness, so many ways to disappear. Still, she couldn't resist the urge to press Audrey further. "But don't you think it's suspicious? Multiple people go missing from the same place a few years apart?"

"Not really. Hundreds of people work there, and so many of them aren't from Alaska. They have no idea how to survive in the cold. One of them gets too drunk and wanders off to pee in the woods and freezes to death. Or goes moose hunting and gets hunted by a bear instead."

"But don't you think they'd eventually be found?"

Nina sensed, by the way Audrey was looking at her, that her sister thought she was being naive. "You know how much effort a wilderness search party is. I think the oil company views a lot of their employees as, you know . . . replaceable. They probably search as much as the family demands. Benjamin's parents were willing to camp out here and pressure the search to continue for as long as possible. If the missing person doesn't have a family, or anyone else who cares . . ."

Nina nodded again, anticipating the end of her unfinished sentence. She drew a breath, picked at the fuzz on the blanket, and dared to ask one more question. "Do you think—the explosion and Clyde's disappearance are connected?"

Audrey's mouth twisted for a moment as she considered the question. "I really have no idea. I guess anything is possible. But I think you have too much free time if you're spending this much time thinking about it."

"But it affects Grant, right? He works there. I want him to be safe."

"And you have no reason to think that he isn't."

Nina resisted the urge to fill Audrey in on all that had happened. It was clear that she had no idea the events were linked, and Nina could imagine no way that Audrey could help the situation. Nina had already done all she could to get the police back to Brooks Valley. "You're right. Tell me how you've been."

"I'm good," Audrey replied, brushing a strand of blond hair from her face. "I've been helping the Harrisons clear out their house the past few days. Well, Mrs. Harrison. Mr. Harrison died last year. Did you know?"

Nina shook her head. She remembered the Harrisons— an older couple, three kids who all grew up and left Alaska. A huge house at the edge of town, custom-built after they moved up to Whitespur from Fairbanks as empty nesters. Wanted to get away from it all. Instead, they found Audrey, Nina, and Grant, as well as all the other local kids, fascinated by a house larger than The Spur. In the summer, friends young and old gathered in the sprawling front yard—the perfect central meeting location. The Harrisons never minded.

"That's too bad. I remember Mrs. Harrison had the best snacks. She always had that homemade granola. How's she doing?"

Audrey waved her hand. "Oh, she's coping. Her house is overflowing with all his stuff, so she asked me to help her box it up. She's going to have someone drive it down to Fairbanks to donate, whenever the roads are clear again. So, probably the spring."

"That's nice of her," Nina replied, failing to stifle a yawn.

"Sorry if I'm keeping you," Audrey said. Nina supposed that in her sober state, Audrey considered herself a burden to everyone she spoke to. How backward—Audrey was the firstborn, the one who should rule over their family. She had first claim to their parents, to their home, to this life. Yet she was afraid of taking up too much of Nina's time.

"You're not," Nina replied. "I'm just tired. I went to Fairbanks yesterday and I guess I didn't sleep enough last night."

"It was nice of you to visit." Audrey finished the last sip of her coffee and stood up. She held out a hand to take Nina's mug, and it crossed her mind that perhaps Audrey wanted her to leave, that she'd overstayed her welcome. Audrey didn't seem on edge, but maybe she had somewhere to be. *The bar*, Nina thought, followed by a flash of guilt for making the assumption.

"Can I stay a little longer?" Nina asked. "I'm almost done."

Audrey nodded and touched Nina's shoulder lightly as she passed her, heading back to the kitchen. Tears sprang to Nina's eyes—that simple gesture, reversing her thoughts about their relationship. She was still Audrey's little sister, had still lived two fewer years on earth, even if her life had a more expansive trajectory.

She pressed her right palm against each eye in turn, stifling her tears before Audrey returned. When she did, Nina asked, "That guy I was talking about on the phone, Frankie Campbell? Do you know him?"

She shook her head, settling into the chair again. "I would have told you if I did. There's Frank Barrett who has a cabin on the river. He comes up to trap in the winter."

The name jogged Nina's memory. Frank Barrett had bought the cabin while she was still in high school and tried to sell animal hides around town every winter. But he was a big man, with white-blond hair, stark against his leathery tan skin. He looked nothing like the man who'd taken Honey and Wilder.

"Yeah, I know Frank Barrett. That wasn't him." Disappointment swept through her. She stayed for another half hour, talking to her sister and allowing herself to appreciate the time together, time that wasn't spent worrying that Audrey was on the verge of drinking herself to death. Instead, her mind tumbled with thoughts of Frankie Campbell, of Waylon Turcotte, of Honey and Wilder, wherever they were. Her search wasn't yet over. She would find the dogs, and Frankie, no matter how long it took.

18

NINA PARKED THE SNOW MACHINE BESIDE THE OTHERS and turned off the engine. She had only driven the vehicle a few times since she'd arrived home and still thought it was too fast, too loud, compared with traveling by dogsled. But she couldn't leave the dogs unattended outside the bar for hours, so she had made the sacrifice.

Nina tucked her helmet under her arm and pushed open the door to The Spur. A blast of warm air greeted her. The bar was packed more than Nina ever remembered it being, even on a Saturday night—but the half-empty days of The Spur were over. The oil field had brought hundreds of newcomers to Whitespur in the six years it had been operating. Nina wondered how much time would pass before another restaurant, another bar, were opened in town. It might not be bad for the tourist crowd to have more options, whenever it was safe to travel again. When she had the patience to load the news on her phone, Nina read articles about how the vaccines in development were close to being approved. Life in most of the world was still far from normal. But if Whitespur could hold out with the influx of money from the oil field, maybe the tourists would one day return.

She paused near the entrance, stepping closer to the bulletin board. There it was—another missing person poster, half covering Eric Riley's, which covered Benjamin Weber's, like a layer cake of missing men. His expression was difficult to read—his mouth set in a grim line, eyes covered by sunglasses. Was that really the only photo they could find? She skimmed the details, including his full name—Clyde Lee. Last seen on October 22nd. Her heart ached at that false information, with the knowledge of his death that she carried. Nina stepped back, unable to look at it any longer, and chose a booth near the back of the restaurant, away from the loudest part of the floor. When she glimpsed Ila, she lifted a hand to flag her friend down.

"Hey! It's been a while," Ila said as she approached, setting a glass of water on the table.

Nina thought of how relative time was—nine years or two weeks could both feel like too long. "Sorry. I've been busy."

"I'm sure you have. What can I get you?"

"I'll have a caribou burger and fries," Nina said. She waited while Ila jotted her order down and then leaned closer. "Listen. I want to ask you about something."

Ila blinked, calibrating Nina's conspiratorial tone, and then glanced behind her. "Okay. But let me do a round."

Nina sipped her water while she waited, letting her gaze drift to the bar, where, as she had predicted, Grant sat. One arm slung over the back of his chair, drinking a beer and talking to his friends, he was at ease, unaware that his sister was observing him. He was seated with a few other young men like him—lean, bearded. She recognized most of them from the three-room school they'd all attended—a room for elementary, middle, and high school kids each. Plus the cafeteria, but that was more like a hallway at the back of the building. Indoor plumbing, although that occasionally stopped working and they had to use the outhouse around back. Seven kids in her graduating class.

But a couple of the men she didn't recognize. *They must be from out of town.* More experienced oilmen, maybe, brought in by the company to show the Whitespur newbies the ropes. It stung that in the time she'd been away, her younger brother had grown up and become one of these men, hardened by life in Alaska. When he was a kid, she used to find him asleep in the dog kennel, curled up in a pile with the retired sled dogs. He still had that soft side, still loved the animals just as much, but he seemed different now. More anxious, more willing to maintain the status quo. Afraid of losing a job that he would have sworn against as a teenager, willing to sacrifice so much for his family.

Ila approached the table again, setting a white plate with the caribou burger and fries in front of Nina and drawing her focus from Grant. The smell enticed her—she hadn't eaten much since that morning. After she'd returned home from visiting Audrey, she'd spent the afternoon running a few different dog teams, trying to distract herself. Ila slid into the seat across the table and leaned forward, affixing her curious stare on Nina.

"Okay," Nina said, taking a deep breath. "Has a man named Frankie Campbell ever come in here?"

Ila tilted her head up, no doubt running through a mental list of customers, and then shook her head. "That name doesn't ring a bell. What does he look like?"

Nina thought back to that night, to Frankie's face illuminated beneath the harsh kennel lighting. "Middle-aged. Tall and thin. He had a beard. A shortish one. And graying hair. Super blue eyes, but nothing else distinct about his face."

"He had . . . ?" Ila trailed off, a question. "Who is this?"

"It's a long story," Nina said, wary of starting in case Ila got called away. "He came by the kennel the other day and wanted to buy some dogs. But when I looked him up yesterday, I couldn't find anything."

"And did he? Buy some dogs?" Ila asked, one eyebrow raised.

"Yeah," Nina said. "He did. Two of them."

"Well, it's not a big deal, right? I know your mom has that contract system. Don't you have his contact info?"

"He didn't sign one, that's the problem."

Ila exhaled. "Yikes. Well, I'm sorry, but I can't say I've seen him. A lot of tall, thin, bearded men come through here."

"I figured. Promise me you'll keep an eye out, okay? I'm worried about the dogs."

Ila glanced over her shoulder, then back at Nina, nodding. "I will. Promise. But I'd better get back to work before Harry notices."

"Of course," Nina replied. The Spur's owner had a reputation for giving ruthless chew-outs. "Thank you!" she called after Ila's retreating back.

Nina pulled out her phone. To her surprise, there was a text from August that read, Are we still on for Monday?

Nina closed the message without responding. She hadn't yet searched for Waylon Turcotte, but all day she had wondered if his name might lead her to more concrete information about Frankie, or if they might be the same person, and she couldn't wait any longer to find out. She was beginning to feel like she'd been visited by a ghost—no one knew who Frankie was. Maybe he really was passing through, had made the kennel his only stop on the way back to Fairbanks. Maybe he kept company with criminals and kept his online presence nonexistent.

The search took a long time to load. She ate another bite of the burger and set it down when the results popped up. A headline— WAYLON TURCOTTE ARRESTED ON DRUG TRAFFICKING CHARGES. Below it—a link to a page listing Montana's most wanted fugitives.

His name was highlighted in bold beneath the title. She tapped the first link to the news article.

When it loaded, she held in a gasp. A pair of familiar blue eyes stared back at her from a mug shot. The man wasn't identical—he had recently shaved, just a hint of stubble on his jaw, his skin clear and less weathered. But those eyes—those startling blue eyes; she would recognize them anywhere. Frankie Campbell. Waylon Turcotte. The names were different, but the man was the same.

She skimmed the article, taking in as much information as she could. Millions of dollars of cocaine seized from a home in Billings. Turcotte, a respected businessman, was among three arrested and later released on bail. The other names were listed, but they weren't Frankie, or Frank, or any variation. There wasn't much to the article—a quote from a police officer involved in the operation, but nothing more.

Slowly, the search page reloaded after she tapped the back arrow. Then the second link—Montana's most wanted fugitives. There, at number three on the list, was Waylon Turcotte's now-familiar mug shot, those vivid blue eyes staring back at her. He had disappeared after being released on bail, suspected of fleeing Montana and possibly the country. The drug trafficking charges were listed beside his photo. She took a screenshot. Fear tumbled through her veins as she forced herself to close the tab. She still had no idea why this man—this criminal—wanted sled dogs. The article about the arrest was from nearly five years ago. How long had he been in Alaska for? Perhaps he'd recently reached Alaska and wanted to hide out through the winter, to trap and hunt and survive off the land. Suddenly, his imagined aversion to a hunting license made sense. But there was a darker possibility—maybe he was still trafficking drugs, this time through the wilderness. Brooks Valley, or any other oil field, might make a profitable customer, all those bored and lonely workers isolated far from home. Whatever his reason for buying the dogs, he was a man in hiding, a man with a lot to lose if his location was discovered. An electric pulse of dread swept through Nina at the thought of stumbling across him out in the forest.

But what could she do about him? Traipse back to the trooper station for the third time in less than a month and make another vague report? They would put a little picture of her on the wall, with a note: "Don't listen to anything this woman says."

Before she put her phone away, she typed a quick text to August. I've got a lot going on right now. Rain check for later this week? She hit Send, and hoped he would understand.

19

MICHAEL ELBOWED GRANT'S SIDE. "DUDE. YOU LOOK miserable."

"Just thinking," Grant replied. Thoughts that gave him an outward appearance of misery, clearly, as his brain bounced between the cover-up he had witnessed—no, participated in—and the fact that the oil field was crawling with troopers the last few days. Since his conversation with Fisher, Grant had remained even more unsettled, picturing Elias waiting in the hallway outside the room, that unreadable gaze trained on Grant as he left the building. He traced his fingers over the grain in The Spur's wooden bar top. "Hey, shouldn't you be miserable, too? Don't all the cops make you nervous?"

"Nah. As long as I'm making money, I'm happy. And Tom said he'll get me a job at the North Slope next year."

Grant raised his eyebrows. "You want to go to Prudhoe Bay?"

Michael shrugged. "Why not? It's good money. Besides, if Brooks Valley gets shut down, I want to have somewhere to go. I'll keep saving and then move to fuckin' Florida while you guys are still breaking your backs into your forties."

On Grant's other side, Orson snorted. "Yeah right. It's not like Brooks Valley doesn't pay well. And you'd hate Florida. You'd have to sweat."

"Hey, I've lived in Florida, remember?"

Grant and Orson exchanged a look. It was hard to forget all the places Michael had lived, because he talked about them so often. His father had been in the army and had last been stationed in Fairbanks. He'd fallen in love with Alaska, permanently moving his family up to Whitespur when Michael was a teenager.

"I loved it. Palm trees, fishing, girls in bikinis. You only get one of those here."

"As long as you'll let us visit," Grant said, and took a sip of his beer. "You think they're going to close Brooks Valley?"

"I wouldn't be shocked," Michael said. "I mean, with how many investigations they've had over the years. Multiple missing people reported, and rig malfunctions? I think they'll at least get another company to take over the contract. All we need is one more injury, one more disappearance to make the news, and our jobs are toast."

After a moment, Orson cleared his throat. "Grant. Have you been called in to talk to the troopers yet?"

Grant set his glass down. He felt suddenly trapped between his two closest friends. He sensed Orson's eyes on him, expectant.

"Yeah," Grant said. "The first day they showed up. Why?"

"I overheard some guys the other day saying that you were out at Site Fourteen when the explosion happened," Orson said. "You didn't mention it."

"Oh." Grant tried to arrange his thoughts. Michael leaned on the bar top to Grant's left, propped up on his elbow, equally curious. "Yeah. Doc had me drive some pipes out there."

"And?"

"And what?"

Michael laughed. "Come on, man. I can't believe you didn't tell us sooner."

Grant tried to laugh, too, play along. "It wasn't a big deal. It was like, bam, a big burst of fire, and then it was out. I mean, it was loud. A little scary. But I don't think it warranted shutting down the entire oil field."

"No one does," Orson said, taking a long swig of his beer. "But those guys I heard talking? They think you're the one who reported it."

Grant's blood went cold. He had to answer, quickly, to laugh it off, but his tongue was leaden, his brain sending panic signals. "I don't know why they'd say that," he managed.

Orson brushed a strand of long black hair away from his face. "I don't, either. I don't even know their names. They live in the dorms and they kind of walk around in a pack."

"Probably the guys who work at Site Fourteen," Grant mumbled. "I figured Elias reported it. You know, following protocol."

"Isn't that the foreman you worked under your first year?" Michael asked.

"Yeah. He's a weird guy. But I didn't speak to him that day, when the explosion happened." A half-truth. "I parked the truck and helped unload the pipes so I could get out of there faster. And, like I said. The explosion didn't seem like a big deal."

Orson nodded. "Well, it's turned into one."

"I think the troopers are back about that guy who was

reported missing. He used to work at Site Fourteen." Grant let his words hang in the air, as much of the truth as he was willing to tell. For a moment, he wondered if he should let his closest friends know about the cover-up, about what the police might find if they drove to the end of the scout road. But he couldn't bring himself to say it. They would judge him, Michael and Orson both. They had been the ones to beat up bullies in school, to break up fights between the younger kids or at least help the losers win. He couldn't imagine either of them agreeing to drive a body to the woods and say nothing while it was dumped. His friends would have refused, would have driven the truck straight to camp and alerted the highest authority that a man lay dead at Site Fourteen. But not Grant. He'd been too weak, too easily influenced by fear. And it had all happened so fast— the explosion, the dead man, Elias's careful plan. If he could go back in time, of course he wouldn't have gone along with the cover-up. But it was easy to say that now, with an awareness of exactly how much guilt he carried.

Orson finished his beer. "Watch your back, okay? These guys have a whole lot of time on their hands, and it sounds like you're not their favorite person right now. If you see them in town, maybe go the other way."

"Thanks," Grant said, "that's reassuring." He kept his tone dry, measured, which didn't match how he felt inside: like part of his brain had calved off and gone crashing into the sea below. Orson didn't joke.

But Michael did. He clapped a hand onto Grant's back, jarring his lungs. "You know, Orson and I have a lot of time on our hands, too. You could hire us to be your personal bodyguards."

"Yeah. But no drinking on the job," he replied.

"Pass," Michael said, signaling Shauna over for a refill. Grant wished for an easy excuse to slip away. His snow machine was parked at Michael's house; they had walked over together an hour or so ago. Twisting in his seat, he spotted a familiar head of blond hair at one of the central tables. Audrey, sitting opposite of Katrina.

He looked for a beat too long because Michael and Orson both turned, too. Orson squinted. "Is that a glass of . . . water?"

Despite Grant's disbelief, it did appear that Audrey had only a glass of water beside her plate of food. In Katrina's hand was some sort of mixed drink in a cocktail glass.

"You're going to be an uncle," Michael said, elbowing Grant's rib cage.

"Or maybe it's straight vodka."

"Shut up. Both of you," Grant said, just as Audrey's head turned toward the bar. She spotted Grant immediately and lifted a hand to wave. He held in a sigh; now he had to go say hello and prolong his night here. That his friends treated Audrey's alcohol problem as a joke bothered him, but he lacked the energy to set them straight right now.

"Thanks for coming over," Audrey said as he reached her table, standing up to pull him into a hug. Grant hugged her back, resting his hands on her bony shoulder blades. "Are you okay?" Audrey peered up at him as she sat back down, her eyes flooded with concern. He wondered how she could be so quick to sense the distress he tried to hide.

"Yeah," Grant said, attempting a smile. "Stressed from work."

"I bet."

Katrina kicked Audrey under the table and leaned forward in her seat. "Tell him," she hissed.

A sheepish smile crossed Audrey's face. "You probably noticed I'm not drinking."

"I did," Grant said carefully. Upon closer inspection, it did indeed appear to be a glass of water.

"I've been sober for two weeks. Since the day after Nina saw me here." Her expression fell, her eyes shimmery with tears. "I felt awful about that. Lower than I've ever been. I just— I just can't let her see me like that. I thought I'd try to get sober again. Morgan runs those AA meetings at the Protestant church three times a week, you know? And when I make it to thirty days, I'm going to apply for a job at Los Padres. Alma told me they're short on waitstaff."

"Wow, Audrey, that's huge." Trying to muster all the enthusiasm he had to offer, and hoping that he sounded sincere, Grant laid a hand on her left shoulder, which dropped half an inch as Audrey exhaled. Though he was glad to hear her announcement, he wasn't sure if he was supposed to. Did they tell you, in AA meetings, to let other people know about your burgeoning sobriety, to hold you accountable? Or was it supposed to be a secret, a promise kept only to yourself until you had proven that you were capable of overcoming your addiction? Maybe that was only Grant's inclination toward privacy, or toward hiding the truth—as he had hidden his relationship with Ila from Nina, as he continued to harbor the truth of Churchy's death. He couldn't let his own shortcomings cloud his judgment of Audrey, though it wasn't the first stint of sobriety she'd had in the last few years, all unsuccessful. He couldn't recall if she'd ever made it past two weeks before. Besides that, she was at a bar, and he couldn't imagine a worse place for her to be, though Whitespur didn't offer many other options. As the night slunk on, would the temptation of free-flowing beer and liquor grow too strong?

"I was nervous to tell you. I thought . . . well, it hasn't been that many days."

Katrina pointed her fork at Audrey. "Hey. Every fucking day

counts, girl." To Grant, she said, "I'm keeping her accountable. No alcohol in the house."

"And while you're out?" Grant asked, nodding at Katrina's drink.

"Kat has always been able to control herself. Not like me." Audrey's tone could have slipped into self-pity, but there was something triumphant about it, like it gave her power to acknowledge her shortcomings. "We're here for dinner. We're not staying long. I want to do this. I don't want Nina to be afraid of me."

"I don't think she was afraid. I think she was worried—"

"It doesn't matter," Audrey said, cutting Grant off with a wave of her hand. "I don't care what she thinks, because I want to show her a new me in a few weeks. I thought maybe, when I make it to a month, when I have a job at Los Padres . . . maybe Mom and Dad would have me over for dinner."

Grant swallowed around the lump in his throat. "That would be great, Audrey. I think that would make them really happy." He didn't add that he doubted their parents would be open to having her home again. A month wasn't much against the years of failed sobriety, of drug abuse. He remembered the way that Audrey and his mother had screamed at each other in the days leading up to Audrey being kicked out. But maybe he could talk to them, offer his support on her behalf, if she kept her promise and made it to thirty days.

"Nina's here, by the way," Audrey said. "In one of those back booths. I saw her on the way to the bathroom, but she wasn't in much of a mood to talk."

Grant processed this, that both his sisters were present, and that one could slip by completely unnoticed by him. He wondered if Audrey had shared the same information with Nina. He'd have to ask before he left.

After saying goodbye to Audrey and Katrina, he returned

to the bar. "What time are you thinking of leaving?" he asked Michael.

"Why? The night's young."

"I've got some stuff to do at home. And I want to keep an eye on my dad. He's been in a bad mood and I don't want my mom to have to deal with him alone."

"I'll give you a ride to Michael's," Orson said. "I need to swing by home and grab a few things."

"What, you're both abandoning me?" Michael said, eyes wide.

"I'm sure Holly wouldn't mind if you were home a couple hours early."

"She likes when I'm gone," Michael replied. "She says I follow her around like a lost puppy."

Orson snorted. "I believe it." He glanced at Grant. "Let me finish this drink and then we'll go."

"Alright. I'll be right back."

He found Nina in the back of the restaurant, as promised, staring at the table in front of her as she picked at a plate of fries and a half-eaten burger. She startled when he slid into the booth seat across from her, flinching hard and then letting out a long breath.

"What, you're going to hide out back here and not say hello to me?" Grant took a fry from her plate and ate it in one bite, though he wasn't particularly hungry. There was a comforting familiarity in the undersalted, perfectly crisp strip of potato, cooked the same as they'd been when he was a kid.

"I was going to," Nina protested, indicating her plate of food. "I saw you on my way in, but I was starving. Sorry."

"I guess that's an acceptable reason to ignore me." He stole another fry. "How are you?"

"Okay. It's been a long day." Nina closed her eyes, then dragged a hand across her face. "I got too used to the luxury of sunlight all day, even in the winter."

Nina did look tired, and a little anxious. Grant guessed that their father's reaction to the dogs being sold still weighed on her. Ted had been sulking around the house, the dark cloud building to a thunderhead. "Must be weird to have so much light year-round," Grant replied, trying to keep his tone casual. He leaned back in his seat, putting distance between himself and the rest of her fries. "Audrey told me you were here."

"Yeah, I talked to her for a minute. I went to her apartment earlier today. She's in a good mood." Nina pushed the plate toward him. "Here. I'm full." Queasiness clouded her expression, like the greasy meal had made her sick. The same exhaustion she'd carried home with her, after the long journey from Maine to Alaska, hadn't left.

"What?" he asked, trying to decipher her expression.

"Do you know a man named Frankie Campbell?"

Grant let his eyes drift to the ceiling, running through the list of names he knew from work, but it didn't sound familiar. "Nope. Why?"

"He's the man who bought the dogs. He said he worked in the oil industry so I thought maybe he was involved with the Brooks Valley field." Disappointment was clear on her face.

"Nah. No Frankies, Franks, or anything of the like that I can think of. Although half the guys go by dumb nicknames. And, of course, I haven't met everyone." Grant tried to tamp down a growing wave of concern. "What's wrong? You look upset."

Nina blinked. "I'm not upset. I have a bad feeling about the guy. Don't tell Mom, but he didn't sign a contract."

Grant snorted. "Like Mom won't notice. She's a stickler for paperwork. What happened? You forgot?"

"No. He . . . he left while I was in the house. Took the dogs and left an envelope of cash."

For all the dogs his family had sold over the years, he couldn't recall someone slipping away without signing the contract. His mother required it even for the retired dogs going off to be pets. He wondered why Nina hadn't told him sooner. "That is strange. Did you ask Ila? She sees a lot of people come through here."

"She didn't recognize the name." Nina rubbed her eyes. "I didn't have much to tell her about him. He was middle-aged. Tall and thin. He had a short beard and grayish hair. I just described half of Whitespur."

Grant tried to ignore the faint alarm bells ringing in the back of his mind. "Anything else notable about him?"

Nina's mouth twisted into a frown for a moment. "His eyes were blue. Like, vibrant blue."

The skin at the back of Grant's neck prickled. "Huh. Sounds like one of the rig foremen. But his name isn't Frankie."

"Weird. I mean, there wasn't anything particularly unique about him. He said he was from Montana. He was on his way back from Prudhoe Bay."

Grant drummed his fingers on the table, looking toward the bar, at the row of his coworkers' backs. The alarm bells had amplified to a deafening racket. He couldn't stop visualizing Elias in his mind's eye, that tall, thin, blue-eyed man. "You're describing Elias exactly."

"Why would he use a fake name to buy sled dogs? Does he have dogs here?"

"I don't know," Grant replied, refocusing on Nina. "He's never mentioned it. He's a quiet guy, keeps to himself. Wants to get the job done, not shoot the shit. I don't work with him anymore, but I was one of his roughnecks my first year." He paused. "He's the foreman in charge of Site Fourteen. Where the explosion happened."

Nina shook her head. "It can't be. I think it was someone who wanted to run an illegal trapline, maybe. Or hunt without a license. Or—" Her sentence caught, left unfinished. She shook her head once, communicating with herself more than with Grant.

Grant knew without her saying it that Nina thought he was being paranoid. Why would a well-off rig foreman buy two race-bred huskies under the table, using a fake name? Elias had no reason to do that, not that Grant could think of. He tried to interpret her stony expression. "Are you worried about the dogs?"

She shrugged. "Yes and no. I don't like not knowing where they are. We have no way to check up on them. But why would he spend so much money to buy dogs to neglect? I think he'll take care of them."

"People with lots of money do bad things all the time," Grant said. Churchy's body came to mind, unbidden, no doubt half buried in the snow now. "But you're right. They're probably fine."

She reached into her pocket and produced her phone. "Can I show you something?"

Grant was about to say yes, but he heard his name being called, and craned his neck to spot Orson waving at him from across the restaurant, his booming voice turning everyone else's head, too. He looked back at Nina. "Sorry. I gotta leave with Orson."

"Wait—" Nina started, but Grant was already out of the booth.

"I have to go, okay? Show me tomorrow." He'd likely be asleep by the time Nina came home.

Her description of the man played on a loop in Grant's mind as he made his way back to the bar. Elias couldn't be the only tall, thin, blue-eyed man in Whitespur. Besides, Nina said the man had claimed to be from the lower forty-eight. Maybe he really was passing through on his way back from Prudhoe Bay, headed to the airport in Fairbanks. Maybe Nina hadn't searched for him enough, or maybe he had managed to leave no traces of himself on the internet—unusual, but not impossible. Halfway to the bar he realized he hadn't asked Nina if she knew about Audrey's sobriety. Another conversation for tomorrow.

"Hang on a sec," Grant said to Orson. "I'm almost ready." There was one more thing he needed to do.

A quick visual sweep of the restaurant floor revealed no Ila, though he couldn't see the part that curved back toward the restrooms and pool tables. He tried to think of how long ago she'd joined him at the bar on her ten-minute break—an hour, two? She might be on another.

Grant found Ila leaning against the wall in the hallway that led from the restaurant to the kitchen, scrolling on her phone. A smile briefly crossed her lips but was replaced by an expression of concern. "What's up?"

"Nothing. Are you on another break?"

"No." She sighed. "I would have come to see you. I'm just stealing some time."

"I wanted to let you know I'm heading home."

After another glance at her phone screen, she turned it off. "So early?"

He caught himself about to lie to her, too, to tell her he had chores to do. But there was no reason not to be honest with her. "I'm not in the mood for sitting around at the bar, getting drunk."

"Fair enough. Get home safe, okay? I love you."

He said it back, still surprised, even a year later, that he had someone who cared about him that much. He didn't want to walk away from her, but they had plans to see each other the day after tomorrow, and the urge to leave The Spur was greater than his desire to be near Ila.

He met Orson at the bar again and wove through tables toward the front door. Audrey smiled at him and waved from her table as they passed. At the door, Grant stole one last look over his shoulder. In the warm yellow light, Audrey's bleached hair shone close to golden. Katrina's mouth was open in laughter, and though Audrey's back was to him, Grant imagined she was laughing, too. Two weeks sober—not nothing. She was as clear-headed and bright as he had seen her in years.

Grant walked into the sparkling, frigid air with a spark of something like hope in his chest.

20

AT 5:42 P.M. GRANT RETURNED HIS WRENCH TO THE toolbox and said goodbye to Doc, who, tireless as ever, was still underneath one of the trucks. Grant sometimes wondered if the man ever slept, but he also understood the pull to stay busy, especially in winter. People got itchy fast without enough daylight if they weren't occupied. He had hung back to finish repairs on one of the trucks, not realizing how far past the end of his shift the clock had ticked. Only a couple people staffed the shop overnight; he hadn't noticed them drift in. Only his growling stomach had clued him in that it was past time to head home.

Grant pulled his hat on as he shouldered the door open and stepped outside. The evening was almost balmy, hovering around twenty degrees, and he took his time walking to the warehouse. A vivid blanket of stars covered the cloudless sky, bright even against the lit-up oil field. Light pollution was still

a foreign concept in so much of Alaska. Grant had yet to see
the aurora borealis this year, but each time he stepped outside
in the dark he hoped that blue-green lights would shimmer
above. For now, it was only the stars against the black velvet
abyss like a handful of snowflakes tossed upward.

In Warehouse A he punched out and went straight to the
locker room, shrugging off the jumpsuit and grabbing the gray
wool sweater he'd worn that morning. He still missed the orange
one he'd had for years, hadn't been able to find it in his mess
of a room. He tugged the sweater over his white T-shirt and
followed it with his thick canvas jacket. He didn't anticipate
freezing on the ride home that night, but didn't know what the
weather would be like in the morning. Despite the clear sky,
the air outside smelled like snow.

The warehouse was quiet instead of the usual bustle of the
changing shifts. There was something eerie about all the empty
space, the rows of lockers left untouched. He was used to having
to angle his body to squeeze through the crowd, but tonight he
moved unimpeded.

Outside Grant headed straight to his snow machine. He
paused beside it, patting through his jacket pockets for his keys.

Grant was jerked off his feet so quickly he didn't have time to
shout, to make any sound. The breath was knocked out of him
as his arm was twisted backward, excruciating pain rocketing
through his shoulder. A gust of cold air brushed his forehead
as his hat was ripped away. His feet scrambled for traction in
the snow but he was dragged back, slammed onto the ground,
and kicked in the stomach again and again. Another pair of feet
joined in, kicking his back, and Grant thought again of falling
asleep as a child on his sisters' bedroom floor. Only this time he
desperately wished to be there, awoken gently by their high-
pitched voices, admonishing him through giggles. Grant flailed

his arms and legs, tried to crawl away, but there was another boot between his shoulder blades, holding him down.

A hand yanked a fistful of his hair, lifting his head and slamming it down on the concrete parking block. Grant suppressed a cry and tried to twist away, but whoever was beating him repeated the gesture again, and Grant couldn't think for the searing pain that spread from his right eye to his forehead and everywhere beyond. He barely registered the final emphatic kick to his back, the shuffling footsteps retreating. He tried to sit up and see who had attacked him but all he caught was a blurry, tilted image of three pairs of legs before his vision crumbled and he collapsed into the snow, breathing hard. The coolness soothed his burning face and he lay there for a moment, trying to gather the strength to move, nausea rolling in his stomach to match the waves of pain. Finally, he pushed up, gagging at the pain in his rib cage, anticipating broken bones. He managed to right himself, to stand, shakily, to pull off a glove and run his hand across his face. A little blood came away on his fingers.

There was a spattering of red on the snow, too. His hat lay a few feet away and he bent to reach for it, grimacing at the burst of pain in his shoulder. Dizziness swept through him and he stumbled, his vision erupting into static and stars before clearing. He pressed his fingertips to his face again, aware that the pain he couldn't yet pinpoint would arrive later, when the adrenaline and disorientation had worn off. How long had the men waited in the shadows for him? He shouldn't have hung back. Michael and Orson had warned him this was coming, yet he'd wandered out to the parking lot alone, without the safety of a crowd.

Despite the lack of a mirror, Grant could imagine the blood and bruises marring his face. He couldn't show up at home looking like he did. Nina would ask too many questions.

He couldn't go to The Spur, either; his battered appearance would draw too much attention. And Ila would want to know what happened. When he drove the snow machine away from the oil field, he steered in the direction of town instead, toward Michael's house.

21

INSIDE LOS PADRES, CHEERY MARIACHI MUSIC PLAYED through the speakers around the room. During a family meal years ago, Nina and Audrey had figured out that the music played on a loop, something like an hour and a half of songs before it started over. The soundtrack never changed, but the consistency was comforting, the same voices crooning Spanish lyrics over the years. The decor hadn't changed, either—colorful red, orange, and green walls, smiling metal suns, vibrant paintings of women in embroidered dresses. And it smelled *good*— simmering garlic and onions, rich chilis, and the bright acidity of tomato salsa. Nina's mouth watered. She hadn't eaten much variety since she'd returned home, just whatever was in the refrigerator, usually some combination of toast, eggs, and jam for breakfast and lunch and some kind of meat for dinner. And since March, back in Maine, as her trips to the grocery store dwindled to every two weeks instead of daily, she felt more and more like a scavenger picking over the scraps of her pantry. Food for survival, not pleasure.

Nina had texted August from the general store that morning to ask if he'd be able to meet for dinner, two days later than they'd originally planned. To her relief, he'd been available. She was hopeful that the dinner would offer a small amount of normalcy that she desperately needed. She still hadn't decided what to do about the fact that Frankie Campbell was Waylon Turcotte, a wanted man in Montana. She had been about to show Grant his mug shot on Saturday night, before Orson called him away. Maybe that was for the best—he had too much else to worry about; finding the dogs was her problem to handle, even as it became more complicated.

It took her a minute to spot August. He was seated near the back, reading a menu, wearing a black coat and gray hat.

"I'm meeting someone," she told the hostess, a bored-looking teenage girl, who merely nodded and handed Nina a menu to carry to the table herself. There were already two glasses of water on the table, and as Nina slid into the booth across from August, he raised his head, a smile spreading across his face.

"You made it."

"Did you think I wouldn't? Is that why you're dressed to leave at any moment?"

His smile dropped, replaced by a flush of embarrassment. "Sorry. I'm still cold from walking over."

"I'm kidding," Nina said, but he pulled off his hat and coat anyway. "Thanks for being cool about me having to reschedule."

"It worked out better for me anyway. Like I said the other day, I've been trying to finish paperwork for a vegetation research project we did over the summer and—" he paused, flipping up his palms "—it's been a nightmare. I had to hunker down and finish it."

"I understand. I'm very distracting."

August smiled again. "How was your day? I realized I don't have any idea of what you've been up to since you came home."

Nina turned the question over, trying to think of a good answer. So much of her time, recently, had been consumed with thinking about Frankie Campbell, about Waylon Turcotte, and about the body lying in the snow at the oil field. "Not that much. I've been taking care of the dogs a lot to take some of that off my mom's plate. I made it to Fairbanks last week to apply for some jobs."

August widened his eyes. "You mean you don't want to stay here? And work at Los Padres?"

Nina laughed. "A Mexican restaurant could be fun. But I want to work with seafood again. I was thinking Homer, or something else coastal and touristy. I figured it'd be easier to get a job here and then work my way out of Alaska again."

He took a sip of water. "You don't want to stay?"

"Not really. Come on," she said, as his expression fell further. "Don't tell me you don't understand."

"No, I do," he said eventually. "But I've learned to love it. The refuge has given me a purpose here."

"You always had a purpose here. Or a sense of belonging, at least."

"You never felt that?"

Nina shrugged. "Not the way everyone else does. You, Grant, even Audrey. I always felt like I had to grab any opportunity to leave and run with it. But other people think of it as home."

"And what's home to you? Maine?"

"Maybe." Nina shifted and picked up the menu, ready to redirect the conversation. The topic of home made her uncomfortable, because she couldn't imagine what it was like to have a sense of belonging. All the places she'd lived, even Whitespur, felt temporary. "What are you getting?"

"I was going to ask you that. What does the chef suggest?"

Nina was about to tell him that she always got the chicken fajitas as a kid when something caught her eye. A couple had entered the restaurant and were being led by the hostess in their direction, toward the other clear tables. Nina blinked. It was Grant and Ila, no mistaking them, but Nina couldn't square Grant's appearance with the last time she'd seen him. Purple and blue bruises covered most of his face, with a darker ring around his right eye. His cheeks had several small, scabbed-over cuts. Before she knew what she was doing she was halfway out of her seat, her voice strained when she called his name.

He turned his head, and the strangest expression flashed across his face. Fear, Nina thought. But then his expression turned neutral, even sheepish, as he lifted a hand to wave, as if nothing was wrong, as if he was only embarrassed of not spotting her first.

"We should invite them to sit with us," August said.

Nina glanced at August, trying to read his expression. If Grant and Ila joined them, their dinner would lose all intimacy. She couldn't catch up with August in the way she'd wanted to, not when she needed to know the story behind Grant's bruised face. But August didn't look disappointed; he looked like he understood that she would worry about Grant the rest of the evening if she didn't talk to him. She flashed him an apologetic smile and waved over Grant and Ila before they were seated at another table.

"Sit with us, please," Nina said. Grant and Ila made eye contact with each other, some unspoken communication, and walked over. The teenage hostess rolled her eyes and tossed their menus unceremoniously on the table.

"Are you sure we're not intruding?" Ila asked, gaze flicking between Nina and August. She could hardly contain her smile, and Nina suspected she'd want to hear everything later, how Nina and August had reconnected.

"Not at all," August said, getting up to take the other booth seat on Nina's side. Once Grant and Ila were seated, Nina tried to catch Grant's eye, but he wouldn't look at her, intently studying the menu instead.

She exhaled. "Grant, obviously I'm going to ask. What happened to your face?"

He didn't lift his head. "Michael and I broke up a fight at The Spur."

"That's what you look like after breaking up a fight? You must not have done a good job."

"Yeah, well. You should see the other guys."

"Who was it?" Ila and Audrey both spent a lot of time at The Spur. She wondered if either of them had witnessed the fight.

Grant looked up, finally, clearly annoyed by her imploring questions. "Some guys from work, I don't know who. Probably got too drunk."

"Michael got away without a scratch. Can you believe that?" Ila said, her tone mischievous. But irritation sliced through Grant's sharp response.

"I told you—"

"I know," she said quickly, laying a hand on his arm. "I'm not mad at you for making sure some drunk idiots didn't kill each other."

Nina sensed August's attention on her, possibly regretting his decision to encourage Grant and Ila to sit down. A waitress breezed up to their table and deposited more glasses of water, two bowls of salsa, and a giant platter of warm chips. Grant dived in, apparently glad for a distraction from the conversation. Nina struggled to tear her eyes from him, still disturbed by his injuries. She didn't believe his story, not one bit, especially because Ila—who worked at The Spur—seemed to know nothing about the fight.

"So, August," Ila said, "I haven't seen you at The Spur in a while. What have you been up to?" She shot Nina a look, as if trying to remind Nina who she should be making conversation with.

"I've been busy at the refuge," August replied. "Finalizing data from summer research, and going through applications from some biologists who want to come study tundra plants next year. I'm also thinking about buying one of those cabins up Back Creek. The refuge house is fine, but I want my own place."

This caught Nina's attention. "Which one?"

"Probably Morgan's. He bought a place in town and he's been talking about selling his cabin for a year now. I finally told him I can cough up the money next spring."

Grant had stopped eating and was now also focused on August. As kids, Nina and Grant had talked about buying one of the cabins themselves, a grand fantasy that Audrey frequently shot down, asking why they never considered moving somewhere else. *Dream bigger*, she always told them, rolling her eyes, and eventually Nina had. But now she wondered if Grant still dreamed of one of those secluded, off-grid cabins nestled in the spruce trees, a cozy fire burning in the woodstove, a home for him and Ila. Ila was only looking at August with minor interest, no indication that Grant had ever shared such plans with her.

The waitress returned and took their orders. Nina couldn't ask the questions of August that she wanted to, not with Grant and Ila present, but she found she enjoyed his company anyway. He relaxed as the evening went on, joking more, hints of his younger self shining through. Ila and Grant shared stories of things that had happened in the nine long years Nina had been gone, August chipping in for the years he'd been home. But Nina couldn't stop studying the bruises on Grant's face, the cuts on his cheek. She didn't doubt that he would break up a fight, but how had he gotten so injured? Why had Ila made that comment, about Michael not having a scratch on him? She thought about tracking down Michael to ask him, but Michael's loyalties lay with Grant, not her. He would either lie to cover Grant's tracks or tell Grant that his sister was being nosy, poking around for information. Grant already seemed annoyed with her, with the situation at Brooks Valley. She'd have to let this sleeping dog lie.

Later, after dinner, she stood in the falling snow with August in front of Los Padres as Grant and Ila retreated toward her house, leaving footprints in the fresh powder. The lights outside the restaurant illuminated the street with a soft yellow glow.

"Did the food live up to your memory?"

"Not exactly. The fajitas were a little underseasoned. Or like, lacking any flavor at all. I don't want to be too hard on Los Padres, though. I'm sure it's even harder to get ingredients shipped with the pandemic going on."

"My enchiladas were okay. I guess I'm glad I didn't listen to your recommendation."

Nina opened her mouth to respond and yawned instead, exhaustion settling into her body. August smiled.

"Sorry if I wore you out."

"No," Nina said, "this was nice. I'm sorry about . . ." She trailed off, realizing she didn't know how to phrase it, and gestured in the direction Grant and Ila had gone. "I know you didn't plan for this dinner to involve more than just us."

"It's a small town," he replied with a shrug. "Besides, I've always liked your brother. And obviously I consider Ila a friend." He paused, his eyebrows rising. "Are you worried about him?"

"Grant? No," she lied, hoping she sounded certain. "I mean, I didn't know he got beat up. He hasn't been home in a couple days. It feels like something he should have told me. But his life was a mystery to me for years. I can't be mad at him for not sharing every detail with me."

"You're an older sister, though. I think you get to be protective." He stepped closer, reaching to brush a few snowflakes from her hair. Nina's heart skipped a beat, but his hand dropped back to his side. "Can we do this again? Maybe later this week?" He paused. "Maybe just us?"

"I'd like that," Nina said. "But I think we'll have trouble with that. Like you said, it's a small town."

He smiled again, although there was something guarded in his expression. "Why don't you come to my place? You know where the refuge visitor center is, right?" When she nodded, he continued. "There's a road past it. My cabin is about half a mile up it. There's a little sign for the driveway and you'll see the lights. I'll make us dinner."

"Are you sure you don't want me to cook?"

August laughed, a warm and familiar sound. "No. I'm going to try my absolute best, and I want you to give me a full culinary school grading. Tell me if I flunk or pass."

"Sure," Nina said. "I'll bring my lowest expectations."

"Hey. I'll have you know I've been scouring the general store. I mean, you have proof of that. I'm cooking the best of what this town has to offer. How's Sunday?"

"If that works for you."

"Perfect," August said, and Nina's heart squeezed with the familiarity of him, of the ease with which he had always fit her into his life. Even now, so many years later, both of them in adulthood, she didn't feel as if she burdened him.

They parted ways without touching again. Nina sat on the

snow machine for a long moment after August's truck backed up and rumbled down the road, heading out of town, headlights cutting through the darkness and then disappearing, swallowed by the night. She fought the urge to go to Ila's, to corner Grant, to ask him for the truth. She had to leave him alone; she had to trust him. Her brother had been through so much, the trauma of the recent weeks turning him anxious and guarded. Chasing him down with more questions wouldn't help.

22

GRANT'S CONFUSION ON MONDAY HAD QUICKLY
turned to anger as he drove to Michael's house. Hadn't he been
warned about this? Michael and Orson knew that the Site
Fourteen men were talking about him. He had been naive to
think that he could let his guard down for a second, that it was
safe to stand alone in the dark parking lot without any kind of
protection. At first, his anger had been directed inward. But
then he'd received the news of another closure at work yesterday, and his anger had turned to Nina. Sitting through dinner at
Los Padres had been agonizing. When he was still upset at Ila's
that night, he understood he needed to talk to his sister again,
to give her one more chance to come clean.

A week ago, she had denied reporting the cover-up to the
police. He had allowed himself to believe her. But since Monday,
he had questioned again if it was her, if she had lied to him,
if she didn't understand the danger she had put all of them in.
When Michael had seen Grant's bruised and bloody face, he

had connected the dots instantly. Grant didn't tell him the full story, but he didn't need to. Michael had come up with the bar fight fib. Not only had Nina clearly not believed it, but she also had a distinct aura of guilt, Grant thought, as if she had somehow been responsible. He planned to continue staying with Ila or Michael, switching between their houses like a stray dog, but he needed clean clothes and another pair of boots.

He drove his snow machine back in the evening, shrouded in darkness. His mind circled the same thought that it had circled all day, like a wolf closing in on its prey. It was Nina. She had gone to the police, against Grant's plea, and told them everything. Who else knew? Who else besides the Site Fourteen men, who were united by the incident, sworn to secrecy?

He parked the snow machine, lifted his helmet, and watched his breath fog for a minute, trying to calm himself before he went inside. He had trusted Nina. And she had betrayed that trust.

Inside the house smelled buttery and earthy. Nina was at the stove, stirring something in a large pot. The TV screen bathed the living room walls in weak light. Their mother was nowhere to be seen.

Nina looked over her shoulder at the sound of the door shutting, her face lighting up in a smile when her eyes landed on Grant. "Oh, good. I didn't know if you'd be home tonight, but I'm making—"

"I need to talk to you."

Nina glanced at the pot. "Uh. Right now?"

He knew better than to pull her away from her cooking. "After you eat, I guess."

"You're not hungry?"

Grant was far from hungry, but he had to play along. "I'll eat."

Thirty minutes later all four of them sat at the table. Nina had made mushroom polenta and even though food was the last thing on Grant's mind, it tasted good. His mother had baked a fresh loaf of bread and they ate warm slices of it slathered with butter. At least his family wasn't one for conversation. Neither his mother nor father mentioned the bruises on his face. They were less visible than they had been even yesterday, beginning to fade from blue-green to a sickly yellow color, but he wasn't sure if his parents even noticed. By the time they were finished they had exchanged few words. Grant helped Nina wash the dishes and waited for their parents to drift away. When his mother picked up a book from the counter and headed down the hallway, he turned to Nina.

"Now?"

"Okay," she said, still nonchalant. "What's up?"

"Let's go to the kennel."

"Okay . . . Is something wrong with one of the dogs?" She was more hesitant now, watching him closely. Grant didn't care. He had barely kept a lid on his simmering temper throughout dinner.

"Just come," he said, grabbing his heavy coat off a hook in the mudroom and opening the door. He walked across the yard, kicking up loose snow with each step, listening for Nina's footsteps behind him. In the kennel, he had to wait for the dogs to quiet their racket before he could speak. Nina said hello to a few of them, sticking her fingers through the chain-link gates, but Grant couldn't focus on the dogs right now.

Nina took a seat on one of the worn chairs pushed up against the wall. "Well? You're being mysterious, what's up?"

"The oil field is shut down again." He could barely say the words without spitting them out. Doc had told them all at the end of the shift yesterday. *Don't come to work tomorrow.*

Nina's eyebrows rose the tiniest bit and she leaned forward. "You didn't mention it last night. What happened?"

"You fucking know what happened," Grant said, his voice too loud, too angry. Nina flinched. He hadn't meant to yell. He ran his hands through his hair, trying to control his breathing. "I told you about the accident—about all of it—because I trusted you. I know you told the troopers, Nina. I know it was you."

He waited for her to deny the accusation, to shift the blame. But she only stayed quiet, and when she finally spoke, her voice was barely audible. "I had to."

"Why?" Grant's hands fell to his sides. At least she had admitted it. But he wished, fiercely, that she hadn't been the one to tell. Now he had no way of proving that he, and by extension his family, hadn't been involved.

"Because it's the right thing to do," Nina said. Her jaw was firmly set but her eyes shone with tears and Grant felt a flare of guilt for cornering her. But it was short-lived.

"It was a fucking stupid thing to do." He drew a breath. "Do you have any idea the kind of people we're dealing with? They don't give a shit about us. They only care about their jobs. And now their jobs are being disrupted for a second time. Without that income, they have nothing. Probably most of them want nothing more than to get out of Alaska."

"Wait," Nina said, her eyes growing wider. "Your face— there wasn't a fight at the bar. Someone did that to you."

"Yes," he said, irritated. "I don't know who did it. But I think I know why."

"How do you not know—"

"It was dark. Some guys grabbed me when I got off work and beat me up. I didn't see their faces." He felt weak admitting it, but she needed to know the truth. "It's not only me, Nina. Once they realize we're related, they'll come after you, too. Especially if they find out that you're the one who went to the police."

"I wasn't planning on telling anyone."

"Yeah, I can tell."

They remained in silence for a moment. Some of the dogs were whining, either upset by the tense conversation or seeking attention, maybe a treat or a chance to leave the kennel. Sage was staring at Nina intently, her golden eyes fixated on her.

"I think you should talk to the troopers," Nina said.

"What?"

"I'm serious. When I went—I've been twice—I told them everything came from an anonymous source. But I think if it came from you, they might be sympathetic. They might understand that you were afraid."

Grant snorted. "Yeah, or I'll be thrown in jail. And then who will take care of Mom and Dad?"

"Me," she said evenly, as if Grant getting locked up was the least of her worries. "I just think there's no good end to this situation unless people come forward."

"No one's going to. You know what people around here are like. As soon as word got out at work that I'd been at Site Fourteen that day, they came after me. I guess they trust each other not to have told, but not me." He paused. "How'd you get the troopers to come here, if you had to go twice?"

Nina flushed. "Don't get mad."

"No promises."

"The other week, when you left your phone here? I—I took the video off it."

Grant's blood ran cold and his pulse pounded in his ears. "I can't believe you did that. It has a password."

"It wasn't hard to guess."

Grant's hands shook, the low current of energy threatening

to spill over. He half turned away from his sister. "I don't know what to say. I don't care if you thought it was the right thing to do. You put us in danger. Me especially, but . . ." He trailed off, trying to collect his thoughts. "This?" he said, turning back to her and indicating his face. He unzipped his coat and pulled up the side of his shirt, showing her the blue-black landscape across his ribs. Her face paled. "This? It could happen to you, too. It could happen to any of us."

"I still think you're being dramatic," Nina replied, although she didn't sound convinced by her own stance. "Please come clean. I think it'll make everything better."

"Why? So you can gloat that you were right all along?" Grant zipped his coat and shoved his hands into its pockets. "Nina, I was glad when you came back home. Really. I've missed you. But now I've realized that you remember nothing about what Whitespur is like. And you don't understand the oil field. It's like you're living in a different reality. It's just . . . God." Her expression turned sorrowful again, tears brimming in her eyes. Her show of emotion did nothing to him. "I won't be home for a while. And don't come looking for me. I don't think I've ever been this mad."

Nina opened her mouth to speak, but Grant turned away and strode toward the door. If she said anything, the chorus of dogs drowned her out, leaping to their feet to bark and howl at Grant as he left. *Let them cry*, he thought. The dogs were as useless as Grant felt.

23

GRANT HADN'T BEEN HOME SINCE THURSDAY. HE'D
spent the last three nights at Michael's, sleeping on the ratty
living room couch. Michael and Holly cooked dinner each
evening, and Grant did the dishes. It wasn't a bad existence,
but on Sunday evening he went to Ila's apartment instead. Her
landlord kept a watchful eye on how many visitors Ila had over,
and for how long they stayed—usually just Grant, and usually
not for more than one night, since Ila's landlord had vaguely
threatened to raise her rent if she "wanted a third roommate."

"You can't stay mad at Nina forever," Ila said.

"You don't know that."

Ila looked down at her hands for a long time. They were
sitting beside each other on Ila's newer, cleaner couch. Her hair
was pulled back and Grant noticed the dark circles beneath her
eyes—she'd been working six days a week at The Spur, which
was perpetually short on staff these days.

"I told her to report it."

"When?" Grant said in disbelief.

"Right after it happened. I know you told her, and she told me, and . . . well, she didn't say your name, but I could piece it together. I understood why you didn't report it, but I thought someone needed to, and it seemed like Nina knew the truth." Ila exhaled and picked at the fuzzy blanket on her lap. "I shouldn't have gotten involved. I wouldn't have, if I'd known you'd get hurt." She reached over to touch his face, the light pink scars on his cheek. Her hand was warm despite the cold goose bumps that rose on his arms. "Don't hold it against her. Please. If anything, you should be upset with me."

Grant stared at the floor, tracing the wood grain patterns until he became dizzy. He didn't feel mad at Ila, which told him that he shouldn't feel mad at Nina, either. Perhaps he'd been blinded by his own fear. Maybe they were both right—he should have simply told the police the truth. The entire mess might have been resolved in a few days instead of dragging on and growing increasingly complicated.

"I'm not upset," Grant said, hoping it was enough to reassure her. "I think—I think maybe I overreacted." He paused. "It's been weird enough having Nina back home. And then she goes and inserts herself into this—mess, and I don't know, I didn't want anyone else to get hurt." He looked at Ila. "You don't judge me for not reporting it?"

Ila hesitated, her lips twisting into an unfamiliar expression. "That's a hard question to answer."

"But you didn't say anything about it."

"Neither did you." She exhaled and tilted her head back, training her gaze on the ceiling. "Like I said, I pieced it together. You've been acting so weird, and when Nina knew about an accident . . . I mean, you told me about the fire. Of course, I knew. But I wanted you to come to me on your own. And you didn't." She lifted her hands half an inch, a gesture of frustration that Grant recognized.

"I'm sorry. It's not that I didn't trust you. I was trying to keep you safe."

"You keep saying that. 'Safe.' From what?"

Grant pointed to his face, to the scars she had touched moments ago. "This wasn't from breaking up a fight."

Ila rolled her eyes. "I know that. Michael is a terrible liar. He was trying not to laugh while you told me about it. Besides, I would have heard about a bar fight, even if I wasn't working that night. So, who did it?"

She listened while he recounted the incident of the men in the parking lot. "I'm sorry I didn't tell you the truth about that, either."

"Does Michael know?"

"Yeah, but not the full story. It's . . . God, it's all so complicated."

"That's what happens when you lie."

"Are you mad at me?" Pathetic to ask, but he needed to know where they stood. He could handle whatever Nina was feeling toward him; they were family. But there was nothing stopping Ila from cutting him out of her life forever.

"Sort of. Yes, but I also understand why you did it." She tilted her head. "You always want to make everyone happy, and it must be even harder to resist that when you're afraid. Apologize to Nina, okay? She doesn't deserve the cold shoulder. And think about what you want to do. Maybe we can brainstorm a path through this."

"I'll talk to Nina tomorrow," Grant said as Ila stood up and wandered into the kitchen. "And I'll tell the police what I know, okay?" The words tumbled out before he had a chance to think, to make sure he meant what he said—but now the weight of his promise hung in the air between them. Ila turned to face him, one eyebrow raised. "You're right. I'm afraid. But I don't think that excuses everything I've done. This whole mess. I want out of it."

Ila nodded once, her expression still distant. "Don't do this for me, okay? Make sure it's what you want to do."

Grant understood what went unsaid—that she might not forgive him, even if it all turned out okay. Even if his confession guided the troopers to Churchy's body, and by extension to Elias, who had covered up his death. Ila still viewed him for what he was, a coward who had been too afraid to do the right thing, who had put his own imagined safety above a literal death. He nodded, but couldn't bring himself to speak, worried that if he said too much, Ila might grow tired of listening. She picked up a bag of chips from the counter but hesitated at a faint knock on the door.

"That might be my mom," she said, stepping into the living room to toss the chips to Grant. "She wants me to go through some clothes before she donates them."

Grant set the chip bag aside and picked up his phone, thumb hovering over the screen. He'd changed his password again since Nina revealed she'd gone through his phone, and it always took him a minute to remember it. He couldn't see the front door from the couch but heard muffled voices. Ila appeared in the doorway, and when Grant raised his head, his heart froze. Fear clouded her expression. Behind her, Grant glimpsed a familiar head of black hair, pale brown roots showing through like soft earth in the spring.

"I didn't know where to find you," Katrina said. "It's Audrey."

Grant didn't need to hear what she said next. He already knew.

24

"SO. HERE YOU GO."

The plate in front of Nina held angel hair pasta with a generous spoonful of homemade sauce. Her heart warmed to think of their conversation in the general store, the way he had remembered her favorite pasta—surely it wasn't the same box she had handed him; he must have gone back since then. He had said he was trying to perfect the sauce recipe, and here it was in front of her, though she'd smelled it as soon as she entered the small cabin. Acidic and bright, with plenty of basil and oregano. There were shallots in the sauce too, and little strips of fat-marbled bacon. A slice of bread, warm, from a fresh loaf. Probably from the woman in town who baked dozens a week and sold them for eight dollars each.

"I'm impressed."

"Hold on." August grabbed a large bowl from the counter and scooped a portion of salad onto her plate, then drizzled it with balsamic vinaigrette.

"What did the bacon come from?"

"Shouldn't you be able to guess?" August replied.

"I can tell it's not pork."

"Bear."

"You hunt?"

"Harvey does," August said as he returned the pot to the stove. "I go visit him for a week every summer. He's living in Fairbanks now, has access to way more groceries than we do, but he still likes to stock the freezer. If I'm nice, he gives me half a caribou. If he's in a really good mood, I get bear."

"You need it way more," Nina pointed out around a mouthful of food. "Sorry," she said as August sat down across from her. "I'm starving. Also, I haven't had bear in forever."

"It's good?"

"Amazing. Although maybe it's just nice to have someone else cook for me."

"I'll take it."

"How much did the salad cost?"

"A small fortune," August said, a familiar smile working its way across his face. "You owe me."

Nina glanced at the fireplace, distracted by the popping of sparks and the thud of shifting logs. The cabin was small and rustic, like all the rural cabins she'd been in—not many, but they were all the same. August had layered rugs over most of the floorboards. There was a couch pushed against one wall, a massive desk covered in papers—evidence of the alleged paperwork—and a loft overhead. No bathroom, of course, no indoor plumbing out this way. Massive jugs of water were stacked against one wall.

"You haven't given me your opinion yet. Of my humble abode."

Nina blinked. She glanced down at her plate; she'd devoured most of the meal. "I like it. You get to live here for free?"

"Not free. They take a bit out of each paycheck. But I like being away from town. Especially after the oil field opened."

Nina winced at the mention of the oil field. Grant's confrontation was still fresh in her mind. Thursday was the last time she'd seen him, but she'd mostly stayed home, avoiding places where she might run into him, like The Spur. Though part of her was relieved that she was no longer carrying a secret, she hoped that they could talk about it again, more calmly, so Grant could grasp that she'd only been trying to help—and understand how much thought she'd put into reporting. He'd specifically asked her not to look for him, and she didn't want to go against his wishes again.

In the meantime, she'd helped her mother reorganize the filing cabinets in the kennel office and called a couple of leads for possible dog purchases. Both were busts, had already found what they needed at other kennels, but it had given her a sense of purpose. The next day she'd gone through the family phone book, cold-calling numbers and giving her best sales pitch. She'd gotten a couple people to say they'd come out in the spring. They wanted young dogs, ready to begin training—the city litter would be the perfect age by then. But her mother was still uncertain that they could afford to keep the full kennel of dogs through the winter. Maybe in a few weeks she'd be going door-to-door in town, asking people if they wanted a new pet.

In the evenings she watched TV with her dad, mostly sports, sometimes the news. She studied his face, lit by the ever-changing colors of the screen. He rarely looked at her or spoke above a low grunt, but sometimes Nina made conversation anyway, if something on the TV reminded her of a memory. She told him about the time Micah dragged her to a Mets game, and about the time she was stuck on the subway in a dark tunnel for hours, wondering if the world was ending overhead. She waited for him to tell her some piece of his life from the past nine years, but the bridge was too long to cross in only a few nights, and she sensed he wouldn't meet her halfway.

"What's wrong?"

Her emotional turmoil must have been visible on her face. Nina shook her head and set her fork down. "Sorry. Nothing. Grant and I got into a fight about his job. It's stupid." It wasn't stupid, but she still had a sense of loyalty to Grant. She didn't want to unravel the threads holding the last few weeks together.

"Is it about the drilling shutting down? It's been a pain. I've been out there most days, coordinating with the police. They want all kinds of maps. They told me they're investigating a possible death. Does Grant know anything about that?"

Nina hesitated. She could tell August everything, but she didn't know where his loyalties lay. If he took the information to the police, it would be worse for Grant. She still believed that Grant had to be the one to tell them. "I don't know," she replied. "He won't tell me much."

August nodded slowly. "Well, it's a big oil field," he said, his tone neutral. He stood up and reached across the table to take Nina's plate. "They searched the woods yesterday and today. Hard work, with all this snow. They brought in bloodhounds."

Nina tried to keep any tension out of her expression. "I hope they find what they're looking for." She pushed her chair away from the table and stood, wandering to the couch, closer to the warmth of the fire. August piled the dishes in the sink and joined her, his left thigh pressing against her right, igniting a spark of something both familiar and new. She'd known him so well, but he'd become akin to a stranger again, blurry around the edges. She didn't know where the night was headed and wasn't sure she wanted to. August was an unexpected but not unwelcome complication to her time back home.

August glanced at her and asked, as if reading her mind, "Do you still want to leave Whitespur again?"

Nina nodded, surprised at the lump in her throat. "It's not—it's not for me. It never has been. It's home, but it's not . . . where I belong."

August's mouth twisted in a frown and he lowered his head. Nina wanted to comfort him, but it was all too familiar, like the conversation they'd had years ago when she'd left for the first time. "I guess I shouldn't have gotten my hopes up."

"I wish I felt differently. I wish I could stay. But there's so much more of the world to see, and I can't be a chef here. I mean, who would come to my restaurant? I can't compete with The Spur and Los Padres."

August smiled briefly, the reaction Nina had been hoping for. "It's true. You can't do better than those two stellar institutions." After a pause, he added, "Tell me more about your life while you were away."

"Like what?"

"Your restaurant. Living on the East Coast. Your friends."

Nina thought about where to begin. "In culinary school, I made a friend. His name is Micah. Before you ask, it was never anything more than friendship. I think we were about as far from each other's types as we possibly could be. But I've heard people talk about the friendship version of a soulmate, and for me, that's Micah."

Nina told August about the times she and Micah had gotten in trouble for laughing too much in class, whispering their inside jokes back and forth. She told him about moving to New York, how they'd barely slept for weeks as they took inventory of all the closest specialty food stores during the day and dive bars at night, slowly venturing out to other boroughs. How, despite living in different apartments, they'd spent most nights together at one or the other, cooking and gossiping. She told him about 4950, their shared dream, the physical manifestation of their passion and hard work. And about how, though they didn't blame each other for its closure—the pandemic was such an unpredictable wild card, a sweeping sword that severed so much of society that places to eat felt like an afterthought— they'd had to go their separate ways, Micah to Texas and Nina back home, though she'd held on tooth and claw to the bitter end.

"And," she added, sheepishly, "I think I'm most thankful that he was there for me during my first year away, because those first few months, I was struggling. Homesick."

"Really? You?"

"Believe it or not, I cried myself to sleep most nights. I missed my family, and Whitespur, and the dogs, and the snow, and you. I had the feeling that I'd taken scissors to everything I loved and willingly cut it away." She paused. "Micah helped me through that. He helped me see that I would have new friends, new experiences, new memories. It's not like he was there for everything, but every significant part of my time away was because of our friendship. I know it's selfish, but sometimes it feels unfair that we didn't get to end that chapter on our own terms."

"I don't think that's selfish. You went from living closely with someone, working on the same project, to being thousands of miles apart and having limited communication." He reached for her hand and she let him take it. "I know what it's like. Maybe not to the same extent, but I had good friends at UAA who left to different states, different countries, after graduation. It's hard to stay in touch. It feels like little pieces of my memory spread all over the world."

That's exactly what it's like, Nina thought. Like she'd left slices of herself in New York, in Portland, and in Austin, though she'd never been there. In an unfamiliar city, her closest friend was experiencing life without her, and she kept on living without him. A year ago, it would have seemed inconceivable, but then again, she couldn't have predicted so much of what her life looked like now.

August was looking at Nina, his gaze unwavering, his hand still holding hers. "I feel like an idiot for saying this. But while you're here, for however long that might be, can we at least pretend?"

"Pretend what?" Nina asked, but he was already moving toward her, his lips meeting hers, cool and soft like the snow. She let herself kiss him, noticed the warmth of his hand on her jaw, buried a hand in his hair. She almost didn't register the knock on the door.

August pulled away, the confusion plain on his face. "I have no idea who that could be."

"Better go see," Nina replied, smoothing her hair back down. As he walked to the door, her heart thumped with the implications of their kiss. Did she want to do what he'd asked—to pretend? It would only end with both of them getting hurt, or Nina slipping into complacency, deciding that she would remain in Alaska for August's sake. She had tried often, the first time around, to picture their life together: hunting and fishing, smoking moose meat and cleaning trout, spending every evening in front of a roaring fireplace. She had always been able to visualize a future version of August, but not herself—a white outline beside him, a void of her absence.

Nina blinked when August opened the door, unable to understand why Grant stood on the other side.

"Is—oh. Nina." Grant peered into the cabin and spotted her. She couldn't read his expression and stood up, crossing the living room slowly. Snow fell outside, a billowing white curtain behind her brother, who was dimly lit by the light beside the door.

"What are you doing here?"

"I, uh . . ." He glanced at August. "I'm sorry. I really need to talk to Nina alone."

"Sure. I'll wait in the truck for a few minutes." August grabbed his keys from the counter and shot Nina a look, confused, but she could only raise her shoulders half an inch. She guessed Grant had come to apologize and didn't want August to overhear.

Grant stepped across the threshold so August could pass him, shutting the door as he left and cutting off the cold air. To Nina's shock, Grant started crying.

"What's wrong?" she asked, a million possibilities running through her mind. She didn't think a simple apology would make him so emotional. But she would never have guessed what he said next.

"Audrey's dead."

He choked out the words in a sob. Nina froze. A wave of disbelief washed over her. Audrey couldn't be dead. Nina had seen her just last week. She'd been talkative at her apartment, her cheeks awash with color. Alive. Nina's mind couldn't locate a question to ask.

Grant rubbed his hands against his eyes and glanced at the door. "I'm sorry about— I thought it would be better if I told you alone."

"Oh my God, don't worry about him," Nina said. She took Grant's arm and led him to the couch, heart hammering in her chest. She didn't have the urge to cry, not yet, not when Grant was so distraught. The grief would come soon enough, but for now she needed to take care of him.

"Do Mom and Dad know?"

"Yeah," Grant managed. He swiped a hand across his damp cheeks. "I went straight home. I figured you'd be there, but they told me you were out. It wasn't hard to guess where." He paused. "So. She's dead. Katrina found her. She—she, uh, got home from work and found Audrey . . ." He drew a few deep breaths. "Unresponsive, I guess. No pulse. Passed out on the bathroom floor. She did everything she could, but Audrey didn't wake up." He lifted his head with a look so full of grief that Nina's own wall began to break. "She wasn't using, Nina. I know she wasn't. She stopped drinking, too. I don't understand."

"She was an addict," Nina said. Grant half turned away, anger darkening his expression. "I mean, Grant, she probably hid things from you. From us. It's not hard to relapse."

"I know that. But she was careful." He paused again. "I should have done more for her. I should have given her more money. She needed it more than Mom and Dad did. I thought about . . ." He trailed off and pressed his palms against his face. "I thought about renting a place a year or so ago so she could live with me. Because Mom and Dad wouldn't let her come home. I could have kept an eye on her, helped her get back on her feet. But then—but then she was doing okay. It was almost spring, and she sounded optimistic every time I talked to her. She had just moved in with Katrina. I thought she'd do better if I left her alone." He dropped his hands to his lap. "How fucking stupid of me."

"You couldn't have done anything more," Nina said, but her words sounded empty. "Sometimes people are . . . well, the way that they are."

His voice brittle and sharp, Grant said, "You have no idea, Nina. You weren't here."

He was right. She hadn't been here for so many years, hadn't been a firsthand witness to their sister slipping away, like Grant had. She couldn't guess at what had happened in those years;

she'd been given only fragments and no set of directions to connect them. She felt unmoored, disturbed by her own lack of feeling. She suspected it was twofold—partially a panic response, her brain granting her with calmness to deal with Grant's trauma, and also that she didn't know her older sister well. The Audrey she remembered hadn't existed for years, and all that was left was a blank space, partially filled in by Grant's memories and the recent, brief time spent with her—a half-finished pencil sketch with no color, just lines.

"Did you see her?"

Grant shook his head. "Katrina found me at Ila's and told me. Like I said, I went straight home. Mom had the idea of driving over to the oil field and getting one of the troopers there to—you know. Take her somewhere else."

Nina squeezed her eyes shut. That part, she could picture all too well. Audrey's lifeless body, wrapped up and carried out of that rickety old apartment by a couple of indifferent men. Driven down the Dalton to a bigger town, one with a funeral home, where they'd cremate her body. Whitespur was too cold to bury bodies most of the year. For a short window in late summer, it would be possible to dig a shallow grave. But who wanted to keep a body around for that long? Sometimes, out in the bush, people left a body on the porch all winter to bury in the summertime. Nina shivered at the thought.

"Fuck," she muttered, and Grant nodded.

"I know. Fuck."

"Are they going to investigate the cause of death?"

Grant blinked. "I hadn't thought about that. I guess, maybe? I mean . . . something caused this." He pressed his palms against his eyes again, though he wasn't crying any- more, and exhaled. "I wanted to apologize to you, about this entire situation, and then . . . this happened. I can't believe she's gone."

"Me either," Nina replied. "It doesn't feel real."

"You aren't upset?"

"It's complicated," Nina said. "I'm upset, of course I'm upset. But I didn't know her well anymore. I need time for it to sink in."

"Yeah. I don't feel like I knew her well anymore, either, and I saw her all the time."

Nina's focus caught the wall clock and she realized how much time had passed. "Can I go get August?"

"Yeah, of course." Grant drew a deep breath and sat up straighter. "I guess I'll head home."

Nina touched his arm. "Wait a minute. I'll go with you. We should be with Mom and Dad."

"Yeah. Prepare yourself mentally for that."

Nina paused, halfway off the couch. "Why? They're upset?"

"They're angry."

"That's a given. Their first child just died of an overdose."

Grant flinched, but he nodded slowly. "Yeah. It's just that they skipped the denial and went straight to anger."

"We'll deal with them later. Together. I'll be right back."

Nina grabbed her coat by the door and stepped into the snow squall. The night was pitch black and windy and the snow stung her cheeks. She closed her eyes for a moment and felt it, the dam breaking, her grief pouring out like a raging river. Her older sister was dead. Bright-eyed, whip-smart, troubled Audrey was dead.

Nina squatted down and sobbed on the threshold, illuminated by the weak light. She didn't care if August saw her. The truck was idling a short distance away, headlights off, windows fogged from the heat. After allowing herself a minute to cry, she stood up, stifling the tears with her already red hands. Nina walked to the truck and tapped the window before opening the passenger-side door.

"There you are," August said. "I thought there'd been a coup and I'd lost my house forever." He paused, taking in her expression. "What happened?"

Nina breathed, suddenly in Grant's position, the one to break the news. "Audrey's dead. An overdose, her roommate thinks."

"God. I'm so sorry."

"It's . . ." The foggy window absorbed her attention, like the mist shrouding her own emotions. "I don't know what to think. Or say. Grant is devastated."

"Of course."

"I feel so distant from her. I mean, if you asked me yesterday if I loved Audrey, I'd have said yes. But I didn't *know* her."

"It'll take time, Nina," August said. "You just found out. You've barely had time to brush the surface of what you feel."

"I know. It's that right now I feel numb."

August was quiet for a moment. "What are you going to do?"

"Go home, I guess. It sounds like my parents got the troopers involved after Grant told them. I mean, you know, they have to take her somewhere. I asked Grant if they're investigating the cause of death and he said he didn't know." She paused. "I could follow them to Cold Creek and ask, but this storm . . ."

"Don't worry about that tonight. Go home, be with your family, and tomorrow you or Grant can go to the oil field and talk to them. Figure out who's involved and what they know."

A reverse investigation, Nina thought. How ironic that they'd end up in this position. She didn't want to talk to any of the troopers. They'd brush her off, as Peterson had.

"I'm so sorry, Nina. I can't imagine."

She let him wrap his arms around her for a moment, stretched awkwardly across the two seats, but her racing thoughts created mental distance between them. She and Grant needed to get home, to be with their parents. Later, maybe she could finally convince him to come clean. He had nothing left to lose.

25

AUDREY CAME HOME A FEW DAYS LATER. THAT'S HOW
Nina thought of the box on the counter, the one that contained Audrey's urn, which contained Audrey's ashes, because Audrey was no longer alive. Nina repeated these facts to herself methodically. She still felt far away, removed from such an intimate event of her family's life, as if she was still in Portland and had received a phone call instead of a knock on the door, Grant's tearstained face at August's cabin. She wondered if she would have flown home, had she received a call about the news, and concluded that she would have, of course she would have. Maybe if the pandemic had never existed, she would have insisted the restaurant close for a week and brought Micah with her, let him taste fresh salmonberries and wild moose meat and serve as a cheerful buffer between her and her family. But that wasn't reality, and besides, it seemed morbid to imagine a more pleasant version of Audrey's death. Instead, she'd called Micah from outside the general store, late in the evening, when she

knew he'd be off work but still awake. In their first conversation since she'd moved back to Alaska, she broke the news of her sister's death and recounted, vaguely, what she'd spent her time doing. He'd listened in silence, which was unusual for him, prone to interrupting as he was.

"Nina," he had said, "you've got to get out of there. You sound so sad."

She was sad, but it wasn't that simple. Even her closest friend couldn't understand why she needed to stay.

Darkness had descended upon Whitespur. The sun now rose around 10:30 a.m. and set around 3:00 p.m., less than five hours of daylight. Thanksgiving was one week away. Grant had been home all week because Brooks Valley was still shut down. The police had yet to make a statement or, as far as anyone knew, find what they were searching for. Grant had been the one to open the door when the trooper arrived with the box. Perhaps he had thought, for a second, that they were there to arrest him. She had been out in the kennel tending to the dogs, the only thing that allowed her to forget, even momentarily, that her sister was dead. The dogs were still alive, still full of personality and needs. When they'd been fed and run and fed again, she sometimes sat and brushed their fur mindlessly, soothed by the way the bristles disappeared inside their thick coats. Sage, the most recalcitrant of them all, sometimes lay her head in Nina's lap and fell asleep. Inevitably someone would come fetch her, either her mother, who wanted help making dinner, or Grant, who didn't want to be alone.

"Are you two going to scatter her ashes?"

Nina flinched at the sound of her mother's voice. She turned away from the counter, unfolding her arms and letting them fall to her sides. Her mother leaned against the doorframe, holding her morning mug of coffee. It wasn't the first time she'd mentioned the ashes. In fact, she'd been talking about them before they'd even arrived, hinting that perhaps Nina and Grant had somewhere in mind for their sister's final resting place. But it was the first time she had asked so directly.

"Are you sure you and Dad don't want to be there?"

Mary frowned. "I don't think your dad could handle it. And me . . ." She trailed off. "I don't know, Nina."

Nina hesitated. She had wanted to ask, all week, what her mother genuinely thought about Audrey. If her addiction and alcoholism had been simply unforgivable, or if part of her always hoped her oldest daughter would come back, struggles and all, to allow her parents to help her.

She sensed what Nina was thinking. "I love her, Nina, I do. She was such a bright light in my life for years. But she should have known better. I tried to help her for so long. Let her live here, gave her money, supported her. But when I found her taking those pills here, that was it. Grant was still young. I didn't want him finding her stash and accidentally killing himself." She shook her head. "I gave her chances, too, after she left. But she never got clean, not that I'm aware of."

"Grant said she was trying to, these last few weeks. And he thought she had only been drinking, not using any drugs. I'm not sure if I believe him."

Her mother coughed once. "Look at how they found her. What does that tell you?" She paused. "I'm proud of you, Nina, for getting out of here. I wish you'd stayed in contact more, maybe helped us if you could, but—well, I'm not sure I would have kept too close a tie to home if I were you, either."

"What do you mean?"

She sighed, switched the mug to her left hand, and gestured around the kitchen, though Nina suspected she meant the house, Whitespur, Alaska—all of it. "I never left. Always wanted to, but I never did. Growing up the way I did, no electricity, no running water, there was never time for anything else besides staying alive. Every summer minute was spent preparing for winter, and every winter minute was spent making sure you didn't freeze to death or starve. It was a miracle when I met your dad. It was his goal in life to make sure I would one day have those comforts, even way out here in the North. I know what you think of him now, even if you've never said it. But you have to understand that in his eyes, he's accomplished all he ever wanted. All those race wins were icing on the cake."

Nina nodded, savoring what her mother had to say. It was rare for her to speak so much at once. She hadn't gotten more than a few clipped words here and there since she'd come home. "I'm worried about him, that's all."

"We all are." She paused. "The pain medication has helped, but he needs that surgery. I'd tell you to try convincing him, but I don't think he'd listen to you." A hint of a smile crossed her face. "I know he threw a big fit about those dogs, but he admitted to me last night that the money is a huge relief. Maybe he'll say it to your face one day."

Nina forced herself to smile. She couldn't tell her mother about Waylon Turcotte, at least not now. If her father was coming around to the fact that Honey and Wilder were gone, she couldn't throw such troubling news into the mix. Still, she longed to tell her mother everything. She was a fixer, self-sufficient, the most capable woman Nina knew.

"I'll mention it to him," Nina offered. "Not in a lecturing way. I'll just ask him if he's thought about it any more." Her eyes drifted back to the box on the counter, the reason they were having the conversation at all. "We'll do it. Scatter her ashes, I mean. Tomorrow. I'll tell Grant."

"Thank you." She straightened up and started to turn around, then paused. "I think Bow Lake would be nice."

"That's what I was thinking, too."

"Great minds, Nina." A softness, a sadness, in her expression, but something like love, too. Without hesitating, Nina pulled her into a hug, feeling the bones beneath her layers of clothing. Her mother's body shared similarities with Audrey's—had carried her as it had carried Nina and Grant. For a second Nina's throat caught as she thought of the woman Audrey might have become, middle-aged, with smile lines and crow's feet. When Nina looked at her mother, she saw a reflection of herself, too, the older woman she would one day become, if she was lucky. Brown hair streaked with gray. A perpetual cough from woodsmoke, a softness in her body.

They would get through this, all of them. Though she couldn't see the path through the dark forest, Nina had no doubt it was there.

"Are we going to do Thanksgiving this year?" she asked, letting go. They'd never celebrated the holiday in a traditional way, mostly because staples like turkey and sweet potatoes weren't always readily available. But every year her mother would cook something special—moose or caribou stew with more vegetables than usual and heaps of mashed potatoes on the side. A crowberry pie, if she'd harvested enough berries that season.

Mary shook her head slowly, not quite a no, noncommittal. "I'm not sure. We haven't for the past few years. Grant is usually working, and your dad hasn't been up for it. Why don't you ask him what he thinks? If he wants to, we can plan the menu together."

Nina smiled, even as her chest constricted. "I'd love that."

She found Ted in the living room. The TV was off, and he was holding a thin stack of papers in his hand, reading the top sheet. She paused in the doorway, hesitant to interrupt. "Dad?"

"I'm not busy," he responded, setting the papers down. "What is it?"

He still spoke with a familiar gruff rumble, but Nina sensed that something was different about him—perhaps a willingness to engage signaled by the darkened television screen. She lowered herself to the armchair beside his, and gestured to the papers. "What are you reading?"

"Medical paperwork," he said after a moment. "The recommendations from my doctor to get another surgery."

"Are you thinking of doing it?"

He took longer to reply this time. When he raised a hand to brush against his cheek, she noticed that his hand trembled, though his eyes remained dry. "Maybe in the spring."

Nina drew a breath. "I think you should," she said. "If you're up for it. Even if you're not." She recalled her conversation with her mother. "I think Mom wants to see you back on your feet again. We all do."

"I can walk," he huffed, but seemed to consider her point. "The money from the dogs you sold. It might make it possible. I didn't want to put us in too much debt."

Nina reached for him, and to her surprise, he let her take his right hand. She squeezed it, feeling the rough skin of his palm, the ridges of his knuckles. "I'm sorry about Wilder. I should have asked you. I know the dreams you had for him."

"They were just dreams, Nina," he said, withdrawing his hand. "I'm not the man I used to be."

"But maybe you could mush again after the surgery. After you're healed."

"Maybe," he conceded. His eyes held a faraway look.

Nina cleared her throat. "Mom wanted me to ask you about Thanksgiving. If you want to celebrate this year."

"Do you miss your restaurant?"

She blinked, surprised at the question. "I do. That restaurant was my dream. I miss my friend, Micah, who ran it with me.

Every day that I'm not there . . . it's hard. I don't feel like myself, sometimes." She drew a breath, startled by how much she had just revealed to her least-forthcoming family member. "But I try to imagine that maybe I'll have something even better one day."

He nodded once without meeting her eyes. "We haven't paid much attention to the holidays since all you kids grew up. This year, without Audrey, it's hard to think about celebrating. But if you want to cook for us, I would like that."

Nina swallowed the lump in her throat. "I'm sorry about Audrey," she said, her voice barely above a whisper.

"Me too," he said, "me too." And for a few more minutes they sat in silence, accompanied only by the ticking of the clock on the wall. From the photograph opposite them, a different version of Ted Sanford gazed down, a triumphant smile on his face. Nina stared back, willing her father to remember some spark of that younger, wilder self. For the first time since arriving home, she felt hope that he one day might. He hadn't truly apologized, or thanked her, but he had acknowledged that she had helped the family, and acknowledged Audrey's absence, and that was enough for now.

"HERE, YOU THINK?" Nina stepped off the sled runners and checked the dogs quickly before lengthening her strides to catch up with Grant. He didn't seem to have heard her. He walked down the slope of the lakeshore, covered in snow like the surrounding landscape. It was impossible to tell that it was a lake, but Nina knew the contours of the shore like the back of her hand, from summers of lounging and winters of skating.

They all did, Audrey included, which was why her mother had suggested Bow Lake.

The afternoon quiet was broken only by the sound of their boots crunching over the snow. The darkening sky hovered low over the earth. A few half-hearted clouds drifted overhead, but the rolling span of undisturbed snow drew more attention. Nina had bundled up against the cold, but now she was on the verge of sweating beneath her layers.

Finally, Grant stopped, near where Nina guessed the water might begin. He turned back to her. He held the urn in his gloved hands gingerly, as if afraid of dropping it, though the snow would cushion its fall. "Yeah. I think here is good."

Nina skidded on the slope, catching her balance before she fell. She stepped onto the flatter area of the shore and took in the wide expanse of snow and the dark line of spruce trees far in the distance. The enormity of the silence settled over her. Behind them, most of the dogs had lain down, but Sage, as always, sat stoically upright in front. One of Grant's dogs barked, briefly shattering the quiet.

"Are we supposed to say something?"

"Like what?"

"I don't know." Grant looked like he wanted to be anywhere else, and Nina felt a flash of sympathy for him. She reached over and took the urn.

"It's Audrey. She would hate a speech."

"Yeah. She'd make fun of us for sure."

"Do you remember when Mom asked us to make rags, and you went into Audrey's dresser and cut up a bunch of her favorite shirts?"

Grant laughed. "I thought she was going to turn *me* into rags. Mom had to pry the scissors from her hands." He paused. "I remember her trying to train puppies when we were kids. She would give them such a full, detailed explanation of what she wanted them to do, sometimes demonstrate it herself, and then get so perplexed when the dogs didn't understand her instructions."

"She couldn't fathom anyone else not being as smart as her."

Grant exhaled, a wave rushing up the shore. "I miss her."

"I do, too." Nina paused. "It's hard not to keep picturing what her life might have been like if things had been different. But this was her life, you know? She was loved by a lot of people."

"I know. Every time I've been at The Spur this week, people kept coming up to me to tell me how sorry they were and how much Audrey always brightened their day. Apparently, she wasn't just cleaning houses, she was organizing them, helping people go through their belongings and get rid of stuff they didn't need. One woman—I didn't recognize her, she must be the wife of someone at the oil field—she told me that she was so overwhelmed by how messy her house was. Constant despair whenever she looked around. And Audrey came in without any judgment and helped her through it. She said it changed her life."

"I had no idea she was doing that."

"I feel like she lived a life we'll only ever understand pieces of."

"I wish we could hear it all from her." Nina willed herself to remove the lid from the urn in her hands. One of the dogs howled, a piercing cry overhead. "I guess they miss her, too," she said. "Should we?"

Grant nodded. Nina lifted the lid from the urn and tilted her head, indicating for Grant to reach in and take the small tube they'd filled earlier that day. Nina had told her mother they would scatter the rest in the summertime, when Bow Lake came back to life. For now, a small part of Audrey could rest.

Nina dug a shallow trench and Grant scattered the ashes,

turning the snow a soft gray. Nina brushed some of the loose snow back over the trench. They worked silently, a few minutes ticking by as twilight fell, the first stars becoming visible in the sky. Grant handed the empty tube back to Nina and she tucked it inside the urn, which she'd set in the snow beside her.

She straightened up and pulled the mitten from her right hand, pressing the back of her gloved hand against her eyes, more to stop the tears from freezing than to stop the crying. Grant wrapped his arms around her shoulders and they stood for a moment, both crying, the sounds muffled by their jackets. Grant let go and Nina stepped back, blinking, and drew a shaky breath.

"This sucks."

"I was thinking the same thing."

Nina gazed at the frozen lake. "We'll be back," she said quietly, a promise both to Audrey and herself. She'd given up hope of leaving Whitespur before winter, but even if she found another job in the spring, she would return in the summer to finish dispersing Audrey's ashes. She owed it to her sister, and to Grant. Maybe even to herself.

Grant placed a hand on her shoulder, steering her gently away from the shore and up the slope. But after a few feet he dropped his hand and stopped in his tracks. "I'm going to talk to the police. Tomorrow."

Nina turned to face him. "You are?"

He nodded. "I've been thinking about it a lot this last week, since . . ." He trailed off and gestured at the lake, which Nina knew meant Audrey, as if by dying their sister had become the body of water, the trees, the snow. "I kept thinking what she would say if she knew. 'What the hell are you doing, kid?'" His voice became more gravelly in an imitation of Audrey's, and Nina loved him more for it. "I can't keep being afraid of what might happen. I keep thinking about that guy, Clyde, and whoever might be waiting for him back home. They deserve to know the truth."

For the second time, Nina blinked back tears. "I'll go with you tomorrow. If you want. And I'll be there for you, no matter what happens."

"I'm not sure if I want you to come with me. It might be better if you don't. But thank you."

He resumed trudging up the slope and Nina followed, a tentative spark of optimism warming her chest. The dogs on both teams were restless, biting at each other's faces and pacing in small circles as their tug lines allowed. Sage still sat, staring into the distant forest with undivided attention.

"I guess we should head back," Grant said. "Unless you want to go the long way. They might appreciate getting to burn off some more energy."

If Nina had gotten a chance to respond, she would have said yes. She would have said *that's a great idea, I don't want to go home yet*, because going home meant leaving part of Audrey behind. It was morbid to think, but they still had most of her—Nina had nestled the urn into the sled basket as soon as they'd crested the hill—but her death had finality now. There was no coming back from dust.

But Nina didn't get a chance to respond. Her ears were ringing with an impossibly loud sound. *An earthquake*, Nina thought, though it made no sense. Grant stumbled and righted himself, one hand on his sled. Another crack echoed through the valley. The dogs whined and barked, agitated. Nina's brain leaped. *A gunshot*. Too close, but it could be nothing else.

Grant lifted the bag from his sled and tossed it into the basket of Nina's. She couldn't understand why he had done it. She said his name but he ignored her. In disbelief she watched as he kicked the snow hook loose behind his sled and shouted to his dogs, urging them to go. His lead dog took off, paws scrambling in the snow, moving faster than ever with the lightened sled. Nina's dogs howled and strained against their harnesses, desperate to follow. Grant turned and stumbled to Nina's sled, bumping into it, clutching his right side. His hand moved, revealing the tattered hole in his jacket, the edges frayed like arm hairs standing on end. Gripping the side of the sled, he choked out the words.

"They shot me."

26

A HUNTER, NINA THOUGHT, THE ONLY THING THAT made sense. And if it was a hunter, they would realize their mistake and rush over to help. Even as it crossed her mind, Nina acknowledged the absurdity of the idea. She needed to help Grant, now, as he clung to the sled to remain upright.

Nina rushed to him but stopped, hands shaking, afraid to touch him. "What should I do?" She wasn't sure who she was asking. Grant's face was pale, his expression contorted in pain. He almost certainly didn't have the answer.

Now that Grant's team was out of sight, the dogs were somewhat subdued, no doubt unsettled by the gunshot. A few still spun in circles, whining, but it was Sage who drew Nina's attention. The leader sat motionless, facing forward, but her head turned back toward Nina, golden eyes locked on her. Nina stared back for a moment, attempting to interpret what Sage meant to communicate.

She inched closer to Grant. "Where?" she asked, and Grant responded by pointing a single finger at his stomach.

Nina let out a breath, relieved she'd gotten through his fog of shock. "Can you get into the basket?"

Grant stared down at it, as if asking himself the same question. Finally, he nodded. Another gunshot echoed through the valley and Nina lunged forward, grabbing Grant's arm and pulling him down. He wrenched free and clambered into the basket, shoving the bags and the shotgun aside, as Nina crouched behind the sled, terror gripping her body. Adrenaline forced her upright again and she centered Grant's body in the basket as much as possible, positioning the urn between his feet. She remembered the blanket stuffed into her sled bag. Digging into the tan canvas sack, she pulled out the thick wool blanket and spread it over Grant. Another gunshot made her flinch and drop low, squatting beside the sled. Whoever was shooting must have no idea they'd hit someone. She braced for the impact of another stray bullet as she smoothed down the blanket, blinking against the rapidly falling darkness.

Grant's eyes snapped open.

"Nina," he managed to say, each word an effort through the pain. "Don't go." He paused to breathe. "Back home." His right hand lifted in a feeble gesture, pointing at the woods. "Go there."

Nina froze, processing his directions. The woods led away from civilization, away from any help they could easily get. The woods were part of the refuge—no one lived on that land, and there were no structures save for a few hunting cabins, likely unoccupied at this time of year. She wanted to ask why, but Grant's eyes were closed again, his breathing labored. She sneaked a glance up at the trees, and thought about Grant's directions. The gunshots had come from the direction of home. But if they headed away from home, further into the wilderness, Grant wouldn't receive treatment as quickly. Nina had been sure of where to go—to the oil field, where they had a doctor on staff and several EMTs. Grant had told her before about the safety training he went through yearly, how the EMTs would teach everyone CPR because the ambulances couldn't travel quickly in the snow.

Grant's eyes flew open again, the intensity of his stare difficult to break. *He knows something*, Nina thought. Maybe the bullet hadn't been a random accident. Grant had been paranoid for weeks, and those men had attacked him—suddenly, his recent fear made much more sense. "We'll go to the woods," she agreed, and it calmed him.

They could still get to Brooks Valley, Nina knew, by circumventing the woods. Eventually they would reach the service road that ran past all the drilling sites. After Grant had taken her to see the oil field from above, Nina had peppered him with questions until he had shown her a map, pointed out all the different buildings and drill sites. The image in her mind was faint, but it was there. Even though operations were shut down from the investigation, Nina hoped that at least one of the medical staff remained. If they couldn't treat him, they could at least help get him to a hospital somewhere else.

As Nina pulled her headlamp on and climbed aboard the runners, concern for Grant's dogs surged through her. So many things could go wrong on their way home—the sled could get stuck, the dogs could get tangled. Whoever had shot at them might hurt the dogs. Still, their parents knew Nina and Grant were out, knew exactly where they were. If the dogs hadn't returned in another hour or two, they might start to worry. And they would definitely worry if Grant's team came careening into the yard, pulling an empty sled. His dogs had headed in the right direction. She couldn't think about them, not now, not when her brother was injured and her own dogs had become frenzied again, eager to run once more.

Nina kicked the snow hook free and shouted to the dogs, braced for the jolt and the rush of air as they sprinted in the night. A last glance over her shoulder revealed nothing but the great white valley and the huge navy-blue sky, the landscape bathed in the faint orange glow of the oil field lights.

And then another gunshot echoed through the trees.

27

NINA CURSED AS THE DOGS LEAPED SIDEWAYS, pulling the sled off-kilter. She leaned all her weight to the left, counterbalancing as the runners slammed back onto the ground. A moment passed before she realized she hadn't been shot. But whoever it was didn't just want Grant dead. They were after her, too.

She noticed that a few of the dogs moved with tucked tails and hunched shoulders—a bad sign. If the dogs quit pulling, they could influence the whole team to stop, and what they needed to do now was keep moving. Out in the open, trotting along the shoreline toward the forest, they were totally unprotected. The valley was silent—no sign of a gun-toting snow machiner hell-bent on chasing them down. Headlamp switched on, Nina returned her attention to the now-illuminated dogs.

"Go on, Wren. Good boy, Moose, keep pulling." The large chocolate-brown husky in wheel position glanced over his shoulder at her and gave the slightest tail wag. She kept talking to him and a few minutes later he was pulling better, leaning into his harness. Wren, one of the team dogs, still wavered, drifting left and right instead of pulling straight ahead. Nina knew if Wren dropped off, she'd have to unclip her and release her into the wilderness. She couldn't risk the rest of the team stopping. Wren would meet whatever fate was in store for the other dogs Grant had sent in the direction of home.

On the bright side, Sage was moving at an incredible pace, head down, loping over the packed-down snow. Nina was proud of the cagey dog—three weeks ago, Nina's mother had been skeptical about her plans to train Sage as a leader. But Sage had needed no training; she had a natural instinct to lead a team. Even in Nina's distracted state—she'd hardly given the dogs any commands—Sage guided them down the familiar training route.

Too familiar, Nina realized. Whoever was after them would have an easy time tracing their path down the wide, well-packed trail. Once they reached the woods, they needed to get off trail. The deep snow should cover most of the brush; she could only hope that it was packed enough that the dogs wouldn't break through. They couldn't pull the sled through deep snow, and breaking trail was a slow, arduous process that Nina didn't wish to perform at the best of times.

She stared down at Grant's body for a moment. Mostly covered by the wool blanket, he was disguised as any other cargo. But she couldn't tell if he was breathing.

Up ahead, the forest loomed. The dogs swung right without Nina's command, following Sage's lead. To Nina's relief, Wren had picked up her pace, matching strides with Raven beside her. Nina let them glide through the forest, welcoming the relative cover of the gnarled spruce trees. When she spotted a denser stand, she called to the dogs.

"Whoa," she repeated, drawing out the word until the excited dogs gradually slowed. Nina hopped off the sled, a risky move, and jogged to grab the nearest tug line, gradually working her way up until she reached Sage. She guided the dog into the stand of trees, carefully winding around until she hoped they were no longer visible from the trail. She retraced her steps and set the snow hook. As long as the dogs didn't tangle, they were in a safe spot.

Beside the sled basket, Nina peeled the blanket back from Grant. His chest rose and fell, though his face was pale. Nina hadn't even registered the temperature—cold, surely, though her body was hot from both adrenaline and from manning the sled.

Grant's eyes opened, though they took a second to focus on her. "Why'd we stop?"

His voice sounded clearer—maybe some of the shock had worn off. "I wanted to make sure you were still alive," Nina replied.

"I am."

"Okay, well. I'm not taking that for granted."

Grant wriggled, attempting to sit up higher in the basket, and gasped in pain, a frightened look in his eyes. Nina touched his shoulder.

"Don't move."

"Shouldn't have stopped here."

"Okay. Where do you suggest we go?" Nina suspected he had a good reason for not wanting to go toward home—the direction the gunshots had come from—but now their path headed into nearly a million acres of uninhabited land. "And I need to look at your wound. We should find a cabin."

"You're not a doctor," Grant said.

Nina opened her mouth to reply, and then shook her head. "That is a ridiculous response."

"I'm just saying. You might make it worse."

"I want to take you to the oil field. To the doctor there.

But I don't know if you can wait that long. What do you want me to do?"

Grant closed his eyes, and when he didn't reopen them, Nina failed to tamp down a wave of guilt. She'd exhausted him. She should have taken charge, told him they were circling back and heading back home. He had no power to stop her.

"I'm not certain who did this," Grant said, his voice low. "But I have an idea, and we can't go back. Not now. Not to the oil field, either." He paused and drew a few labored breaths. "When this trail comes out of the woods, go left instead of right. Up the mountain . . ." He trailed off, a full minute of nothing but the sound of his breathing. One of the dogs whined. "Cabin. No trail. I go there sometimes."

Nina nodded, although Grant's eyes were still closed.

"And turn off your headlamp. Too visible."

She squeezed his shoulder and covered him again with the blanket. One of the dogs began to bark and Nina shushed them, terrified of drawing attention. She retraced her steps, lifted the snow hook, and then darted to grab the dogs before they realized they were free. It was a tedious process to turn them around in the narrow woods, but a few minutes later the dogs were lined up on the trail, pointing away from home. This time there was no fooling them—the dogs surged forward as soon as Nina released them, and she caught the sled as it went by, planting her feet firmly on the runners.

Night wrapped its arms around them, carrying them through the dark woods. Nina kept her eyes peeled for moose or wolves, but spied no other creatures moving through the forest. After a few minutes of navigating the inky dark, her eyes had adjusted, and now the quarter moon above shed more than enough light, illuminating the soft undulations in the snow. The dogs' paws pounded a steady rhythm, their pewter shadows sliding silently over the ground beside them. Nina made a mental note to check their feet at the cabin; they likely had balls of ice in their paws. Then her stomach sank. Pulling a sled burned an enormous number of calories, and she had no food to give them. The sled bags contained a few human snacks—protein bars, jerky—things the dogs could eat in a pinch, but she had to feed herself and Grant, too. Maybe the cabin would have something. Otherwise, the dogs would go hungry and quit pulling.

The silent woods comforted Nina somewhat. Her mind felt tethered by a kite string, drifting off on nonsensical thought paths. She kept tugging it back. The darkness strained her vision. Eventually, a thin gray light would brighten the world. But only for a few hours.

The dogs emerged from the woods and began to bear right, following the familiar path back toward home. "Haw!" Nina called. "Haw!"

Sage flicked an ear back and altered her course to the left. Nina held her breath, waiting to see if the swing dogs would follow. They did, and the rest of the team too, sweeping left to begin climbing up the mountainside. Pride rushed through Nina's chest, again, for how well the team, who she'd put together three weeks ago, worked.

There was no clear trail up the mountainside, which Nina took as a good sign. No one had been frequenting the cabin. Still, the sled glided along smoothly without sinking through the snowpack.

Nina kept her head on a swivel, scanning for signs of a cabin. Grant hadn't given her the clearest directions, and "no trail" didn't sound promising. Nina's eyes burned, afraid she'd miss it if she blinked. Gradually, she noticed the dogs had begun to alter their path and drift right, following Sage's lead. How well could she trust Sage's intuition? A moment later, she had her answer.

The cabin stood on a cliff, sheltered by an overhanging rock mass that protruded from the mountain face above. They were only halfway up the slope, nowhere near the peak, but Nina shivered at the scale of the rock. The cabin itself was tiny, like most hunting cabins, nothing more than a room. Still, Nina was brought close to tears at the sight of it, a place to rest and recalibrate, to wrap her head around the disastrous position they were in.

Sage led the team right up to the front door and sat. Nina knew she expected food and tried to ignore her growing worry. "Good girl!" she called, hoping praise could temporarily sub- stitute for calories.

Nina hopped off the sled, set the snow hook, and peeled the blanket off Grant, placing her hand on his chest as it rose and fell with each breath. He didn't stir or open his eyes.

She circled the sled and pushed the cabin door open, greeted by a dank, musty scent as soon as she crossed the threshold. It was dark inside, but several candles and boxes of matches were scattered around. She lit a few of the candles. On the worn table sat a camp stove and a few containers of fuel. Someone had stacked crates against one wall. They were mostly empty, but Nina glimpsed a few cans of soup and chili. She breathed a sigh of relief and collapsed into a chair for a moment, resting her head in her hands. Exhaustion and anxiety permeated every inch of her body, but she had to get Grant inside the cabin.

Back outside, she repositioned the dogs so that the sled was close to the cabin door. She didn't worry about the dogs running off now—the short time she'd been inside, they had started digging nests out of the snow.

Nina shook Grant's shoulder gently, repeating his name until his eyes opened. "We're at the cabin. We have to get you inside."

He nodded grimly. "I know."

"Do you think you can walk?"

Grant blinked as he considered the question. "Maybe. Worth a try."

Nina positioned herself next to the sled basket, hoisting Grant's legs over the side as he braced. His sharp breaths of pain turned into a cry as his body twisted, contorting the wound on his stomach. Nina lowered his feet to the ground and hauled him upright.

Worried he would pass out, she slipped beneath his arm, slinging it around her shoulders. Though she was shorter, he leaned against her, and together they hobbled the short distance inside the cabin.

Nina helped Grant lower onto the cot in the back corner. Though it was freezing inside, she started to pull away his coat, steeling herself to lay eyes on the wound. Grant pushed her hands away.

"Go take care of the dogs."

Nina nodded and backed away, thankful that he could string together full sentences again. She retraced her steps outside and moved the dogs for the second time, positioning them in a loop to the right side of the cabin, hidden from sight. Digging through her supply bag, she produced a packet of jerky and gave each dog one piece. Moose wolfed down the offering in a single gulp and gazed up at her, unimpressed. Nina rubbed his fur and held back tears at the thought of working the dogs so hard and giving them near nothing in return.

As she retraced her steps, a strange shape against the side of the building caught Nina's eye. Bending over, she swept the snow away until her hands hit a blue tarp and beneath it, a meager woodpile. She doubted the wood was dry enough to burn, and she had no kindling, but she gathered a few small logs anyway. Maybe someone had stashed newspaper inside.

In the cabin, Nina emptied the contents of the sled bags on the table and did inventory.

Two bags of booties, which she counted out to forty-eight pairs.

A thick wool sweater, gloves, socks, and a hat.

A spare headlamp, with batteries.

One container of Black Magic bear slugs.

Fire starter and a lighter, sealed in a plastic bag.

Six packets of jerky, a half-empty bag of trail mix, a can of chili, a Snickers bar, and a jar of peanut butter.

A gallon-sized ziplock bag of dog kibble.

Plus the blanket she'd draped over Grant, which was now thrown across the back of a chair, and the Remington, which she left propped beside the door. Nina took the fire starter and lighter and a few minutes later, a meager fire crackled to life in the fireplace, adding more light to the flickering glow of the candles.

Grant's eyes were closed and his mouth had a grim set, as if he was grinding his teeth, but his chest rose and fell steadily. She grabbed the blanket and laid it over him again, then took the bag of kibble outside. She doled out a handful to each dog, apologizing again for the lack of food. The jerky she saved for later, wanting first to dig around the cabinets and crates inside for anything else suitable to eat. The dogs had settled for the most part; they would be fine for a few hours. Any longer, and she might have to bring them all inside to keep warm.

In the relative warmth of the cabin, Nina grabbed a chair and dragged it over to face Grant's cot. "Hey," she said. "You awake?"

His eyes opened and he nodded.

"I need you to tell me what you think is going on here. Because I don't see any good reason why we're hiding out instead of going home."

"Someone shot me," Grant said, his voice like coarse sand. He drew a labored breath. "I think it's someone from the oil field."

A cold chill ran up Nina's spine. "Because of the cover-up?"

"Because they think I went to the police."

"But how did they know we were out here tonight?"

Her brother grimaced. At first Nina thought it was from pain, but his tone was laced with regret when he spoke. "I talked about it today. When I got lunch with Michael and Orson. Maybe someone there overheard, and reported back to Elias. It was so crowded." He hesitated. "That, or Elias has been staking out our house, waiting for me to leave."

"You think it's him out there?"

"I don't know. He might not be able to mush or shoot a gun. But I think he's behind this."

Nina let the information settle in. Even if it wasn't actually Elias trailing them through the wilderness, she understood that he represented the real threat in Grant's eyes. "Okay. Let's say Elias wants you dead. Am I the complication? He thought you'd be out alone, he'd kill you, and then it's just another death for him to cover up. Because he thought you were the problem. Without you, no one would say anything about Clyde Lee's death, and he could continue doing his job and making good money, forever."

"Maybe." Grant paused. "He might want you dead, too."

"Do you think . . ." Nina hesitated. "Do you think he had anything to do with Audrey?"

"Maybe. I don't know."

Nina absorbed the answer. They might never know the

truth. "Do you think he's following us? Did the gunshots sound like they were getting closer?"

Through gritted teeth, he replied, "I have absolutely no idea."

A light sweat had broken out on Grant's forehead. "Are you too hot?"

"No. I just feel like shit."

"Fair enough," Nina muttered. "What should we do?"

"I don't know. Am I supposed to stay awake?" Grant turned his head in her direction. "I wish Mom and Dad had put us through a wilderness survival course."

"That was our entire childhood, minus the bullets."

"We're probably safe up here for a few hours. Then we should move. Let's take the river. Up," he said, lifting his left arm, "and follow the curve. That'll put us north of the service road. Then we can get down to the oil field."

Nina nodded, drawing a mental map of his instructions. "That'll take days."

"Two."

"Can you make it that long?"

"No clue. But you're right. The oil field is the best place to go."

"Okay. We'll give it three hours?"

Grant nodded. "I might fall asleep. But, you know, make sure I'm still breathing. And, Nina?"

"Yes?"

"Bring the dogs inside."

Nina couldn't hold back a smile. It was just like Grant, to worry about the dogs when his own life hung in the balance. She stood up and returned the chair to its place next to the table before checking the fire—still burning, although the logs were well charred and likely wouldn't hold flames for much longer. A hot pile of embers had formed, though, and Nina acknowledged that now was the time to eat. The thought of food made her stomach rumble—her wristwatch read close to 7:00 p.m., later than they usually ate dinner. Their parents would be wondering where they were, if Grant's team hadn't yet returned to signal a problem.

Before bringing the dogs in, Nina rummaged through the cabinets and crates. There wasn't much—a few cans of soup, chili, and baked beans, and some old packets of tuna and crackers. Nina placed everything she found on the table, including a dingy old pot and a remarkably clean butchering knife. Maybe they could fish the river and get food for the dogs. But ice fishing took hours, and they didn't have a tool to make a hole in the ice. Nina scrapped the idea. She would have to give the dogs tuna, jerky, and chicken soup, a meal that might upset their stomachs but would at least provide some sustenance. She would make the chili for herself and Grant.

Nina drew a breath, registering the severity of the situation. If Grant could hang on for two more days, Nina could get them through the long dark night, back to safety, back to a world she understood. They could prove Elias's guilt. Grant would tell the truth, and he would go to a hospital and be healed, and Nina would finally be able to breathe. Two days. Two days and miles of wilderness to go.

28

GRANT WOKE UP TO A WET NOSE ON HIS ARM.
He turned his head and locked eyes with Moose. The big
brown dog sat beside the cot, gazing at him with a friendly
expression. Grant moved his arm until he made contact with
the soft fur of the dog's side. Moose panted and tilted his head,
pleased as ever with the attention, no matter the circumstances.
The fire crackled and his sister talked to the dogs with a lilting
hum in her voice. If he closed his eyes, he could pretend he
was home, although the mere presence of the dogs inside was
enough to tell him that he was anywhere but home. And the
pain—a thick thrum of pain, a black hole of pain, red-hot pain
radiating from his stomach. Every inhale expanded the pain,
every exhale cooled it slightly, his ab muscles stretching and
receding. He found it difficult to ignore the sirens going off in
his brain, the systems in his body sounding their alarms. *You are
hurt. You are dying.*

Grant had known, moments after the bullet pierced his body, that the shot had been no accident. A tiny part of his mind had wondered if he was being too paranoid, overcome by the fear that had haunted him for the last few weeks. But he kept seeing Elias's cold, blue-eyed stare fixed on him as he left the office after speaking to the trooper at work. What had gone through his mind then? Surely that Grant was an outsider, not one of his own men who he could trust to keep a secret. And then when the police shut down the oil field again—Elias would have known that it hadn't happened because of his own original report. Everywhere Elias turned, from Clyde Lee's death to the police at the field, Grant was there—threatening the cover-up that Elias had tried to execute. In Elias's eyes he was the question mark, the thing preventing Elias from succeeding, from going about his job as if nothing was wrong. Nina had asked if he was certain it was Elias, and Grant admitted that it could be anyone trailing them through the wilderness, but no matter who it was, he knew Elias was holding the strings.

Grant opened his eyes again and turned his head. Nina's back was to him; she sat in front of the fire, doling out pieces of jerky to the dogs, who snapped the food up eagerly. It was a miracle they weren't all at each other's throats. The dogs were delighted to be inside, dispersing to sniff the entire cabin when Nina stood up. Grant tracked her as she crossed the room and gathered two bowls from one of the cabinets. Back at the fire, she ladled chili into the bowls and carried one over to Grant. He tried to sit up, gasping as the pain flared, turning his vision white. Nina grabbed his shoulders and helped him slide upright to rest against the wall. Grant's eyes still swam and his head pounded. Maybe Nina was right. Maybe he couldn't last for two days.

When the pain dimmed, he thanked her for the bowl of food and took a bite.

"How is it?"

"Better than anything you could make."

She pretended to hit him, but relief showed in her eyes, which had been his intention. As long as he cracked jokes, she wouldn't worry as much. "It's almost nine. Should we get out of here soon?"

"Yeah. After I eat." The canned chili did not, in fact, taste good, the tomato sauce sour, but Grant forced it down while trying not to worry about the expiration date. Nina ate quickly, efficiently, the way Grant imagined she might have scarfed down a meal while at work, just enough nutrients to sustain her through a few more hours of constant motion. The image of her in a restaurant kitchen reminded Grant of something he'd been meaning to tell her, at least before their argument. "I want to tell you something."

"Okay?" It came out as a question, her expression briefly flooded with fear. Grant knew how it must have sounded, like the prelude to a deathbed confession, but—maybe that's what it was. He had no idea if he would survive.

"Your restaurant, in Maine? I knew about it. I looked you up last year because . . . well, I wanted to know what you were up to. And I found this whole long article about your restaurant, you and that Micah guy, how you were bringing two new cuisines to the dining scene there."

Nina smiled. "Yeah. That article was cool, but I was so nervous to be interviewed and photographed. Micah said I looked like I was being held at gunpoint in the one where we're standing outside the restaurant." Her smile dropped, as if she realized the unfortunate timing of the gunpoint joke. "The instructions from the photographer were 'smile and relax.' I guess I'm not good at that."

Grant remembered the photo. Nina and the other chef— Micah, a big guy with a shaved head and two full sleeves of tattoos—in short-sleeve chef jackets, standing outside a brick building on a slanted sidewalk. Arms folded over their chests, Micah with an easy smile, Nina—yes, perhaps a little forced, bordering on a grimace, but happy. Brimming with possibility. "I thought the pictures were nice. And the website was cool. Fancy menu." He swallowed the last bite of chili and set the bowl aside. "Anyway, I wanted to hear it in your own words when you got back. But I also wanted you to know that I was thinking of you, all those years you were gone." Nina looked dangerously close to tears, so Grant tilted his head to indicate the wider room. "How are the dogs?"

Nina blinked away the moisture in her eyes. "Fine. Hungry, I'm sure, but they'll survive." Her tone contained doubt, but Grant couldn't say much to reassure her. The dogs would survive, but whether they'd have the strength to pull for two days straight off barely any food was a different question. As much as he wanted to ignore the thought, his survival depended on the dogs. Nina glanced at him. "Do you think they're looking for us?"

"Who?"

"Mom and Dad. Ila. August. Anyone."

Grant considered the question. On the ride from the lake to the cabin, to distract himself from each painful bump and jostle in the sled basket, he'd tried to picture his dogs returning home. Pine had been leading Grant's team for three years and knew all the routes; he'd be able to lead them home. But he worried about the other dogs getting distracted—catching a scent and pulling Pine off-balance or tangling in the lines and freezing to death. It seemed unlikely—the dogs were such bundles of relentless energy, surely they would gnaw through the tug lines before letting themselves freeze or starve. If—when—they made it home, Pine would lead them straight to the kennel door and sit as Grant had trained him to do. Eventually, his mother would look out the window—she would have glanced at the clock several times, wondering what was taking them so long— and see the team.

Then what? She'd tell everyone in town. A search party would form, snow machines and skiers and dog teams spreading out to find them. Maybe they wouldn't even need the two days to reach the oil field, maybe someone would find them sooner. August *lived* in the park and he was still devoted to Nina, it was plain even to Grant. He would search for them as soon as word got out that they were missing. He could picture Ila tearing off her apron and tossing it on the floor of The Spur, ready to join the search. The image made him smile, but it brought a wave of sadness, too. Ila hadn't been happy with him a few days ago and now he was putting her through even more trouble and worry. She deserved an enormous, monumental apology, whenever they were out of this mess. Maybe he'd use his savings to buy plane tickets to somewhere warm. They could take a cheap vacation, stay in a hostel somewhere, visit a beach. Grant had never seen a beach.

The sound of Nina talking to the dogs brought him back to reality. She was performing the tedious task of slipping them back into their harnesses, made more complicated by the wiggling mass of dogs vying for attention. Grant whistled, and a couple of the dogs broke off and bounded over to his bed, in good spirits despite their half-full stomachs. They bumped into the cot and leaned up against it, jostling it and aggravating the wound. Grant gritted his teeth and ran his right hand over their backs, trying to settle them down. Only Sage sat still, staring at Nina with rapt attention from a few feet away.

"Look at Sage," Grant said. "Don't you get creeped out by how she stares at you?"

Nina laughed. "She's different, that's for sure. It's too bad Mom didn't keep any of her siblings. She's such a good dog."

"I think that's why she had no trouble finding homes for them. Even as puppies, they were different."

Nina straightened up and walked toward the door, holding Sage by her harness. "Hang tight. This might take a while."

But by the time Nina returned the rest of the dogs were sitting patiently by the door, tails wagging, ready for the next stage of what they viewed as a fun adventure. Or maybe they were eager to head back home, where a full meal awaited them. Nina took the next two, Cedar and Ocean.

Grant attempted to swing his legs over the side of the cot and rode a wave of nausea from the pain. He collapsed back, sweat beading on his forehead. When he remained still, the pain ebbed—not enough to forget it existed, but he could focus enough to get through a conversation. When he moved, the tide surged back up to cover the shore, washing away all his thoughts. He dreaded another long, bumpy ride in the sled basket. But he would have to endure it.

When Nina finished with the dogs, she stood a few feet away with her hands on her hips, appraising him.

"Did you load the sled bags?" Grant asked. He'd been too overwhelmed to pay much attention to her movements for the last few minutes.

"Yes."

"You took everything?"

"Yes."

Grant lifted his head and pointed to the knife on the table. "Take that, too."

"Why?"

"Just take it. We don't have one in the sled and it might come in handy."

Nina rolled her eyes, picked up the knife, and exited the cabin. She returned a minute later, letting the door bang shut behind her. "There. Are you happy? It can stab you in the leg while you're in the basket."

"It'll be fine. Now help me up."

With Nina's hands on his back and shoulders, Grant had an easier time standing, though his vision still flickered and his stomach turned with nausea. *Maybe I shouldn't have eaten*, he thought, as he walked slowly beside his sister across the cabin. Every breath hurt; every step sparked pain that clouded his ability to think.

Eventually they made it to the sled, which Nina had maneuvered to right in front of the cabin. The dogs were barking and singing, eager to pull, and Nina shushed them to no avail. Grant worried that their calls might carry down into the valley, directing Elias to their exact location. But he said nothing as Nina helped him lower into the sled basket, overcome by pain. There wasn't much room for his legs with the stuffed sled bags, but he found a comfortable enough position.

"I'll be right back," Nina said.

Grant listened to the dogs and breathed the sharp air. The clouds from earlier had vanished, leaving a sky full of so many cold stars. The quarter moon provided plenty of light, though Grant couldn't remember if it was waxing or waning, if they were headed into more darkness or out of it. At least it wouldn't snow. The cabin door shut again, followed by Nina's footsteps. She materialized above him and covered him with the wool blanket. He hadn't even noticed its absence, too focused on the fire burning below his rib cage.

"We'll stop again in a few hours. Can we have some kind of signal if you start feeling worse?"

"Sure. I'll just scream."

"Grant," Nina said, her smile belying the firm tone of her voice. "Lift your arm if you need something, okay?"

"Okay." Between the sounds of the dogs running and panting and the sled sliding over the snow, it was hard to carry a conversation in the best of times. Nina needed to focus on the dogs, anyway, to give them the proper commands to reach the river and beyond. He just needed to keep breathing, which he hoped he could manage.

Nina lingered for a moment longer, as if she wanted to say something more, then turned away to step onto the runners. But something made her pause. She looked into the distance, down at the valley, and then whirled to face Grant. "I think I see something. A light."

"What?"

"Do you have your binoculars?"

Grant nodded and tried to reach into his jacket pocket, gasping with pain as his stomach twisted, frustrated that he couldn't accomplish such a simple task. Nina stepped above him and gently pulled the left side of his jacket back, reaching into the interior pocket. Wordlessly, she turned and lifted the binoculars to her eyes, fiddling with the focus. Grant waited anxiously; a long moment passed before she spoke again.

"It's a dogsled. The light seems brighter than a headlamp." She lowered the binoculars. "I don't recognize the dogs, and I can't make out the person. It's too dark. Do you think it's someone looking for us?"

A sinking feeling joined the pain in Grant's abdomen. He took the binoculars back and tossed them into the sled, his heart beating uncomfortably fast. "We need to go. Now."

Nina stared at him for a second. Something in his expression must have conveyed his fear, because seconds later Nina's boot collided with the snow hook with a *thump* and then they were off with a lurch, the dogs barking a few more times before they settled into their work. Grant closed his eyes. He was exhausted, though he didn't know if his injury would allow him to sleep. Half of him was comfortable—his full stomach, the warm blanket laid over his body. The other half knew only pain, and fear, as a desperate sort of certainty set in. He had thought it was Elias before, but now—he knew. There was more to the equation, but he would have to wait until they reached somewhere safer to tell Nina his theory.

GRANT DIDN'T KNOW how much time had passed before he heard Nina saying his name. He opened his eyes, struck by how his entire body ached. He opened his jaw, testing to see if the muscles still worked. Then he turned his head. Nina came into view, her expression worried.

"Look."

Grant twisted further, trying to follow where she pointed. Something red was attached to the side of the mountain. He blinked, trying to make sense of it. A fire, burning bright and orange. The mountain was some distance away now; they were closer to the river.

"It's the cabin," Nina said, somewhat impatiently.

"Shit. Did you put out the fire?"

"Of course I did. I checked when I went back in for your blanket. I threw snow on it before we left. It was definitely out."

"What about the candles?"

"I blew those out, too."

"So, Elias did that."

"I think so."

"Which means he can clearly follow our trail."

"Right." Nina chewed her lip. "What if I brush over our

tracks once we get to the river? I could park the sled and then backtrack on foot a bit."

"That might work, but he'll know you were headed for the river all along."

"It's still worth a try." Nina's brow furrowed, determination clearly written across her face. "Fuck that guy. I'm not letting him find us."

"Better go, then," Grant said, and it was like all the oxygen left his body. He drew a shuddering breath, thankful that Nina had already gotten back on the runners and didn't notice how weak he had become. Hot and cold all at once, sweating and shivering, he sank lower beneath the blanket. He hoped they made it before infection set in. *I can't die*, he thought. *Not yet. Not before I have a chance to make things right.*

29

AT SOME POINT NINA STOPPED LOOKING OVER HER
shoulder, maybe around the time the burning cabin went out
of view. She told herself that if Elias—or someone else—was on
their trail, seeing him would make no difference. They would
shoot her in the back and that would be the end of it. As long as
she focused on the dogs, they had a better chance of escaping.

And the dogs were running well. Heads down, some trotting,
some loping, flicking their ears back when Nina gave them
commands. She estimated they were traveling at about fifteen
miles an hour, but didn't know the exact distance to the oil
field—only that it would require multiple days and nights of
travel. The dogs were content following Sage's lead, and Sage
seemed to understand where they were headed. Nina didn't
like to think of the dogs as more than what they were, but
she shared a connection with Sage that she couldn't remember
having with another dog, as if Sage could read her thoughts.

Maybe it was the gravity of the situation sinking in, turning her a little giddy and delusional, making her imagine that she alone wasn't responsible for her brother's life, that someone else was watching out for her. Even if that someone was a dog.

The hunting trails had given way to wilderness, and Nina occasionally had to stop and break trail, a slow, laborious process of packing down the snow so that the sled could slide smoothly. The orange glow had faded from the sky, emphasizing how far they were from the oil field, from relative safety. Her work would also only make it easier for Elias to catch them. But it was too much to ask of the dogs, to pull the sled through loose snow up to their chests. And if their drive dipped and they quit pulling, Nina had no idea what she would do. Each stop she checked their paws, too, attaching pairs of booties as needed, a clock ticking loudly in her head.

The third time she broke trail, Nina dug through the sled basket and doled out the last packet of jerky along with a few handfuls of kibble. She checked on Grant, too—he was sleeping, or something like it. His complexion had paled, but maybe it was only the moonlight and snow reflecting off his skin. Nina was overwhelmed by the immensity of her task. She crouched beside the dogs in turn, running her hands over their fur, checking their paws for ice, whispering encouragement into their ears. The dogs licked her face or rolled onto their backs to ask for belly rubs. She indulged them, but only briefly. They had to keep moving.

THEY REACHED THE river in the early hours of the morning. Nina's eyes burned from straining in the dark; her eyelids grated like a fine layer of sandpaper every time she blinked. She hadn't used the headlamp yet, because the sky was clear, the moonlight unimpeded.

"Go on!" she called to Sage, encouraging her lead dog down the riverbank. Sage hesitated, then took a small leap forward, landing on the snow-covered river. The swing dogs followed. Too late, Nina realized that the sled would crash down onto the ice. The ice would probably hold—but it wouldn't be pleasant for Grant.

Sure enough, he cried out when the sled jolted onto the river. Nina called to the dogs until they came to a stop.

"Sorry, sorry," she said, stepping off the runners and peering into the basket.

"Shit," Grant muttered, adjusting his position. "Are we at the river?"

"Yeah. I'm sorry. I should have walked them down."

"It's okay," he replied through gritted teeth. "Go cover the tracks."

"I'm going to," Nina said, trying not to sound indignant. With the snow hook set and the knife in her hand, she walked away from the dogs, though her instincts urged her not to. The snow wasn't as deep on the river; what if the dogs yanked free and took off with Grant? Nina doubted they would leave the riverbed, though, and the dogs were tired. A few of them watched her leave while the others sat panting. Nina hurried up the bank and into a nearby stand of spruce trees. She cut a couple large branches off a tree, thankful that Grant had urged her to take the knife. Using the branches as brooms, she swept over the sled's tracks in the snow, walking as far from the river as she dared. She stood listening for a long minute, but the entire world was quiet. If she hadn't left the dogs and her brother behind, Nina might have believed she was the only living being on earth.

NINA CALLED "WHOA" to the dogs hours later. She had noticed their steady pace slowing. This was an enormous task—they didn't usually pull for more than a few hours at a time. The dogs came to a halt, some turning to face the sled. She stepped off the runners and made her way shakily to the front of the line. It was strange to walk, to take steps, after so long balancing on the runners. She checked the team one by one—all fine, no signs of injury.

She shook Grant awake. His condition had worsened; she couldn't pretend otherwise. His skin looked ghostlike; his eyes were glazed over. Nina wished they had brought more than a single bottle of water.

"I think we should rest," she said.

He blinked once, enough of a response. Nina walked to Sage and slipped her hand through the top of the dog's harness, leading her up the riverbank and toward a stand of trees, where she hoped they would be out of sight. She set the snow hook and told the dogs to stay, then repeated the process of cutting two tree branches to sweep over their tracks. When she was finished, she surveyed her work with dismay. It was obvious where the sled had turned and left the river. If Elias was still following them, he would have no trouble tracing their path. Exhaustion prevented Nina from devoting more energy to worrying. She dropped the branches above the riverbank and trudged back into the trees.

They needed a fire. Nina wished she hadn't used the fire starter already, but she hadn't understood the magnitude of the situation when they'd first set foot in the cabin. The wood of the snow-covered trees surrounding them was probably too moist, but it was worth a shot.

An hour later, one of the twigs finally, finally caught fire. The little flame licked up the twig and burned long enough to catch another on fire. The kindling continued to light and Nina sat back in the snow, breathing a sigh of relief. She'd found a pile of mostly dry sticks after searching the area for a third time. The bigger logs were all branches cut from trees, and she had doubts about those catching. But if the kindling got hot enough, they too would burn. The damp wood released a thick smoke that drifted in Nina's direction, filling her nose and stinging her eyes.

She turned away from the fire. The dogs were already fed, using up most of the supplies. A couple cans of tuna were still tucked in the sled bag. The dogs eyed her hungrily as she walked past them. Nina considered, again, trying to break a hole in the river ice and fish. But it might take hours, and they didn't have that kind of time. Besides, all she really wanted to do was lie down by the fire and rest. Thirty minutes, an hour—it didn't matter, but Nina couldn't stay awake and functioning much longer.

Grant was still in a fitful state between waking and sleeping. Nina didn't dare check his wound again—no matter what shape it was in, she couldn't help him. He was shivering, but when she laid the back of her bare hand against his forehead, his skin was hot.

"What do you need?" she asked him.

He opened his eyes, though they took a long time to focus on her. "I'm cold."

"Okay." Nina dug through the sled bag and pulled out the spare sweater, socks, gloves, and hat. Grant already wore his own gloves and hat, but maybe he could fit two pairs. She laid the sweater over him, beneath the blanket, hesitant to move him too much lest she cause him pain. She couldn't fit the gloves over his other pair, but took the socks and stretched them over his gloves, like makeshift mittens. A smile ghosted his lips when he looked down at his hands.

"Tell me about that man again. The one who bought the dogs."

Nina blinked. She hadn't been expecting the question, but she regretted that she hadn't yet had a chance to tell Grant the truth. Strangely, she remembered Frankie's face more clearly from the mug shot than from when he'd bought the dogs. Those startling blue eyes, the remorseless expression. She gave his physical description again, then squeezed her eyes shut. "I didn't tell you this, Grant, but he's wanted in Montana. I looked him up a couple weeks ago. He's going by a fake name. His legal name is Waylon Turcotte. I found an article about his drug trafficking charges. The mug shot, it's absolutely him. I meant to tell you, but with everything that's been going on . . ." She trailed off and drew a breath. "You were angry at me, and I didn't think it was important enough to risk upsetting you more."

"I wish I could see that mug shot."

Nina patted her pockets, trying to remember where she'd stashed her phone the previous afternoon. "I have a picture of it," she said, once she'd located her phone, sacrificing her right hand to the cold air as she unlocked it and opened her photo app. The phone's battery percentage was low, but there was no service in the wilderness anyway. She pulled up the eerie image of the blue-eyed man and turned the screen to show Grant. Grim recognition crossed his face.

"I knew it."

"What?" Nina leaned forward.

"That's Elias."

The puzzle pieces snapped together. "Elias is Frankie Campbell?"

"I think so." Grant's right hand squeezed into a fist and released. "Your description of him, that photo—it matches perfectly. He must have created another fake identity. I know Elias was one of the first hires at Brooks Valley. I mean, where would you go if you wanted to disappear?"

"Here," Nina said. "But I don't understand. Why did he buy the dogs?"

"For this."

"To . . ."

"Chase us. To chase me."

Nina's eyes widened. It suddenly made sense—why he'd asked for the glass of water. To get inside the house, to take something of theirs. Grant's missing sweater. "Because the dogs know our scent."

"Honey and Wilder do," Grant replied. "I knew he had something to do with it, but I thought maybe he'd sent one of his buddies after us. I guess we won't know unless we see him ourselves, but we know the person following us is on a sled, and now we know the guy who bought the dogs is actually Elias. It makes sense that it's him out here, if he bought the dogs himself."

Ugly, bitter sense, but sense nonetheless. "How do you think he got hired?"

"No idea. I guess he's got a hookup for good fake IDs. He must have created the identity of Elias Woodsman once he got out on bail, and then fled. Maybe the oil company wasn't running the most stringent background checks when they first started hiring."

"Or he has friends on the inside." Nina exhaled. "At least we know who we're dealing with." Despite the myriad of thoughts that swirled in her brain, she needed rest to make sense of them. "Do you think it's safe if I lie down for a bit?"

Grant blinked, slowly. "No idea."

"Yeah. Me either. But the dogs need to rest, too."

"Wait," Grant said, as she started to turn away. "Take the gun."

Nina reached into the basket and pulled out the Remington. She knew how to shoot but didn't think she was a great shot—both her siblings were better. Still, Grant was right. If Frankie caught up to them, she needed to be prepared, whatever that meant. The shotgun was loaded with slugs powerful enough to stop a bear.

Nina carried the shotgun a few feet away, closer to the fire, which to her relief had grown a respectable amount. She mimicked the dogs, digging a soft trench out of the snow to nestle her body into. Grant's realization repeated itself in her brain. A dangerous armed man was chasing them with their own dogs. It was painful to think of Honey and Wilder loping after them, eager to be reunited with their old owners, clueless that they held the key to Elias's—Waylon's—goal of murdering Grant. But they had a plan. She hoped it was good enough, and that they had enough of a lead on Elias to warrant a short rest.

It was freezing, and she spent several minutes shivering before her body relaxed and began to be overtaken by sleep. The fire crackled and hissed pleasantly beside her. It didn't offer much warmth, but Nina welcomed anything it had to give. Overhead, the sky yawned dark and endless, dotted with a staggering number of stars behind the thin veil of smoke drifting past. Nina remembered, as a child, sitting in the backyard on warm nights and trying to count all the stars. Audrey would roll her eyes and say it was impossible, but Nina was certain that there had to be a way to determine the true number. Sometimes her father sat on the back stoop, drinking a beer, awake all night on the summer days that provided only an hour or two of darkness. Nina didn't yet understand, or at least didn't believe, that everyone in the world didn't grow up the way she did, with an endless wilderness for a backyard, huge mountains in the distance, days that went unmarred by darkness. Or the opposite—the long winter nights, a cold that seeped in to inhabit your body. She didn't mind the winters, the nights spent curled up in front of the woodstove with her siblings or playing the familiar set of board games stored in a beat-up cabinet in the hallway. There had been no television then, nothing but the sound of their own voices for entertainment. Sometimes she wondered why she had left it all behind.

THE GROWL CUT through Nina's dreams. An engine thrumming low, the heat of a car melting the snow beneath it. A bear waking up from hibernation. The fur standing up on the back of a dog's neck. She opened her eyes and drew a breath of sharp, cold air, opening her lungs. She smelled something earthy, like a damp forest. The growl sounded again and Nina realized it hadn't come from her dreams.

She flipped onto her stomach and sat up, trying to make sense of the darkness. She had no idea how long she'd been asleep. Her mouth was dry and her eyes ached. Then she caught sight of the dark shape in the shadows and froze.

Bear, she thought, but no—taller. *Moose.* A bull moose at the edge of the little camp, pawing at the snow, bony antlers lowered and aimed at her dogs. At Sage. Who stood bravely, hackles raised, teeth bared, not afraid of the creature ten times her size.

Nina didn't have time to think. Moose occasionally attacked and killed dogs, mistaking them for wolves. It happened on the Iditarod sometimes, if a sled team unknowingly crossed a moose's path. A musher who dispatched a moose was required to gut it before continuing on with the race, so that the meat could be distributed to local families. But no one ever hoped to encounter a moose unless prepared for a hunt. They were aggressive and could easily kill a dog with their antlers or their hooves. *Scary as a bear*, her dad used to say.

Nina swallowed, yanked off her mittens, and reached for the shotgun. All the dogs were on their feet, some growling and barking, some cowering away. Maybe if she fired a warning shot the moose would flee. Nina flipped the safety off and told herself not to hesitate. The moose was still swinging its gigantic head and tossing snow with its right front hoof. If she waited any longer, it would charge.

She aimed the shotgun left of the moose and fired.

The bull startled, but it didn't run. It leaped sideways and then lowered its head and charged right for the dogs. They had no way to escape. In mere seconds, at least one of the dogs would end up with a brutal injury, if not dead. Ignoring the ringing in her ears, she cycled the action and aimed the gun at the moose, at the heart. *Shoot the lungs.* Her dad's voice in her head, from all the hunting trips she had gone on growing up. Nina had never shot a moose, but her father had. Enough meat to last all winter. *I don't want to kill you*, Nina thought, and squeezed the trigger.

The dogs were still producing a deafening chorus of sound. Nina blinked, afraid that one or more of them had been crushed beneath the moose's hooves. The bull took a couple stumbling steps and then fell to the ground, bleeding from a jagged hole behind its right shoulder. The dogs were straining against their tug lines, barking and howling, frenzied by the massive creature that had collapsed a few feet away from them. But their voices sounded muted to Nina, coming from somewhere beyond the wall of high-pitched noise that rang in her ears. She heard, faintly, Grant calling her name, and remembered her brother with a jolt. He might not be able to see the moose; he probably had no idea what Nina was shooting at. She set the Remington down and staggered to the sled, her hands shaking.

"It's okay," she said. "I'm okay. It was a moose."

Grant stared at her through bleary eyes. "A moose?"

"Yeah. I fell asleep and I woke up to it attacking the dogs. Or at least threatening to."

"Cook it," Grant said.

Nina thought she had misunderstood him at first. Maybe he was still only half awake, or his body was too consumed with fighting off infection for his words to make sense. *Cook it.*

"Feed it to the dogs."

"Oh." Nina paused, her mind racing. She glanced over her shoulder to where the huge animal lay, bleeding into the snow. "How?"

"The knife."

Nina didn't know why she hadn't reached the same conclusion. Perhaps because the task seemed impossible, with one old, questionably sharp butcher knife. Nina knew how to field dress small game like rabbits, and even Dall sheep, but it had been years since she had hunted. She tried to remember how her father dressed a moose but couldn't picture where to slide the knife beneath the animal's thick hide. Hadn't he used a handsaw for the task? But Grant was right—they couldn't waste the meat, not when they had no other food to eat. She could feed the entire team. She just had to pretend she was back in the kitchen of 4950, cutting up a roast pig with Micah.

Carefully, Nina dug through the sled bag and pulled out the knife. It was duller than the ones she was used to using, but the cuts didn't need to be pretty, just efficient. She took the head-lamp, too, and switched it on before approaching the moose cautiously, eyeing the shotgun she'd left beside the burned-out fire. Now that the moose was down, she doubted it would get back on its feet, even if it was still alive. But she had heard many stories of moose trampling hunters. She wished it had fallen farther from the dogs, who were still throwing a fit, but she would have to ignore them. The moose's flanks remained still. The bear slug had found its way to the moose's heart or lungs—either way, it was dead. Again, her father's voice came to her. *Touch the eye.* Nina did, gently, and the moose didn't flinch.

She studied the beast for a moment. The bull appeared to be in its prime—palmate antlers that Nina knew would have fallen off by January, should the moose have lived, and a large dewlap beneath its chin. It was probably still full of testosterone from the fall rut, ready to pick a fight. Only it had stumbled across a team of sled dogs instead of another bull.

Nina squatted in the snow, overwhelmed by the enormity of the task. Her father had definitely used a saw, she was certain. She would have to make do without, and not worry about all the other rules, too, all the steps between dressing the moose and skinning it. They needed meat, that was all. As much as the dogs could eat now. The rest would have to be left behind.

Inserting the knife through the moose's right hindquarter, she tilted it, muscles tensing as she sawed the hide loose from the flesh. The sinew gave way and she let out a breath. It would be a long, arduous process, but she could skin this side of the bull. Her father hunted moose with a .243 Winchester; the Black Magic bear slug had likely damaged the meat around the shoulder. But a single hindquarter would be enough.

Nina moved the knife, sawing as she went, flipping back the hide to reveal the glistening meat underneath. Her gloves became slick, but there was another pair in the sled. The dogs had grown quiet, so she listened, too, for the sound of anything else approaching. Now that the adrenaline had worn off, she worried that the gunshots had given Elias an exact pinpoint to their location. That was the worst-case scenario—if anyone was searching for them, they would follow the sound of gunfire, too. An entire night had passed. In a few more hours, weak daylight would spill over the valley. Their tracks would become more visible—again, a bad thing if Elias was still on their trail, but good if anyone else was too, or instead. The valley remained quiet, save for the sawing of the knife beneath the hide. She couldn't see Grant but assumed—hoped—he had gone back to resting.

Her arm muscles ached by the time she removed the hide from the hindquarter. Nina thought of the multitude of ways they'd served moose at 4950—burgers, steaks, roast, curries, meatballs, chili, shepherd's pie, always infused with some spark of Hawaiian flavor. It had been a centerpiece as much as the Pacific Ocean fishes, the opah and opakapaka. Nina had met so many people who had never tasted moose and loved it after trying it. The moose from the farm had an easy life and tasted similar to grass-fed beef. This bull, Nina knew, had been surviving on a winter diet of twigs and spruce needles and would therefore be much gamier. But the dogs wouldn't mind.

She began cutting off strips of meat and stacking them in the snow beside her. Normally her family would be careful not to dirty the meat after a hunt, but she needed to work quickly, and whatever bit of dirt the meat picked up wouldn't harm the dogs, especially after it was cooked. If she could get another fire going. She took in the rest of the bull while she worked, the part still covered in brown hide. She hoped it wouldn't go to waste; perhaps a hungry pack of wolves would catch the scent and come to scavenge. They wouldn't ask questions about the partially butchered moose. But Elias would know exactly what it meant.

30

THE MOOSE CAME TO GRANT IN HIS DREAMS,
towering over Nina, scattering the dogs left and right with
its bloodstained antlers. It had human eyes, blue eyes, and
it bellowed when Nina shot it, not with a gun but with an
arrow. Grant kept waking up, waiting for Nina to tell him
that they were moving again, but each time he heard only
soft sounds, the whispers of the forest. Eventually he smelled
smoke and the rich scent of roasting meat, which meant that
Nina had succeeded in butchering the moose with the old
hunting knife. He still couldn't believe that his sister, a chef,
hadn't thought to take the knife from the cabin. But she had
been distracted, focused on keeping him alive.

Nina appeared above him, holding a cooked strip of meat.
Her gloves were stained with blood. "Are you hungry?"

Grant's stomach turned at the thought of eating. He loved
moose, thought it was the best meat Alaska had to offer, but the

pain in his stomach overrode any hunger he might feel. "I want to stand up," he said.

Nina frowned. The gradually lightening sky spread behind her, the branches of spruce trees framing her face. Grant had the impression of God hovering over him, deciding his fate. If God came in the form of bossy older sisters. "I don't know if that's a good idea."

"Please. I feel like I'm trapped in a coffin."

It was true. He'd been awake most of the night, held in the clutches of fear. Though travel had been much smoother along the river, they still hit occasional bumps, and the sled never stopped rattling. Nina talked to the dogs near constantly too, encouraging them along with her voice. But his brain sought unconsciousness to escape the pain, so as soon as they'd stopped in the stand of trees, he had fallen asleep. Now Grant felt weak, but he had no idea if it was from pain or from hunger.

Nina's expression softened. "Okay. Hold on." She disappeared from view and one of the dog's jaws snapped as it devoured the strip of meat. He held his breath while Nina slipped her hands beneath his legs, helping him over the side of the basket. He knew it was coming and so didn't panic when his vision clouded with stars. A moment later his feet were on solid ground and he stood, swaying a bit as Nina braced him. The world came back into its proper order: ground, then trees, then sky, Nina's face below him rather than above. She helped him lower to a seat near the fire, which was small, but apparently hot enough to cook the meat. He turned his head slowly, trying not to make himself dizzy, and looked at the moose's body. He always forgot how big they were. "Will you eat now?" Nina asked.

Grant nodded, knowing that if he consumed even a bite of food, Nina would relax. She placed a strip of meat in his gloved hand and kept her eyes on him as he chewed, then swallowed. His throat narrowed and he resisted the urge to gag.

He had never had unseasoned moose before. It tasted charred and smoky, and the texture was too dry. It was gamy and difficult to chew. The snow on the ground suddenly seemed more appetizing.

As if anticipating his thirst, Nina held out the water bottle. "There's a little bit left. Then I'll fill it with snow and melt it over the fire."

Grant's vision swam again and he wondered if he was about to pass out. He managed to swallow the water and handed the empty bottle back to his sister. "Do you think he's still following us?"

She hesitated. "I don't know."

"Maybe we were wrong to not go back home." He wished he had worked up the courage to talk to the police sooner. Maybe Nina was right, and they would have protected him. When he thought of the last few weeks, all he pictured was a series of mistakes. He should have never driven the body to the woods in the first place. He should have jumped in the truck and taken off to camp, reported the accident the instant it happened. Then he wouldn't be dying of a gunshot wound in the wilderness, and maybe Audrey would still be alive.

"I think he would have killed us." Nina paused. "Can you hang on for another day?"

"Who knows." He couldn't help being bleak, with the dark turn his thoughts had taken, but Nina understood, or at least accepted his answer. She pulled two more strips of meat off the stick she'd been using as a skewer and distributed them to the dogs.

"I want to wait one more hour before we get moving again. Let them digest."

An hour seemed meaningless; all time did. But for an hour, Grant could sit by the fire, breathing in the fresh scent of spruce and snow. Despite the enormous pain in his stomach, the simplicity of the surroundings still brought him a small comfort. The dogs were in good spirits, tracking Nina as she cooked meat over the fire and fed it to them, occasionally eating a piece herself. It reminded Grant of the camping trips they'd gone on as kids, piling tents and sleeping bags into the truck bed during the summer months and staying up much of the night, reveling in the long sunset. Their father would tell stories about running the Iditarod and the Yukon Quest. Back then, Grant had dreamed about one day becoming a musher himself, but he had lost interest as he grew older. He never became tired of the dogs, but he stopped thinking of them as his future. Now he pondered again what it would be like to set out in the wilderness under different circumstances, with a clear finish line, without a madman chasing them. When all this was over, if he survived, maybe he could convince Nina to train for a long-distance race with him. They'd have to enter as separate teams, but it would be fun to spend days traveling together, testing whose dogs were faster.

Grant noticed that the landscape had gradually become more blue than black, another sign of the coming daylight. For less than five hours, they'd be able to see better. Perhaps they could travel faster, too. A wave of pain washed over Grant again and he gritted his teeth. He hadn't seen his own wound yet; he'd been too afraid. But now, with Nina still distracted by the dogs, Grant unzipped his coat and pulled up the layers of shirts, wincing as the fabric brushed against his sensitive skin. The lower part of his abdomen—red skin, inflamed and angry. He dropped the shirts, unable to look further. Despite his best efforts to overcome it, Grant had always been squeamish. Injuries on the dogs he could handle—alleviating their pain was always the priority—but he remembered covering his eyes or leaving the room whenever Audrey or Nina came inside with a bloody cut, crying for their mother. Audrey had broken her arm

once from falling off an ATV, and their mother had fashioned a
splint and waited until the next day to drive her to the hospital,
hours away. Grant had been impressed by the bubblegum-pink
cast Audrey returned with, and the next day all the kids at school
had lined up to sign it.

Grant glanced at the sled, remembering Audrey's urn, and
marveled at how the three of them were still together. *Nothing
bad will happen to us with Audrey here,* he thought, although he
realized it was nonsensical. Wherever she was, he hoped she was
watching out for them.

31

DAYLIGHT BROUGHT RELIEF AND ANXIETY IN EQUAL measure. Nina no longer strained her vision to find the dogs' path, but she couldn't stop looking back, certain that Elias was right behind them. She walked the dogs and the sled up the riverbank some distance, a quarter mile at least, maybe half—she couldn't tell, but she wanted to make it harder for Elias to pick up their trail. Breaking trail had been exhausting, and now her legs ached as she balanced on the runners. Raven, one of the team dogs, had backed off a bit, and Nina periodically called encouragement, worry rising in her chest. Raven was paired with her sister, Wren, who was particularly susceptible to the other dogs' attitudes. If Raven quit pulling, Wren would too, and Nina had no idea what she would do then. The only logical answer would be to unclip both dogs, but setting them loose in the wilderness this far from home seemed cruel. Maybe they would trail behind the sled.

Sage, at least, was leading as well as ever. Her head was

down, her whitish paws flashing quickly over the smooth snow. Inhaling the cold, sharp air had made Nina's throat raw, but she knew the dogs loved it. *They'll be ready for the Iditarod after this*, Nina thought.

She heard a crack and the sled jolted. A couple of the dogs turned their heads, causing them to bump into each other even as they moved forward. Wren's tail tucked and Nina's stomach dropped. The snow-covered river ice appeared undisturbed. She let the dogs trot for a few more minutes and then called "whoa," bringing them to a halt.

She stepped off the runners and crouched beside Raven, running her hands over the black dog's back and legs. Raven's paws looked fine, and she wagged her tail and licked Nina's face. Raven always made Nina smile—she had the body of a stretched-out black Lab, with long legs, floppy ears, and a sweet expression. It was unusual for her to lack enthusiasm, but maybe it was too much, this relentless run away from home. Or the moose meat had made her sick—Nina had feared that outcome ever since she fed the dogs. Maybe she hadn't cooked the meat well enough, or had fed the dogs too much at once, or made them pull too soon after eating. Negative scenarios flooded Nina's mind, but Raven remained bright-eyed and cheerful, no worse for the wear. Nina reached across to pet the smaller Wren, who bared her teeth in a wolfish smile, her entire body wriggling with the force of her wagging tail.

"Good girl. You're fine, aren't you?" Nina whispered. On the way back to the runners she glanced at Grant, but his eyes were shut. His body had an air of fragility beneath the wool blanket, like an overgrown child. Nina turned her eyes to the sky, to the thick gray clouds that covered it. The air smelled of snow. She shivered, knowing how little daylight remained. Maybe they could camp again tonight, but for now, they needed to press on.

THE SNOW BEGAN to fall with darkness, thick white flakes at first, thinning out to tiny pellets that stung Nina's face. The visibility lessened and the temperature dropped. Nina tried switching on the headlamp but found it only illuminated the falling snow in a disconcerting way, as if she were passing through a million white curtains. Without moonlight it was difficult to see, but at least they were following the riverbed. The dogs wouldn't deviate from the smooth snow to attempt scrambling up the bank, not unless Nina told them to.

An hour passed, then another. In a trancelike state, Nina observed the wheel dogs trot at a steady pace, carrying her into an abyss of white. The fatigue almost made her forget why she was on the sled at all, and for a moment Nina daydreamed they were returning home, back to a warm meal and a pile of blankets in front of the woodstove. With a jolt she remembered Audrey's ashes, the gunshots, Grant's desperate expression. Nina knew she needed a break, to sleep for an hour or two, to let her brain reset itself before she fell asleep standing up and tumbled off the runners, losing the dogs and her brother to the darkness.

They were in an area without trees now. The river ran parallel to the mountains instead of straight toward them, which meant that—eventually—it would curve away from them, in the direction of the oil field. Nina knew the area around the drill sites was forested, but this part of the valley was relatively flat and offered little shelter. But maybe the snowstorm was enough to hide them. She would have to take that gamble.

WITHOUT TREES, there was no fire. Nina's brain came to this realization slowly. She surveyed the area she'd chosen for camp—a soft undulation in the snow, a hill rising away from them, doing its best impression of a little mountain. But no trees. Nina looked down at her hands. She had taken her mittens and gloves off—why? Her fingers were bright red. *The sled bag.* She had needed the extra dexterity to dig through it. A meager number of supplies left—two cans of beans, the Snickers bar, and one of the empty jerky bags that she'd filled with moose meat. At least the dogs could eat that. They were all watching her, their faces dusted with snow, ice on the fur around their snouts where drool had frozen. The wind had picked up, gusting around Nina now as she fed them, listening to the snapping of their jaws. She stumbled and nearly fell on the way back to the sled, eyeing Grant with something like envy, because he occupied the basket. In different circumstances, she'd give anything to curl up in the uncomfortable basket and sleep, just for an hour or two. But she would have to make do with the snow.

Before she let herself sleep, Nina reached beneath the wool blanket and pulled the sweater up, using it to partially cover Grant's face. His forehead was already covered with snow; she brushed it off. He shifted when she touched him, as if to move away, his expression twisted in discomfort. He was getting worse, she knew. Infection was setting in, or whatever organ had been pierced by the bullet was failing. She could get him to the oil field tomorrow, if only he held on.

NINA WOKE UP between two dogs. She didn't remember falling asleep but some unconscious part of her brain must have guided her to the warmest place. Cedar was curled up against her chest, Ocean against her back. Cedar's fur, already white, was covered with fluffy snowflakes. As she sat up, so did Sage—the lead dog had been using her hat as a pillow. Nina removed the layers on her right hand and brushed her face, thankful for the gaiter that kept her relatively warm. Her hand looked okay, too—red, but not frostbitten. She flexed her fingers a few times, stretching out the stiffness, and forced herself to her feet. The snow had stopped but it was still windy, a fine layer of powder blowing across the ground, thin clouds racing across the sky. Nina had the impression that everything around her was moving, as if she were on the water instead of on steady ground.

She walked down the line, checking the dogs one by one—all alive, all happy as ever. Even Raven and Moose, with their thinner coats, appeared recharged from the rest. Nina hesitated beside the sled, afraid to peel back the sweater. The blanket rose and fell once, a tiny movement, a breath too small to fill her brother's lungs. Nina pulled back the sweater and laid the back of her bare right hand to Grant's forehead. He was burning up. His cheeks were red, and his skin was clammy. Nina's heart sank. She wanted to shake him awake, to see greater proof that he was alive, but she stepped back. His body needed to conserve its energy.

Nina turned and froze. Something in the distance caught her eye. A pinprick of light. She squinted, in case it was a trick of her imagination. She didn't know how long she had slept but imagined it wasn't enough to truly rest her mind, especially sleeping on the hard, cold ground. But as she watched, the light moved, bobbing in the distance, like a star hurtling toward her. The light meant one of two things: rescue, or Elias. She couldn't bet on the good option.

Nina dived for the sled basket, gently moving Grant's legs

aside as she rummaged through it. He groaned, and she wondered if she had hurt him, or if he was simply feverish and disoriented. Her hands found the sled bags, the clothes piled around Grant, Audrey's urn. The cold metal of the shotgun. She lifted the Remington and slung it over her shoulder, then looked at the light again. She couldn't tell if it was closer—still a dot in the distance—but she knew it was headed right for them. She couldn't continue to wait as the light approached. Her dogs were swift and well-conditioned. They could outrun the other team.

Summoning her reserves of strength, Nina grabbed Sage's harness and guided the lead dog down the riverbank, back onto the ice. The fresh snow had settled in a light, dry layer over the previous snowfall, and Nina had doubts about how well the sled would glide over it. But there was no alternative; travel anywhere but the river would be near impossible. With the dogs lined up and untangled, she stole one more glance back. For a moment she thought the light had vanished, but then it flashed again. They were lower down on the riverbank, not able to see as far. Nina kicked the snow hook free and shouted for the dogs to run.

And for a while, they did. They were enthusiastic to pull again even on relatively empty stomachs. Raven and Wren matched pace with the others, bounding over the snow, kicking up powder with their paws. Nina let out a breath and pulled the Snickers bar from her coat pocket, holding on to the sled bar for dear life with one hand while she used the other to unwrap and devour the candy bar. It struck her as wrong to eat something so saccharine in such a dire situation, but it brought a small comfort, too. She hadn't had many sweets since returning home. She thought of Micah, of his love for Twix, his indulgence during a long night in the kitchen when nothing seemed to go right. He kept a bin of them nestled among the ingredients, restocked it at the nearest gas station.

A prickle on her skin, the hair on the back of her neck standing up, made Nina turn again. Her stomach dropped. The light was visible directly behind, which meant whoever was following them had reached the long, straight stretch of river they had traveled earlier that day. There was no way the team behind would lose their trail; Nina had been too exhausted to attempt covering their tracks earlier, and besides, there still wasn't a tree in sight. They were too vulnerable, too exposed.

"Go on! Good dogs!" Nina called, hoping her voice would encourage them to keep loping along. She got a few tail wags in response but knew the dogs were probably already putting in maximum effort. The wind gusted, lifting her loose hair from her neck. Thin clouds covered the moon, plunging the landscape into darkness and then pulling back, letting the moon shine its light. And the stars: a brilliant sky above, an astronomer's dream. Nina marveled at the beauty, at how Alaska could still astonish her even when her heart was gripped with fear.

The ice cracked, eerie but familiar, the pinging and twinging like video game sound effects. It was normal for the ice to crack as it expanded and contracted throughout the cold season. But she panicked when the sled shifted.

Nina's stomach looped in the same sensation of driving a car quickly over a hilly road, the hint of defying gravity. The creak and groan of ice shards splitting was deafening, and then came the rush of water—exploding over the break in the ice, rushing with a desperate force downriver, in the direction they were headed. Nina cursed and tried to balance on the runners, but the force of the sled slamming back onto the ice threw her. For a second she was airborne, arms pinwheeling as she tried to catch herself, then her left shoulder crashed onto the ice, followed by the rest of her body. Nina gasped from both pain and surprise, the shotgun leaving its full imprint on her body as she landed on it. Momentarily breathless and terrified that the ice wouldn't hold her weight, she scrambled up, tearing the sling strap from her shoulder and letting the gun fall to the ground. She surveyed the scene: The sled tilted precariously, one side dangling over a moderate hole in the ice from which black water rushed. Grant was still in the basket—thank God—though half the blanket had fallen into the water, soaked through.

And the dogs—Nina leaped up and ran back to the sled, not caring if she broke through the ice, too, because no matter what, she had to try her best to save them. The front half of the team were straining against their harnesses, tails tucked, pure stress visible in their bodies. And one of the dogs—Shadow, poor Shadow—had fallen into the water. His dark paws clung to the ice, damp ears flattened against his head. If she didn't move quickly, Moose would slip in with him, and Nina didn't know if she had the strength to haul out both dogs.

She circled the hole, adrenaline carrying her close to the edge, and yanked the layers off her hands, tossing them behind her. She gasped at the shock of ice-cold water that lapped over her hands as she grabbed Shadow's harness, hauling the dripping dog back to safety. He jumped forward, desperate to have his paws back on solid ground, and Nina realized her mistake.

The rest of the team still faced straight ahead, leaning into their harnesses, and she knew they would lunge forward, pulling the sled straight into the water. Grant would be plunged into the river, and there was nothing Nina could do to keep him from being swept away.

"Whoa!" she called, her voice hoarse with desperation, but it was too late.

In disbelief, Nina watched as Sage arced left, leading the dogs diagonally across the river. The sled runners skimmed the surface of the hole, hitched, and then pulled straight with a jolt. Blinking back tears, Nina called to the dogs again as she ran after them, dizzy with relief. After a moment, Sage stopped, and the others did too, as if wondering why Nina had been left behind. Collapsing on her knees in front of Sage, Nina buried her frozen hands in her fur and whispered, over and over, "Thank you."

Sage licked Nina's face once, bored by the show of theatrics. Or maybe Sage was only reminding her that she wasn't the one who needed attention. Nina went to Shadow and stared at him in dismay. His fur was soaked, clumped together in spikes that stood a few inches off his skin, and he was visibly shivering. He wagged his tail and smiled up at her, but Nina knew his fur would soon freeze into shards of ice. There was no sun to dry him off. Working quickly, she grabbed handfuls of snow and rubbed them against his paws. The dry snow would soak up some of the water, and keeping his paws from freezing was important. But it wasn't enough.

Rummaging through the sled basket, Nina tried to ignore Grant. His condition was the same—eyes shut, breathing shallow, skin hot to the touch; even a near disaster wasn't enough to rouse him. Her hands found the sweater and she pulled it out, whispering an apology to Grant for stealing its warmth. She spent several minutes stuffing Shadow into the sweater. He resisted determinedly, wriggling left and right and mouthing Nina's hands. He wasn't used to wearing clothes, not like the decked-out dogs that trotted New York's streets. Nina had often smiled to herself imagining the sled dogs in pajamas or rain jackets, and now here she was, wrangling Shadow into a sweater. Eventually he relented and she pulled his right front paw through and stepped back.

He'll live.

And then the world lit up. Slowly, golden light poured over the dogs, over the sled, over Nina. She turned in horror, vision overwhelmed by the bright light, bracing herself for the bullet that was sure to come. As she dived for the Remington, which still lay on the ice, she imagined her blood pouring out, soaking the snow, mixing with the river. Grant, killed as he lay helpless. The dogs set free, bounding into the wilderness. Then something smashed into Nina and she was thrown onto the ground, once again pitched into darkness.

32

GRANT OPENED HIS EYES TO THE LOUDEST SOUND
he'd ever heard, a mechanical thrumming that came from all
sides, a great wind blowing snow over the surface of the sled.
His entire body ached. Lifting a hand seemed like a Herculean
task. His mouth was too dry, his body cold and hot at the
same time. The thrumming became the sound of paws striking
the dirt paths in summertime, running full tilt with the ATV
bouncing behind them. Only the dogs wore no harnesses, there
was no ATV, and Grant was running with them, as fast as the
dogs, feet striking the ground rhythmically as his arms pumped
and his heart pounded, propelling him forward not in fear but
in joy, a wild expression of everything that represented hope
to him—the endless summer daylight, the golden mountains,
the red grass growing in the valley, and the dogs. The dogs
who never worried, who greeted each day with bright eyes and
boundless energy, who loved unconditionally, who acted not

out of fear but out of bravery. He was nothing like them, and in his half-dream state he fell behind, ribs constricting as his lungs gasped for air, legs wobbling to a halt as he fell to his knees. Someone was touching him and shouting in a loud voice. Too loud. He closed his eyes again, desperate to retreat from the noisy, unpleasant world he'd woken up to, to catch up with the dogs in his dream. But something stopped him.

The person wasn't Nina. It was a man, with large, broad hands and a clean-shaven face. He was saying something to Grant. Instructions? Grant couldn't make sense of his words. Then another man materialized on the other side of the sled and together they lifted Grant's body and placed him on a stretcher. He caught a glimpse of the source of the sound— a brightly colored helicopter, its rotor blades spinning. He turned his head to the other side. Nina was talking to someone. It was dark except for the lights from the helicopter and another source he couldn't identify. Grant understood that he was being rescued, but he felt terror at the thought of being loaded into the helicopter and carried away. Grant hadn't been in an airplane in years. When he was younger, one of his father's friends had owned a bush plane and sometimes taken the kids on rides in the summertime. Grant remembered the stomach-churning sensation of watching the ground fall away, the landscape he knew so well flattening and turning to shapes and colors, approximations of tundra and mountains. He wanted to call out to Nina, to ask her to come with him, but his voice had deserted him. The paramedics tightened the straps on the stretcher and carried him toward the helicopter, that great beast certain to swallow him alive.

Audrey. Grant hoped Nina remembered her ashes, buried somewhere in the sled. It was too late to remind her. With a jolt Grant was lifted into the helicopter, and then it was a

dizzying flurry of medical equipment, of needles and oxygen
and fluids. The helicopter lifted up, igniting a lurch in his
stomach, but this time there was no view. He was stuck
staring at the ceiling, at the blur of hands and faces that
moved around him.

33

FROM THE HOSPITAL BED NINA WATCHED THE RE-flection of her mother's face in the window. It was strange to see her removed from the context of their home, where Nina was most used to her presence—baking bread, murmuring to the dogs in a low voice. Her expression read like worry, though the doctor had assured her a hundred times that Nina was fine, aside from mild hypothermia and dehydration. When Nina first woke up yesterday and saw her sitting there, her instinct had been to ask about the dogs.

"Ila is taking care of them," her mother had replied. "So maybe they'll be alive when we get back, maybe they won't."

At least her dry sense of humor was still intact. Then Nina had asked about Grant, and the hint of a smile had dropped from her mother's lips.

The memories came back to Nina slowly, then all at once. Being thrown off the sled runners. Pulling Shadow from the river and wrangling him into the sweater. Sage turning the sled away from the hole in the ice. Then the bright light, almost upon them. Nina knocked off her feet, expecting at any moment to stare down the barrel of Elias's gun. And then—tackled instead by Honey, by that sweet old dog who wanted nothing more than to press her paws to Nina's chest and lick her face and bark directly in her ear. Nina had struggled up, incredulous to behold Elias's empty sled. He had a full team of dogs, including Honey and Wilder, and a sled full of supplies with a spotlight strapped to the front, but the man himself was missing. Nina had waited, heart in her throat, half expecting a bullet to rip through the air and pierce her skin, some kind of masterminded ambush. But there were only the dogs, and she'd had the wherewithal to drag Honey, eager for a reunion, away from her team. The rest of Elias's dogs, except for Wilder, were strangers, and a full-blown, eighteen-dog fight on the ice was the last thing she needed.

And then the helicopter came. Nina didn't believe her ears, then her eyes, as the huge mechanical bird came soaring through the dark sky, causing the dogs to turn their faces upward and cower. It had circled, sweeping a light over the valley, and she had jumped and waved her arms and screamed until her throat was hoarse. When it landed, she realized the crew had seen her all along and was only searching for the flattest section of snow. Still, she had run to the helicopter, tripping over her clunky boots, speaking so quickly that one of the paramedics had grabbed her gently by the shoulders and asked her to slow down.

She had managed to say, "My brother's been shot," and he had asked no further questions.

The helicopter had only had room for Grant, but Nina hadn't technically needed an emergency evacuation. She waited with one of the paramedics until several people arrived on snow machines—August among them. He touched her arms tentatively, as if checking that she was real. Then she'd been loaded on a snow machine and driven back to Whitespur, and then loaded into a truck and driven to Fairbanks. During the long, exhausting night she slipped in and out of consciousness in the back seat. The truck drove slowly as the driver navigated the snow-covered roads. They didn't make it to the hospital until the early hours of Monday morning. By asking her mother that afternoon, she'd learned the driver was Morgan, who had helped search as soon as he heard that Nina and Grant were missing.

Grant. She hadn't had a chance to see him yet, though she'd asked plenty of times. He'd been put straight into the ICU, monitored constantly by nurses and doctors. Her mother had visited him, drifting back and forth between her children's hospital rooms like an unsettled ghost.

Someone knocked on the door. Nina lifted her head, aware of the multiple IVs still in her arm, keeping her bedbound. Her mother stood and crossed the room, peering around the doorway, then stepped back as August entered the room.

"I'll go check on Grant," her mother said, disappearing into the hallway.

August glanced after her, then returned his attention to Nina. He smiled, hesitant.

"You're my first visitor. Besides my mom."

"I'm honored. But it would have been Ila, if she wasn't watching the dogs."

Nina laid her head back against the pillow. "I know. Is she okay?"

"She's okay. I stopped by before I drove out here. Hell of a drive, by the way." He stepped closer to the bed, hesitated, and then touched her hand, curling his fingers around hers for a moment. He let go, as if afraid that the pressure might hurt her, and settled into the chair that her mother had vacated.

The warmth of his fingers lingered on Nina's. "Not that I should spend any more time sitting." Nina sensed that he was embarrassed, but by what, she didn't know—maybe the undefined borders of their relationship, how much affection he was supposed to show. She knew that he had been worried about her and would have been even if nothing romantic remained between them. Bound to the hospital bed, she couldn't exactly get up and wrap her arms around him, kiss him, both of which she wanted to do. But she hadn't showered in days and her hair was matted from the arctic wind and from being crushed against a pillow. She was thankful the room had no mirrors, so she could only imagine how rough she must look.

"What time is it?" The wall clock was positioned in a way that required Nina to twist her neck to view it, perhaps to discourage bored patients from counting the minutes.

"Six thirty. I'm starving. How's the food here?"

Nina shook her head. "I wouldn't serve it at my restaurant. But I haven't had much of an appetite. I just want to see Grant."

"How's he doing?"

"My mom said he's awake today. Not talking much, but responsive. I feel so horrible for what happened. Like it's my fault." She caught herself before her emotions surged further.

August cleared his throat. "That's part of the reason I came here, actually. They found Elias's body yesterday."

Nina pushed against the mattress to sit up higher. "What? Where?"

"In some woods, sort of between Bow Lake and where we found you. Not the prettiest scene." He paused, and Nina nodded, indicating that he could go on. "There was a downed moose ripped to shreds, and his body was a few hundred feet from it, dragged away. Best conclusion the troopers and I could reach, based on the bullet hole, is that he killed the moose and a wolf pack traveling nearby caught the scent and came in. They killed him," August said, making a slashing motion across his throat. "And dragged his body away. Didn't eat him, at least. He was easy to identify." He blinked at Nina's expression. "What?"

"He didn't kill that moose. I did."

Realization dawned on August's face. "So, it had been dead for hours when he found it. Maybe the wolves were already there."

"He was probably following our tracks off the river and stumbled right into the wolves." She shivered. "Thank God the dogs made it out okay. I can't believe the wolves didn't go after them. I'm still shocked they followed us for so long."

August nodded. "They led us to you, actually. I got a radio call from a guy staying at the very end of Back Creek, where it leaves the mountainside. Said he spotted two dogsleds following each other, way far apart, and when he looked through his binoculars, the second one didn't have anybody on it. Said he'd never seen anything like it. That was right before it started snowing, but I called in the helicopter, the troopers, anyone I could find, and told them the second the snow let up, we had to go search up the river valley. It was dark by the time the helicopter flew up, but they saw the light on Elias's sled, and then they saw you. We were out before that, of course, but most people had gone home to refuel and rest because of the snow." He paused. "Except your mom. She stayed in the refuge visitor center, pacing around, asking me why I didn't have the governor of Alaska on the phone, why we didn't send out the National Guard."

"She pretends not to be overprotective, but she really is. She told me how scared she was when she looked out the window and noticed Grant's team in the yard with an empty sled. And then we didn't come back. It must have been terrifying for her." Nina exhaled. "I guess I have a lot of letters to write. You know, 'thanks for saving my life the other day.'"

"I think you could offer to cook a meal or two and people would be happy."

She laughed. "I wish I could transport 4950 to Whitespur. I'd host a dinner party for the whole town." After a moment, she asked, "Do you know why the oil field was shut down?"

August hesitated, then nodded. "Yeah, I do, but it hasn't been released to the public yet. They found a body on the outskirts. It's the man who went missing a few weeks ago. Clyde Lee." He paused. "They think it's in connection to that explosion at Site Fourteen."

His words hung in the air. The letters shifted into the bars of a jail cell, because she understood what August was implying. "Grant might be in trouble?"

He shrugged. "Maybe. They'll at least want to talk to him once he's back home. But I'm not that involved. I don't know what will happen."

"I know. Thank you for telling me."

"They also found . . . human remains, about a half mile farther into the woods. Too decomposed to identify right away, but the police are working on that now."

"Do they think it's one of the other missing workers?"

August's brow furrowed. "I don't know. But if I had to guess, I'd say probably."

They both turned their heads at the sound of the door opening. Dr. Pascual entered the room, businesslike as ever. She checked Nina's vitals without even a glance at August and then stood squarely in front of the bed. "Your mom tells me you'd like to visit your brother."

"Yes. I'd love to."

Dr. Pascual gave a curt nod. "He's awake, but not very

responsive. But I think it might brighten his spirits to see you."

Or he'll be reminded of the awful experience he went through, Nina thought, but she held her tongue.

August left the room while Dr. Pascual unhooked Nina from the machines and helped her out of bed. At first, the doctor's presence embarrassed her, because *of course* she could stand up on her own—but her legs buckled beneath her when she stood and a wave of dizziness swept over her.

"Your body is still recovering," Dr. Pascual said. Her eyes darted to the wall clock and she touched Nina's shoulder. "Your mother brought some clean clothes for you. They're in the closet. A nurse will be in any minute." She strode out of the room, her footsteps barely audible against the vinyl floors.

Nina made her way to the narrow closet, slow and hesitant. It was hard to believe that two days ago she had been alone in the wilderness, responsible for the survival of herself, her brother, and nine dogs. Now she understood why the doctor had wanted to keep her under observation. With all the adrenaline gone, her body had turned in on itself, gone completely defenseless, ready to be cared for instead of caring for others. She took a deep breath and opened the closet door, then picked up the worn canvas bag her mother must have brought in yesterday while Nina was sleeping.

She found two sweaters, a pair of jeans, and clean underwear. She changed slowly, marveling at the difficulty of something so simple as pulling clothes over her body. A nurse came in as she was halfway finished dressing and busied herself with filling out a chart on the laptop she'd wheeled into the room.

"I'm ready," Nina said, when she'd closed the button on her jeans. The nurse turned—Anna was her name, Nina remembered, reminded by both her name tag and her particularly friendly smile—and gestured for Nina to follow her.

It was a long walk to the ICU. With each step Nina gained confidence, remembering how her body moved, though she sensed that the fatigue would set in as soon as she was back in her own room. As she walked, she wondered if she should say anything to Grant about the bodies being found, but decided against it. He wasn't in the best of shape, and besides, she had no idea how the investigation of Clyde's death would play out. Maybe the police would determine it was too much trouble to investigate the death of one single man who wasn't even from Alaska. They could brush it under the rug, especially after what Nina and Grant had been through—Elias was the perfect silent scapegoat, a dead criminal, on the run from another state, hiding his real identity. But the other body—if it turned out to be Eric, or Benjamin, it might make national news again. The dead man's family would finally have some closure, and perhaps the police would be motivated—or forced—to reopen those old investigations.

Nina could at least show them Waylon Turcotte's mug shot. Let them figure out how he had changed his identity, fled Montana, and spent years working on the oil field undetected. Maybe he had some involvement in those disappearances, too, or maybe more than one corrupt man had found his way to Brooks Valley.

They took an elevator down one floor and walked through a set of doors down another quiet, white hallway, sterile and fluorescent. Anna paused, checked the door number, and pushed in.

The room mirrored Nina's own—small, a chair by the window, although with more machines, ones Nina didn't recognize. Her eyes went to the monitor that digitally drew out the steady beating of her brother's heart. She noticed her mother's absence; perhaps she'd gone to get food since it was dinnertime.

"I'll leave you for a few minutes," Anna said. "One of his nurses might be in. Stay here, I'll come get you."

Nina thanked her, glad she didn't have to navigate her way back through the hospital. She walked closer to the bed, less steady on her feet than ever. His eyes were closed, his expression calmer, more peaceful than it had been during their time in the wilderness. She almost didn't want to wake him, but she reached out and touched his hand.

34

THE WEIGHT OF A HAND SETTLED OVER GRANT'S OWN,
but he didn't open his eyes right away.

Everything required effort. Opening his eyes, moving his
fingers, speaking. He hadn't done much of the latter. He remembered the beginning of the helicopter ride and not much
after that. They'd given him pain medicine and fluids and he
had either fallen asleep or his brain had, mercifully, stopped
recording memories. He didn't remember arriving at the hospital or the surgery to repair his intestines. All this had been
recounted to him, by both his doctor and his mother, as if they
were afraid he would forget this critical information about his
own body. Instead, he suspected his body would keep a record of
these events, a personalized map of the trauma he had endured.
He would pay for it later, but for now he only wanted to sleep
for eternity on the uncomfortable mattress, the beep and hum
of machines in his ears.

But some part of him sensed that this hand was different.

His mom hadn't touched him once, only hovered near him and talked. And the nurses were quick, efficient, touching him with exacting purpose to take vitals or inspect how his wound was healing. This hand lingered. So, Grant opened his eyes.

Nina.

Pale and tired, but he probably wasn't much better. She smiled at him, which only emphasized her worn appearance, and reached up to push back a tangled clump of her hair. "Hi," she said.

Grant swallowed, trying to organize his mind enough to respond. This had been the most difficult part, communicating the thoughts to his tongue and then succeeding in speaking them. "Hey," he managed to say.

"You look good. I mean, better than a couple days ago."

"You too."

"I'm sorry," she said after a moment. She wasn't crying, but there was something pained about her expression, her furrowed brow and downturned mouth. She didn't elaborate, but Grant knew what she meant.

"I forgive you."

Maybe it wasn't completely true, at least not yet. He had an ocean of feelings about the last few weeks to wade through. Maybe a lifetime of processing before he could reach genuine forgiveness. But for now, it was what she needed to hear to move forward. And Grant didn't want to leave her hanging.

Nina tightened her grip on his hand, squeezing his fingers for a moment. Her mouth opened, like she wanted to say more, but a nurse bustled into the room, back for Grant's every-fifteen-minute checks. Nina withdrew her hand and stepped back, folding into the chair by the window. Exhaustion swept across her face. Grant waited, wondering why she didn't leave, until the red-haired nurse who'd brought her popped into the room again, cheerfully calling Nina's name.

His sister stood, her expression difficult to read. "I'll see you soon," she said, and he lifted his hand as much as he could, a few fingers imitating a wave. She gave him another unhappy smile and turned away, long hair swaying across her back as she moved. Grant closed his eyes. The nurse still busied herself around him. The machines still beeped and hummed. His mother would be back soon to complain about another hospital cafeteria meal. Maybe he would go to the step-down unit tomorrow, then the floor, then home. He wasn't sure he wanted to. What waited for him back in Whitespur? He could think only of Ila, of the dogs, and of shame.

NINA WAS DISCHARGED the next day. She came to say goodbye to him, and not much more, except for a joke about delaying Thanksgiving by another week. Their mother went with her, another long journey up the Dalton, and Grant was left alone for another week as November gave way to December. Physical therapists came to him throughout the day, helping him out of bed and walking him slowly up and down the hallway as he braced against a walker, visions of his future as an old man, a stabbing pain in his stomach. Audrey walked beside him, slowing her pace to match his.

And Audrey sat in the chair across from his bed, and Audrey talked to him even when he closed his eyes, even when he dreamed. That his oldest sister showed up when the rest of his family left didn't surprise him. She wasn't real, a figment of his medicated, traumatized brain, but he talked back to her anyway, silently, in his thoughts. He told her about getting shot while scattering her ashes, and she laughed. Said it served him right for not paying enough attention, and yes, she could laugh about it, because he was alive. He pointed out that a scoping rifle could hit a target from a quarter mile away, and Elias must have been pretty far because neither Grant nor Nina had seen him. She rolled her eyes.

Audrey talked about Katrina, about The Spur, but mostly she talked about cleaning and organizing. Putting things in boxes, wiping dust off countertops, scrubbing grime from windowpanes. Crafting a bonfire to burn all the refuse of a person's life, an effigy to getting clean. That last part, about the fire, didn't sound right to Grant, but he liked the image of the fire burning in the snow, heat and ice coexisting. Like the cabin on the mountain. He felt bad for it, that old wooden shack that had housed so many hunters and wanderers over the years. Sometimes it felt good to burn up an old life, and sometimes it hurt like you yourself were on fire.

The only question Audrey wouldn't answer was how she had died. Of course, Grant knew from the autopsy—overdose—but he wanted to know what that really meant, if it had been an accident or on purpose or if someone had picked the lock on her front door and crept through the dark hallway into her bedroom and held a gun to the side of her head and forced her to swallow the pills. Whenever he asked, she grew fuzzy around the edges and her voice turned so soft and liquid, like honey dripping off a spoon, that he couldn't make out the words. Or she would shut her mouth entirely. So eventually he understood that it wasn't for him to know, and stopped asking.

Audrey left when Ila showed up later that week, which was around the time they started tapering his pain medication to a more reasonable dose. Ila stood at the foot of the bed, her eyes wide like a startled animal. Grant lifted his hand to show that he was okay, and she burst into tears.

Kneeling beside the bed, she whispered, "I was so scared. I thought for sure something horrible had happened."

Something horrible did happen, Grant thought. Many horrible things, stacked atop one another into a jagged, treacherous tower. But he laid his hand on her arm, and she shook as she cried. "I love you," he said, and she stopped abruptly, as if remembering that he was in fact alive.

"I love you, too."

"It's too warm in here. They keep bringing me more blankets, like they don't realize that I'm sweating my ass off."

Ila smiled through her tears, the reaction Grant had hoped for. "There's a thermostat on the wall. Didn't you know?"

Grant didn't know. Ila stood up and fiddled with the dial, setting it back a few degrees. When Grant asked if they were allowed to change it, she shrugged. "Who cares?"

Not Grant. He didn't care about much at all now that Ila was there, mostly because he was worried she still hadn't forgiven him for keeping secrets—lying—and dragging everyone he loved into his mess. "I know we never had a chance to finish our conversation." After the news of Audrey's death, Grant had barely spent time with Ila, not for lack of want. He'd been too absorbed in trying to comfort his family and distract himself from his sister's death and the oil field closure. He had seen Ila at The Spur, but not long enough for more than a brief conversation. He had no idea where they stood.

She crouched beside his bed again, fingers resting on his arm. "It's okay. We don't need to worry about that right now."

"I hate to tell you . . ."

"What I mean is," she said, pausing to run a hand through her hair, "I do want to talk about all of it. But I almost lost you, and I need a little time for it to sink in that you're still here. And I want you to know that I'm not going anywhere. I'll be here, for as long as it takes, for you to heal from this and make things right, whatever that means to you."

Her response caught Grant off guard. He'd been expecting something more measured, not complete acceptance of his mistakes. Her emotions were still running high—he had tortured himself plenty of times by imagining how he would feel if the roles were reversed. Not good. There was no reason to argue against her earnestness. Grant took her hand and nodded, slowly, the energy leaving his body like melting snow. Ila was the sun.

"I appreciate that," he said. And she did stay, never left; she was the one to drive him back to Whitespur a few days later, crawling through a snowstorm up the desolate highway.

35

ON THE LONGEST NIGHT OF THE YEAR, NINA MADE a plan.

Seated across from Grant and Ila, beside August at his kitchen table, she studied the mess of papers spread before them. Documents from the founding of Brooks Valley national wildlife refuge, land rights, any and all publicly available information on the drilling operation. Also included were personal testimonies, some typed, some handwritten, from residents of Whitespur and beyond, anyone they could reach via snow machine or dogsled. In late January, the Alaska senate was set to hold a hearing on the condition of oil drilling in the state. Nina had submitted a proposal to speak at the hearing. She had no idea if it would be approved—cell service was recently down across town, and the Dalton was near impassable due to a barrage of snowstorms, so she couldn't leave to check her email. But the plan was to show up, anyway, to leave a week early and creep down the Dalton to Fairbanks, then fly to Juneau, where the legislature met.

The oil field resumed operation in early December, much to the irritation of the Whitespur populace, who had rallied doggedly behind Nina and Grant. To the Oil and Gas authorities and the state troopers, the situation was done and dusted—a single bad actor, a fugitive from another state, taken care of in the most Alaskan way possible: killed by a beast in the forest. Grant had told the full story to the police, inside one of the little offices at the oil field while Nina waited in the hallway. She had half expected him to come out in handcuffs, but the officer said they already knew that Elias Woodsman was Waylon Turcotte, and that was that. They'd been unable to link him to the disappearances of the other men, though the other body had been identified as Benjamin Weber. His parents, relieved that he had been found, hadn't wanted to open another investigation, too exhausted from the media circus years before. To everyone else, the drilling now represented an ugly stain on the town, a place where, in theory, a criminal might go to hide out and make boatloads of money while destroying a precious natural resource.

The story had made national news, and a reporter had flown in to interview Nina and Grant, arriving a little shaken from the bumpy bush plane ride.

"What do you want the world to know about this?" he had asked.

"That we want the Brooks Valley oil field shut down."

Nina and Grant had agreed to unite on that front, at least. Grant hadn't gone back to work—he couldn't, even if he wanted to, still too weak for physical labor—but he'd withdrawn somewhat, spending a lot of time in his room or with Ila, rarely seeking out Nina for conversation. She tried not to let it bother her. She knew his words in the hospital—*I forgive you*—were preemptive, Grant extending her a favor for the future. Forgiveness was a sticky, malleable thing, and she couldn't have expected him to know then, exhausted and pumped full of medication, how he truly felt. But it had been a kindness, and she clung to those three words, desperate to make them true. Perhaps Audrey's death played a role in Grant's desire to forgive, too. He'd told Nina that he'd spent a lot of time thinking about her in the hospital. After Grant's confession, Trooper Peterson had pulled Nina aside and divulged that a source had reported seeing a man who matched Elias Woodsman's description buying pills in an alleyway behind the general store. Though they'd never know for sure, it seemed likely that those were the pills Audrey overdosed on. The why was also unclear, though Grant had guessed, after Nina told him, that it was a way of threatening their family, a death that no one else would blink twice at—an addict overdosing—but that would mean something to her family, who knew about her recent sobriety. The thought had crossed Nina's mind at the cabin. But maybe there was more to it, something from Audrey's past that happened to surface at the same time and get her in trouble. They could only speculate, and that was never enjoyable, so they let the topic of Audrey's death rest.

Without Grant's income, it had quickly become clear that keeping all the dogs through winter was no longer an option. Elias's team had been handed over to the kennel at Denali National Park when no one claimed them, but her family had taken Honey and Wilder back. Luckily, Nina and her mother had found a handful of people willing to care for a dog or two through the winter and give them back in the spring, assuming that the tourists returned, even if at a slower rate. The dogs were confused about being handed over to strangers, but excited to live inside houses, with humans—whenever Nina bumped into someone in town who'd taken a dog, she received a glowing update about how well they were doing. Sage and the other dogs who had pulled Nina and Grant through the wilderness remained at home. She couldn't bear to part with them, even for a few months.

"I think we need to appeal to their sense of what Alaska truly is," Nina said, tapping the stack of refuge papers. "Sure, we have this valuable resource underground. But isn't the true resource all the space? All the unobstructed nature? Wilderness, as a resource, is becoming scarcer and scarcer."

August nodded. "But someone might ask, 'why Brooks Valley?' As in, there are eight national parks here already and dozens more protected areas. Why can't a few thousand acres be used for drilling?"

It went on like this for a while, August and Ila asking questions, Nina and Grant scribbling the answers, piecing together the history of the place where they had all grown up through legal documents, government forms, and stories. By the end of the first night—relatively speaking—Nina didn't feel any closer to the solution, but they had somewhat of a baseline: Brooks Valley deserved respect, as did the people of Whitespur. By disrespecting the land, they disrespected the people who both loved it and relied on it. When the oil had all been taken, no matter how far in the future that might be, the town would be left poor and desolate, the way it had been before the drilling began, except now it would have even less to offer. Instead, a better investment would be to protect the Brooks Valley, perhaps designating it as a national park, offering a reason for tourists to visit interior Alaska. Nina had no idea what went into creating a national park, but she imagined the first step was raising awareness. The four of them—Nina, Grant, Ila, and August—could start the chorus, uniting their voices until others joined in, chanting for protection of the place they all loved.

"We should get going," Ila said, her gaze sliding from Nina to Grant. She had been protective of him since he'd returned home from the hospital, which Nina appreciated and understood. She sometimes worried that Grant had lost an undefinable part of his personality in the weeks between the cover-up and their time in the wilderness, that he'd lost some fundamental spark of joy or confidence. Grant had always been a people pleaser, the family glue, but at least he had cared. She hoped the Brooks Valley project was enough to keep him going through the winter. Grant had always loved summertime, basking in the near endless daylight and the soft colors of the sky.

Her brother and her friend shrugged their coats on and waved as they left, brushing past the stringy spruce tree decorated with warm white lights in the living room. Christmas, just a few days away. From outside came the faint roar of the snow machine engine firing up. Beside her, August shifted.

"You never answered my question."

A few days ago, August had pitched her an idea too absurd to consider at the time, and she had told him so. They had been spending more and more time together since she'd returned from the hospital, his cabin providing a quiet retreat from her family's house. Not that her family's house was loud—but the silence there was oppressive, too many uncomfortable emotions piled atop one another. Audrey's death, Grant's injury, Nina's role in all of it. At August's she could slip in during the day while he was at work—she had his spare key—and read one of the many worn paperbacks that lined the single bookshelf in the cabin. She found herself eager to cook more, scrounging up ingredients from his pantry and eventually bringing an armful of groceries with her each time. But there was nothing overtly romantic about their time together—they hadn't done more than kiss, and Nina never spent the night—which was why she'd been surprised when he had asked if she wanted to move to Juneau together.

"One, it'll be easier to talk to legislators if we live close by. It's not practical to fly to Juneau frequently. I mean, I can't afford it." He had laughed, but his expression had turned serious. "Two, there's a biologist position available in Glacier Bay. I've known about it for a couple of months now, but I've kind of been stringing them along, trying to decide what I wanted to do. They didn't expect me to start in the dead of winter, but I'm sure they'd like to know my decision soon. I could take the ferry or fly depending on the season. Spend my workdays at the park and my days off in Juneau." He had paused to slide a piece of paper across the table to her. "Three, this building is for sale."

A restaurant with a two-bedroom apartment above it. Painted bright blue, with white shutters, a view of the harbor where cruise ships docked and the mountains beyond. A prime location, Nina thought, and cheap. But more than she could ever afford.

"The description says it's in disrepair," she had said.

"Not totally. Nothing we can't fix."

"We?"

August had smiled, as if amused by her inability to connect the dots. "Yes. I'm proposing that we move to Juneau, buy this place, and fix it up. I'll work in Glacier Bay, you'll have your restaurant, and we can fight to protect Brooks Valley."

When she was younger, Nina had always resisted August's desire to plan their life, his sweeping ideas for how they should live together. But now the kindness of his gesture overwhelmed her. She pressed her palm to her forehead.

"I can't afford it."

"I figured, but that part is covered."

She dropped her hand. "What?"

"Come on. You know I've been saving for a place for, like, my entire life."

It was true—even in high school he'd been putting away money for a cabin. "That doesn't mean I feel comfortable taking it."

August cracked a smile. "Well, you wouldn't be taking it. Part of the deal is that I get to live there too, at least when I'm off work." He must have noticed the hesitation still on her face. "I know you might not be entirely comfortable with me buying us a place to live. But once it's done, we'll both be responsible for the mortgage. I'll be out in Glacier Bay five days a week, and once the restaurant is open, you'll be making money, too."

Nina frowned. "That's a lot of work. Like, a ton. We might not have money to get started on it right away." She paused, thinking. "But I could find a part-time job or work as a private chef in the meantime. Maybe it's possible."

The amount of work would be enormous, and would involve construction beyond her capabilities. She had sat in silence for a long time, staring at the listing, trying to imagine the same future he envisioned. Juneau was so far from Whitespur, hugging the border of British Columbia. But she had gone farther before. Opening her own restaurant was a huge gamble, though she had done it once before. But not alone, and it was hard to imagine doing so without Micah by her side. Moving in with August didn't make sense for the speed and trajectory of their relationship, but maybe it didn't have to. Grant—he was her sticking point, the thing she didn't want to leave behind. Nina thought that if more of his support system left, he might crumble away into dust, too.

But for once, she'd sat and looked at the picture of their future that August had painted, and she liked what she saw.

Now she leaned back in her chair, drumming her palms against the table. "Can I have a bit more time? It's a big decision."

August laughed. "I'm not offering you a job. You're not on a deadline. But let's talk about it more, if you want."

"But you do have a job offer."

"Yes," he relented. "I told them I'd let them know by early January. But that doesn't necessarily affect us."

"I can do early January," Nina replied. Maybe she had needed a deadline all along.

Nina didn't expect to find Grant at home that night, but the light in his bedroom was on, spilling into the hallway. She tapped the door with her knuckles and waited.

"Come in."

She pushed open the door, squinting against the light, and closed it softly behind her. Grant was in bed, sitting on top of the blanket, head resting against a stack of pillows. The sight reminded her of the cot in that rustic old cabin—the one that Elias had burned down. Nina pulled the chair away from Grant's desk and sat.

"Did Ila drop you off?"

He nodded. "Her landlord keeps threatening to raise her rent if I'm over more than a few nights a week."

"Ouch. How does he know?"

"He lives next door. And doesn't have anything better to do, I guess. What's up?"

Nina hesitated. She could beat around the bush, try to figure out how Grant was feeling before she pitched the idea, or she could dive right in. "I want to talk to you about something. It has to do with the whole 'save Brooks Valley' thing."

"Okay." Grant replied with only mild interest.

"Last week, August told me about an idea he has. For me and him to move to Juneau together."

Grant almost smiled. "I thought you were just taking a trip there." He paused. "For how long?"

"I don't know. A long time, maybe. He showed me a building for sale. It used to be a restaurant and it has an apartment above it, but it's not in the best shape. He wants us to buy it."

"With what money?" Grant snorted. Nina knew he wasn't being mean, but simply stating a fact: that their family was poor, and that Nina had returned home because she had run out of money, and that since being home, she'd done nothing to earn more—minus selling Honey and Wilder, but that money had gone straight into their parents' bank account.

"He has money for a down payment saved. Remember that night at Los Padres? He talked about buying Morgan's cabin."

"I blocked that night from my memory."

Nina rolled her eyes. "Anyway, the more I think about it, the more . . . I don't know, exciting, it seems. And maybe not just exciting, but right. I didn't want to stay in Whitespur forever. And owning my own restaurant would be a dream, especially in a touristy place like Juneau. It's right across from where the cruise ships dock. It'll be swamped."

"If the food is any good."

"Hey. It'll be good. Probably. I won't have Micah to make it special. I honestly don't know if I can do it without him. I've always pictured us having our own restaurant together again, someday. But maybe I need to move on from that dream. I'll have to serve plain old Alaskan classics. The tourists will prefer that, anyway."

"You can do it without him," Grant said. "But maybe you won't have to. Maybe you could work together on this, too."

Nina frowned. "I doubt it. He's in a good position in Austin. I wouldn't want to give up a sous-chef spot, not when so many restaurants had to close this year. Besides, I don't think we could get his friends to invest in us again. That ship sank with 4950."

Grant nodded, but his eyes betrayed that he was somewhere else. Nina drew a breath. "So. If I do this, if I move away. Juneau is pretty far."

"Not as far as New York."

"But you'll be okay?"

Grant laughed. "Bold of you, to think you're the only thing keeping me alive here."

"That's not what I—"

He lifted his hand, waving off her defense. "I know. Look, I know I've been kind of distant, but I've been thinking a lot, too. I want to stay in Whitespur long enough to see the oil field shut down, permanently. But after that, man—I need to see more of the world. Mom and Dad are fine, for now. I'm going to start picking up odd jobs."

"Getting the oil field shut down could take years," Nina said gently.

"I know. So maybe not even that long. But long enough to get other people here to care about it enough to keep fighting. Maybe next summer, if the tourists come back, that can be part of the tours. You know, here's all this beautiful wilderness, and then bam, a big ugly oil field destroying the environment. The right type of people will write letters to Congress the second they get home."

"You might be right."

"And I'm going to make Dad get that surgery, even if I have to drive him to Anchorage myself. I don't care if he gets it done and then spends the rest of his life watching TV. I just don't want him to be in pain."

"I think he'll do it. After Audrey died, I talked to him. He was thinking about it then. I think he realizes that he doesn't have to live like this forever."

Grant nodded. "Anyway, radicalize the tourists, save Brooks Valley, make Dad get surgery, maybe ask Ila to marry me." He collapsed back against the pillows as he ticked off on his fingers. "And then, I can go anywhere."

"Well, please let me know when that last one happens," Nina replied, unable to suppress a smile. Grant was fine. Better than fine. He had a plan, too, another vision for the future that Nina could see perfectly. Grant was the right kind of person to talk about preserving interior Alaska—big, bearded, a gentle voice, a passion for the land. He could tell his own story when he was ready, and Nina was certain that tourists would hang on every word. "And if you're thinking of going *anywhere* . . ." She trailed off, adding another brushstroke to the painting. "I might have a job to offer the best waitress in Whitespur."

Nina thought Grant would laugh at the idea, but his eyes lit up again. "Oh, Ila would love that. I won't say anything to her yet, but if this ends up working out . . ."

Bolstered by his optimism, she continued, "I think I'll tell August we can look at this place when we visit Juneau. I don't want to buy it sight unseen, in case it's a total dump. But if it's not . . ."

"Then I think it's meant to be."

ONE MONTH LATER, Nina stood in front of the little Juneau restaurant in disbelief. Not because it was the first time she'd seen it, but because Micah sat on the front stoop, smoking a cigarette, a wool hat pulled low over his forehead.

In her right hand she held the keys to the property. In her left hand she held the deed. It dangled loosely from her fingers, swaying a little in the cold wind. The sun was bright in the blue sky, and Nina still wasn't used to it, an acceptable amount of daylight even in January. Seabirds drifted on the breeze overhead. Micah still hadn't noticed her. August's footsteps stopped beside her.

"Man. That guy's gonna have to move before we take the picture."

They'd come straight from the attorney's office, fresh from closing. As much as she'd wanted to resist it, Nina had fallen in love the first time she'd laid eyes on the property in person. That day clouds had hung low over town, unleashing fat snowflakes. They had walked along the Gastineau Channel from the cheap hotel that August had booked for the week to the restaurant, pointing out clusters of bald eagles along the banks. The building's bright blue color cheered Nina instantly, like the clouds parting to reveal a dazzling sky. Inside it smelled dusty, but the hardwood floors were in good shape, would clean up well with some sanding and polishing. The kitchen was a mess—old, dirty equipment, some of which could be cleaned, some of which would need to be replaced. But Nina saw it only as it could be: sizzling pans of meat and vegetables, a handful of cooks whirling between the stoves and counters, waitstaff ducking in and out to deliver plates of steaming food to both tourists and locals. She imagined a green and brown interior, earthy colors like The Spur, because everyone would be sick of nautical white and blue.

And upstairs—upstairs, all the rooms had big windows, and even when the clouds came down to touch the earth, gray light flooded in and softened the scuffed floorboards. She could only imagine it in the sun. Again, it needed cleaning, and the apartment kitchen was even more outdated, but she didn't care. The bedroom window overlooked the channel and the mountains of Douglas Island. August didn't say much, but he stood in the doorway, eyes on Nina, his expression unreadable.

"What do you think?"

He shook his head. "I want it to be your decision."

It went unsaid: She already knew what he thought. So, she said yes, tentatively, and after the building passed an inspection, she said yes, for real.

Though she'd been back in the land of technology for two weeks, Nina hadn't done more than exchange a few texts with Grant. She tried to send pictures of Juneau, but his service was too poor to download them, so she compensated with emojis and exclamation points in her descriptions. But she hadn't talked to anyone else, even Micah—she hadn't had time to, too busy exploring Juneau, preparing her legislature speech, and talking with August for hours about plans for their new home. She blinked rapidly, but Micah was still there, still smoking, still hunched against the cold. Without a word, she shoved the keys and the deed into August's hands and ran.

Micah flinched at the sound of her footsteps and scrambled to his feet. She'd never seen him move so fast outside of a kitchen. Nina flung her arms around him and breathed in his familiar scent—a little spicy, a little smoky.

"Shit," he muttered, "you're going to knock me over."

Nina pulled back, holding him at arm's length. "What the fuck are you doing here?"

"I should be asking you that. Come on, New York, Austin,

to this?" he asked, gesturing around. "This is the least exciting place I've ever seen."

"Wait until you see Whitespur. But seriously. *What?*"

He grinned. "I got a call last week from a number I didn't recognize, but it said, 'Alaska.' I thought it must have been you. I answer and it's some guy telling me I have to go to Juneau, stat. I said, 'Where the fuck is Juneau?' He kept saying, 'I'm Nina's brother.' And I thought, I only know one Nina." Micah waved the cigarette as he talked, trailing thin tendrils of smoke through the air. "And then he tells me you're buying a restaurant in Juneau, Alaska, and you can't do it without me. His words. I guess I've been in that shitty Austin kitchen for so long I'm not thinking straight anymore, because I thought, what the hell, why not. Booked a ticket, and here I am."

Nina shook her head. "When did you get here? What is your *plan?*"

"This morning. My *plan*, Nina, is to crash in your unfurnished apartment and help you fix this place up. After that, who knows. I didn't think that far ahead."

Nina ran her hands through her hair. She remembered the conversation she'd had with Grant back in December, how she'd mentioned wishing that she could work with Micah again. "I can't believe Grant called you. How did he even get your number?"

Micah shrugged. "We live in the age of the internet, even in the middle of fucking nowhere." He tilted his head past Nina's shoulder. "Are you going to introduce me?"

"Oh!" Nina turned and beckoned August closer. "August, this is Micah."

"I gathered. Sorry, it was hard not to eavesdrop. Also, I've heard so many stories from Nina about you."

Micah's eyes narrowed, then his face cracked into a smile.

"Hey. This is that guy you were crying about freshman year of CIA."

Nina felt her cheeks redden. "No. I never did that."

August's face lit up in delight. "No way. Nina was stone-cold when she broke up with me. 'I don't align with your version of our future.' I thought I was the only one crying."

Nina had a sudden urge to melt into the ground. "Micah, if you say one more thing about my emotional state back then, I'm kicking you out of the apartment we literally don't live in yet."

"My lips are sealed," he said, zipping his fingers across them.

IT WASN'T THE ending, nor the beginning, that Nina had expected. October was a lifetime ago, that long, silent ride up the Dalton, her parents' cold welcome, trying to heal her relationship with Grant. Audrey had died, she and Grant had somehow lived. And she'd ended up here—in a previously dust-covered kitchen that now smelled of artificial lemon cleaner and sizzling hamburger. They'd practically bought up the cookware section of the closest grocery store. Thankfully, Micah was willing to donate cash to the cause, though he had insisted on buying mangoes to make salsa with. Nina and August had gagged at the price, but Micah hadn't batted an eye.

In the checkout line, August had left to grab a last-minute bottled coffee from one of the aisles, and Nina had turned to Micah.

"You could stay here, you know. Work with me."

Micah regarded her for a moment. "For free?"

"Well, I don't have a way to pay you right now. I understand if you'd need a second job for the time being. That's my plan, too. But whenever I thought about having a restaurant again, you were always there beside me. And you're here, and I'd hate for you to leave."

He nodded, his expression more serious than usual. "I don't usually work for free. But for you, Nina, I'll make an exception."

A smile, fueled partially by happiness and partially by disbelief, spread across her face. "You uprooted your entire life so easily."

"The roots were shallow." He shrugged.

So maybe that's how it would have to be—Micah plunging fearlessly ahead, Nina hanging on for dear life and sometimes proving to be the more rational one. And August—he looked blank at some of their inside jokes that bubbled up, but he was game to laugh along anyway, and during dinner he and Micah fell into a long conversation about the native plants on Oahu. Nina listened, pouring over with happiness, as they sat on the kitchen floor, eating deconstructed tacos out of two-dollar bowls that were bound to chip in days. Once Grant and Ila arrived—and she was sure they would, one day—she wouldn't ask for anything more.

The long dark night wasn't over yet, but Nina thought she could see the faintest hint of dawn.

ACKNOWLEDGMENTS

BEFORE PUBLISHING THIS BOOK, I HEARD THE PHRASE "book two blues" so many times from fellow writers. It's true that this book, my second, was hard. *A Long Dark Night* came from an idea that I briefly worked on and then set aside for almost a year, unsure if I would ever return to it. One thing all books require, no matter how difficult to write, is a team capable of enthusiastically seeing the publishing process through to the very end. I appreciate this time and space to give them my gratitude.

Thank you to my agent, Jessica Faust, and my editor, Meredith Clark. Jessica, your excitement about this pitch inspired me to go back to this story, once abandoned, and try again. Your support and passion help me continue putting words on the page. Meredith, your understanding of these characters and their world steered this story in a darker, richer, more emotionally complex direction. I am thankful for your invaluable guidance as this book found its footing.

Thank you to the Park Row team, including but not limited to production, design, marketing, publicity, and sales, who were a pleasure to work with and who brought this book beautifully to life.

To my writing group, the B52s, thank you for generously allowing me to skip the critique queue so many times in the process of drafting and editing *A Long Dark Night*. For more than four years now we've been swapping stories, commiserating, and celebrating, and for that, I am so grateful. David, Jordan, Judith, and Teresa—*A Long Dark Night* is shaped by each of you.

To Nicole and Carter, who kindly read early versions of this book and offered brilliant suggestions. There comes a time when every book must take its first steps; thank you for being there to catch it.

The following books informed the dogsledding scenes, and the Alaskan setting, in this novel: *Iditarod Alaska: Life of a Long Distance Sled Dog Musher* by Burt Bomhoff; *Cold Hands, Warm Heart: Alaskan Adventures of an Iditarod Champion* by Jeff King; *One Second to Glory: The Alaska Adventures of Iditarod Champion Dick Mackey* by Lew Freedman; *Fast into the Night: A Woman, Her Dogs, and Their Journey North on the Iditarod Trail* by Debbie Clarke Moderow; *Winterdance: The Fine Madness of Running the Iditarod* by Gary Paulsen; *Race Across Alaska: First Woman to Win the Iditarod Tells Her Story* by Libby Riddles and Tim Jones; and *Mush!: A Beginner's Manual of Sled Dog Training*, edited by Bella Levorsen for the Sierra Nevada Dog Drivers, Inc. All mistakes are my own.

Thank you to my family, for never getting tired of hearing about my books, and for always being excited to read the next one.

To Adam. When I feel like I'm not capable, you always remind me that I am. I'm lucky to share my life with you each and every day. I love you.